STAR WARS

THE HIGH REPUBLIC

CHILDREN OF THE STORM

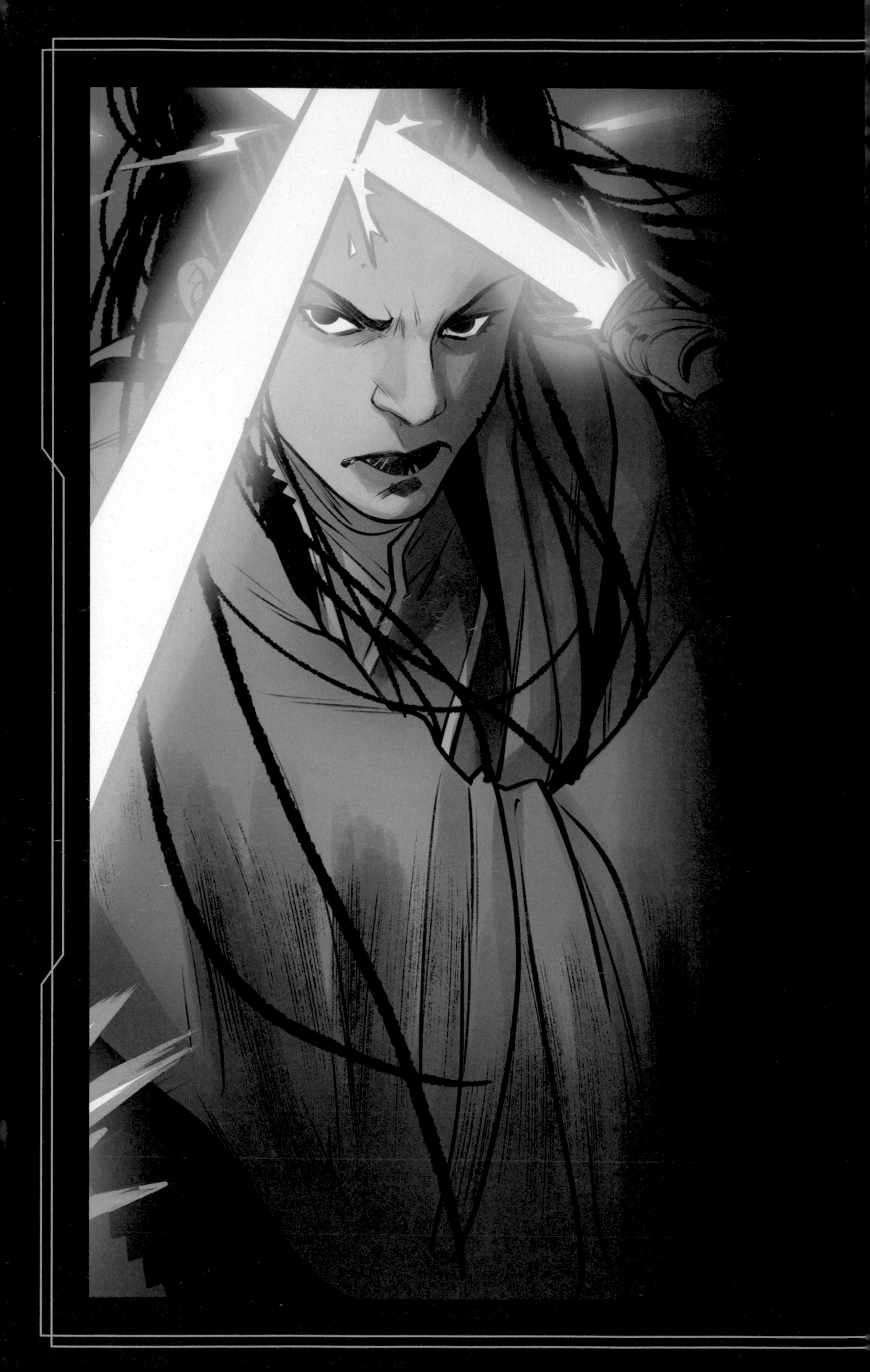

STAR WARS
THE HIGH REPUBLIC

CHILDREN OF THE STORM

Writer
CAVAN SCOTT

Pencilers
ARIO ANINDITO (#1, #5), **JIM TOWE** (#1-4) &
MARIKA CRESTA (#3-5)

Inkers
MARK MORALES (#1, #5), **ARIO ANINDITO** (#1),
JIM TOWE (#1-4) & **MARIKA CRESTA** (#3-5)

Colorist
JIM CAMPBELL

Letterer
VC's ARIANA MAHER

Cover Art
PHIL NOTO

Assistant Editor
MIKEY J. BASSO

Associate Editor
DANNY KHAZEM

Editor
MARK PANICCIA

Collection Editor	JENNIFER GRÜNWALD
Assistant Editor	DANIEL KIRCHHOFFER
Assistant Managing Editor	LISA MONTALBANO
VP Production & Special Projects	JEFF YOUNGQUIST
Book Designer	ADAM DEL RE
Lead Designer	JAY BOWEN
SVP Print, Sales & Marketing	DAVID GABRIEL
Editor in Chief	C.B. CEBULSKI

For Lucasfilm:

Senior Editor	ROBERT SIMPSON
Associate Editor	GRACE ORRISS
Creative Director	MICHAEL SIGLAIN
Art Director	TROY ALDERS
Lucasfilm Story Group	MATT MARTIN
	PABLO HIDALGO
	EMILY SHKOUKANI
Creative Art Manager	PHIL SZOSTAK

STAR WARS: THE HIGH REPUBLIC PHASE III VOL. 1 — CHILDREN OF THE STORM. Contains material originally published in magazine form as STAR WARS: THE HIGH REPUBLIC (2023) #1-5 and STAR WARS: REVELATIONS (2023) #1. First printing 2024. ISBN 978-1-302-95499-4. Published by MARVEL WORLDWIDE, INC., a subsidiary of MARVEL ENTERTAINMENT, LLC. OFFICE OF PUBLICATION: 1290 Avenue of the Americas, New York, NY 10104. **Printed in Canada.** KEVIN FEIGE, Chief Creative Officer; DAN BUCKLEY, President, Marvel Entertainment; DAVID BOGART, Associate Publisher & SVP of Talent Affairs; TOM BREVOORT, VP, Executive Editor; NICK LOWE, Executive Editor, VP of Content, Digital Publishing; DAVID GABRIEL, VP of Print & Digital Publishing; SVEN LARSEN, VP of Licensed Publishing; MARK ANNUNZIATO, VP of Planning & Forecasting; JEFF YOUNGQUIST, VP of Production & Special Projects; ALEX MORALES, Director of Publishing Operations; DAN EDINGTON, Director of Editorial Operations; RICKEY PURDIN, Director of Talent Relations; JENNIFER GRÜNWALD, Director of Production & Special Projects; SUSAN CRESPI, Production Manager; STAN LEE, Chairman Emeritus. For information regarding advertising in Marvel Comics or on Marvel.com, please contact Vit DeBellis, Custom Solutions & Integrated Advertising Manager, at vdebellis@marvel.com. For Marvel subscription inquiries, please call 888-511-5480. **Manufactured between 4/5/2024 and 5/7/2024 by SOLISCO PRINTERS, SCOTT, QC, CANADA.**

10 9 8 7 6 5 4 3 2 1

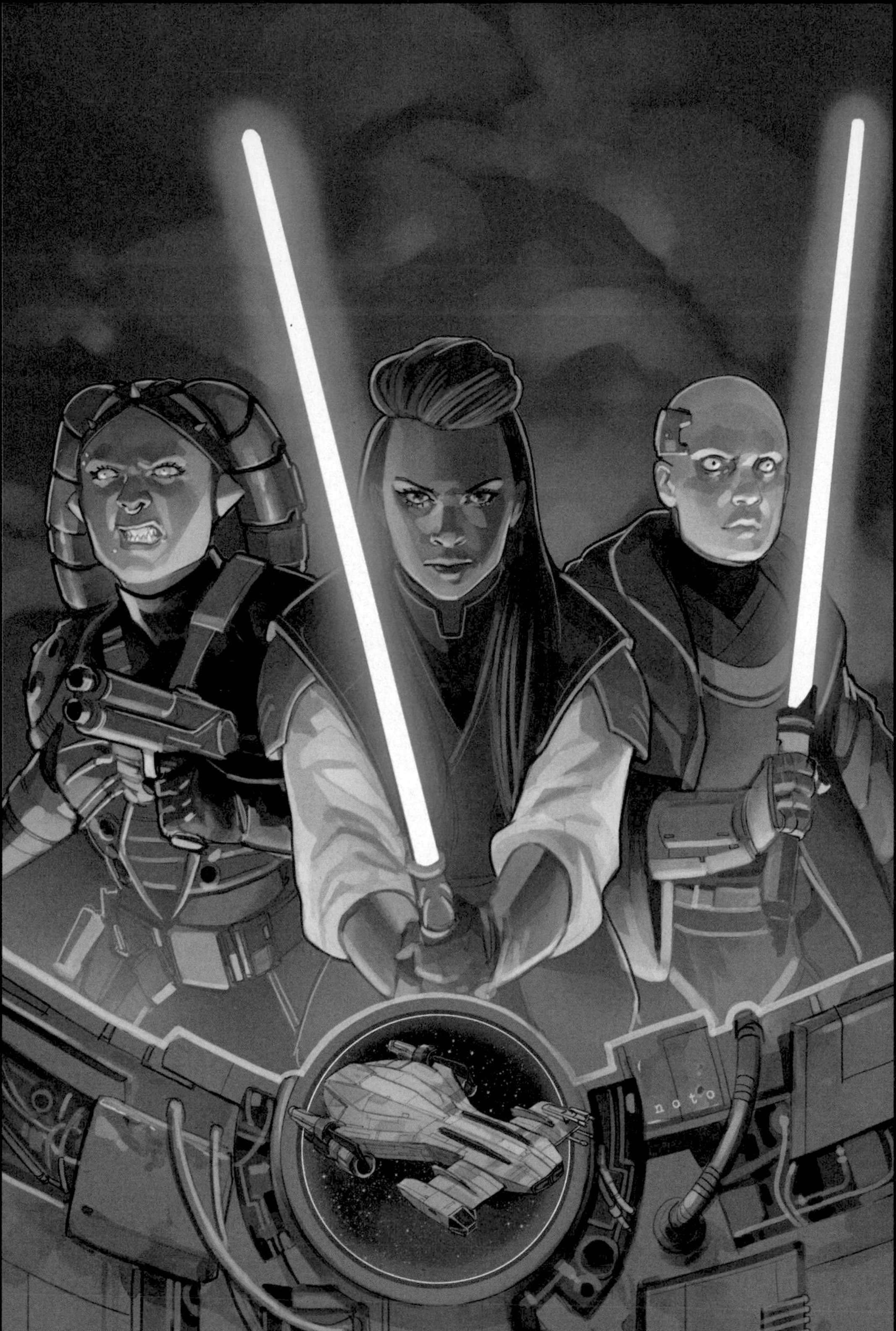
noto

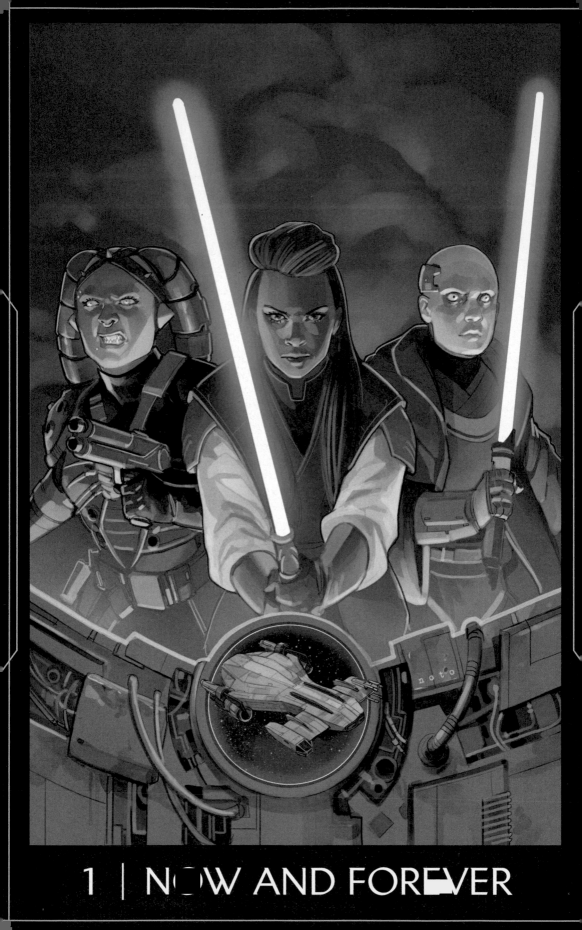

1 | NOW AND FOREVER

STAR WARS TIMELINE

THE HIGH REPUBLIC

FALL OF THE JEDI

THE PHANTOM MENACE

ATTACK OF THE CLONES

THE CLONE WARS

REVENGE OF THE SITH

REIGN OF THE EMPIRE

THE BAD BATCH

SOLO: A STAR WARS STORY

OBI-WAN KENOBI

AGE OF REBELLION

REBELS

ANDOR

ROGUE ONE: A STAR WARS STORY

A NEW HOPE

THE EMPIRE STRIKES BACK

RETURN OF THE JEDI

THE NEW REPUBLIC

THE BOOK OF BOBA FETT

THE MANDALORIAN

AHSOKA

RISE OF THE FIRST ORDER

RESISTANCE

THE FORCE AWAKENS

THE LAST JEDI

THE RISE OF SKYWALKER

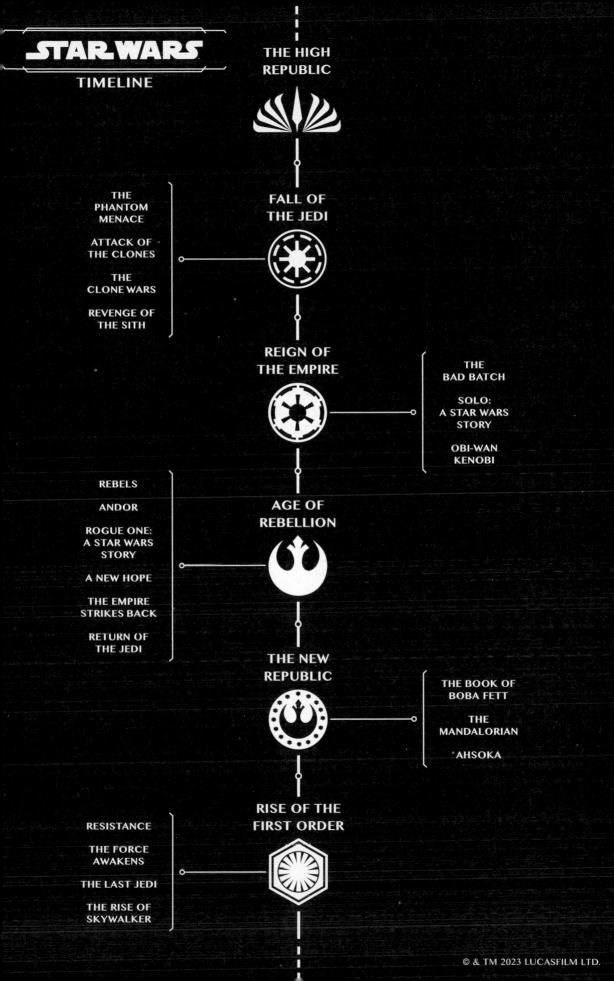

THE HIGH REPUBLIC

A year has passed since the destruction of the *STARLIGHT BEACON* station by the nefarious *Marchion Ro* and his Nihil marauders.

The Nihil have established an OCCLUSION ZONE in the Outer Rim, stranding hundreds of worlds behind their Stormwall. Communications are blocked, and ships that enter are lost to the void or destroyed by the Nihil.

The Republic is helpless against this sinister threat, and the brave and wise JEDI KNIGHTS remain fearful of Ro's fabled NAMELESS creatures, which the Jedi have learned are very real, and very deadly....

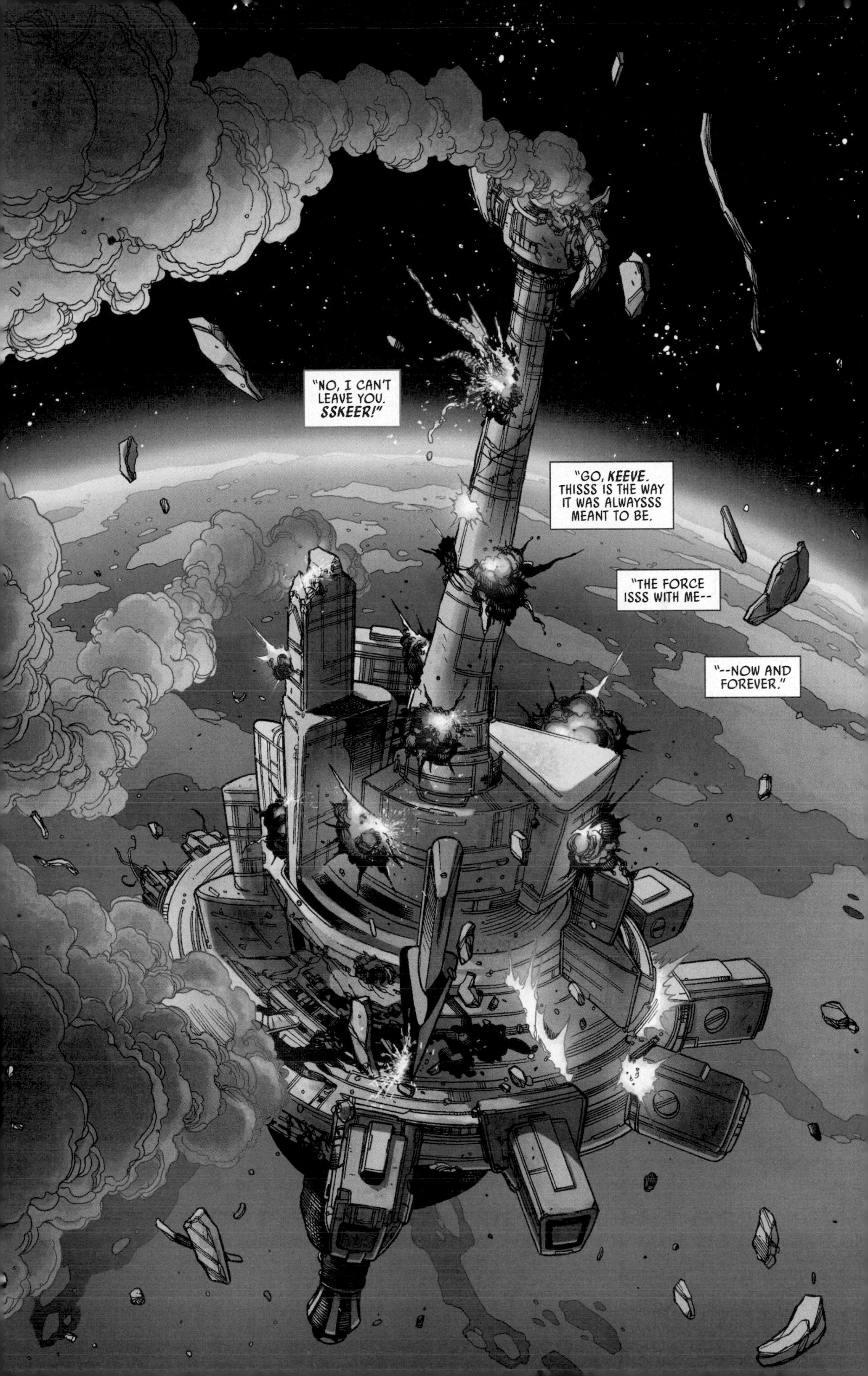
"NO, I CAN'T LEAVE YOU. SSKEER!"
"GO, KEEVE. THISSS IS THE WAY IT WAS ALWAYSSS MEANT TO BE.
"THE FORCE ISSS WITH ME--
"--NOW AND FOREVER."

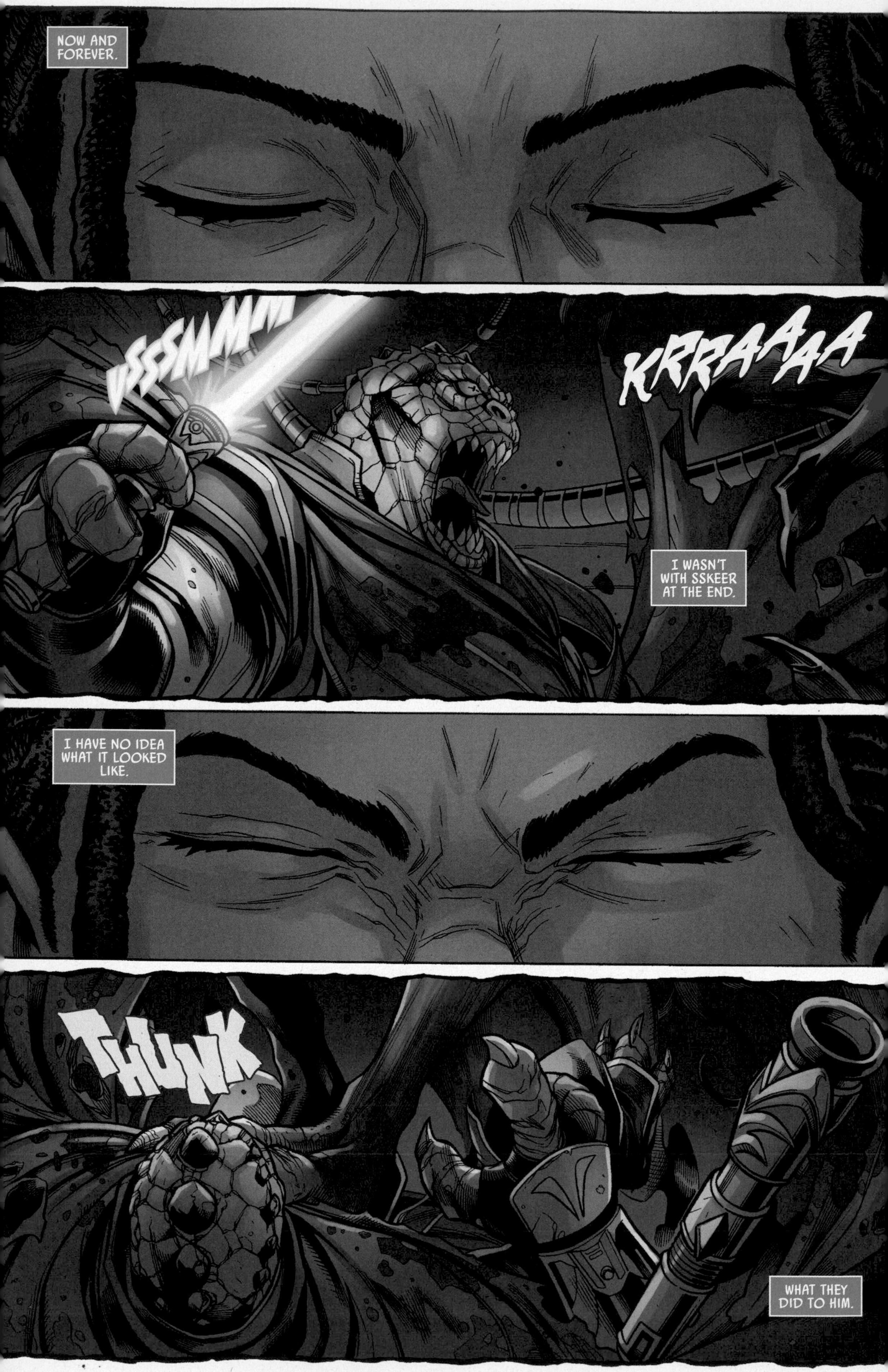
NOW AND FOREVER.
VSSSMMM
KRRAAAA
I WASN'T WITH SSKEER AT THE END.
I HAVE NO IDEA WHAT IT LOOKED LIKE.
THUNK
WHAT THEY DID TO HIM.

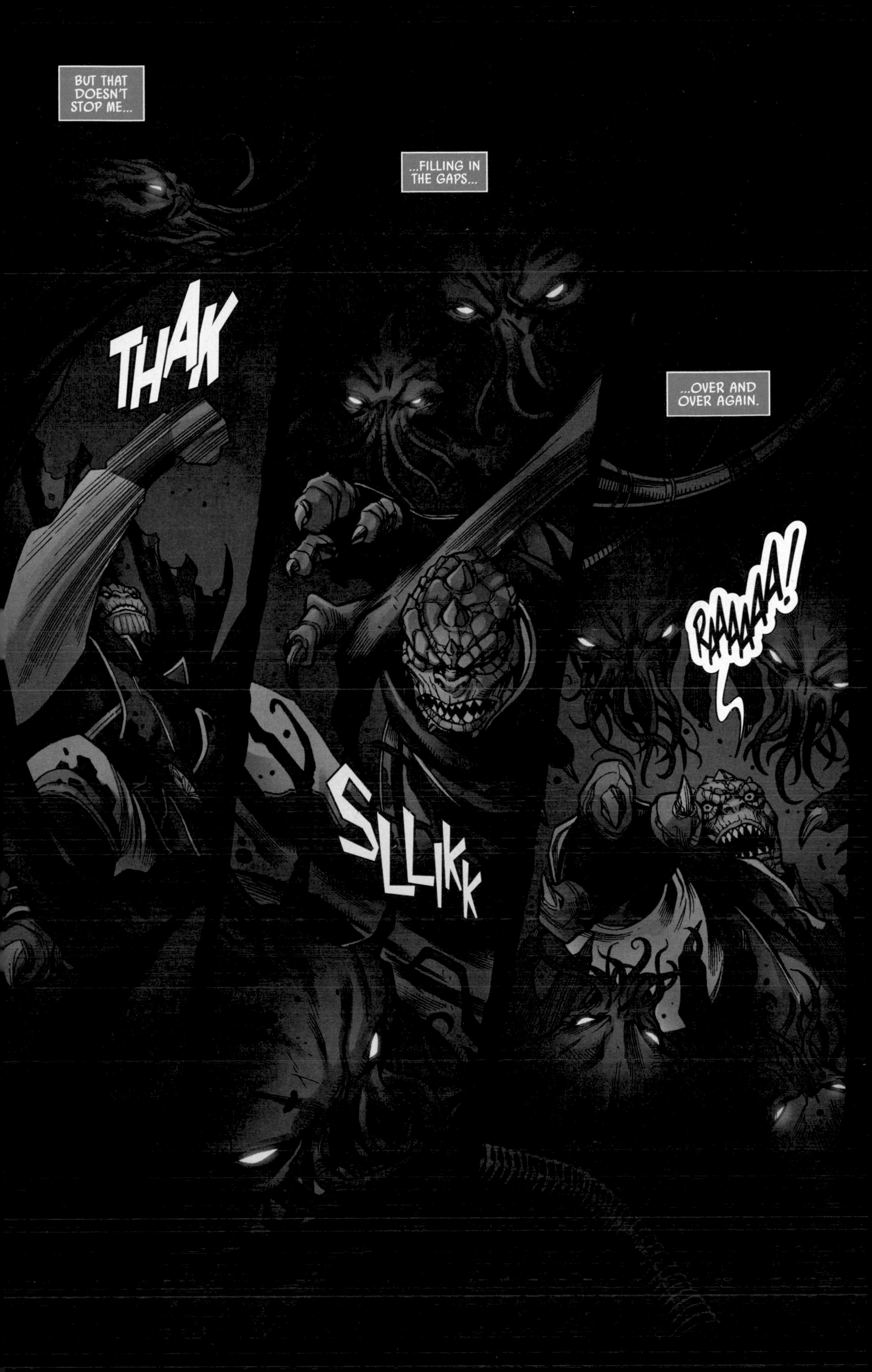
BUT THAT DOESN'T STOP ME...
...FILLING IN THE GAPS...
THAK
...OVER AND OVER AGAIN.
RAAAAA!
SLLIKK

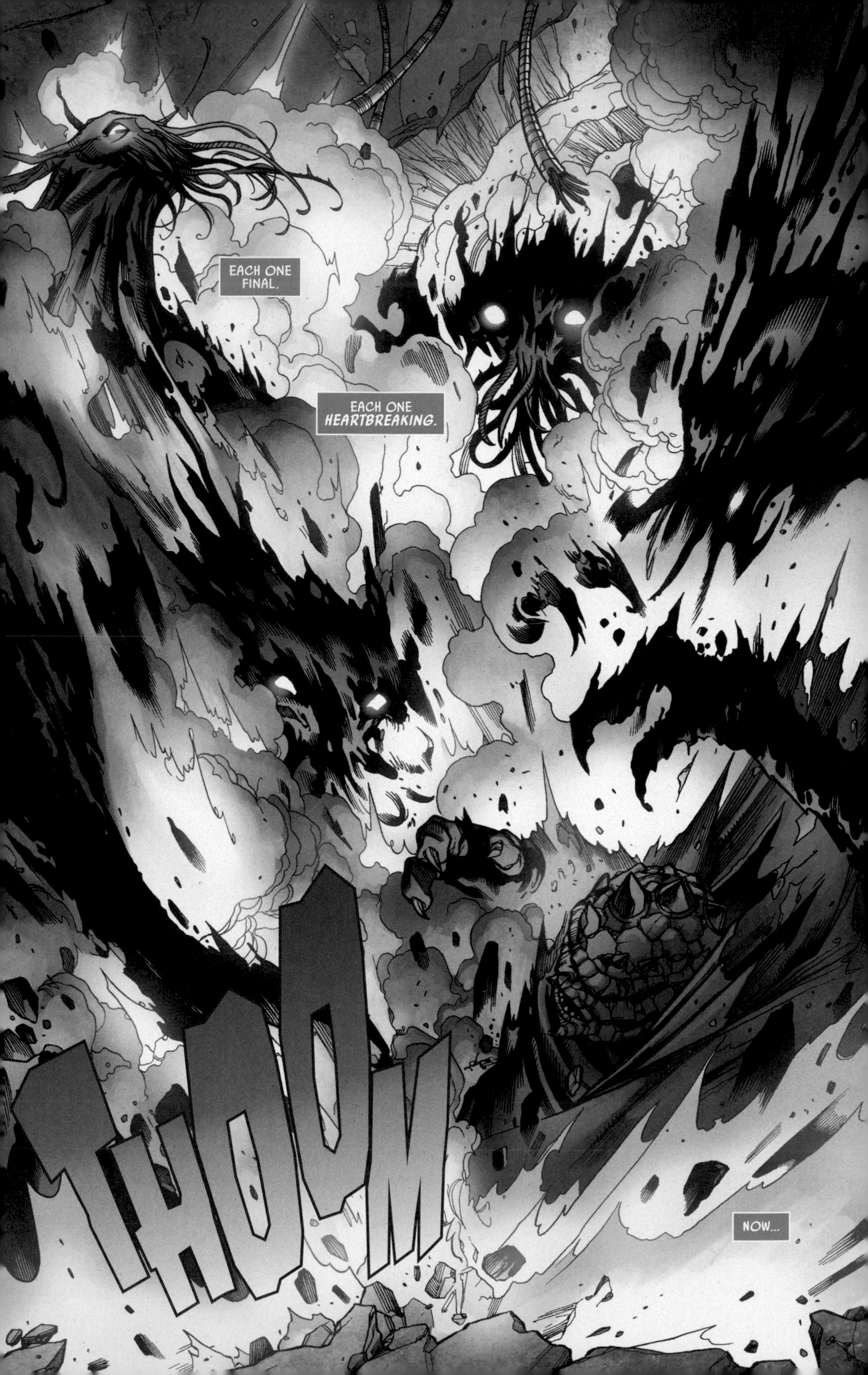
EACH ONE FINAL.
EACH ONE HEARTBREAKING.
THOOM
NOW...

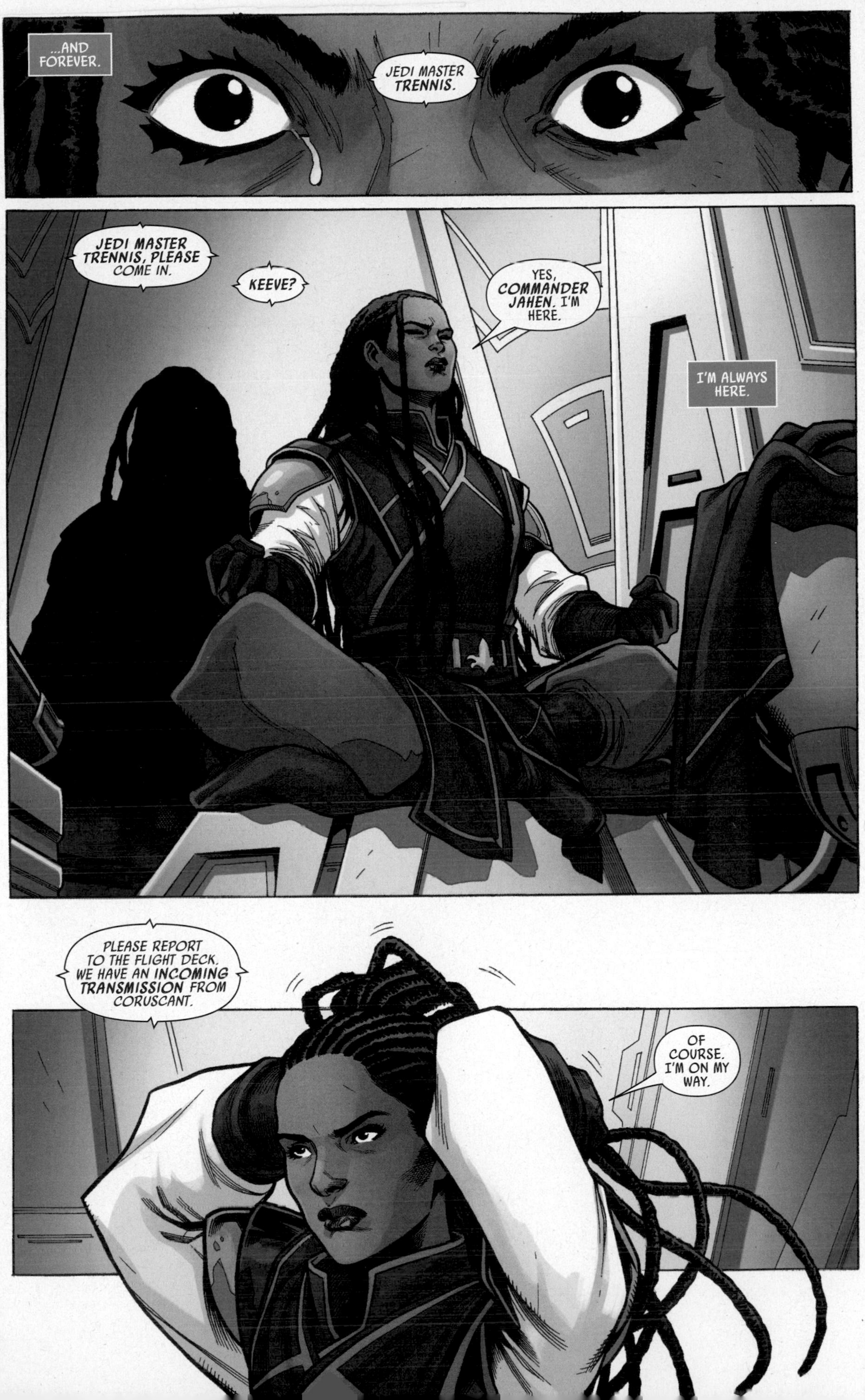
...AND FOREVER.
JEDI MASTER TRENNIS.
JEDI MASTER TRENNIS, PLEASE COME IN.
KEEVE?
YES, COMMANDER JAHEN. I'M HERE.
I'M ALWAYS HERE.
PLEASE REPORT TO THE FLIGHT DECK. WE HAVE AN INCOMING TRANSMISSION FROM CORUSCANT.
OF COURSE. I'M ON MY WAY.

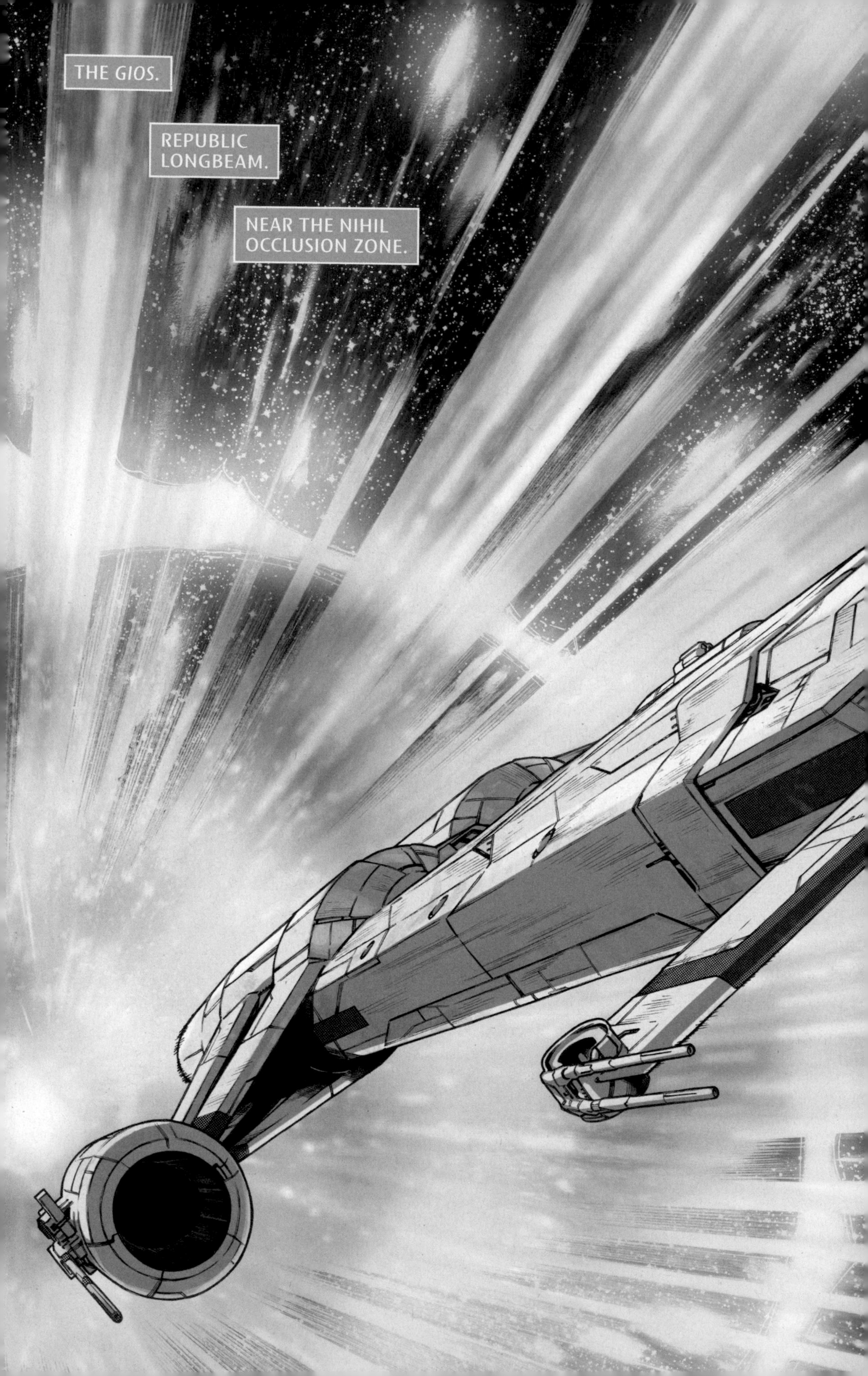
THE *GIOS*.
REPUBLIC LONGBEAM.
NEAR THE NIHIL OCCLUSION ZONE.

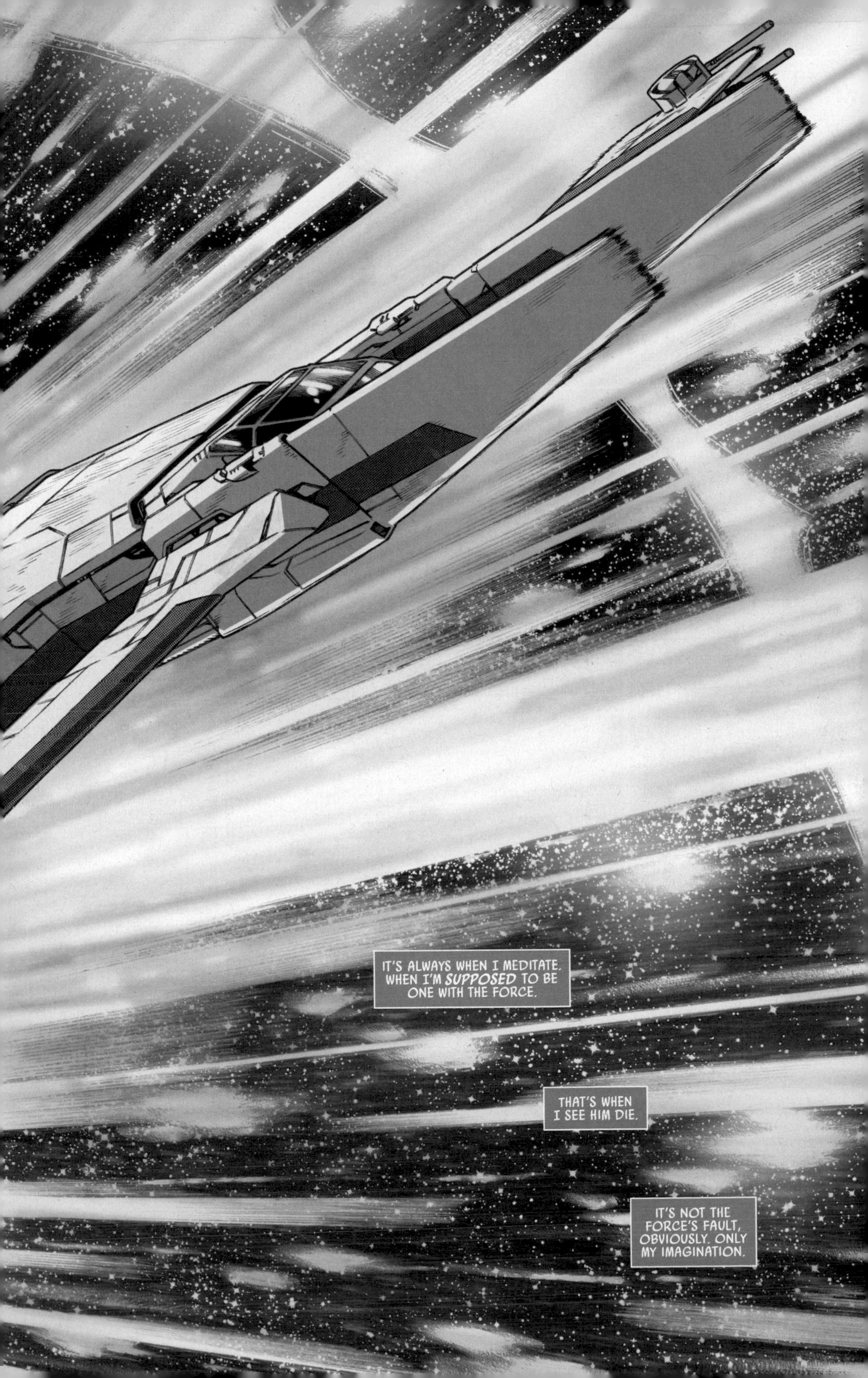
IT'S ALWAYS WHEN I MEDITATE. WHEN I'M *SUPPOSED* TO BE ONE WITH THE FORCE.
THAT'S WHEN I SEE HIM DIE.
IT'S NOT THE FORCE'S FAULT, OBVIOUSLY. ONLY MY IMAGINATION.

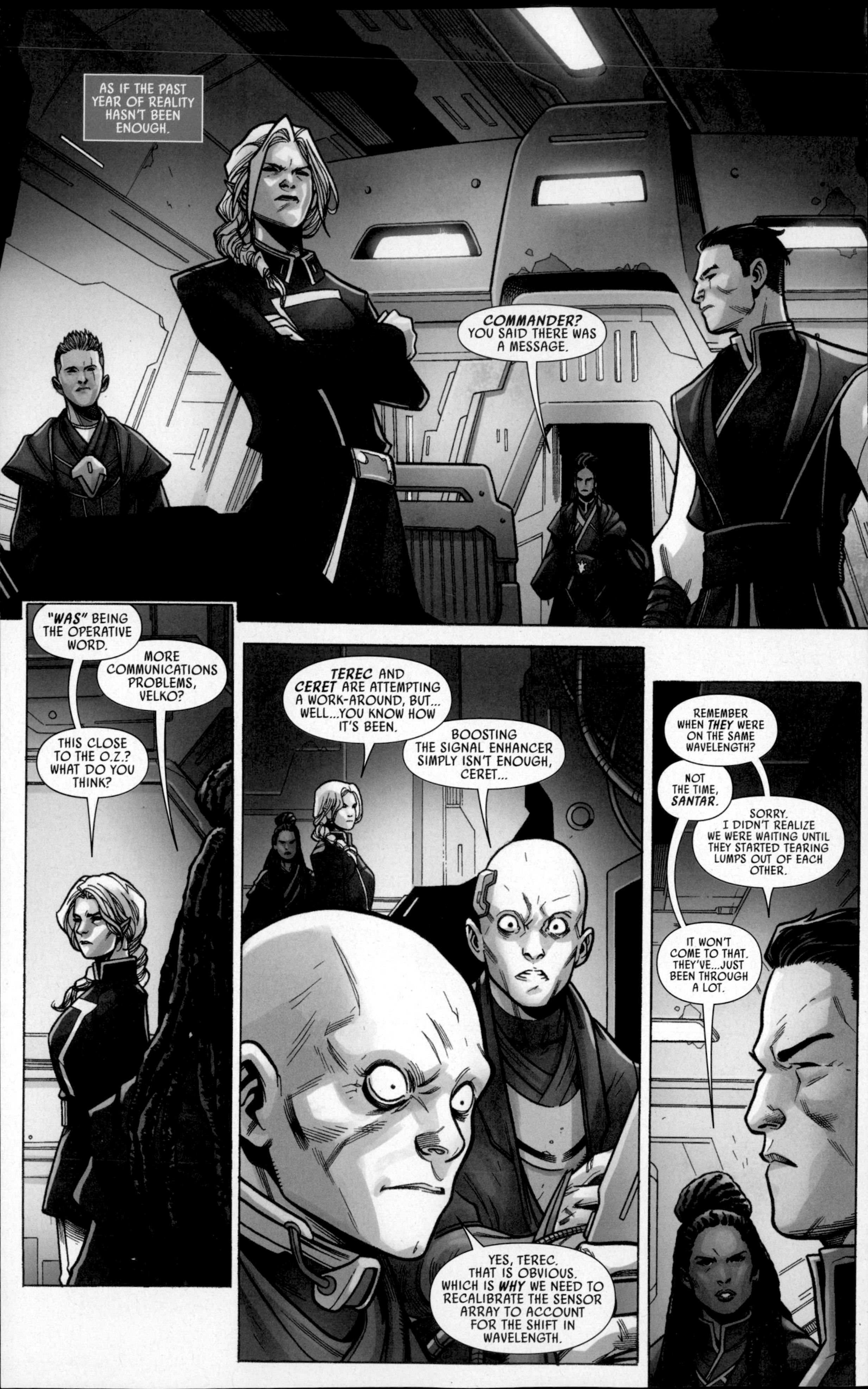

AS IF THE PAST YEAR OF REALITY HASN'T BEEN ENOUGH.
COMMANDER? YOU SAID THERE WAS A MESSAGE.
"WAS" BEING THE OPERATIVE WORD.
MORE COMMUNICATIONS PROBLEMS, VELKO?
THIS CLOSE TO THE O.Z.? WHAT DO YOU THINK?
TEREC AND CERET ARE ATTEMPTING A WORK-AROUND, BUT... WELL...YOU KNOW HOW IT'S BEEN.
BOOSTING THE SIGNAL ENHANCER SIMPLY ISN'T ENOUGH, CERET...
YES, TEREC. THAT IS OBVIOUS. WHICH IS WHY WE NEED TO RECALIBRATE THE SENSOR ARRAY TO ACCOUNT FOR THE SHIFT IN WAVELENGTH.
REMEMBER WHEN THEY WERE ON THE SAME WAVELENGTH?
NOT THE TIME, SANTAR.
SORRY. I DIDN'T REALIZE WE WERE WAITING UNTIL THEY STARTED TEARING LUMPS OUT OF EACH OTHER.
IT WON'T COME TO THAT. THEY'VE...JUST BEEN THROUGH A LOT.

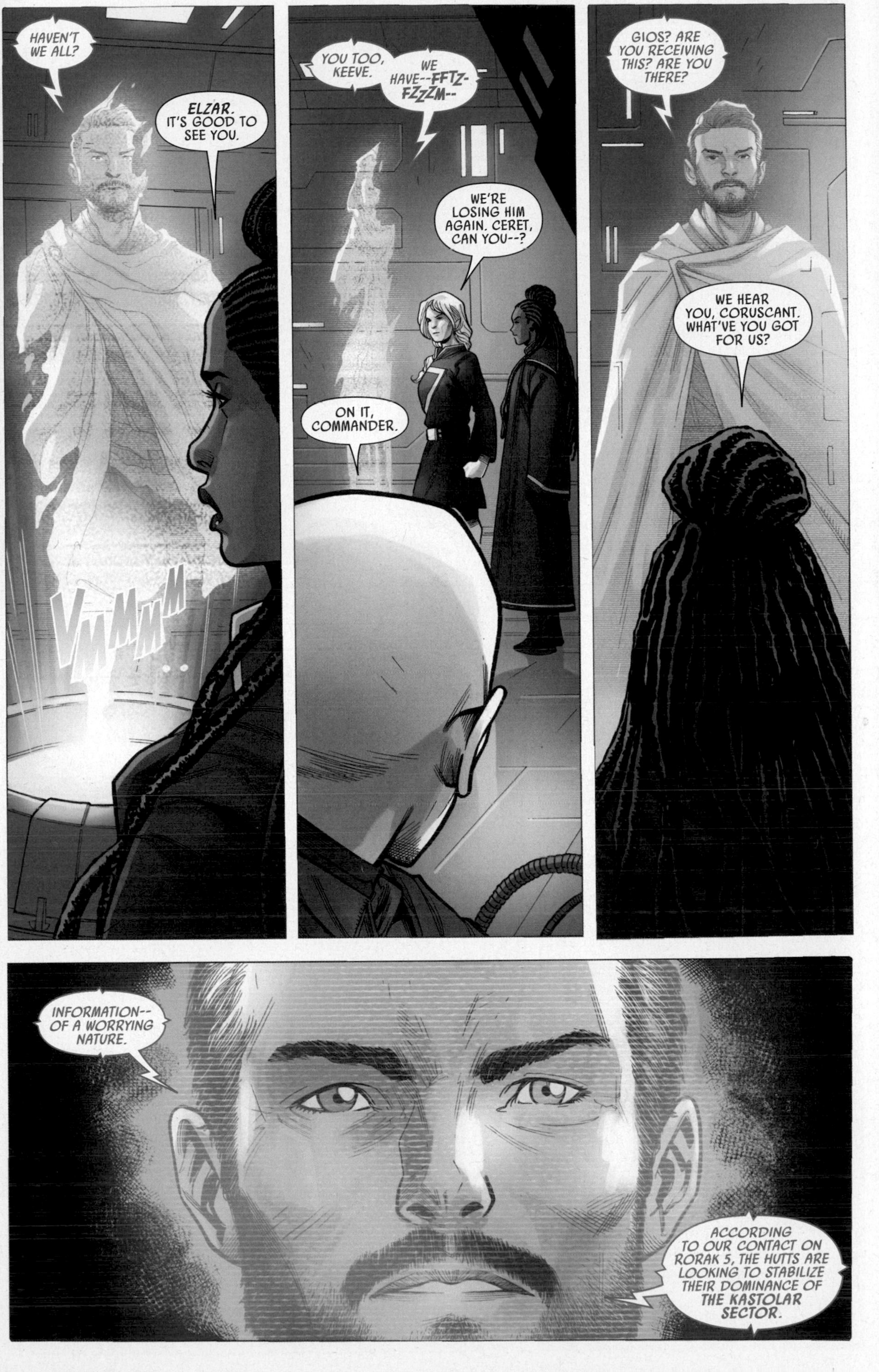

HAVEN'T WE ALL?
ELZAR. IT'S GOOD TO SEE YOU.
VMMMM
YOU TOO, KEEVE.
WE HAVE--FFTZ-FZZZM--
WE'RE LOSING HIM AGAIN. CERET, CAN YOU--?
ON IT, COMMANDER.
GIOS? ARE YOU RECEIVING THIS? ARE YOU THERE?
WE HEAR YOU, CORUSCANT. WHAT'VE YOU GOT FOR US?
INFORMATION-- OF A WORRYING NATURE.
ACCORDING TO OUR CONTACT ON RORAK 5, THE HUTTS ARE LOOKING TO STABILIZE THEIR DOMINANCE OF THE KASTOLAR SECTOR.

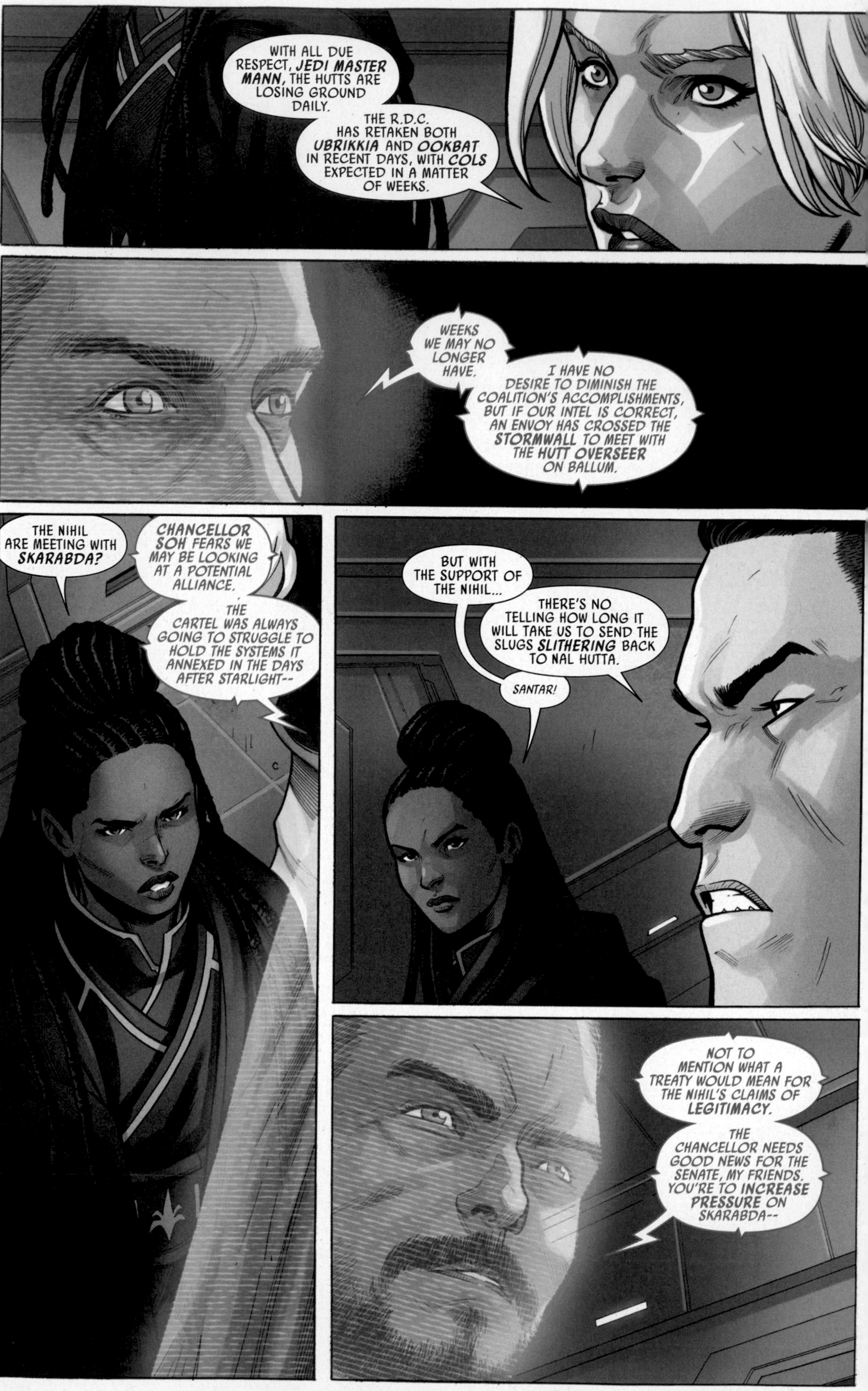
WITH ALL DUE RESPECT, JEDI MASTER MANN, THE HUTTS ARE LOSING GROUND DAILY.
THE R.D.C. HAS RETAKEN BOTH UBRIKKIA AND OOKBAT IN RECENT DAYS, WITH COLS EXPECTED IN A MATTER OF WEEKS.
WEEKS WE MAY NO LONGER HAVE.
I HAVE NO DESIRE TO DIMINISH THE COALITION'S ACCOMPLISHMENTS, BUT IF OUR INTEL IS CORRECT, AN ENVOY HAS CROSSED THE STORMWALL TO MEET WITH THE HUTT OVERSEER ON BALLUM.
THE NIHIL ARE MEETING WITH SKARABDA?
CHANCELLOR SOH FEARS WE MAY BE LOOKING AT A POTENTIAL ALLIANCE.
THE CARTEL WAS ALWAYS GOING TO STRUGGLE TO HOLD THE SYSTEMS IT ANNEXED IN THE DAYS AFTER STARLIGHT--
BUT WITH THE SUPPORT OF THE NIHIL...
THERE'S NO TELLING HOW LONG IT WILL TAKE US TO SEND THE SLUGS SLITHERING BACK TO NAL HUTTA.
SANTAR!
NOT TO MENTION WHAT A TREATY WOULD MEAN FOR THE NIHIL'S CLAIMS OF LEGITIMACY.
THE CHANCELLOR NEEDS GOOD NEWS FOR THE SENATE, MY FRIENDS. YOU'RE TO INCREASE PRESSURE ON SKARABDA--

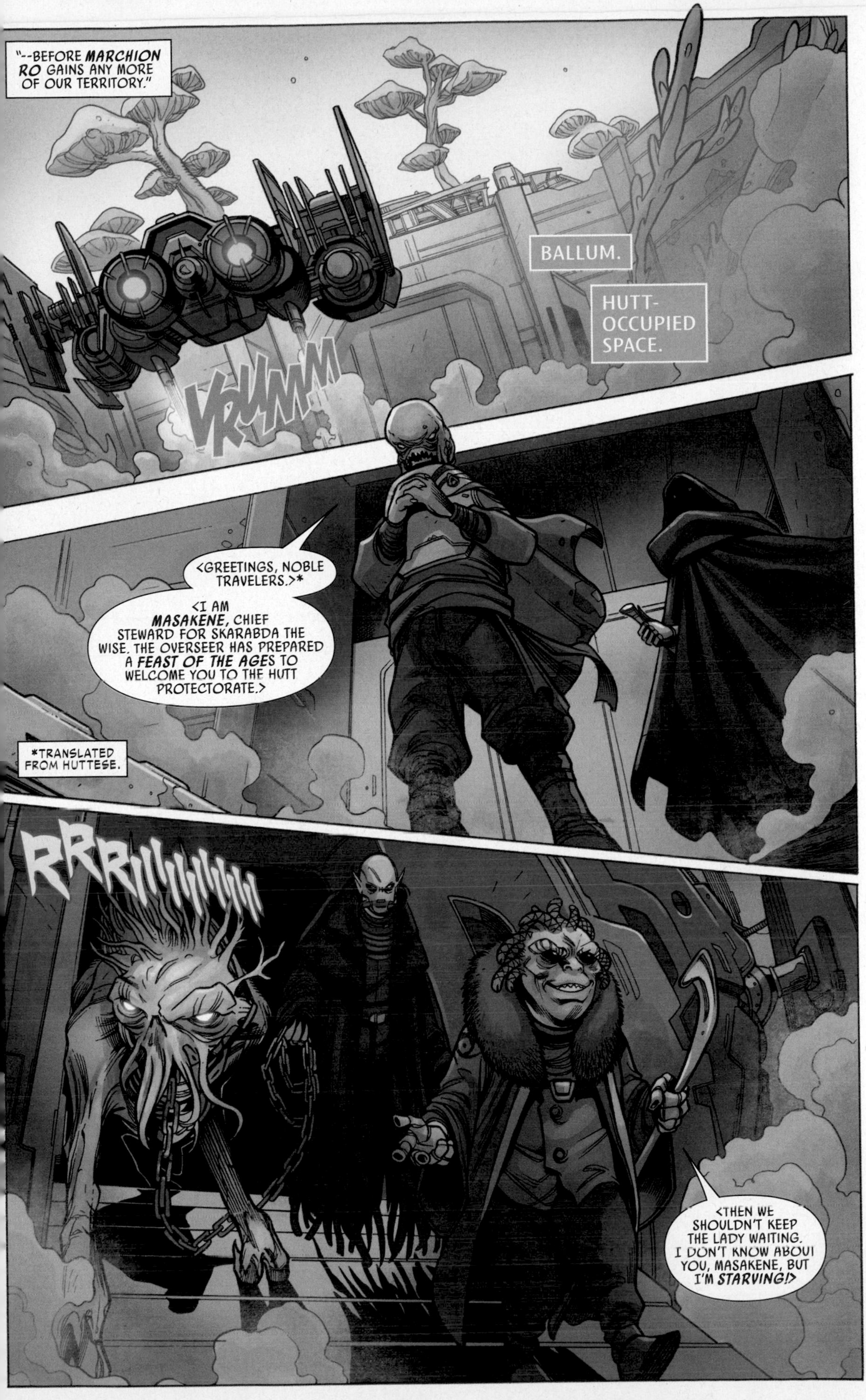
"--BEFORE MARCHION RO GAINS ANY MORE OF OUR TERRITORY."
BALLUM.
HUTT-OCCUPIED SPACE.
VRUMMM
<GREETINGS, NOBLE TRAVELERS.>*
<I AM MASAKENE, CHIEF STEWARD FOR SKARABDA THE WISE. THE OVERSEER HAS PREPARED A FEAST OF THE AGES TO WELCOME YOU TO THE HUTT PROTECTORATE.>
*TRANSLATED FROM HUTTESE.
RRRIIIIIIIII
<THEN WE SHOULDN'T KEEP THE LADY WAITING. I DON'T KNOW ABOUT YOU, MASAKENE, BUT I'M STARVING!>

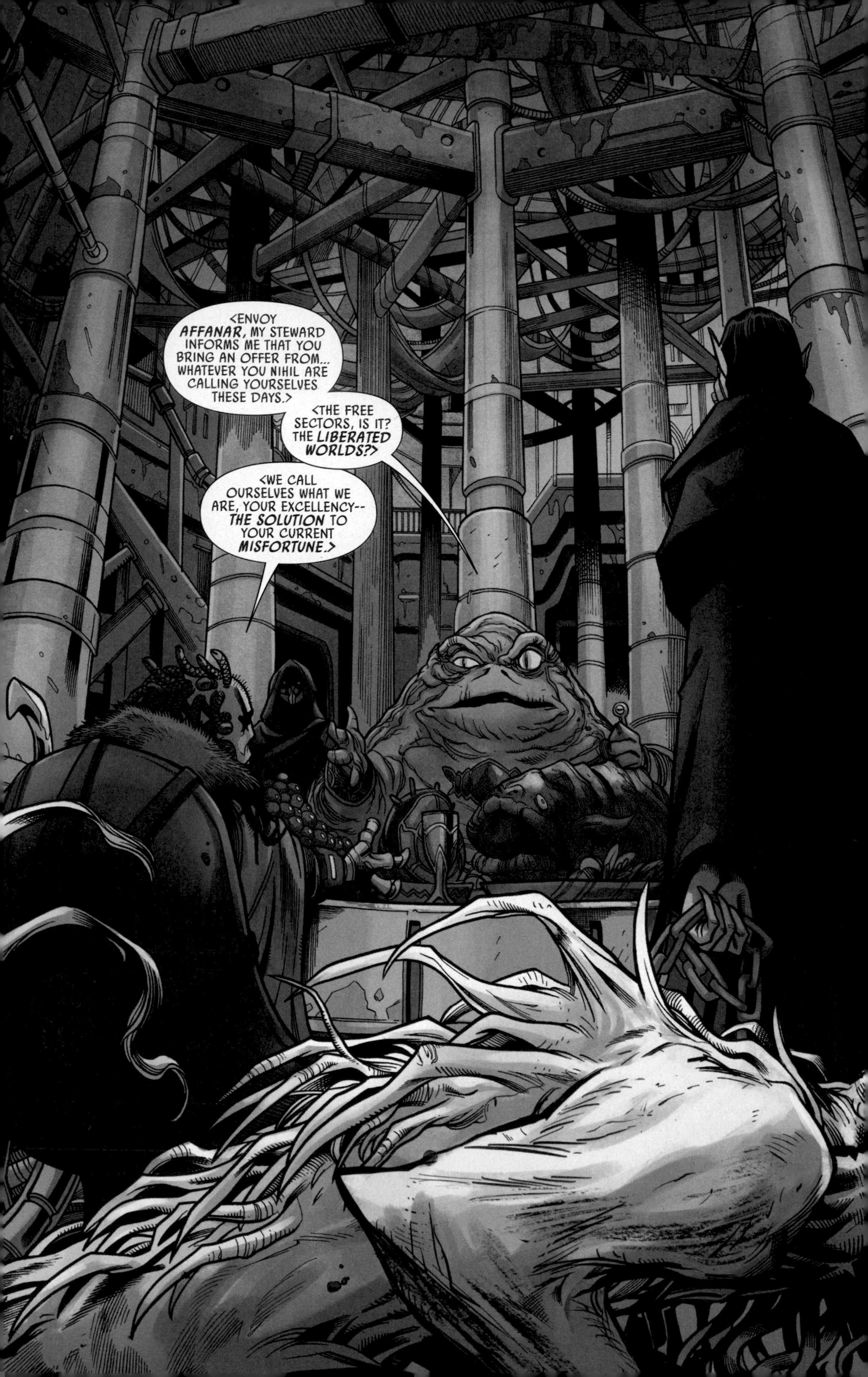
<ENVOY AFFANAR, MY STEWARD INFORMS ME THAT YOU BRING AN OFFER FROM... WHATEVER YOU NIHIL ARE CALLING YOURSELVES THESE DAYS.>
<THE FREE SECTORS, IS IT? THE LIBERATED WORLDS?>
<WE CALL OURSELVES WHAT WE ARE, YOUR EXCELLENCY-- THE SOLUTION TO YOUR CURRENT MISFORTUNE.>

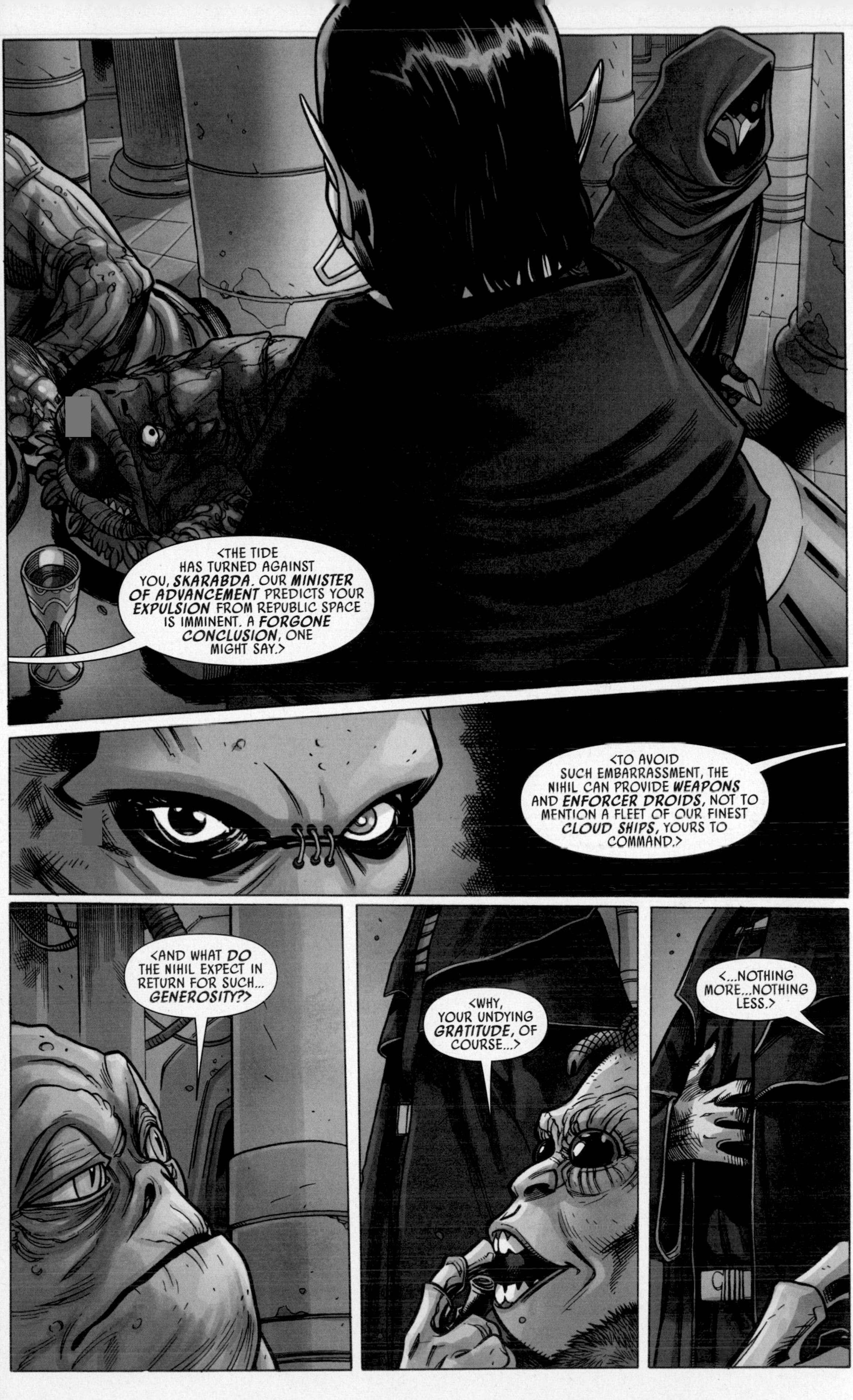
<THE TIDE HAS TURNED AGAINST YOU, SKARABDA. OUR MINISTER OF ADVANCEMENT PREDICTS YOUR EXPULSION FROM REPUBLIC SPACE IS IMMINENT. A FORGONE CONCLUSION, ONE MIGHT SAY.>
<TO AVOID SUCH EMBARRASSMENT, THE NIHIL CAN PROVIDE WEAPONS AND ENFORCER DROIDS, NOT TO MENTION A FLEET OF OUR FINEST CLOUD SHIPS, YOURS TO COMMAND.>
<AND WHAT DO THE NIHIL EXPECT IN RETURN FOR SUCH... GENEROSITY?>
<WHY, YOUR UNDYING GRATITUDE, OF COURSE...>
<...NOTHING MORE...NOTHING LESS.>

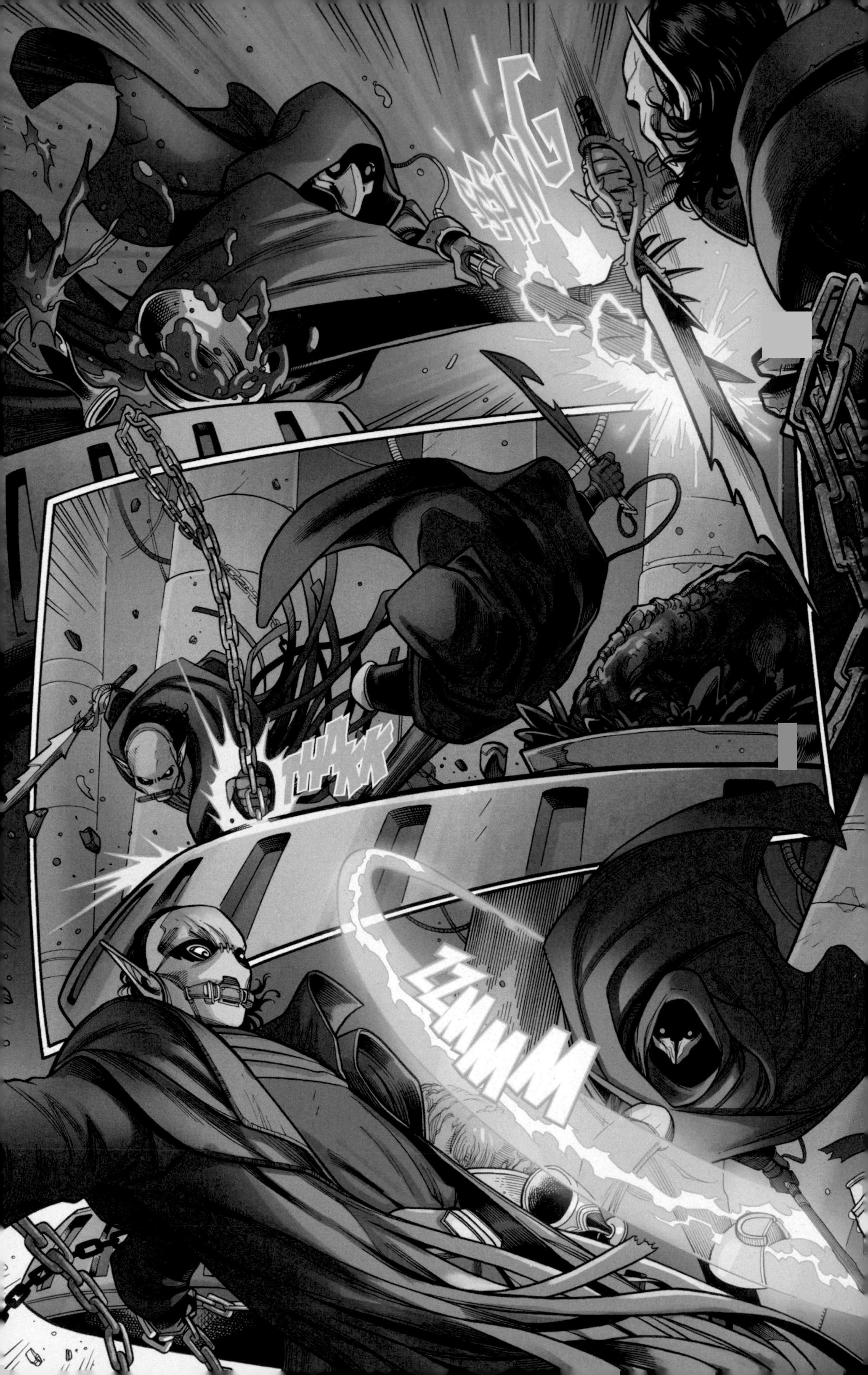
THAKK
ZZMMM

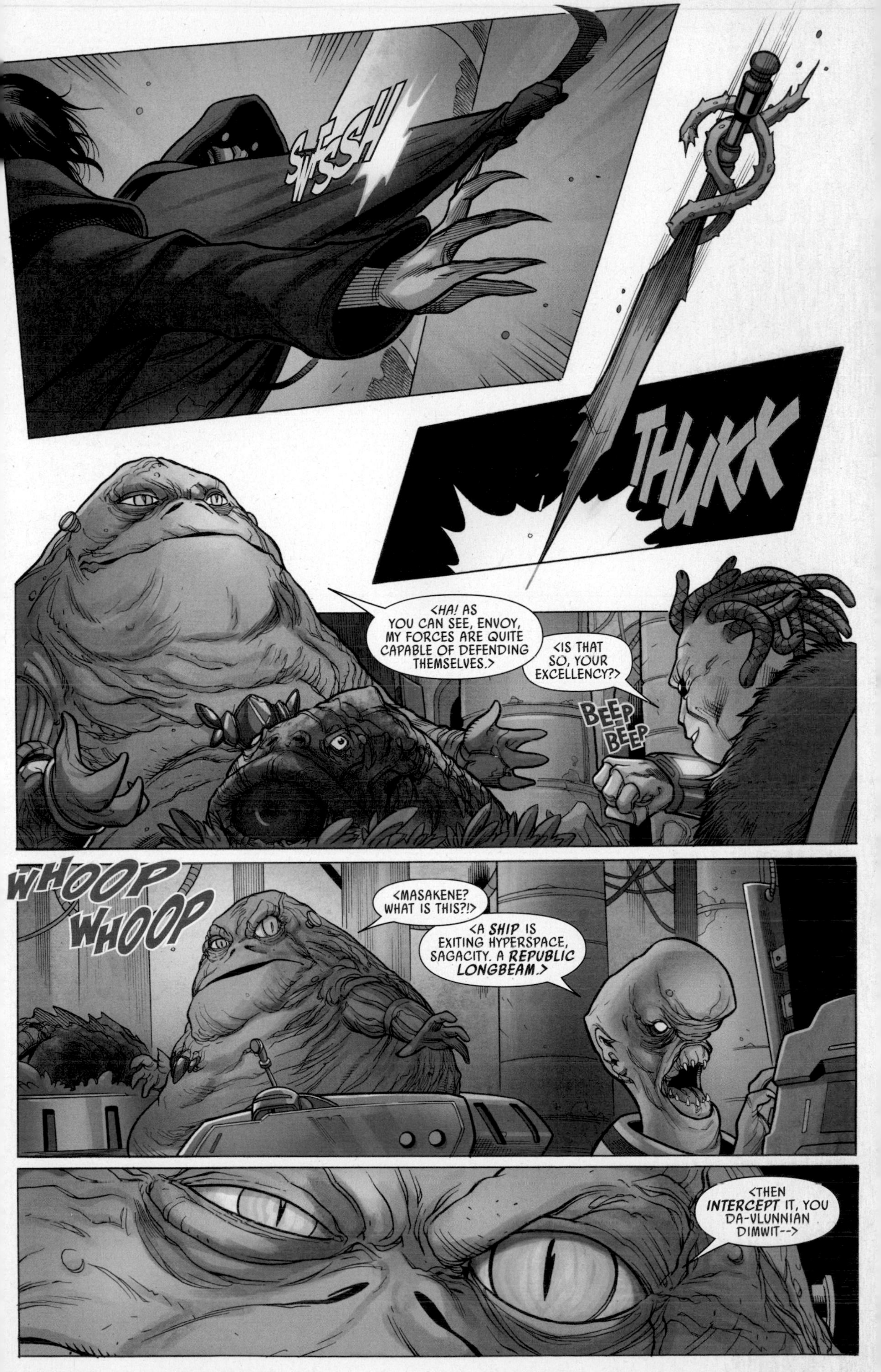
SWSSH
THUKK
<HA! AS YOU CAN SEE, ENVOY, MY FORCES ARE QUITE CAPABLE OF DEFENDING THEMSELVES.>
<IS THAT SO, YOUR EXCELLENCY?>
BEEP BEEP
WHOOP WHOOP
<MASAKENE? WHAT IS THIS?!>
<A SHIP IS EXITING HYPERSPACE, SAGACITY. A REPUBLIC LONGBEAM.>
<THEN INTERCEPT IT, YOU DA-VLUNNIAN DIMWIT-->

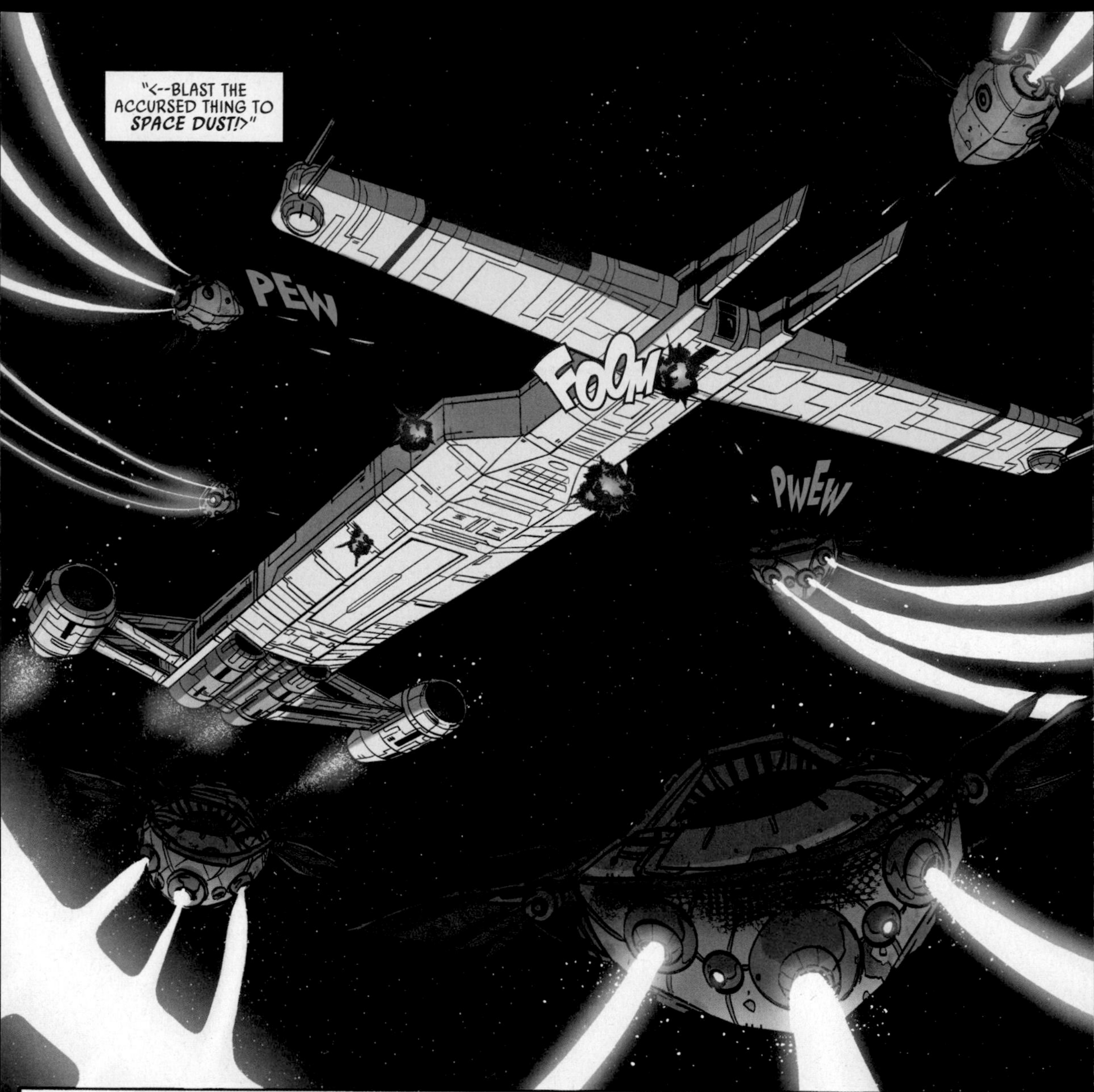
"<--BLAST THE ACCURSED THING TO SPACE DUST!>"
PEW
FOOM
PWEW
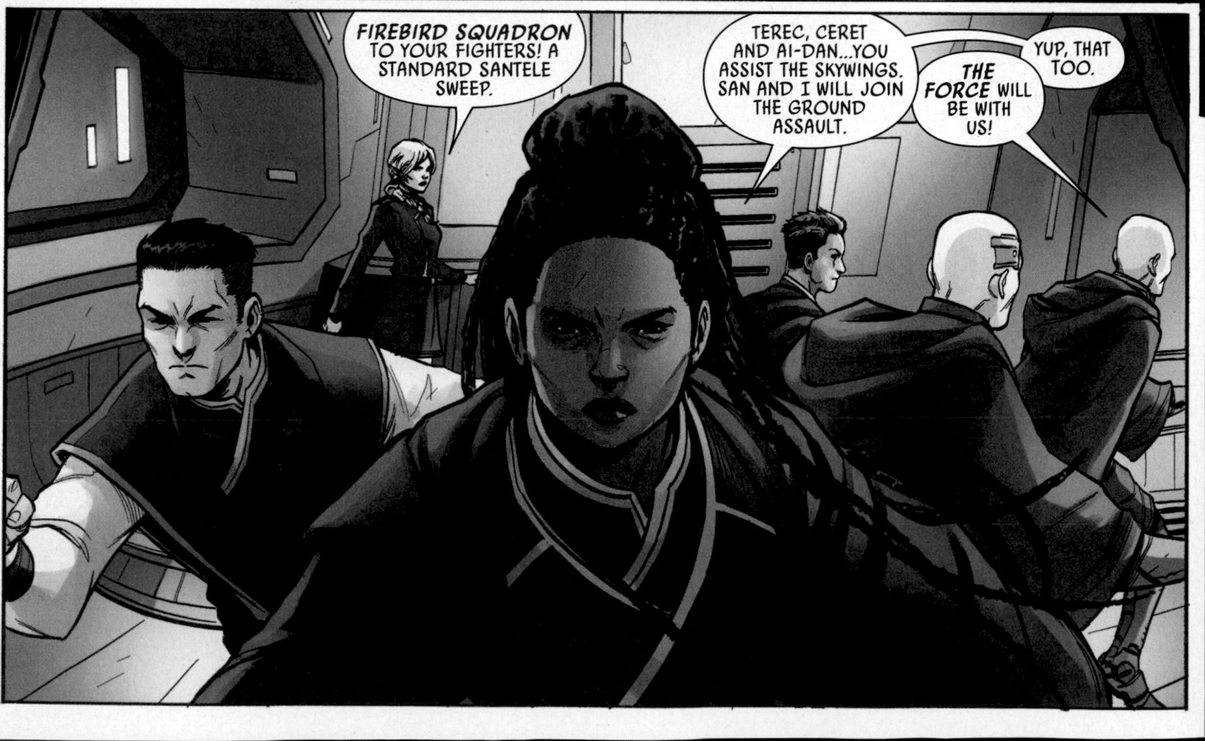
FIREBIRD SQUADRON TO YOUR FIGHTERS! A STANDARD SANTELE SWEEP.
TEREC, CERET AND AI-DAN...YOU ASSIST THE SKYWINGS. SAN AND I WILL JOIN THE GROUND ASSAULT.
THE FORCE WILL BE WITH US!
YUP, THAT TOO.

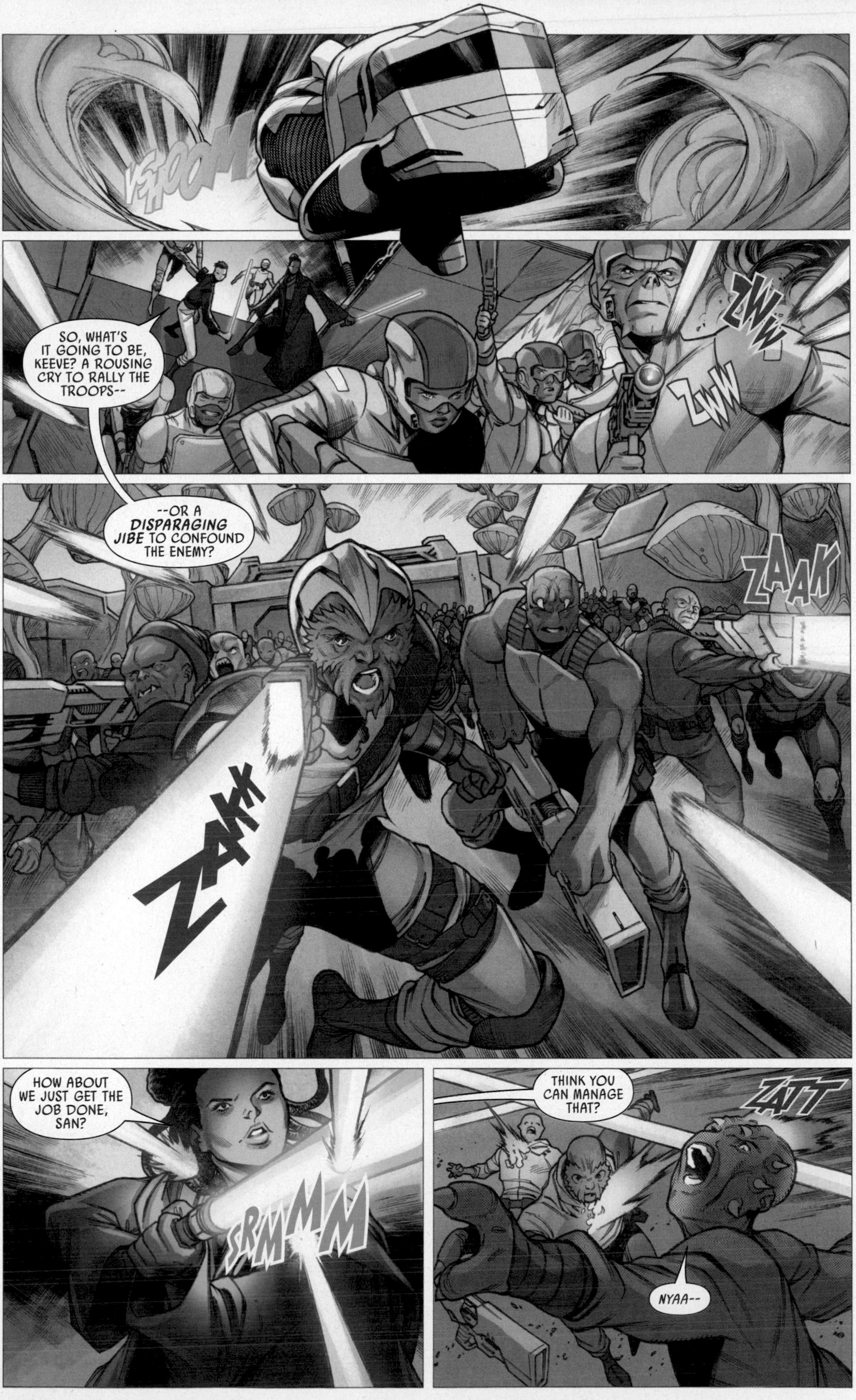
VSHOOM
SO, WHAT'S IT GOING TO BE, KEEVE? A ROUSING CRY TO RALLY THE TROOPS--
ZWW
ZWW
--OR A DISPARAGING JIBE TO CONFOUND THE ENEMY?
ZAAK
ZAKK
HOW ABOUT WE JUST GET THE JOB DONE, SAN?
SRMMM
THINK YOU CAN MANAGE THAT?
ZATT
NYAA--

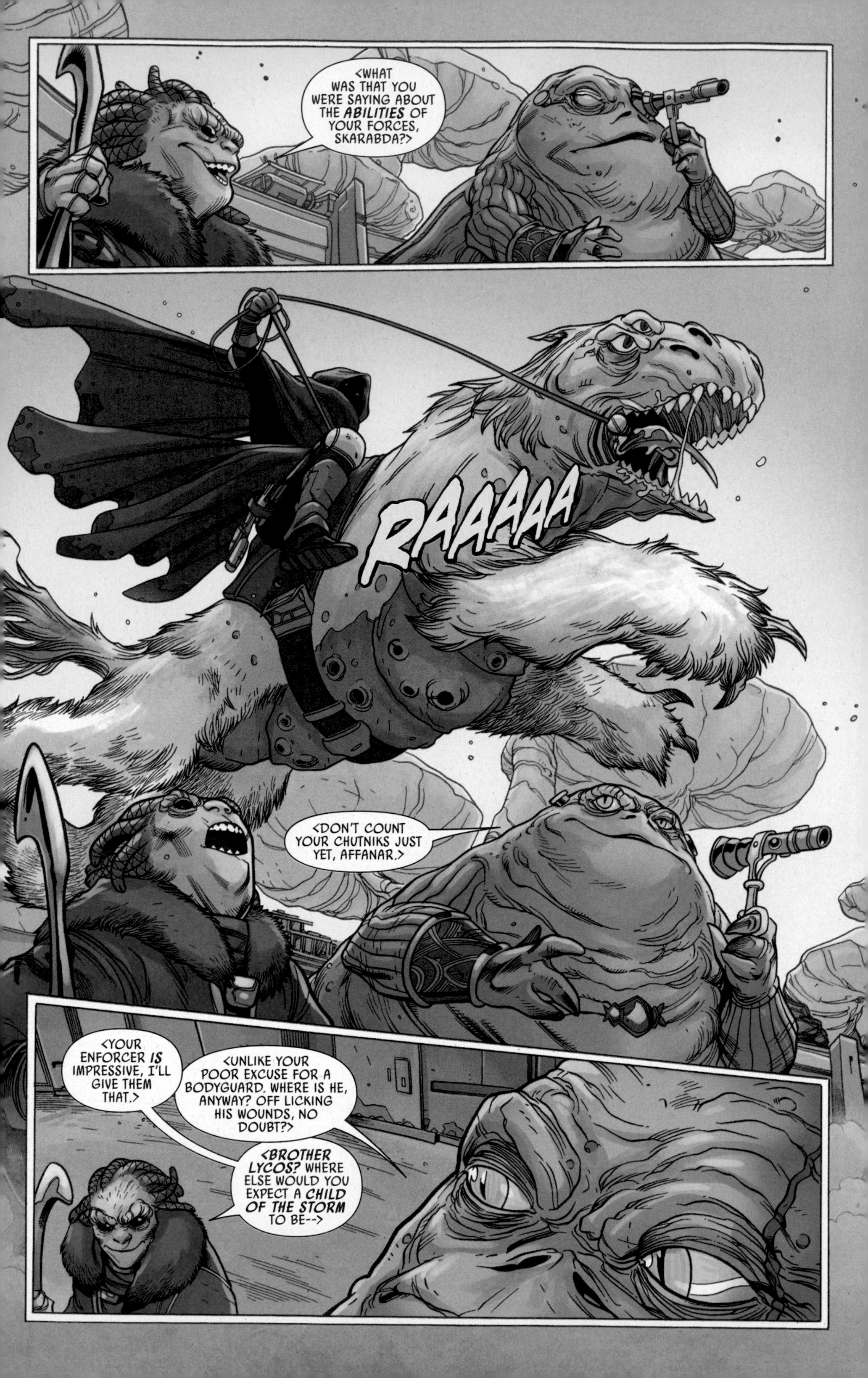
<WHAT WAS THAT YOU WERE SAYING ABOUT THE ABILITIES OF YOUR FORCES, SKARABDA?>
RAAAAA
<DON'T COUNT YOUR CHUTNIKS JUST YET, AFFANAR.>
<YOUR ENFORCER IS IMPRESSIVE, I'LL GIVE THEM THAT.>
<UNLIKE YOUR POOR EXCUSE FOR A BODYGUARD. WHERE IS HE, ANYWAY? OFF LICKING HIS WOUNDS, NO DOUBT?>
<BROTHER LYCOS? WHERE ELSE WOULD YOU EXPECT A CHILD OF THE STORM TO BE-->

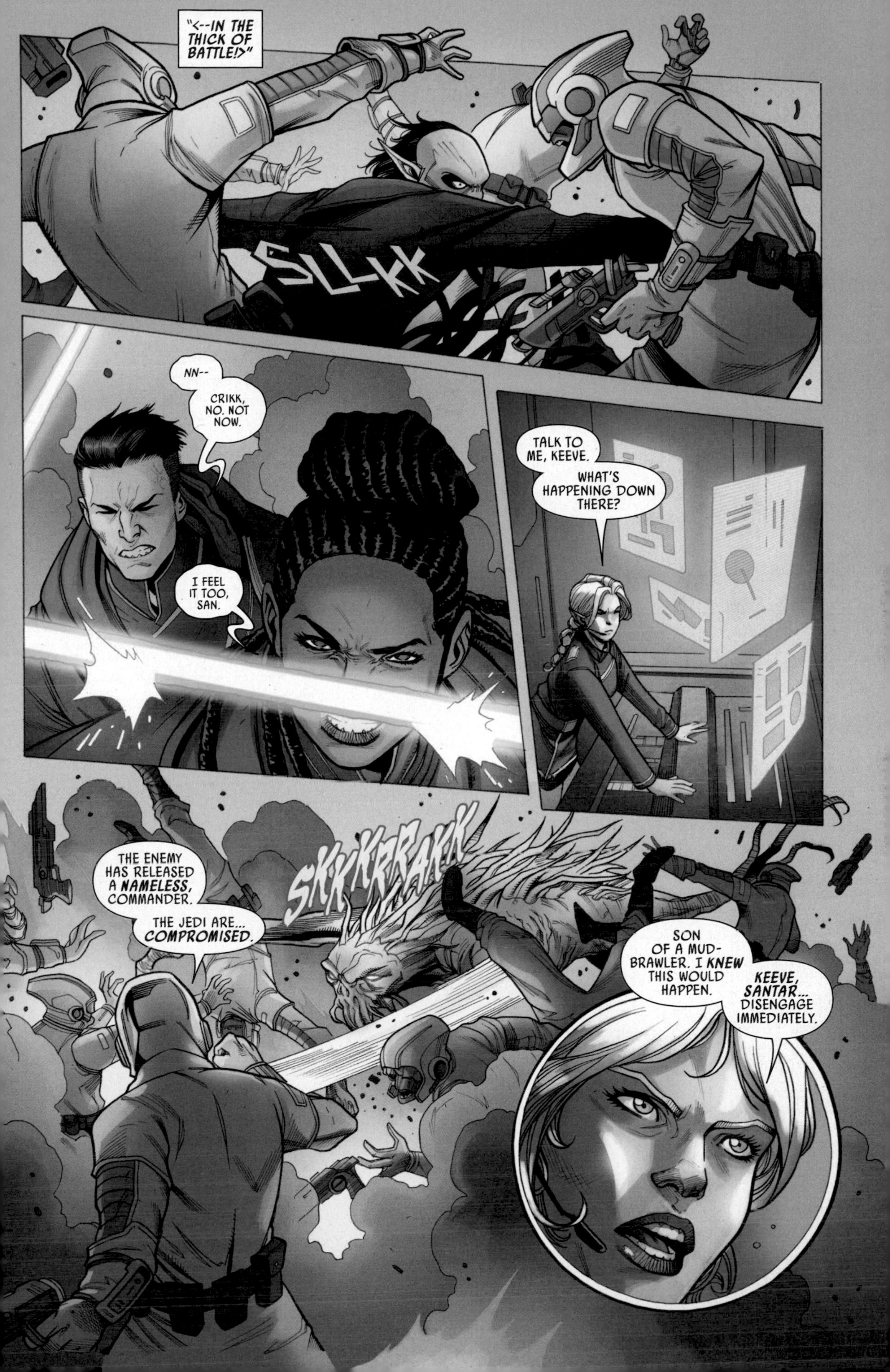
"<--IN THE THICK OF BATTLE!>"
SLLKK
NN--
CRIKK, NO. NOT NOW.
I FEEL IT TOO, SAN.
TALK TO ME, KEEVE.
WHAT'S HAPPENING DOWN THERE?
THE ENEMY HAS RELEASED A NAMELESS, COMMANDER.
THE JEDI ARE... COMPROMISED.
SKKRRAKK
SON OF A MUD-BRAWLER. I KNEW THIS WOULD HAPPEN.
KEEVE, SANTAR... DISENGAGE IMMEDIATELY.

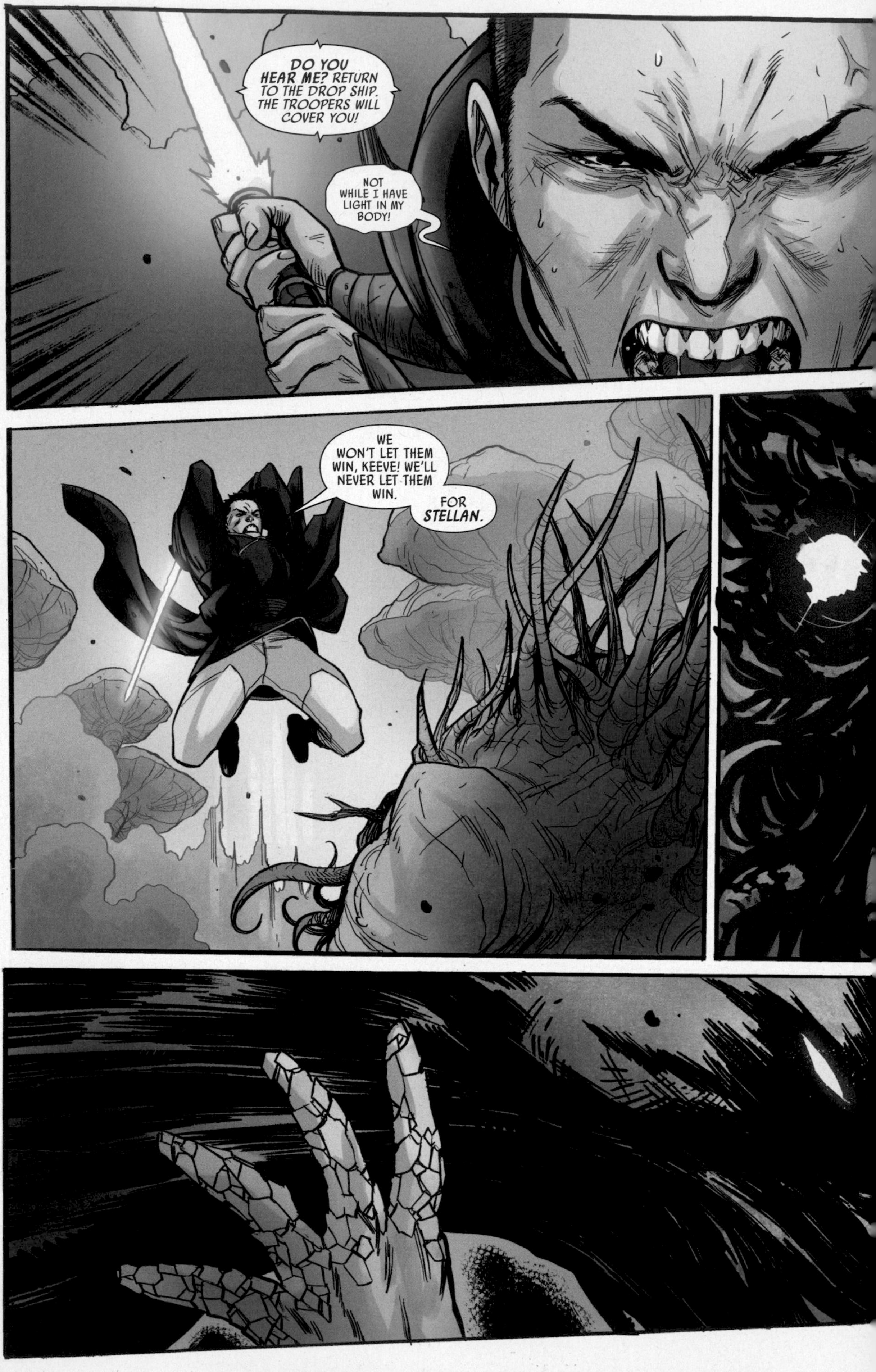
DO YOU HEAR ME? RETURN TO THE DROP SHIP. THE TROOPERS WILL COVER YOU!
NOT WHILE I HAVE LIGHT IN MY BODY!
WE WON'T LET THEM WIN, KEEVE! WE'LL NEVER LET THEM WIN.
FOR STELLAN.

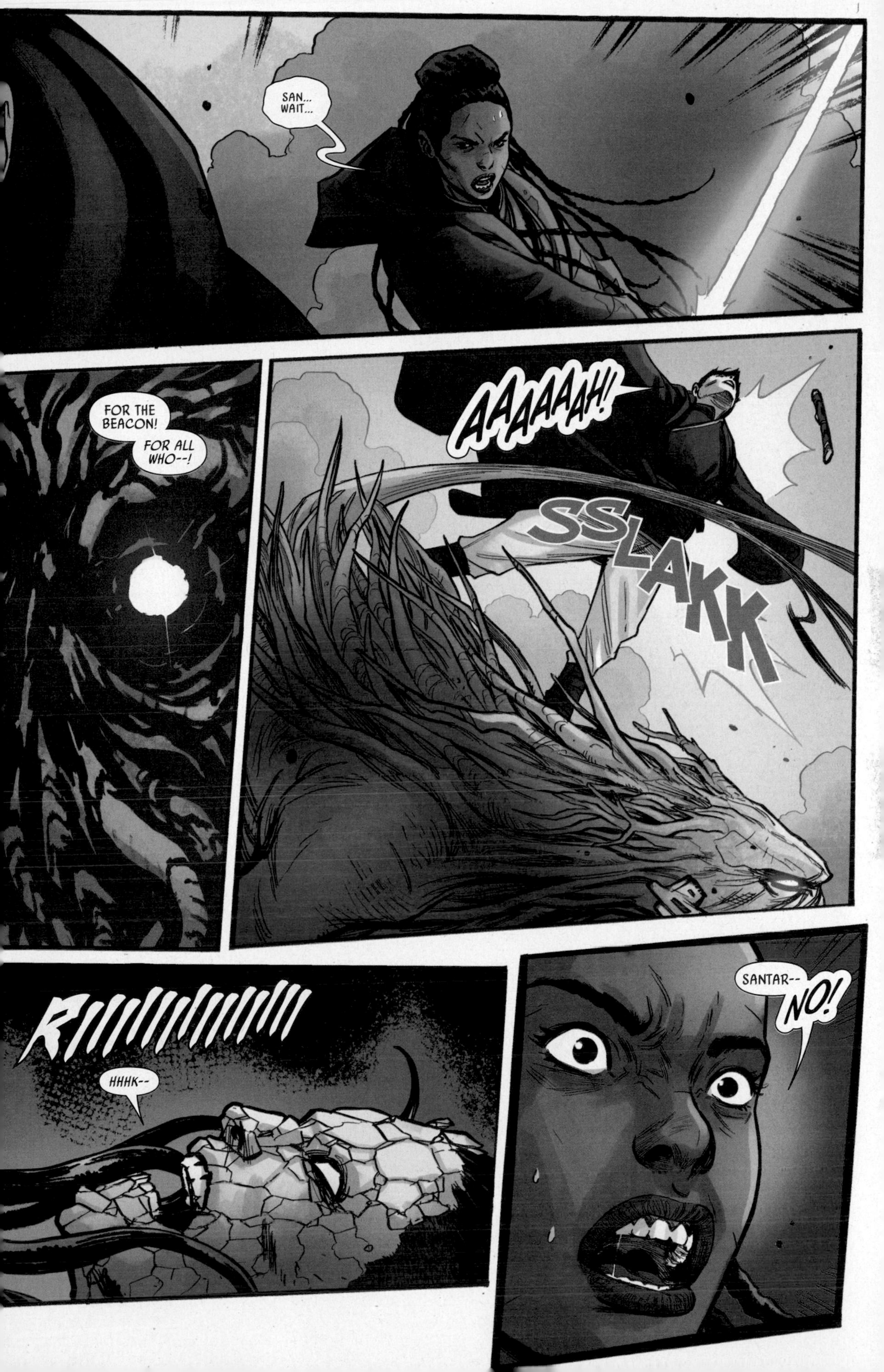
SAN... WAIT...
FOR THE BEACON!
FOR ALL WHO--!
AAAAAAH!
SSLAKK
RIIIIIIIIIIIII
HHHK--
SANTAR--
NO!

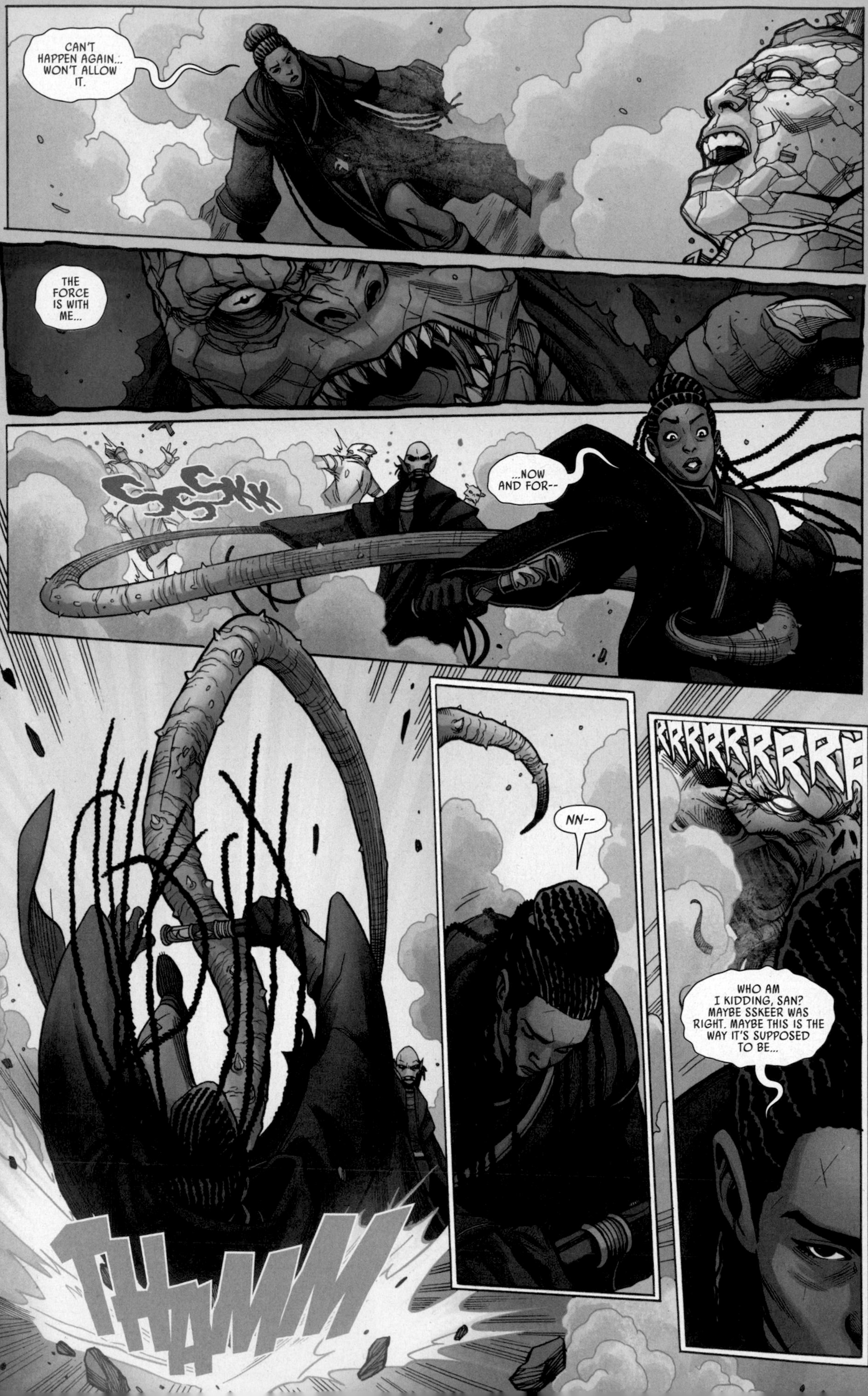
CAN'T HAPPEN AGAIN... WON'T ALLOW IT.
THE FORCE IS WITH ME...
SCSKK
...NOW AND FOR--
THWM
NN--
RRRRRRRRRRR
WHO AM I KIDDING, SAN? MAYBE SSKEER WAS RIGHT. MAYBE THIS IS THE WAY IT'S SUPPOSED TO BE...

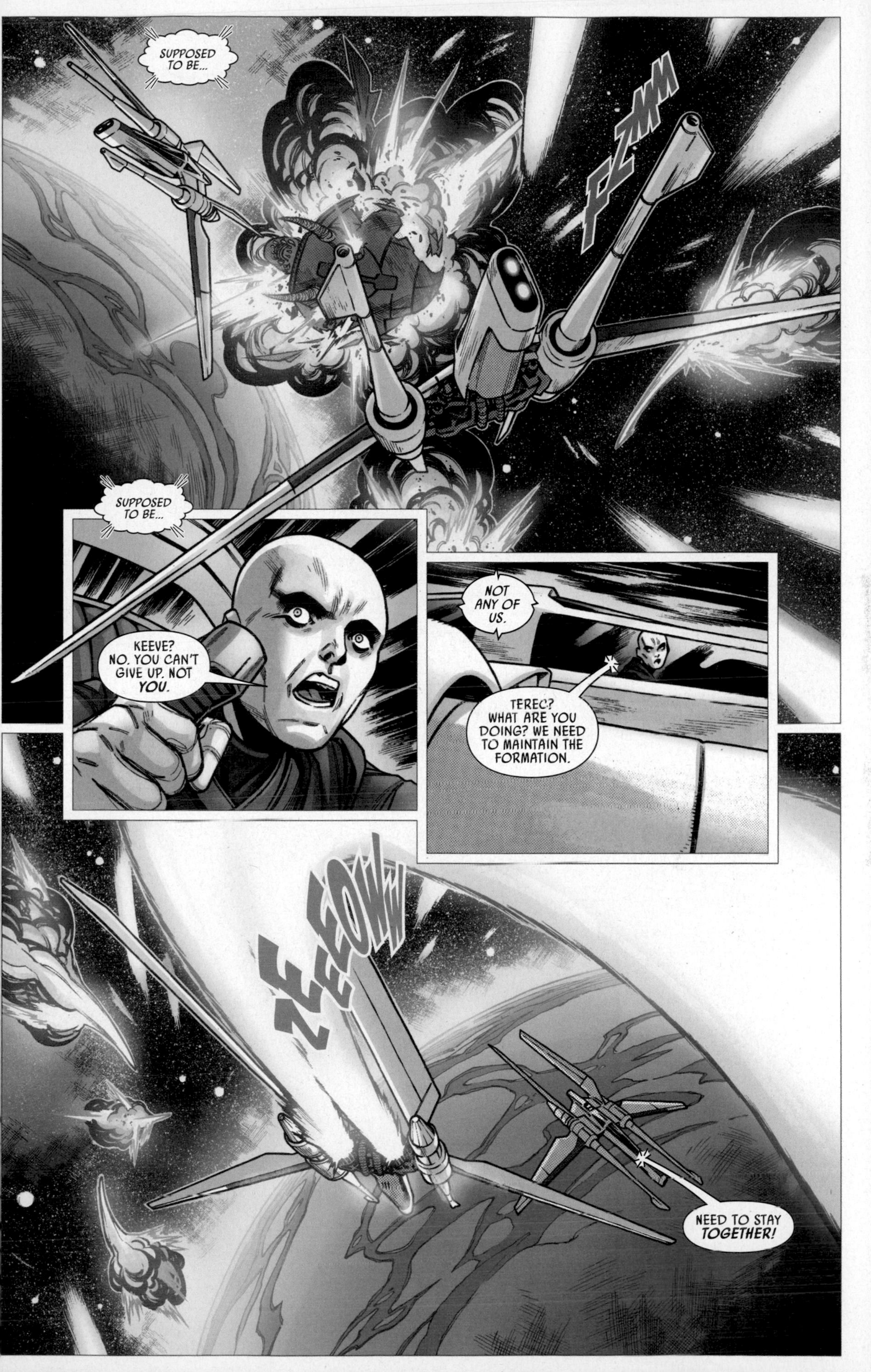
SUPPOSED TO BE...
FZZMM
SUPPOSED TO BE...
KEEVE? NO. YOU CAN'T GIVE UP. NOT YOU.
NOT ANY OF US.
TEREC? WHAT ARE YOU DOING? WE NEED TO MAINTAIN THE FORMATION.
ZZEEOWW
NEED TO STAY TOGETHER!

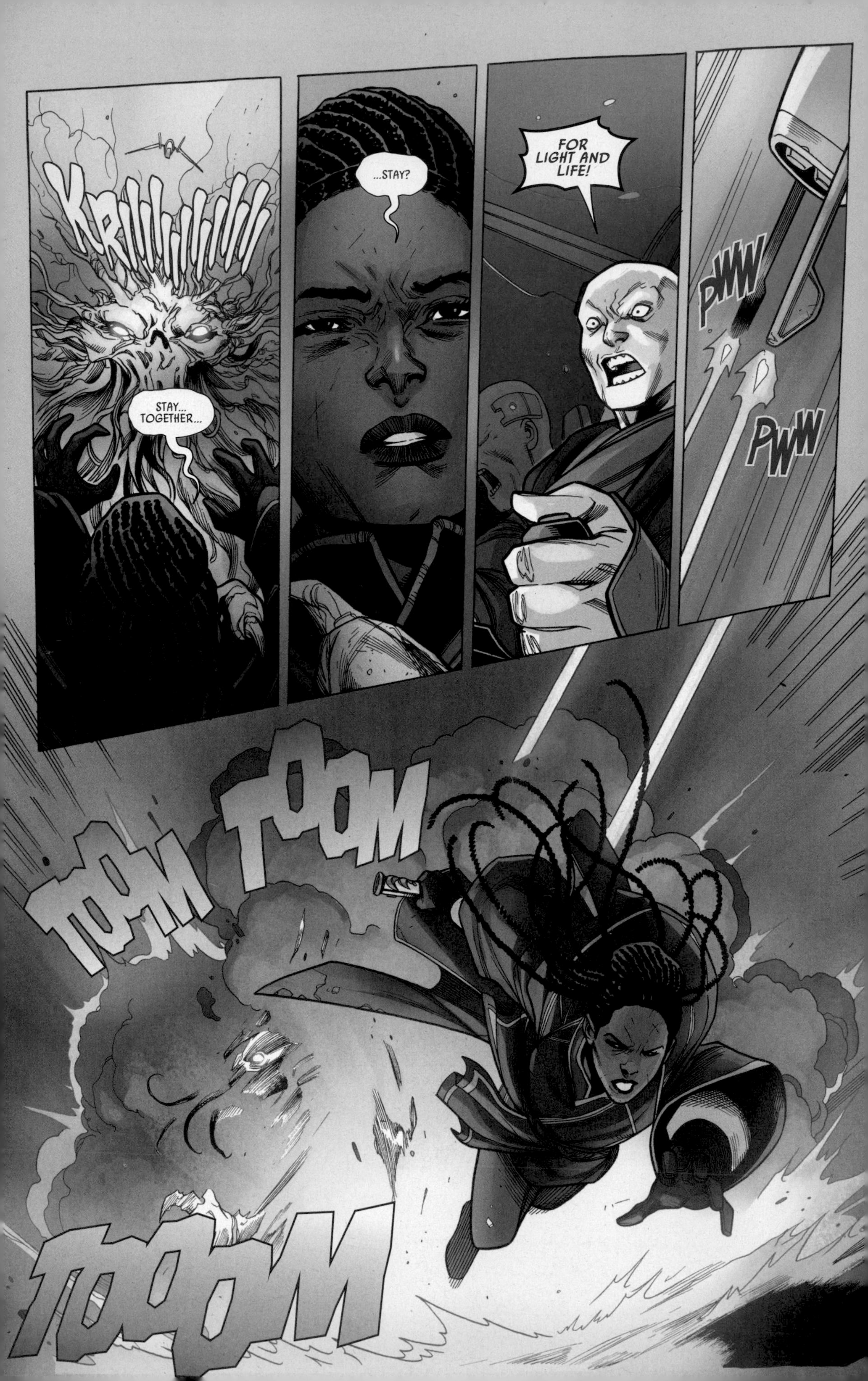
KRIIIIIIIII
STAY... TOGETHER...
...STAY?
FOR LIGHT AND LIFE!
PWW
PWW
TOOM
TOOM
TOOOM

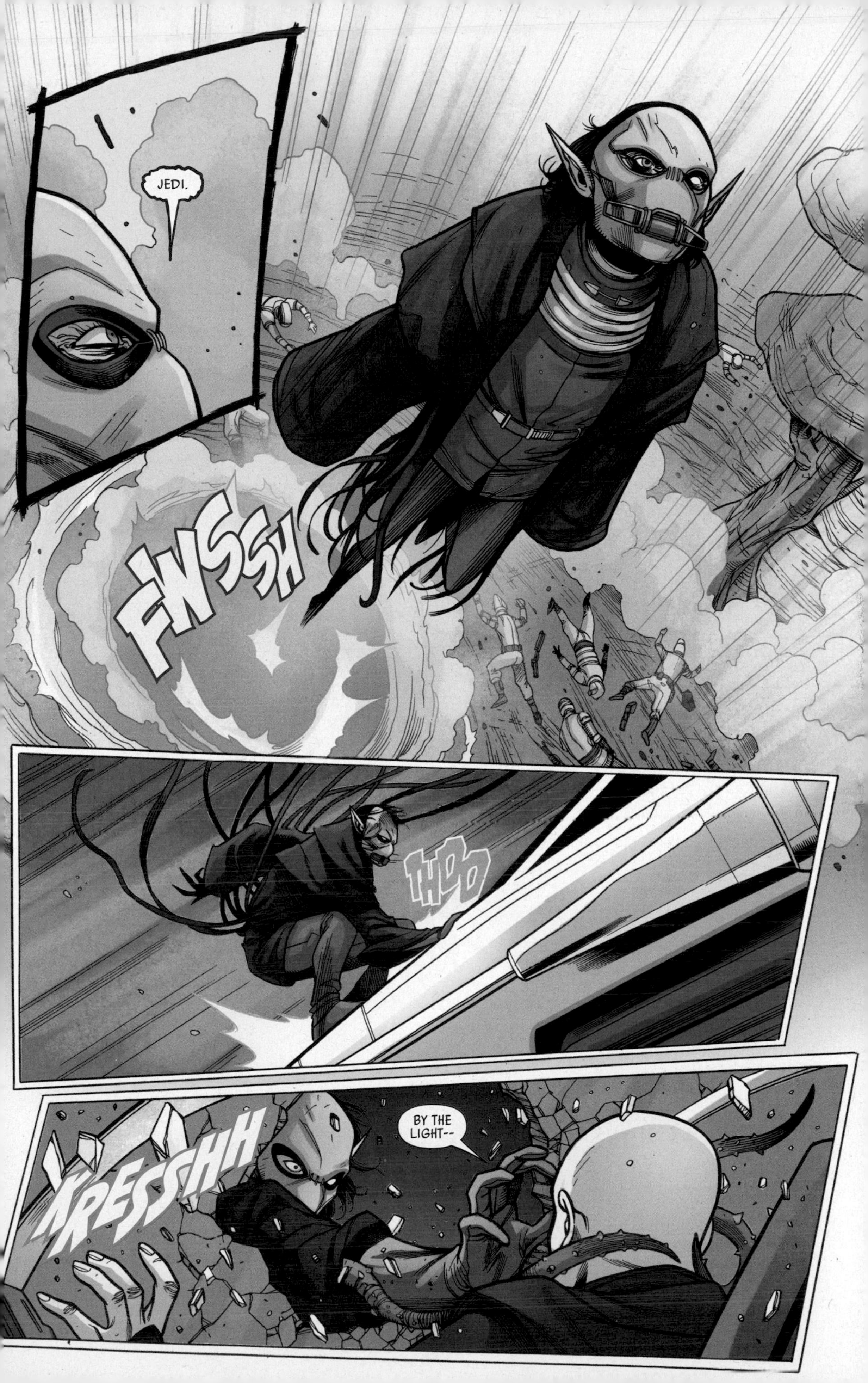

JEDI.
FWSSH
THOD
KRESSHH
BY THE LIGHT--

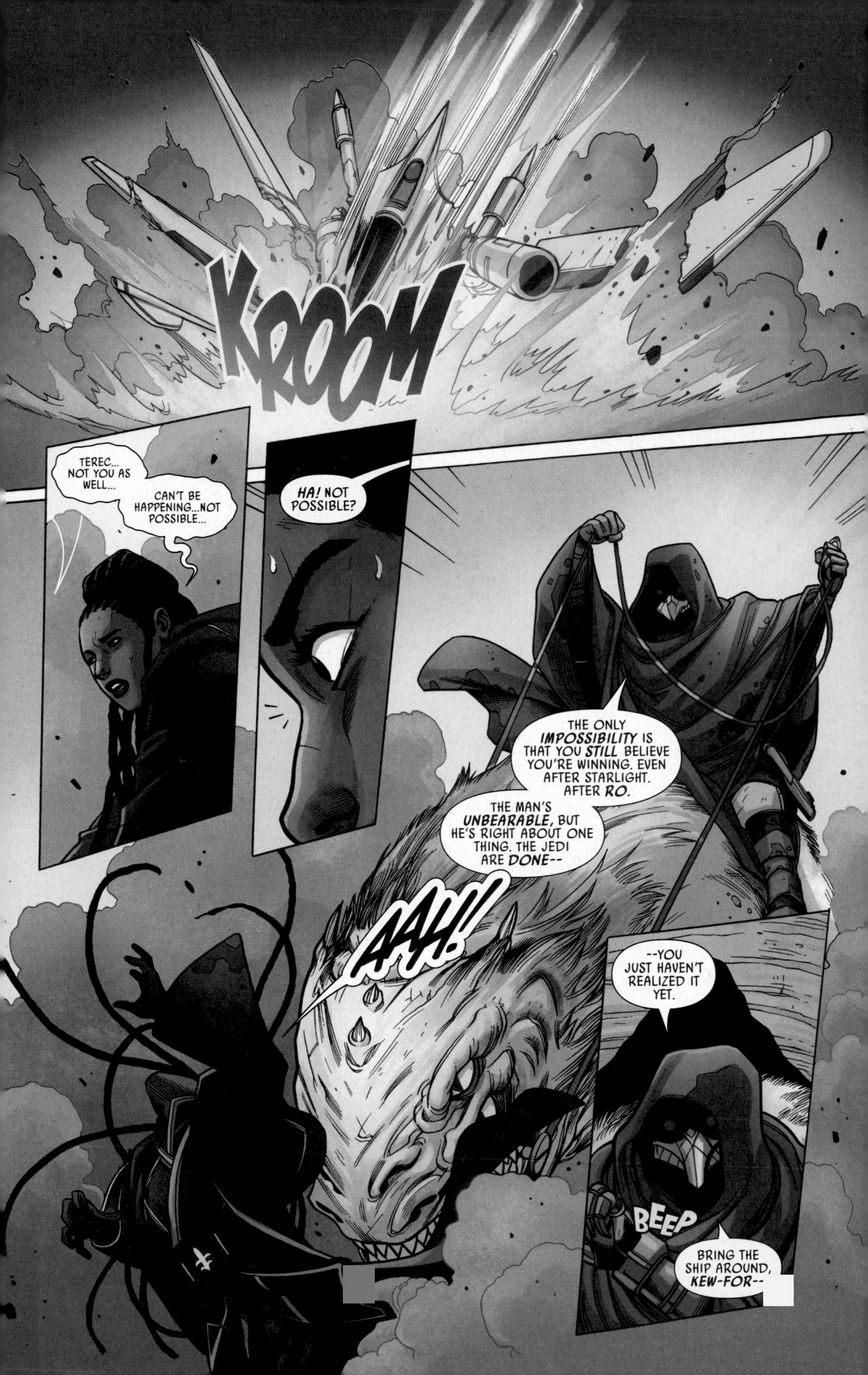
KROOM
TEREC... NOT YOU AS WELL...
CAN'T BE HAPPENING...NOT POSSIBLE...
HA! NOT POSSIBLE?
THE ONLY IMPOSSIBILITY IS THAT YOU STILL BELIEVE YOU'RE WINNING. EVEN AFTER STARLIGHT. AFTER RO.
THE MAN'S UNBEARABLE, BUT HE'S RIGHT ABOUT ONE THING. THE JEDI ARE DONE--
AAH!
--YOU JUST HAVEN'T REALIZED IT YET.
BEEP
BRING THE SHIP AROUND, KEW-FOR--

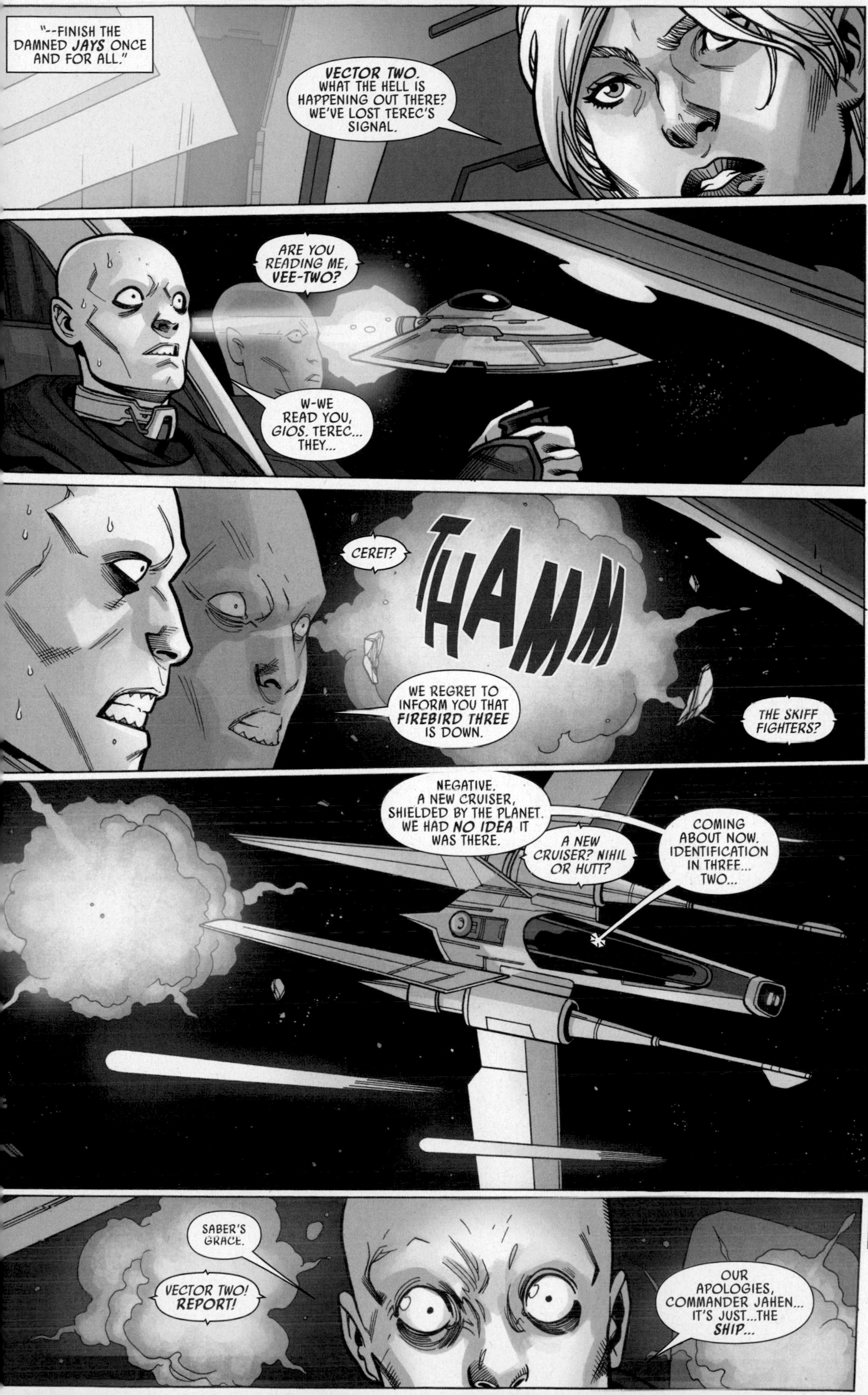
"--FINISH THE DAMNED JAYS ONCE AND FOR ALL."
VECTOR TWO. WHAT THE HELL IS HAPPENING OUT THERE? WE'VE LOST TEREC'S SIGNAL.
ARE YOU READING ME, VEE-TWO?
W-WE READ YOU, GIOS. TEREC... THEY...
CERET?
THAMM
WE REGRET TO INFORM YOU THAT FIREBIRD THREE IS DOWN.
THE SKIFF FIGHTERS?
NEGATIVE. A NEW CRUISER, SHIELDED BY THE PLANET. WE HAD NO IDEA IT WAS THERE.
A NEW CRUISER? NIHIL OR HUTT?
COMING ABOUT NOW. IDENTIFICATION IN THREE... TWO...
SABER'S GRACE.
VECTOR TWO! REPORT!
OUR APOLOGIES, COMMANDER JAHEN... IT'S JUST...THE SHIP...

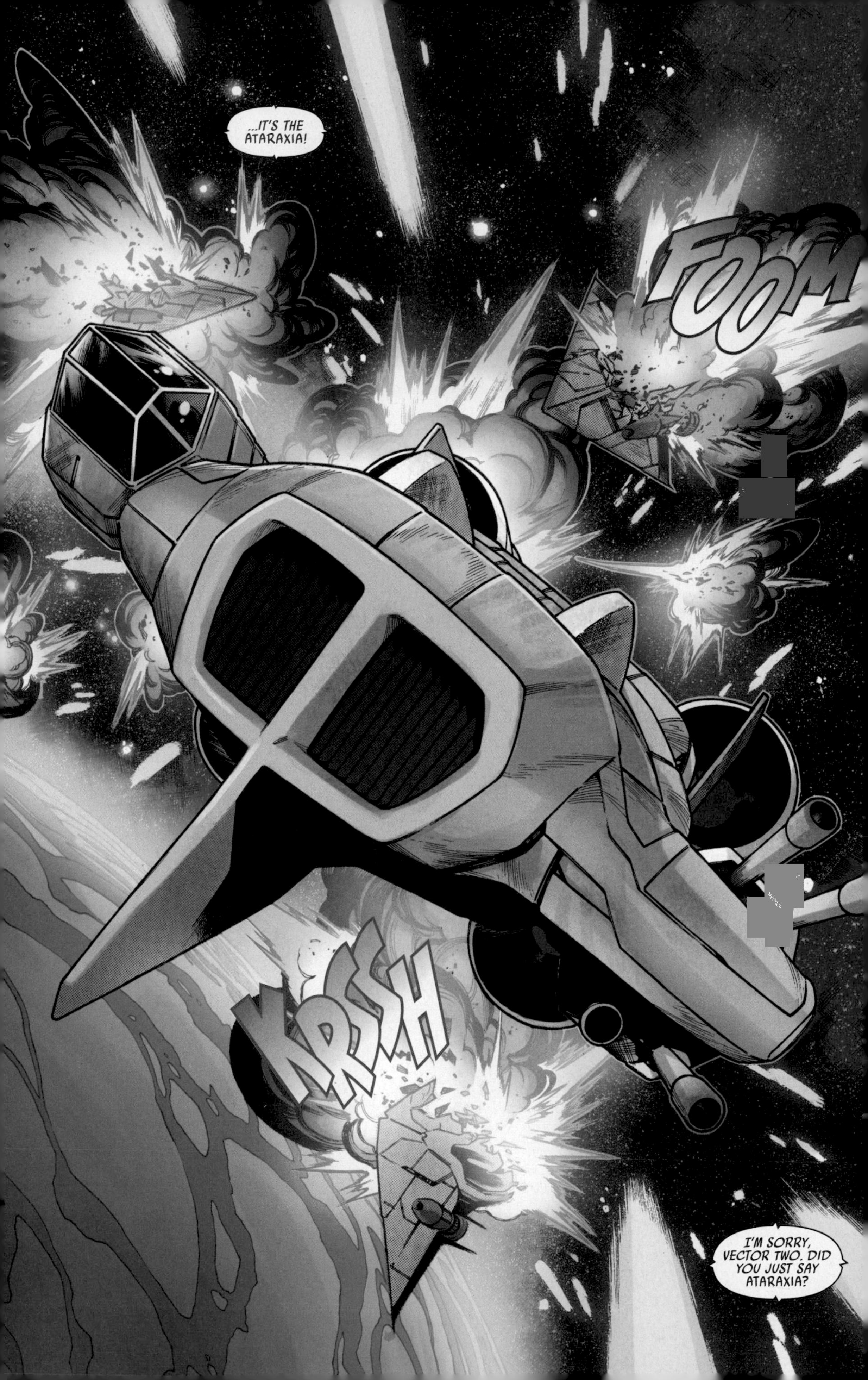
...IT'S THE ATARAXIA!
FOOM
KRSH
I'M SORRY, VECTOR TWO. DID YOU JUST SAY ATARAXIA?

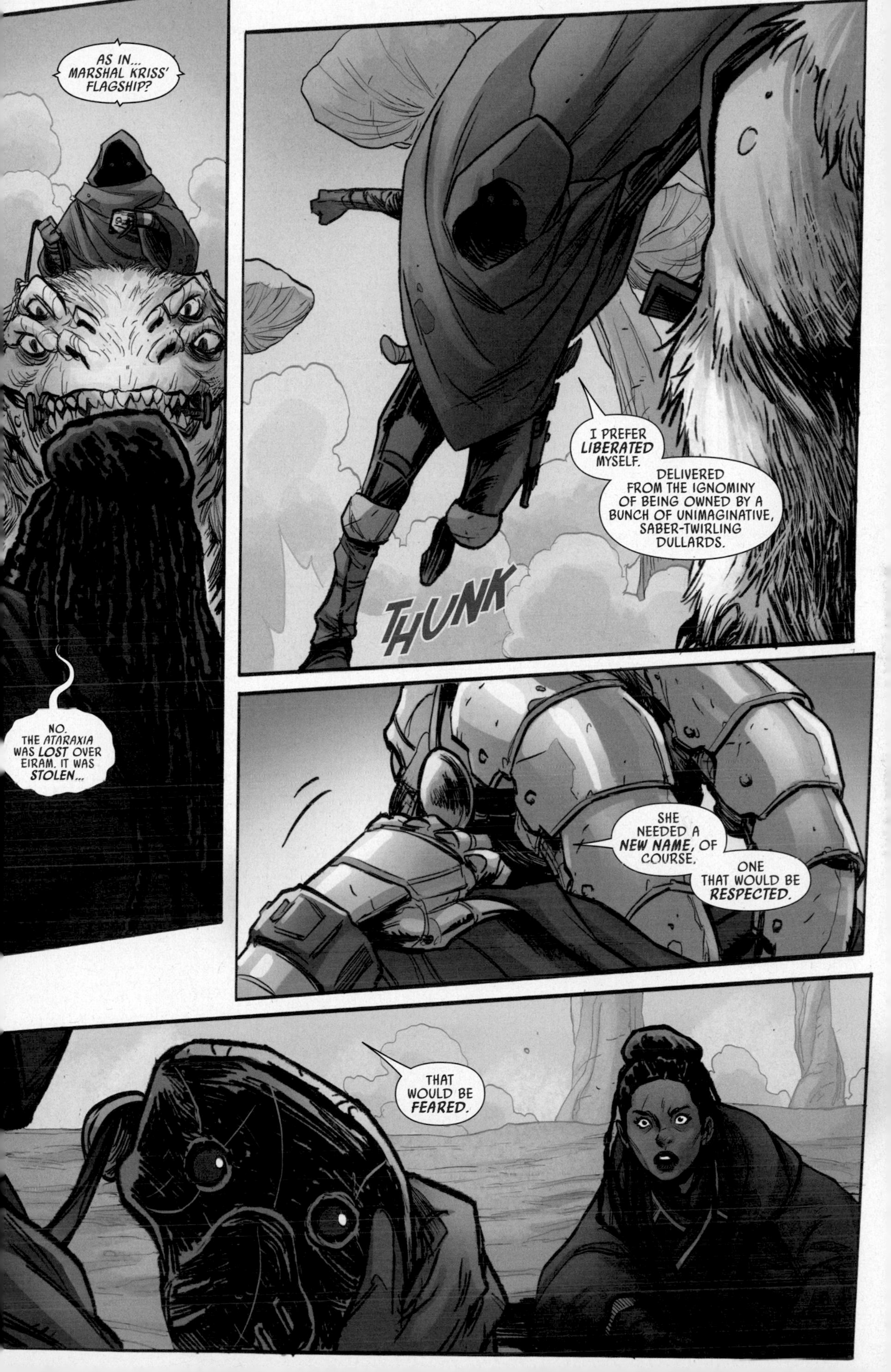
AS IN... MARSHAL KRISS' FLAGSHIP?
I PREFER LIBERATED MYSELF.
DELIVERED FROM THE IGNOMINY OF BEING OWNED BY A BUNCH OF UNIMAGINATIVE, SABER-TWIRLING DULLARDS.
THUNK
NO. THE ATARAXIA WAS LOST OVER EIRAM. IT WAS STOLEN...
SHE NEEDED A NEW NAME, OF COURSE.
ONE THAT WOULD BE RESPECTED.
THAT WOULD BE FEARED.

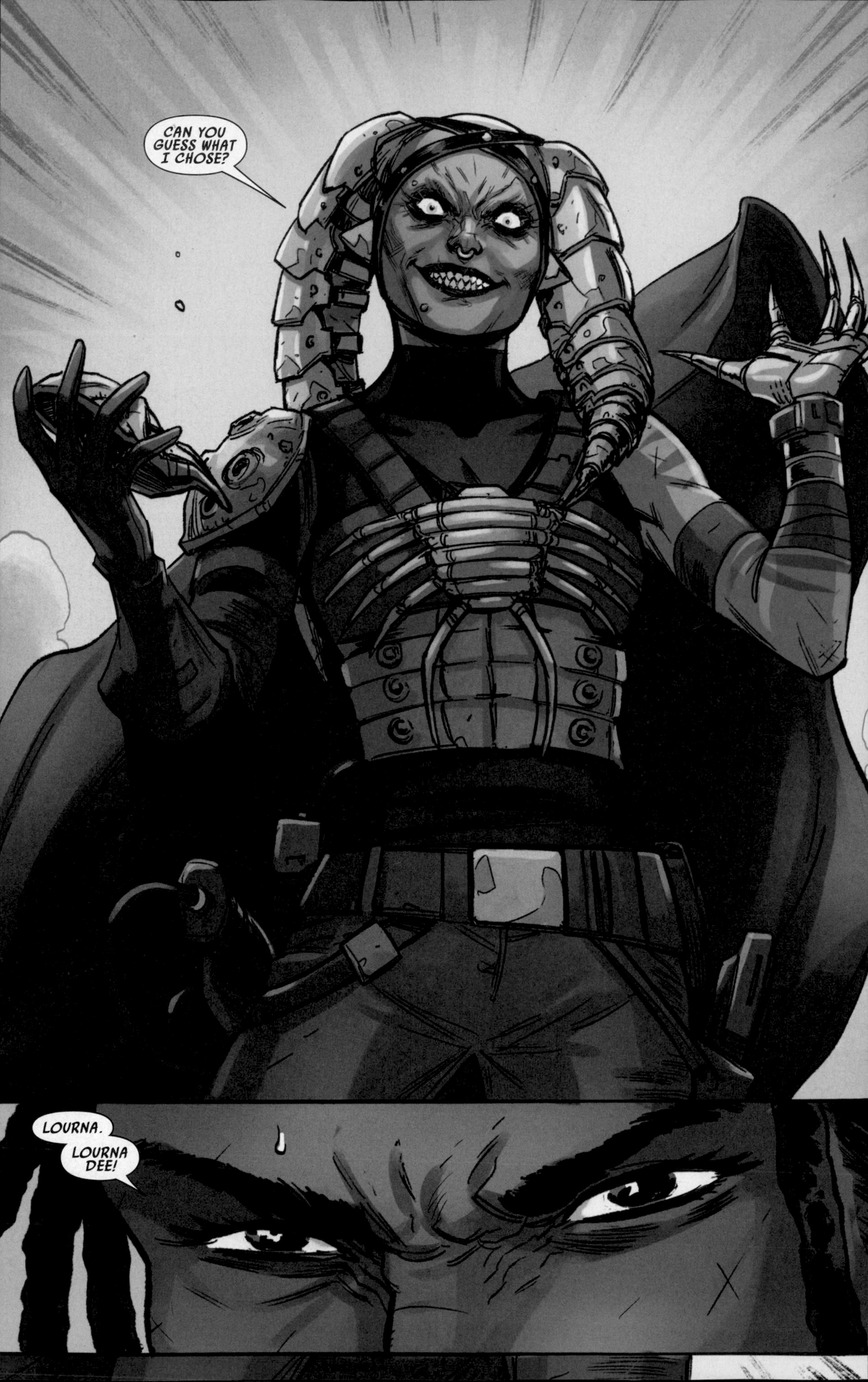
CAN YOU GUESS WHAT I CHOSE?
LOURNA.
LOURNA DEE!

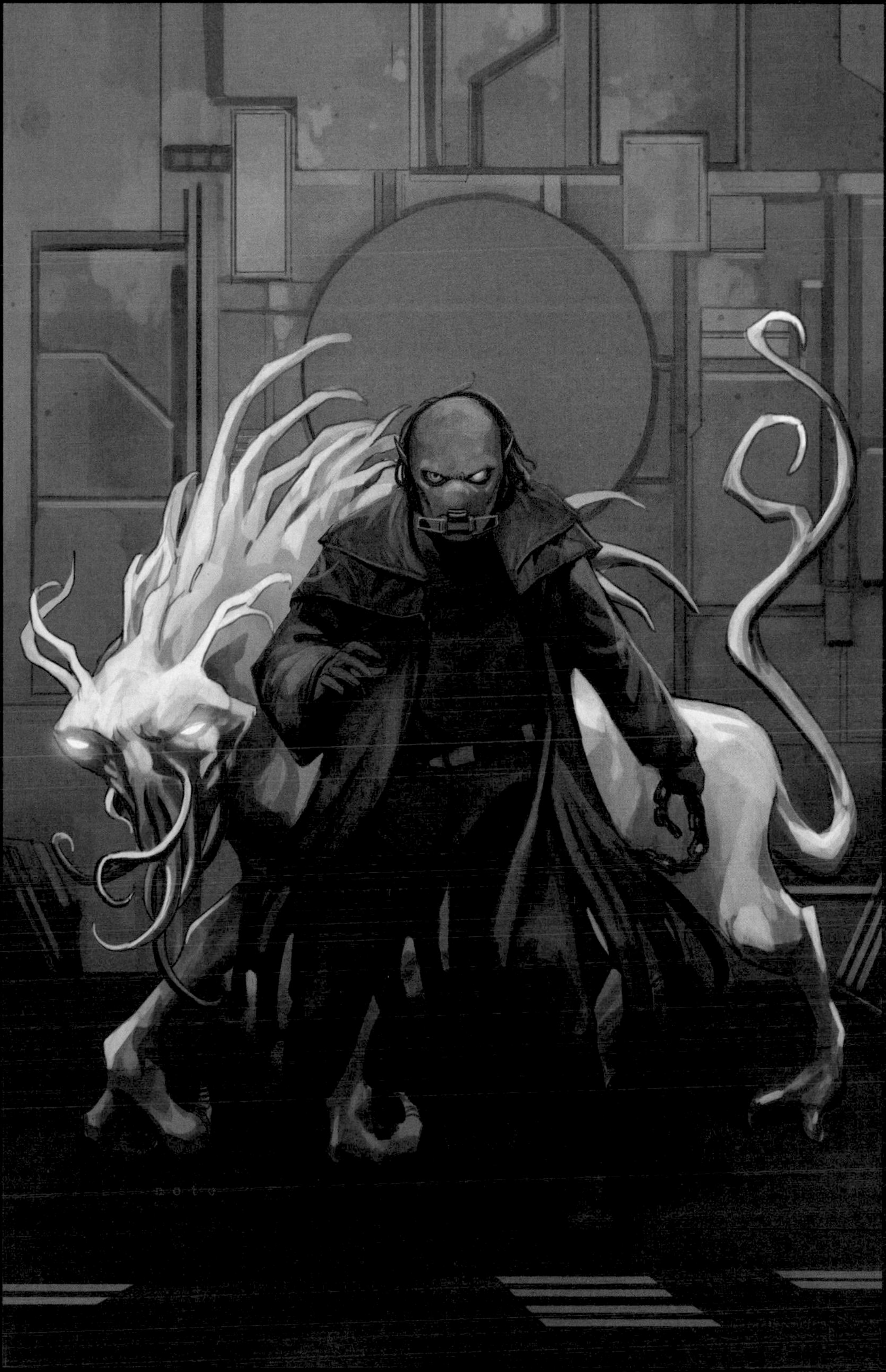

2 | SINS OF THE PAST

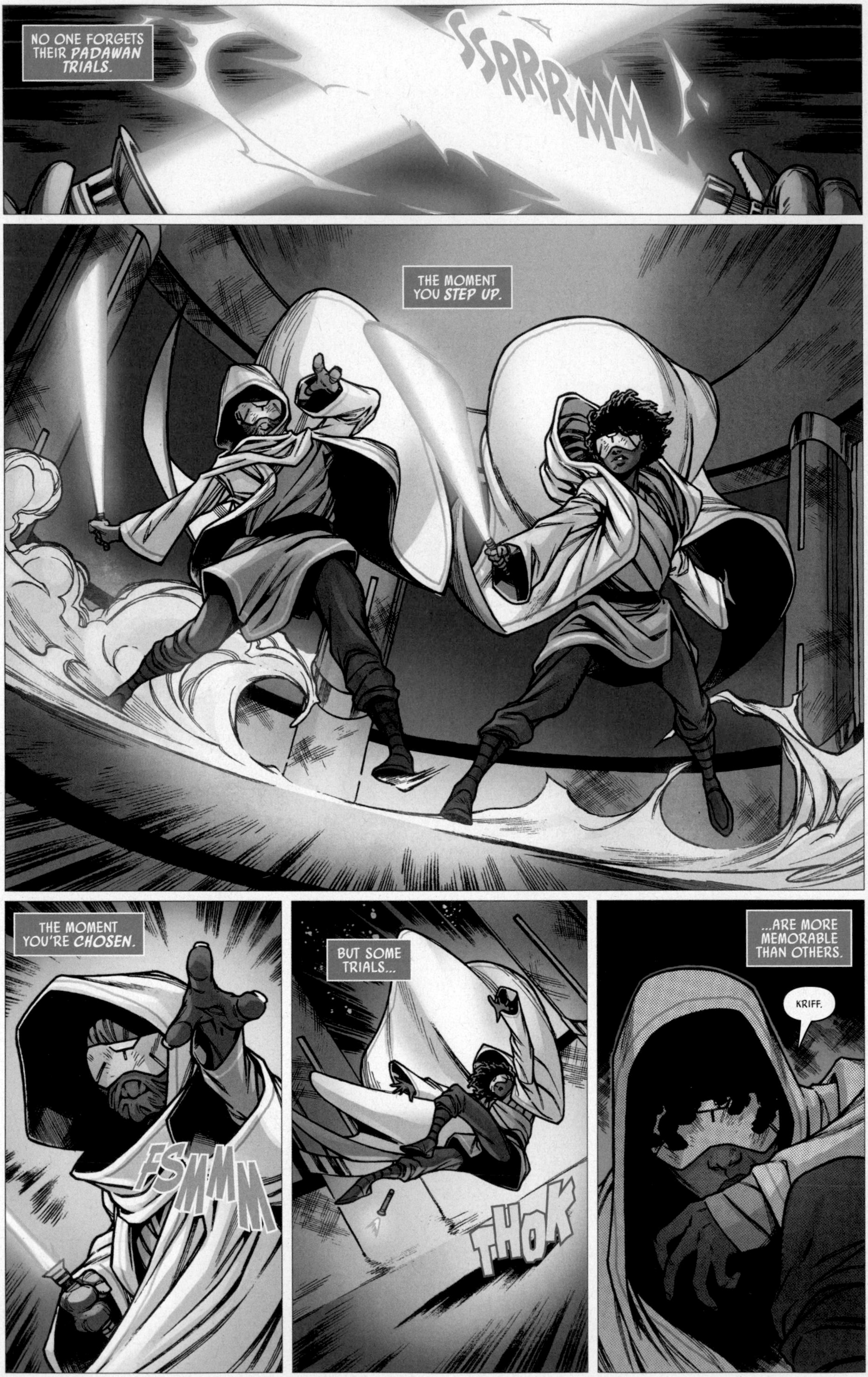
NO ONE FORGETS THEIR *PADAWAN TRIALS.*
SSRRRMM
THE MOMENT YOU *STEP UP.*
THE MOMENT YOU'RE *CHOSEN.*
FSMMM
BUT SOME TRIALS...
THOK
...ARE MORE MEMORABLE THAN OTHERS.
KRIFF.

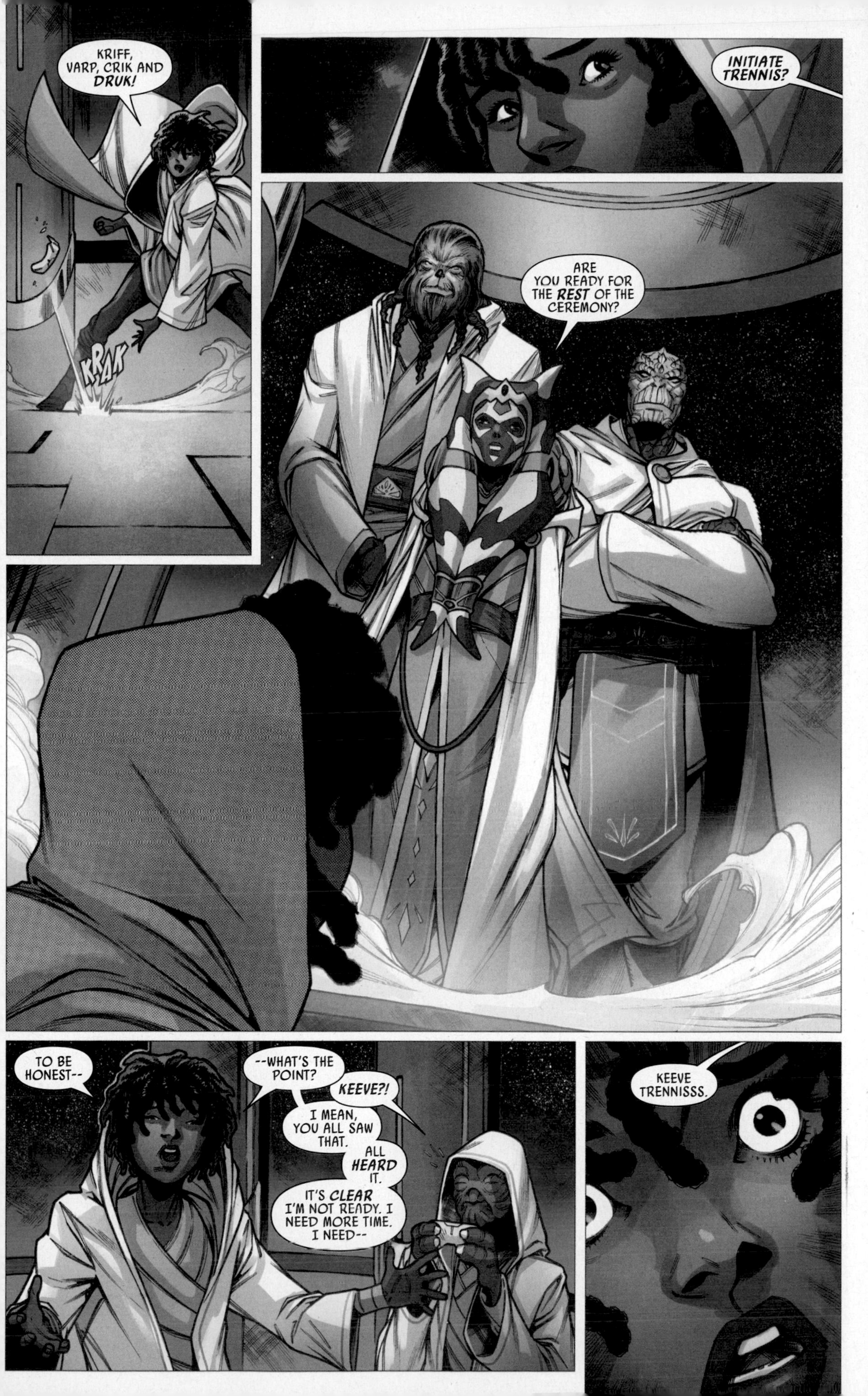

KRIFF, VARP, CRIK AND DRUK!
KRAK
INITIATE TRENNIS?
ARE YOU READY FOR THE REST OF THE CEREMONY?
TO BE HONEST--
--WHAT'S THE POINT?
KEEVE?!
I MEAN, YOU ALL SAW THAT.
ALL HEARD IT.
IT'S CLEAR I'M NOT READY. I NEED MORE TIME. I NEED--
KEEVE TRENNISSS.

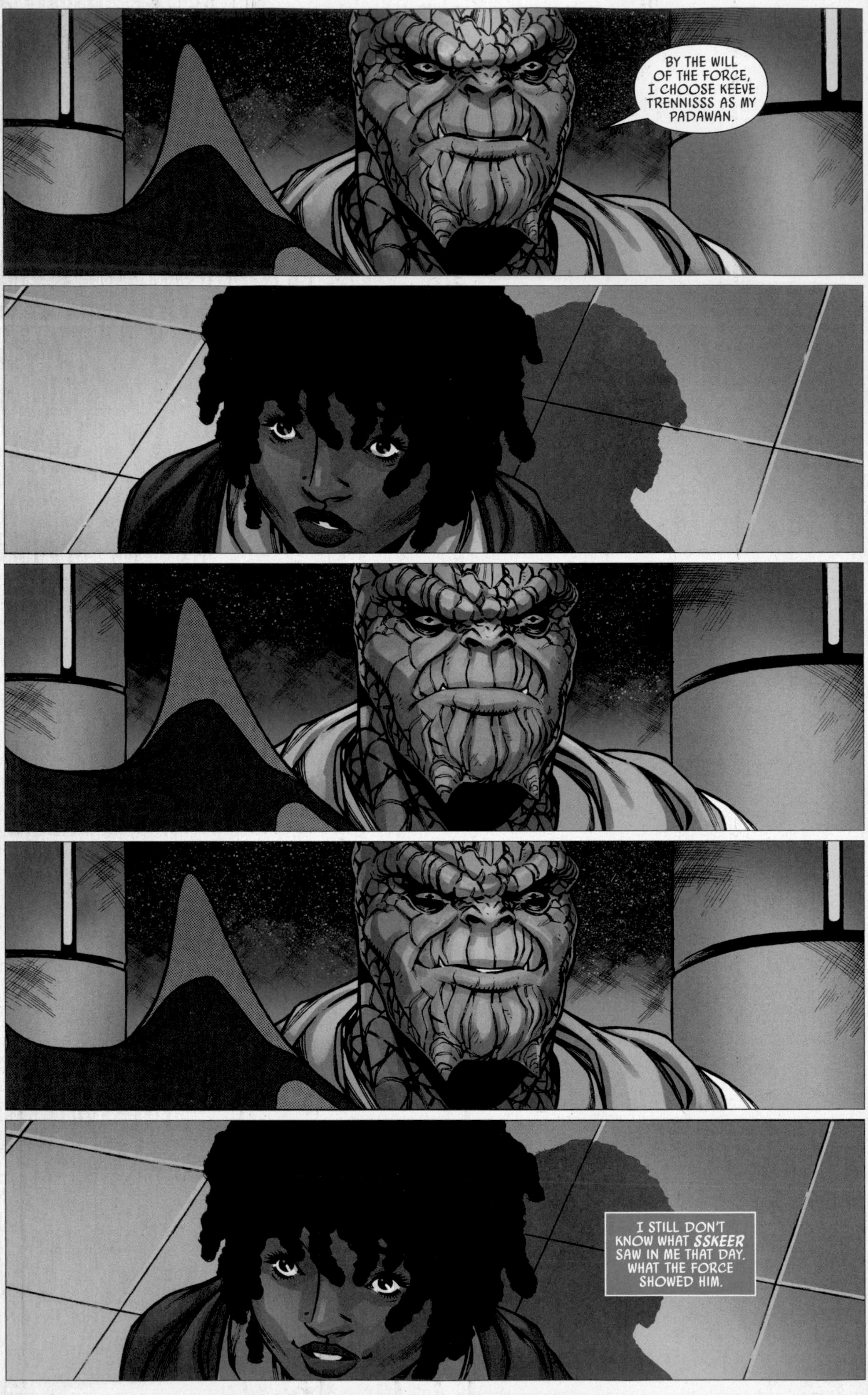
BY THE WILL OF THE FORCE, I CHOOSE KEEVE TRENNISSS AS MY PADAWAN.
I STILL DON'T KNOW WHAT SSKEER SAW IN ME THAT DAY. WHAT THE FORCE SHOWED HIM.

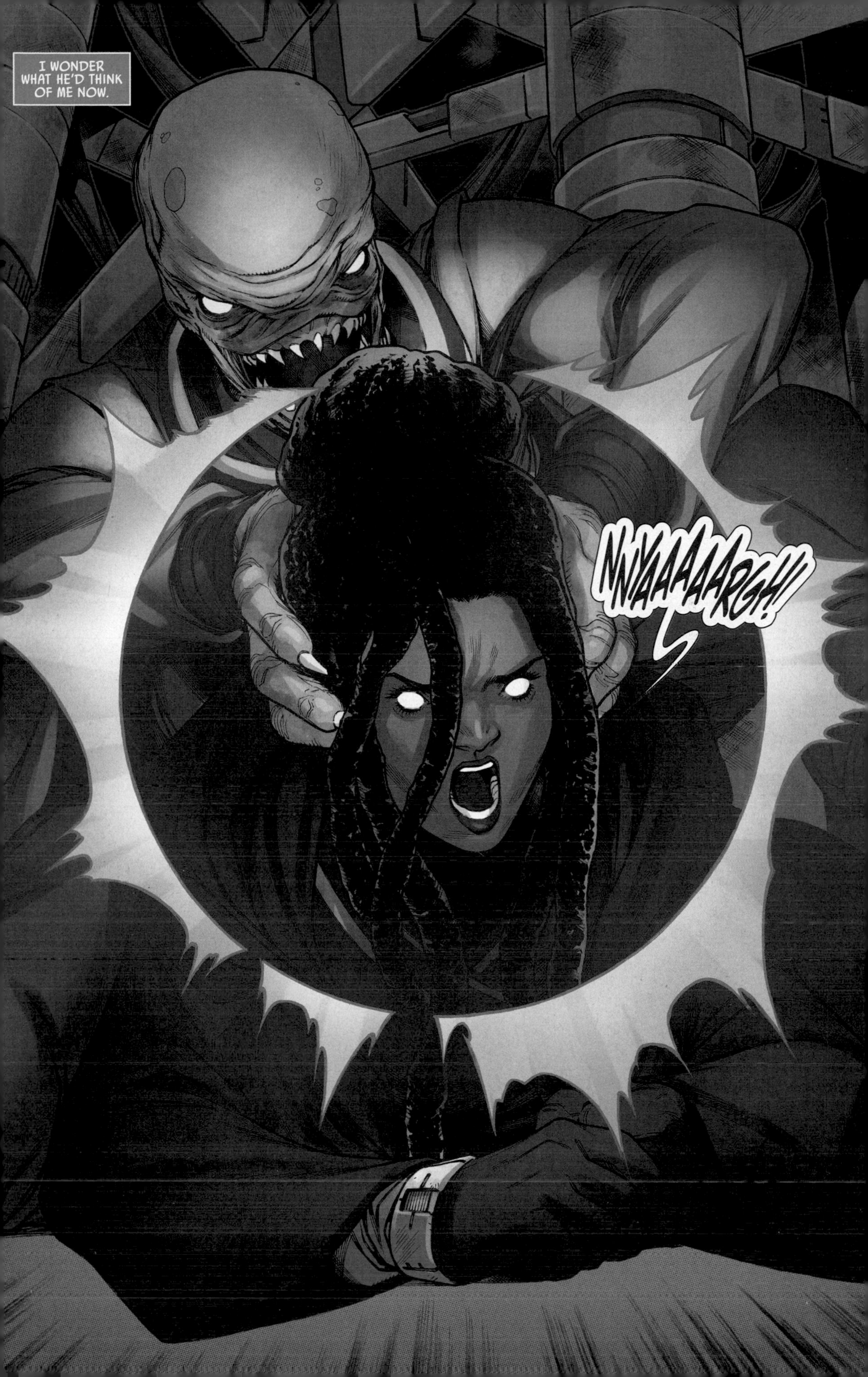
I WONDER WHAT HE'D THINK OF ME NOW.
NNiYAAAAARGH!!

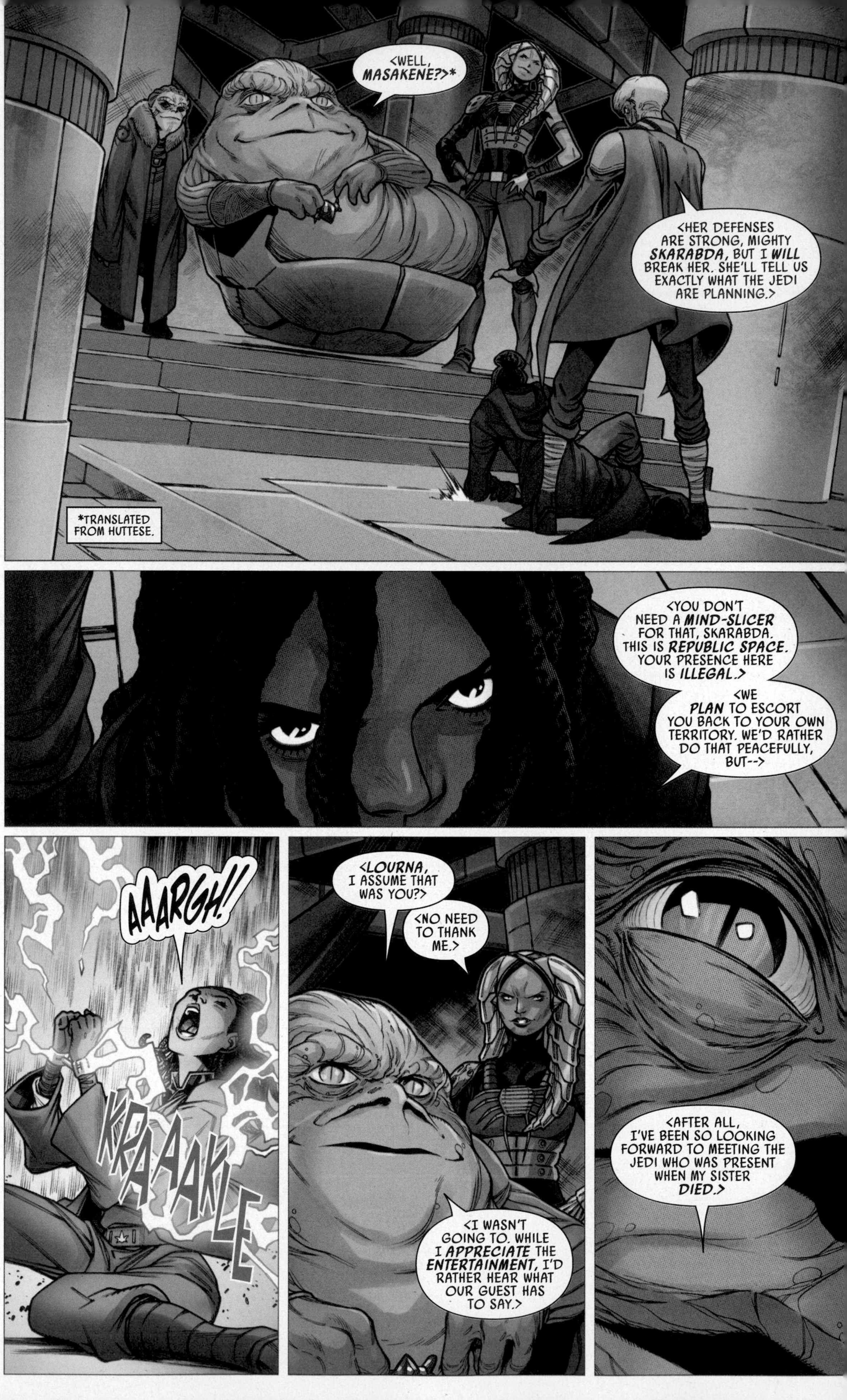
<WELL, MASAKENE?>*
<HER DEFENSES ARE STRONG, MIGHTY SKARABDA, BUT I WILL BREAK HER. SHE'LL TELL US EXACTLY WHAT THE JEDI ARE PLANNING.>
*TRANSLATED FROM HUTTESE.
<YOU DON'T NEED A MIND-SLICER FOR THAT, SKARABDA. THIS IS REPUBLIC SPACE. YOUR PRESENCE HERE IS ILLEGAL.>
<WE PLAN TO ESCORT YOU BACK TO YOUR OWN TERRITORY. WE'D RATHER DO THAT PEACEFULLY, BUT-->
AAAARGH!!
KRAAAKLE
<LOURNA, I ASSUME THAT WAS YOU?>
<NO NEED TO THANK ME.>
<I WASN'T GOING TO. WHILE I APPRECIATE THE ENTERTAINMENT, I'D RATHER HEAR WHAT OUR GUEST HAS TO SAY.>
<AFTER ALL, I'VE BEEN SO LOOKING FORWARD TO MEETING THE JEDI WHO WAS PRESENT WHEN MY SISTER DIED.>

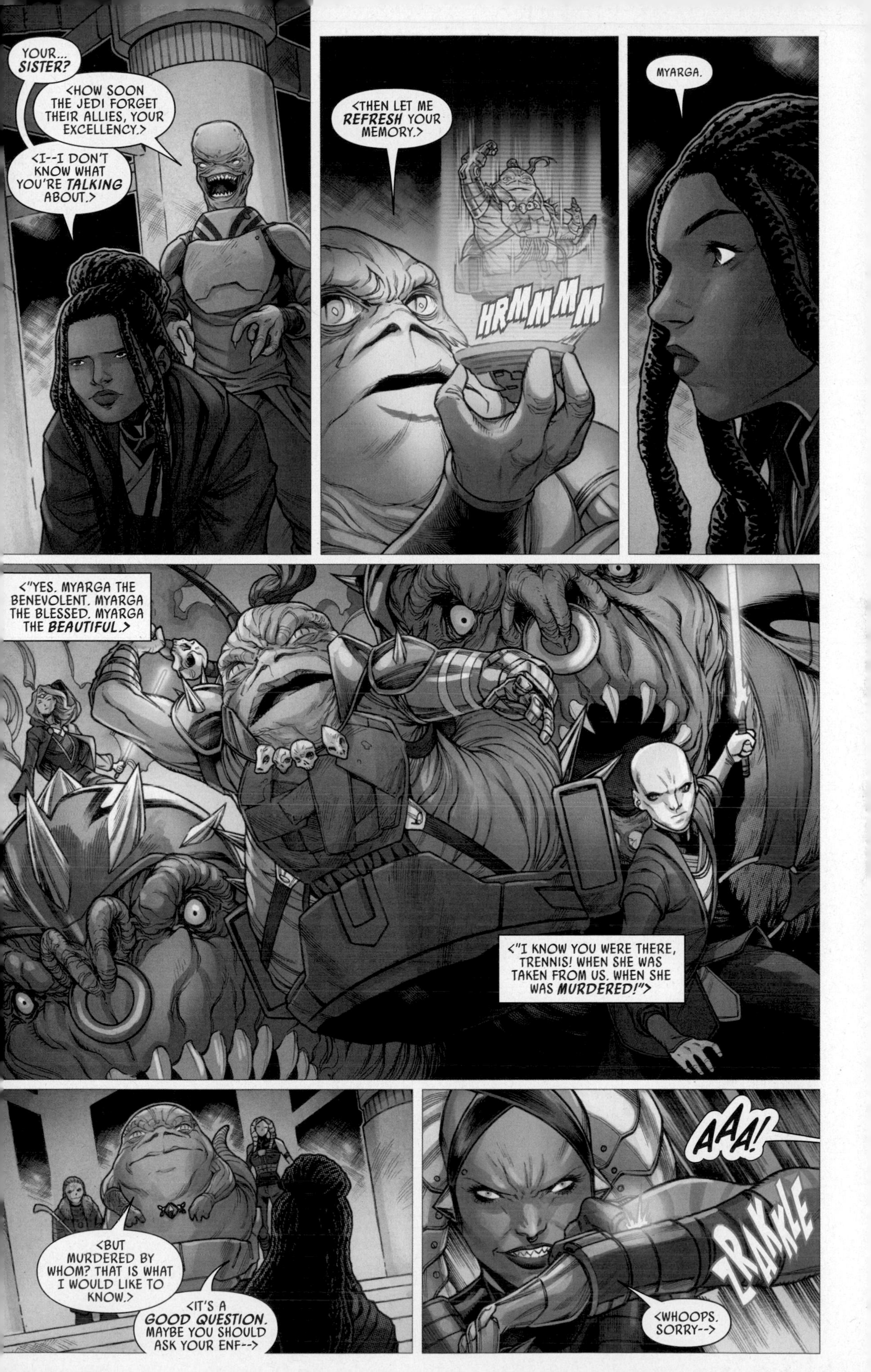
YOUR... SISTER?
<HOW SOON THE JEDI FORGET THEIR ALLIES, YOUR EXCELLENCY.>
<I--I DON'T KNOW WHAT YOU'RE TALKING ABOUT.>
<THEN LET ME REFRESH YOUR MEMORY.>
HRMMMM
MYARGA.
<"YES. MYARGA THE BENEVOLENT. MYARGA THE BLESSED. MYARGA THE BEAUTIFUL.>
<"I KNOW YOU WERE THERE, TRENNIS! WHEN SHE WAS TAKEN FROM US. WHEN SHE WAS MURDERED!">
<BUT MURDERED BY WHOM? THAT IS WHAT I WOULD LIKE TO KNOW.>
<IT'S A GOOD QUESTION. MAYBE YOU SHOULD ASK YOUR ENF-->
AAA!
ZRAKKLE
<WHOOPS. SORRY-->

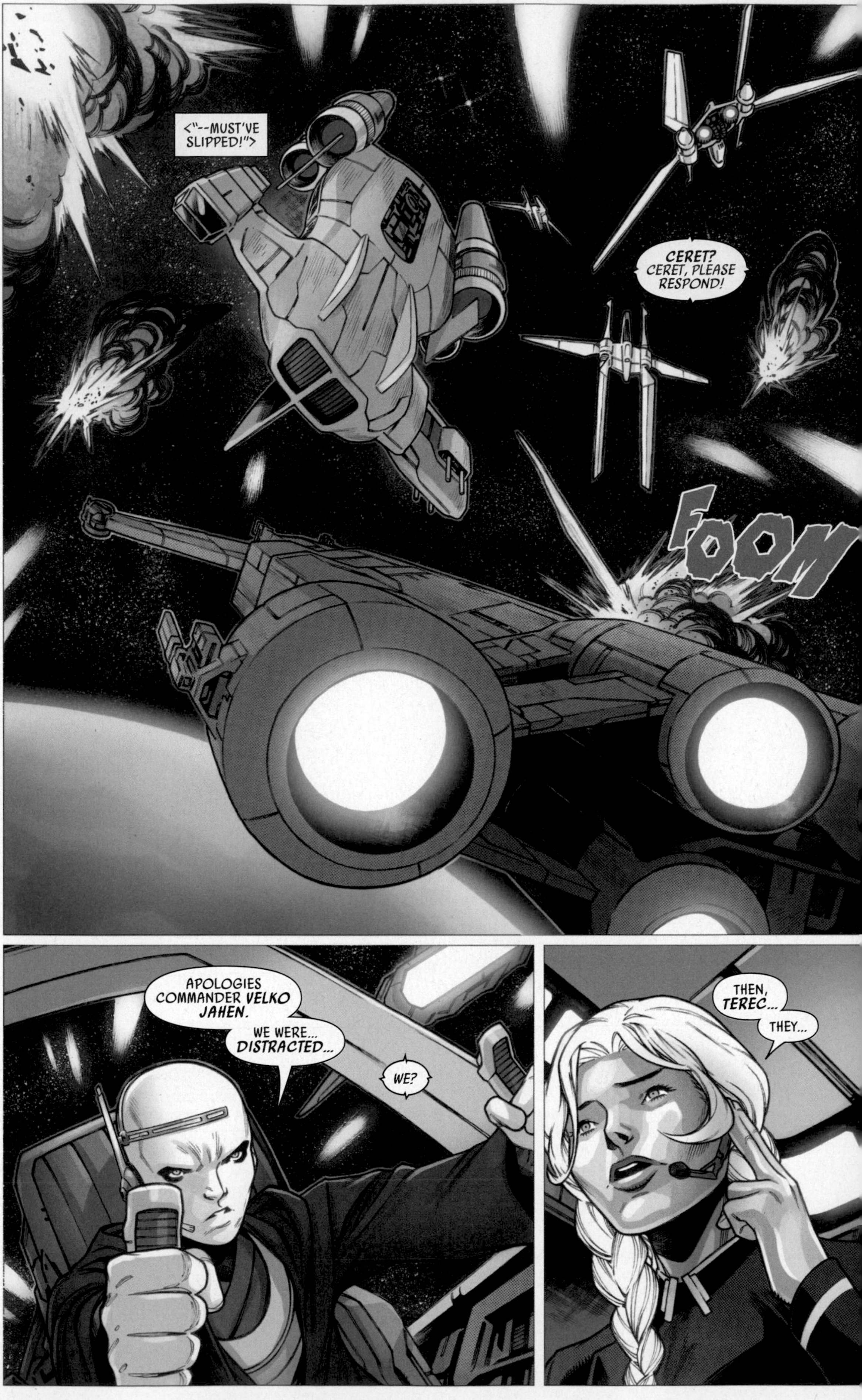

<"--MUST'VE SLIPPED!">
CERET? CERET, PLEASE RESPOND!
FOOM
APOLOGIES COMMANDER VELKO JAHEN.
WE WERE... DISTRACTED...
WE?
THEN, TEREC...
THEY...

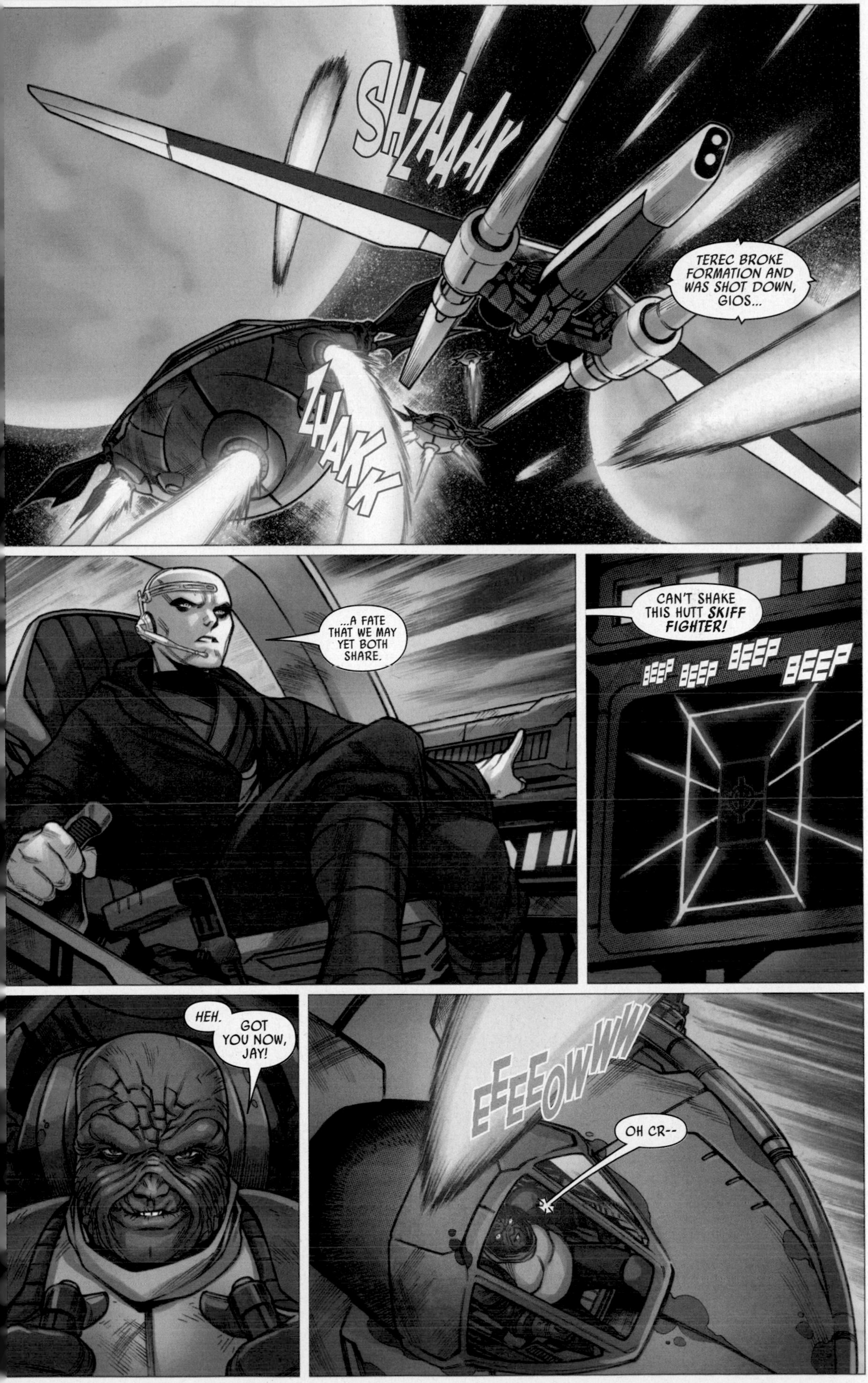
SHZAAAK
ZHAKK
TEREC BROKE FORMATION AND WAS SHOT DOWN, GIOS...
...A FATE THAT WE MAY YET BOTH SHARE.
CAN'T SHAKE THIS HUTT SKIFF FIGHTER!
BEEP BEEP BEEP BEEP
HEH.
GOT YOU NOW, JAY!
EEEEOWWW
OH CR--

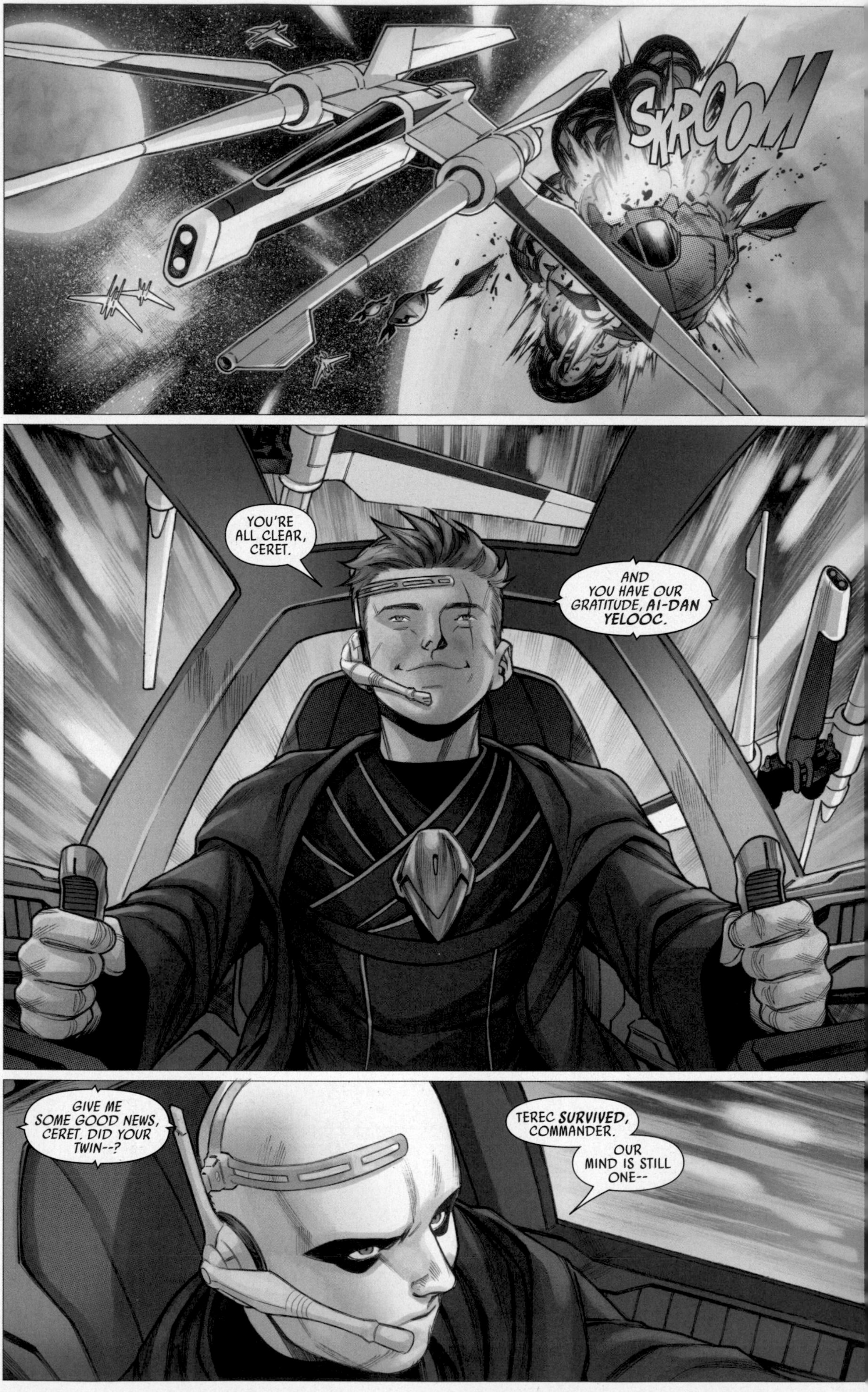
SKROOM
YOU'RE ALL CLEAR, CERET.
AND YOU HAVE OUR GRATITUDE, AI-DAN YELOOC.
GIVE ME SOME GOOD NEWS, CERET. DID YOUR TWIN--?
TEREC SURVIVED, COMMANDER.
OUR MIND IS STILL ONE--

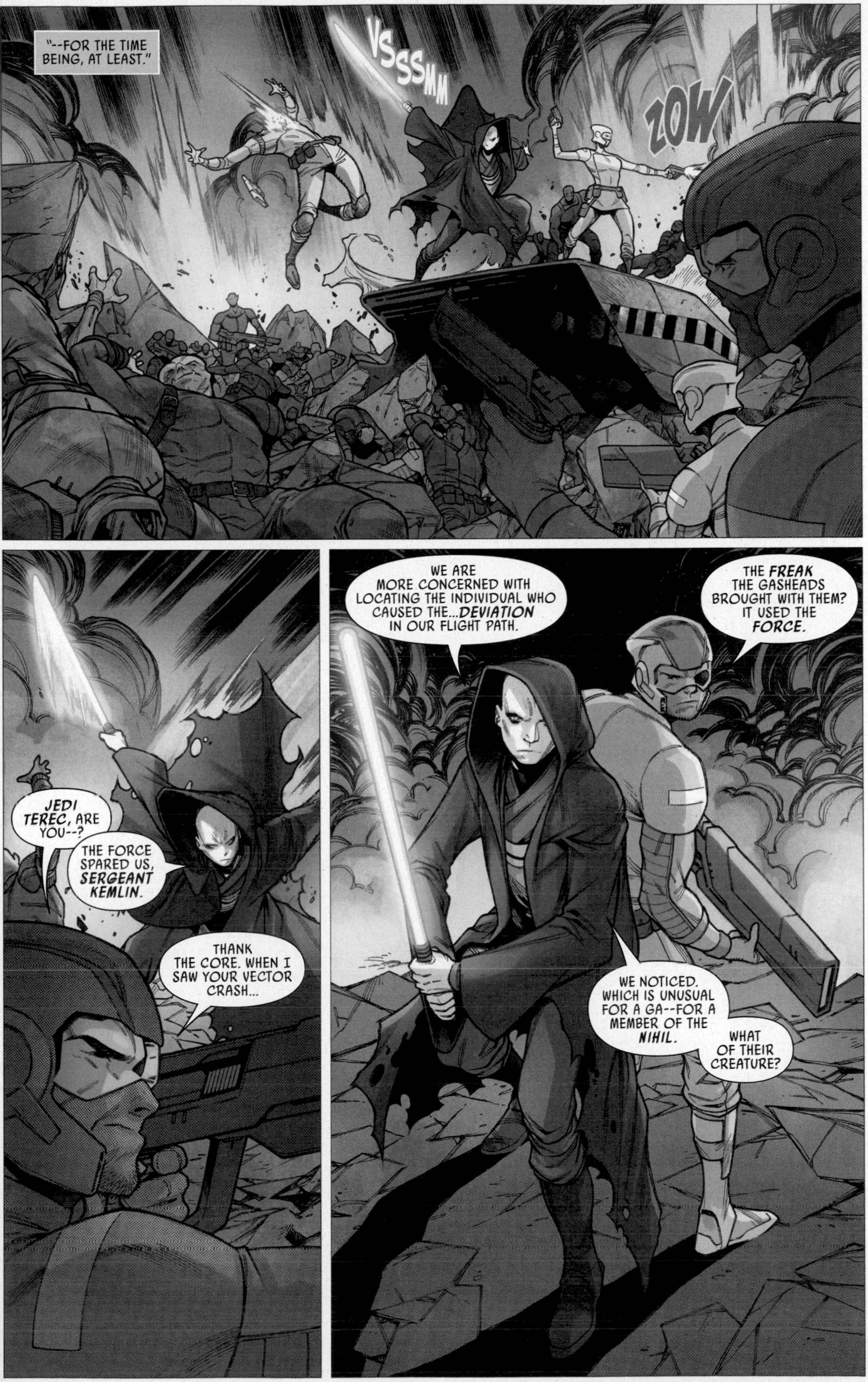
"--FOR THE TIME BEING, AT LEAST."
VSSSMM
ZOW
JEDI TEREC, ARE YOU--?
THE FORCE SPARED US, SERGEANT KEMLIN.
THANK THE CORE. WHEN I SAW YOUR VECTOR CRASH...
WE ARE MORE CONCERNED WITH LOCATING THE INDIVIDUAL WHO CAUSED THE...DEVIATION IN OUR FLIGHT PATH.
THE FREAK THE GASHEADS BROUGHT WITH THEM? IT USED THE FORCE.
WE NOTICED. WHICH IS UNUSUAL FOR A GA--FOR A MEMBER OF THE NIHIL.
WHAT OF THEIR CREATURE?

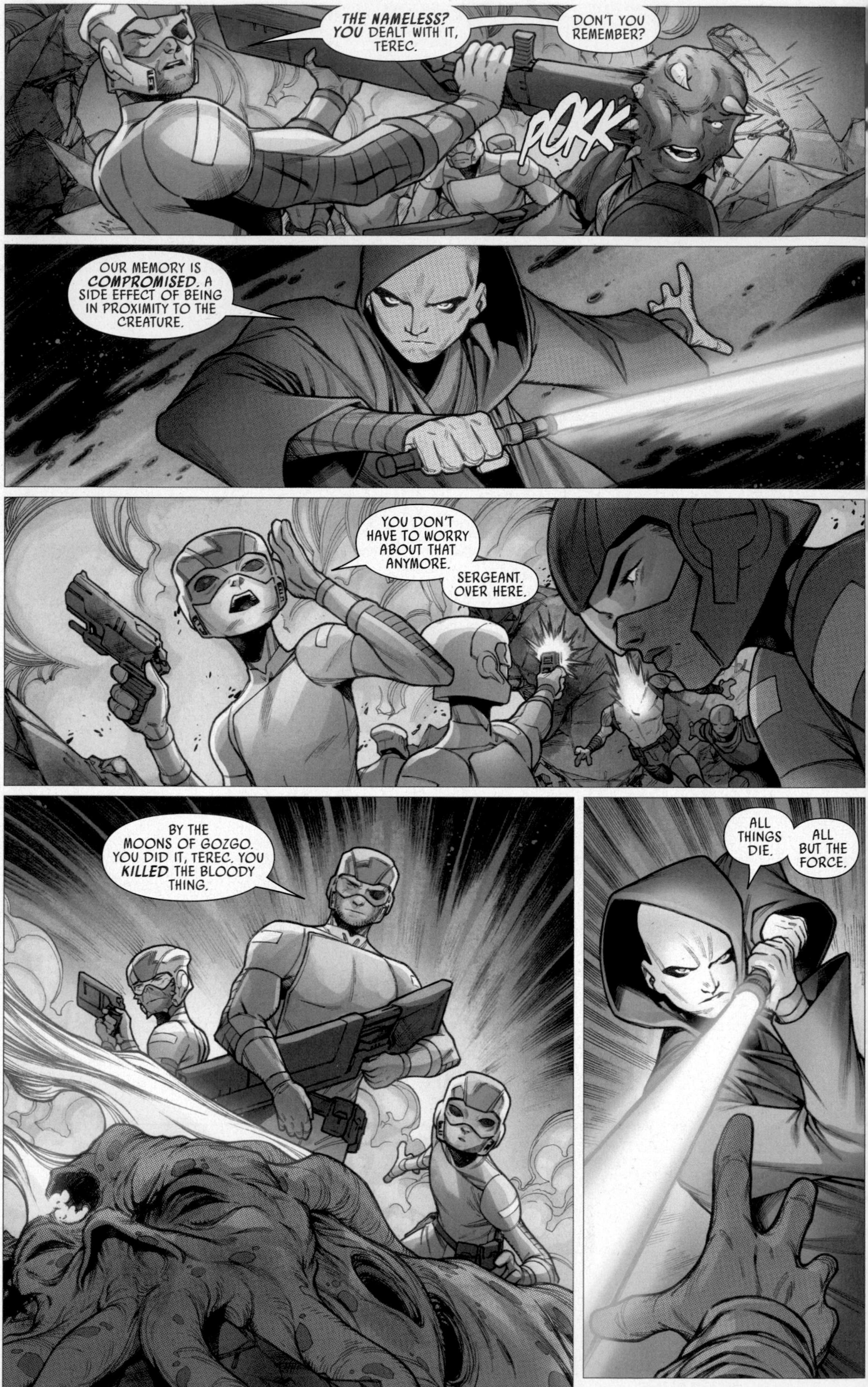
THE NAMELESS? YOU DEALT WITH IT, TEREC.
DON'T YOU REMEMBER?
POKK
OUR MEMORY IS COMPROMISED. A SIDE EFFECT OF BEING IN PROXIMITY TO THE CREATURE.
YOU DON'T HAVE TO WORRY ABOUT THAT ANYMORE.
SERGEANT. OVER HERE.
BY THE MOONS OF GOZGO. YOU DID IT, TEREC. YOU KILLED THE BLOODY THING.
ALL THINGS DIE.
ALL BUT THE FORCE.

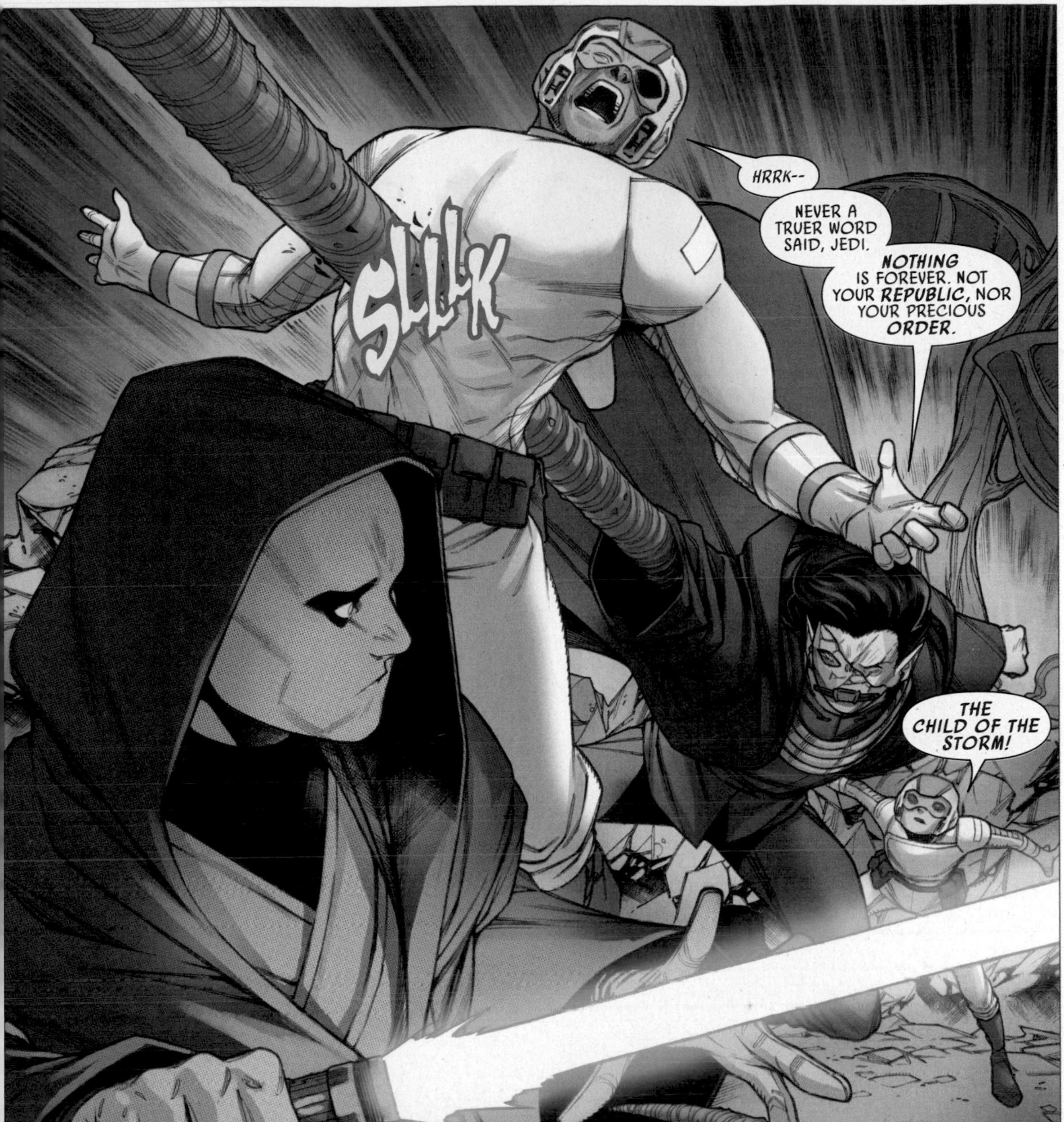
HRRK--
NEVER A TRUER WORD SAID, JEDI.
NOTHING IS FOREVER. NOT YOUR REPUBLIC, NOR YOUR PRECIOUS ORDER.
SLLLK
THE CHILD OF THE STORM!

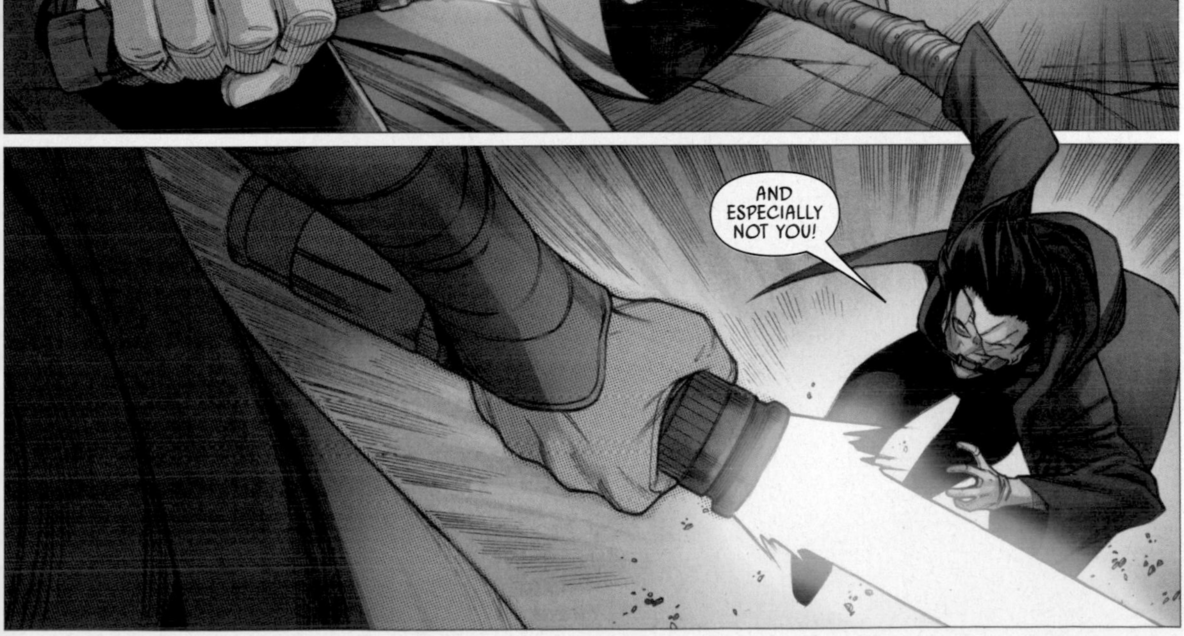
AND ESPECIALLY NOT YOU!

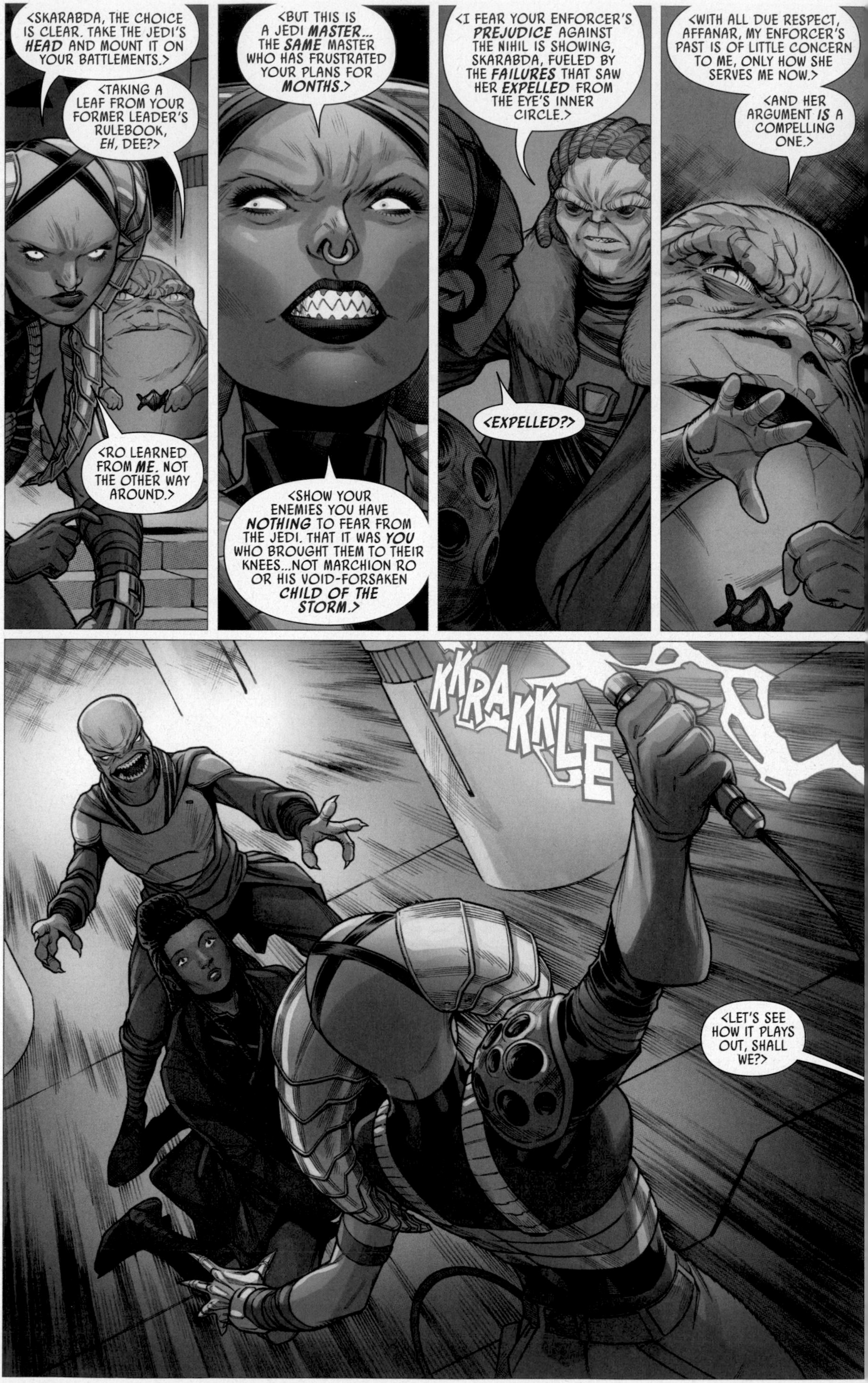

<SKARABDA, THE CHOICE IS CLEAR. TAKE THE JEDI'S HEAD AND MOUNT IT ON YOUR BATTLEMENTS.>
<TAKING A LEAF FROM YOUR FORMER LEADER'S RULEBOOK, EH, DEE?>
<RO LEARNED FROM ME. NOT THE OTHER WAY AROUND.>
<BUT THIS IS A JEDI MASTER... THE SAME MASTER WHO HAS FRUSTRATED YOUR PLANS FOR MONTHS.>
<SHOW YOUR ENEMIES YOU HAVE NOTHING TO FEAR FROM THE JEDI. THAT IT WAS YOU WHO BROUGHT THEM TO THEIR KNEES...NOT MARCHION RO OR HIS VOID-FORSAKEN CHILD OF THE STORM.>
<I FEAR YOUR ENFORCER'S PREJUDICE AGAINST THE NIHIL IS SHOWING, SKARABDA, FUELED BY THE FAILURES THAT SAW HER EXPELLED FROM THE EYE'S INNER CIRCLE.>
<EXPELLED?>
<WITH ALL DUE RESPECT, AFFANAR, MY ENFORCER'S PAST IS OF LITTLE CONCERN TO ME, ONLY HOW SHE SERVES ME NOW.>
<AND HER ARGUMENT IS A COMPELLING ONE.>
KKRAKKLE
<LET'S SEE HOW IT PLAYS OUT, SHALL WE?>

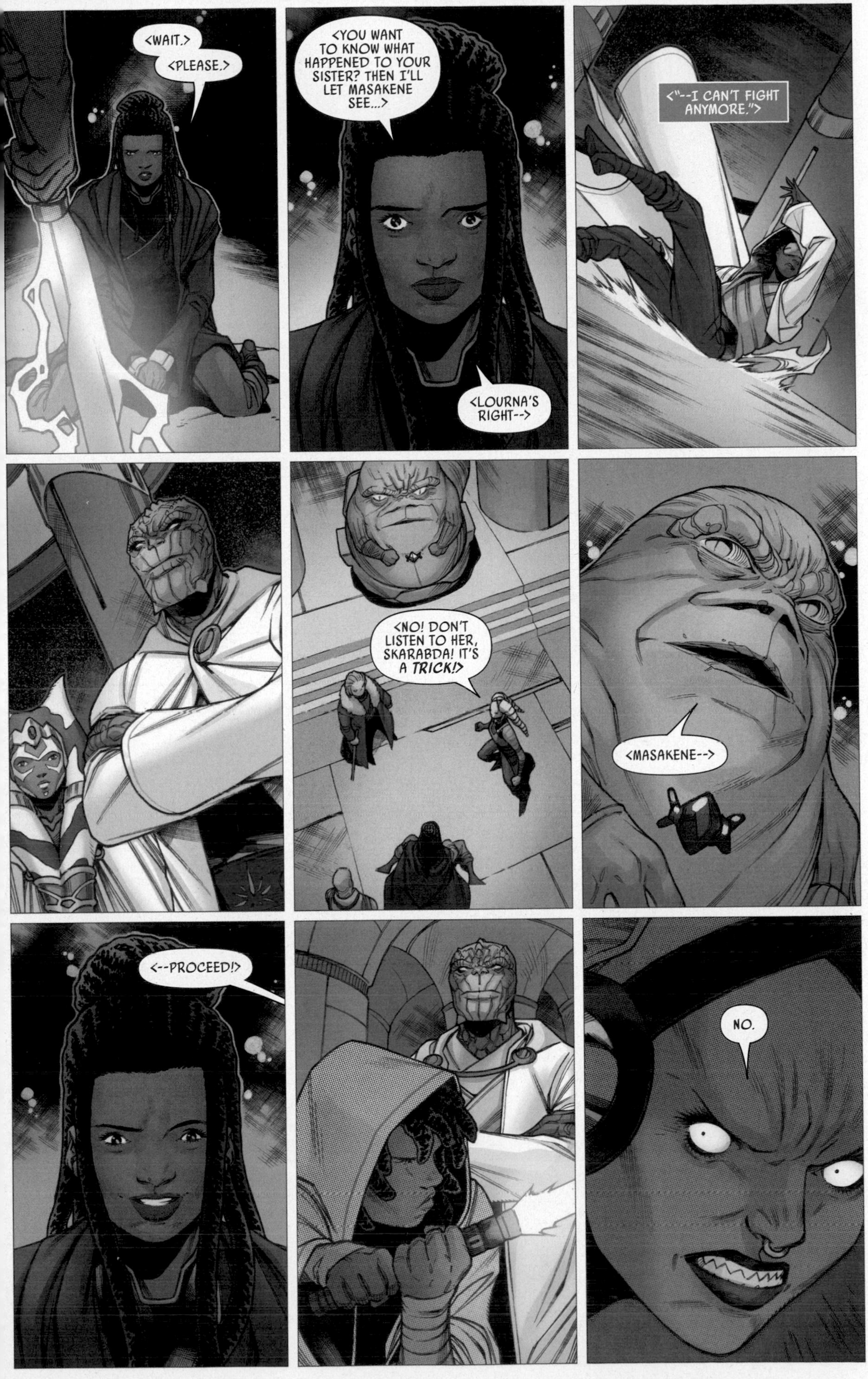
<WAIT.>
<PLEASE.>
<YOU WANT TO KNOW WHAT HAPPENED TO YOUR SISTER? THEN I'LL LET MASAKENE SEE...>
<LOURNA'S RIGHT-->
<"--I CAN'T FIGHT ANYMORE.">
<NO! DON'T LISTEN TO HER, SKARABDA! IT'S A *TRICK!*>
<MASAKENE-->
<--PROCEED!>
NO.

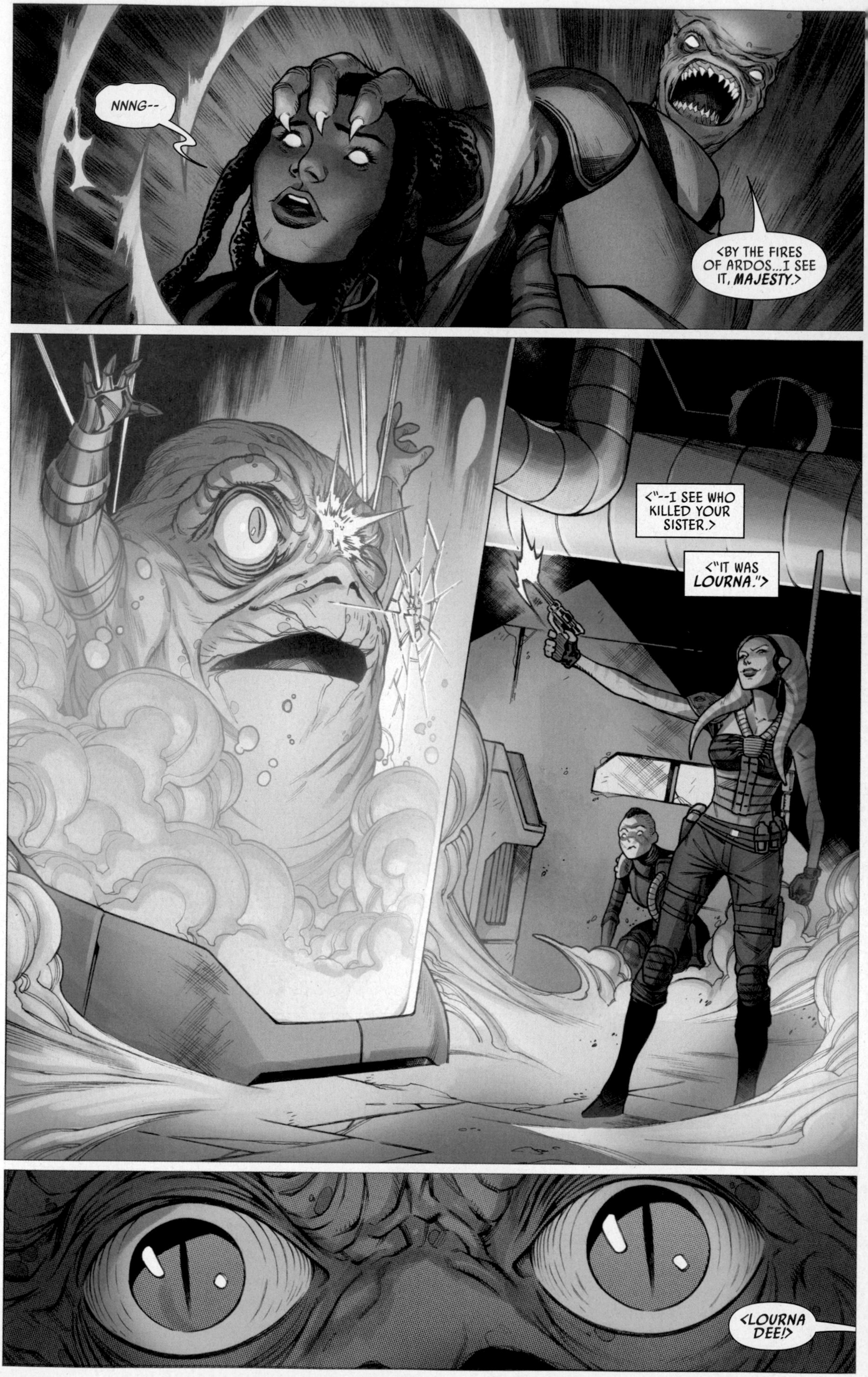
NNNG--
<BY THE FIRES OF ARDOS...I SEE IT, MAJESTY.>
<"--I SEE WHO KILLED YOUR SISTER.>
<"IT WAS LOURNA.">
<LOURNA DEE!>

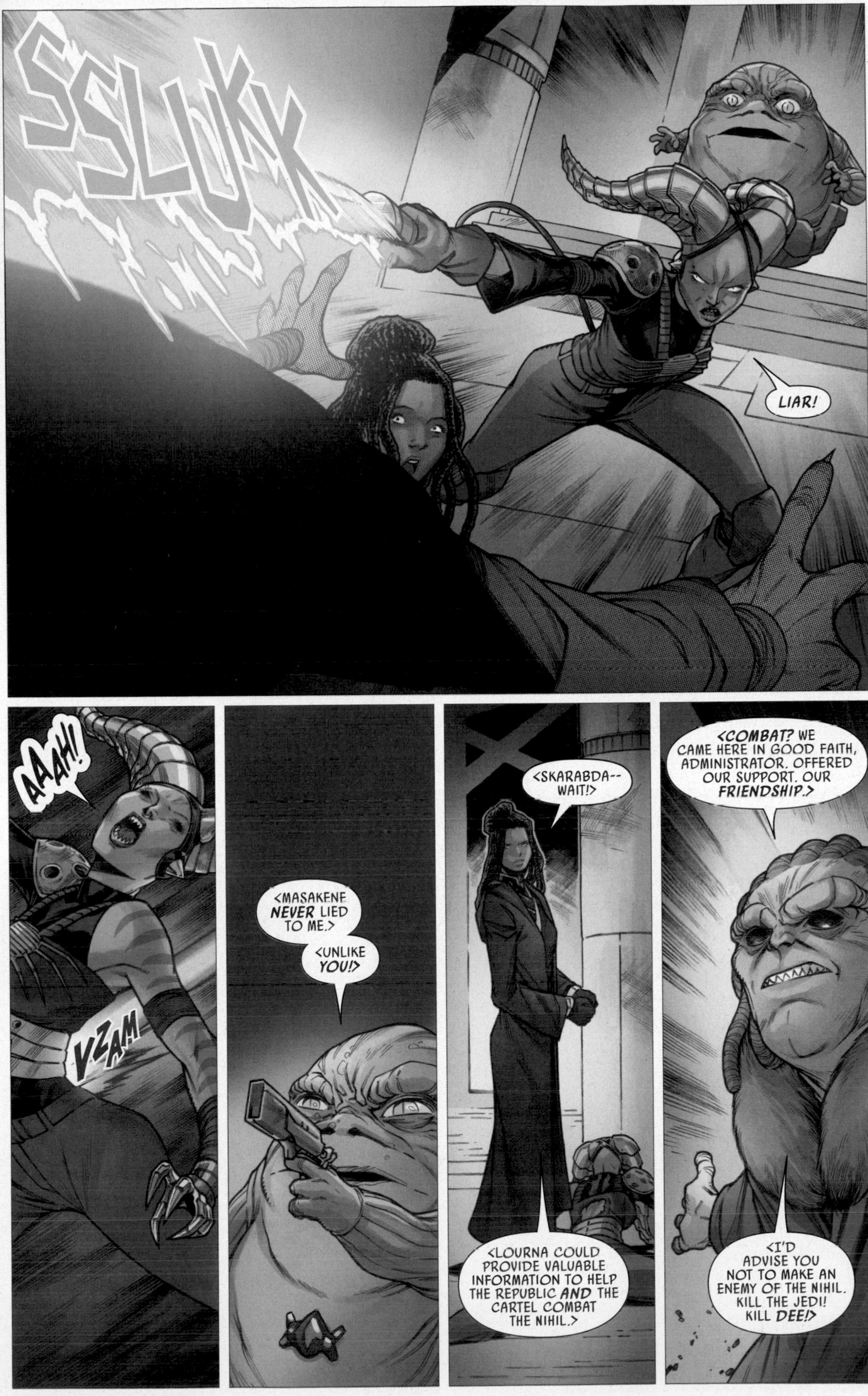
SSLUKK
LIAR!
AAAH!
VZAM
<MASAKENE NEVER LIED TO ME.>
<UNLIKE YOU!>
<SKARABDA-- WAIT!>
<LOURNA COULD PROVIDE VALUABLE INFORMATION TO HELP THE REPUBLIC AND THE CARTEL COMBAT THE NIHIL.>
<COMBAT? WE CAME HERE IN GOOD FAITH, ADMINISTRATOR. OFFERED OUR SUPPORT. OUR FRIENDSHIP.>
<I'D ADVISE YOU NOT TO MAKE AN ENEMY OF THE NIHIL. KILL THE JEDI! KILL DEE!>

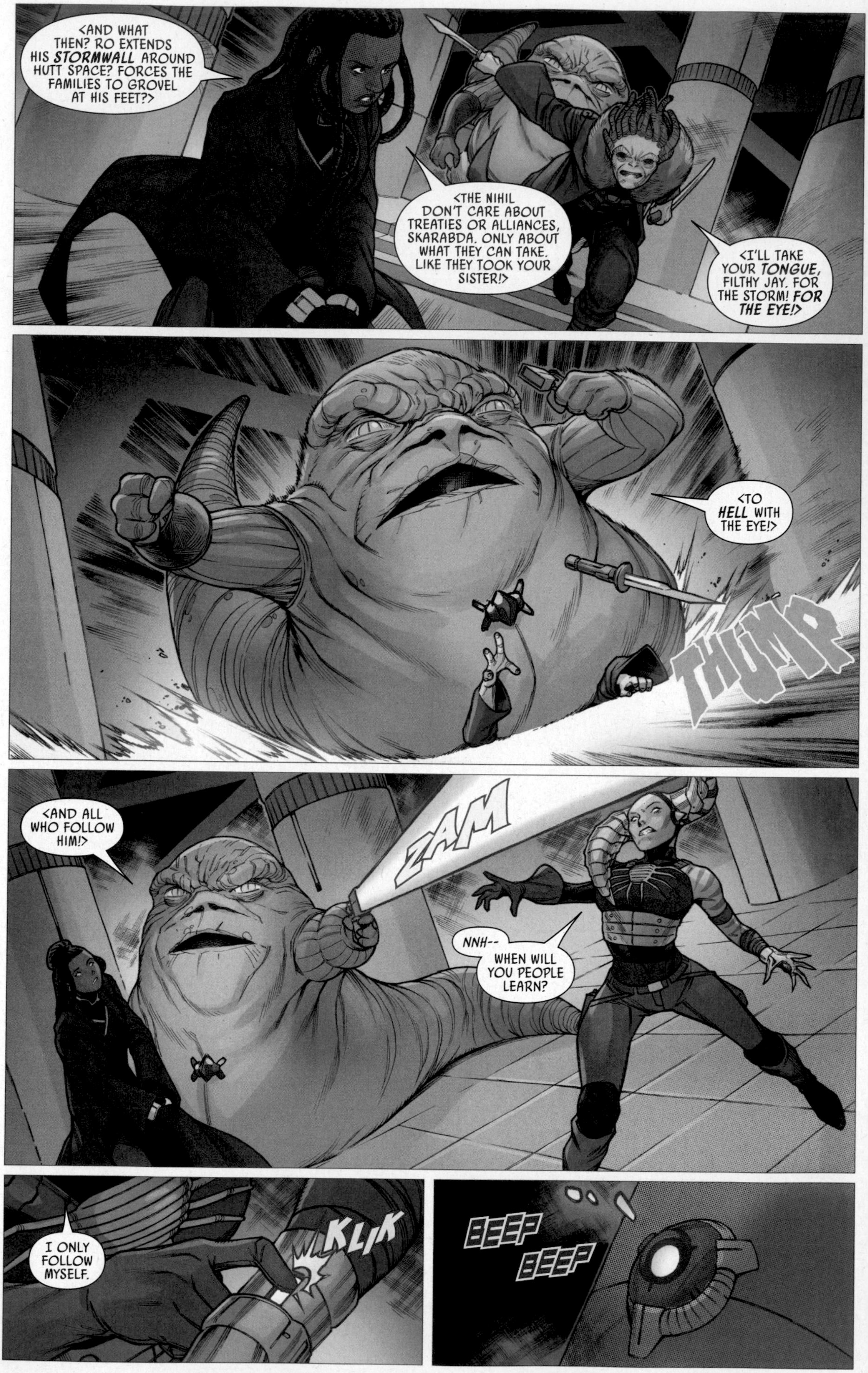
<AND WHAT THEN? RO EXTENDS HIS STORMWALL AROUND HUTT SPACE? FORCES THE FAMILIES TO GROVEL AT HIS FEET?>
<THE NIHIL DON'T CARE ABOUT TREATIES OR ALLIANCES, SKARABDA. ONLY ABOUT WHAT THEY CAN TAKE. LIKE THEY TOOK YOUR SISTER!>
<I'LL TAKE YOUR TONGUE, FILTHY JAY. FOR THE STORM! FOR THE EYE!>
<TO HELL WITH THE EYE!>
THUMP
<AND ALL WHO FOLLOW HIM!>
ZAM
NNH-- WHEN WILL YOU PEOPLE LEARN?
I ONLY FOLLOW MYSELF.
KLIK
BEEP
BEEP

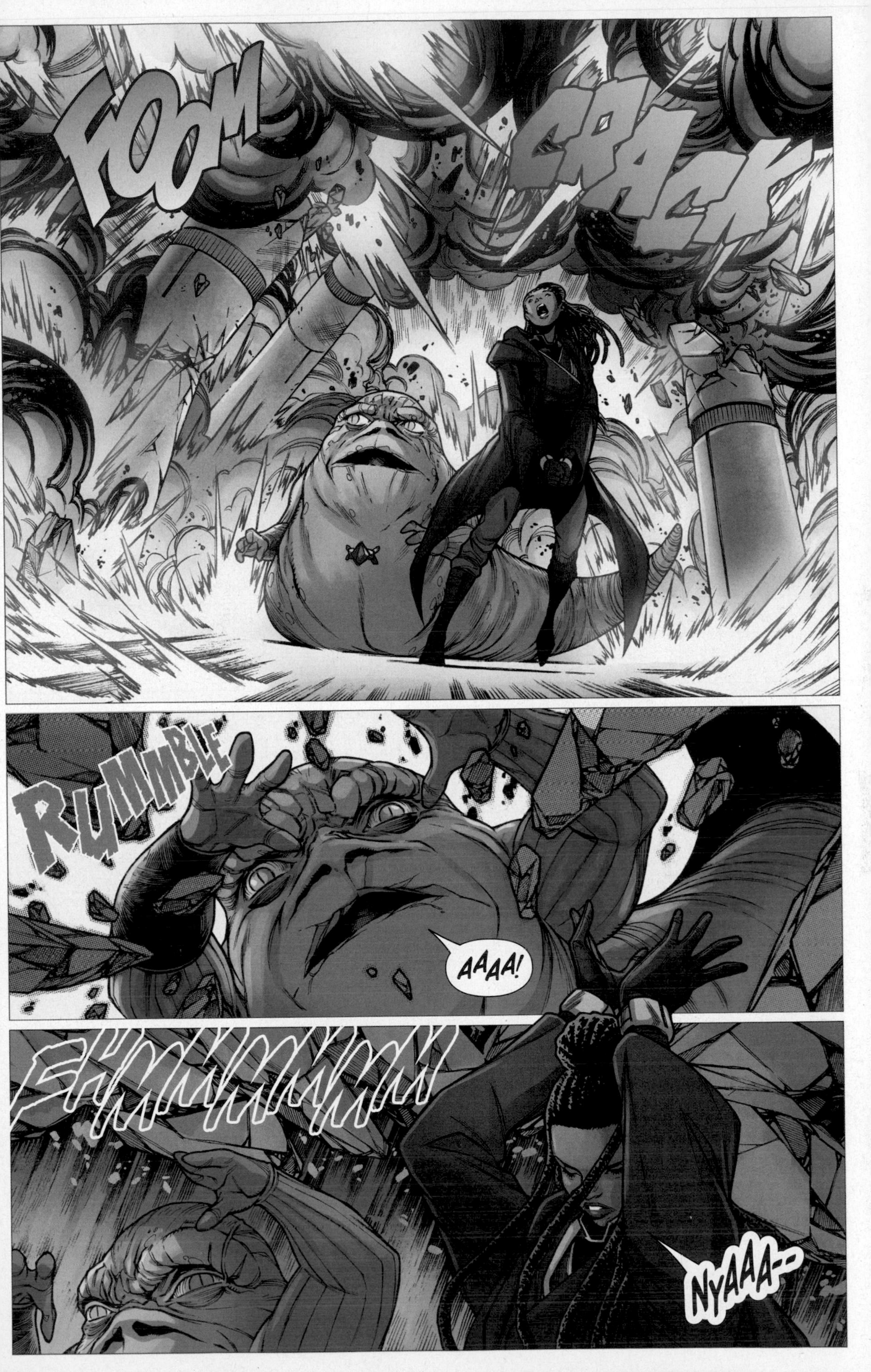
FOOM
CRACK
RUMMBLE
AAAA!
NYAAA-

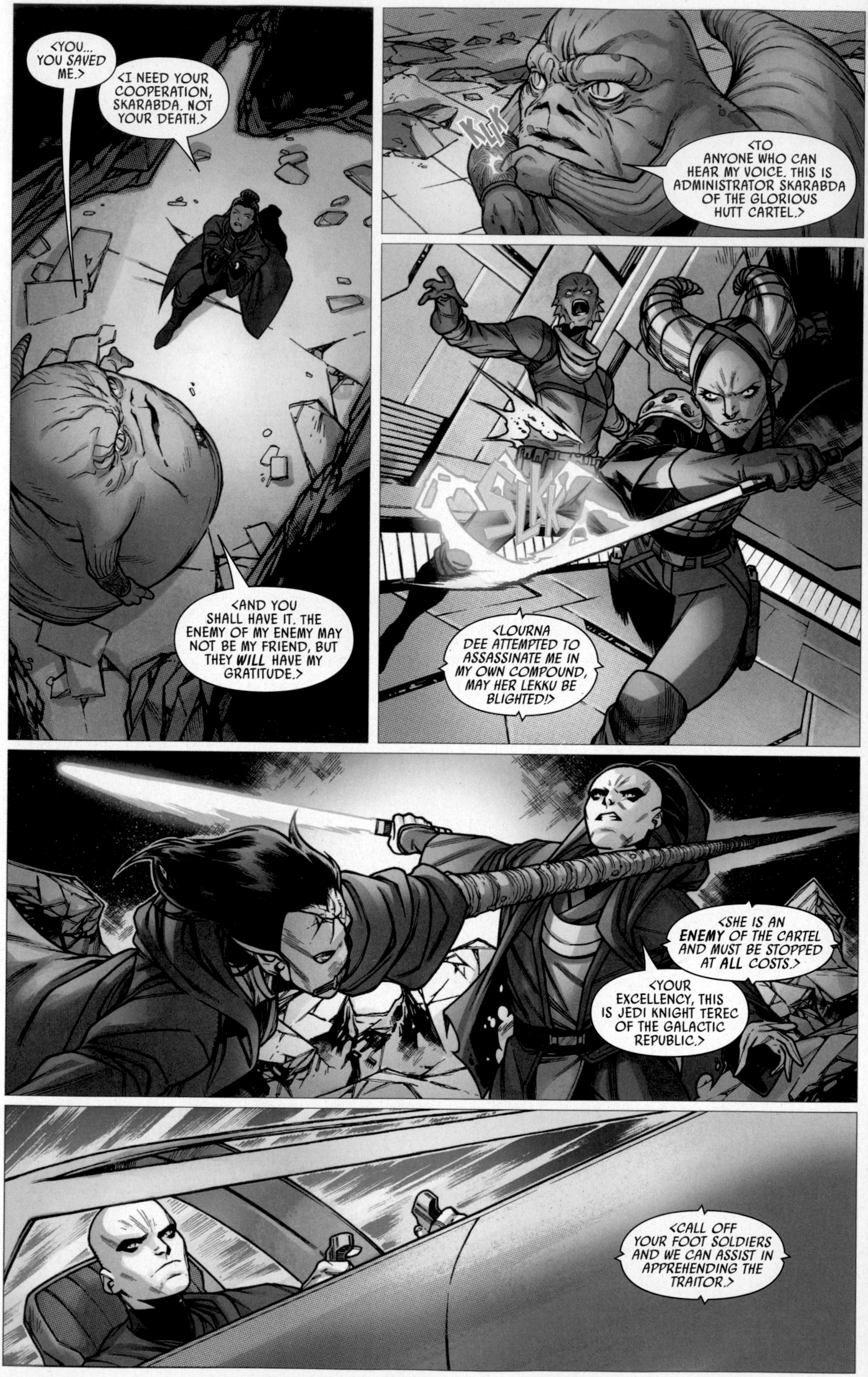
<YOU... YOU *SAVED* ME.>
<I NEED YOUR COOPERATION, SKARABDA. NOT YOUR DEATH.>
<AND YOU SHALL HAVE IT. THE ENEMY OF MY ENEMY MAY NOT BE MY FRIEND, BUT THEY **WILL** HAVE MY GRATITUDE.>
KLIK
<TO ANYONE WHO CAN HEAR MY VOICE. THIS IS ADMINISTRATOR SKARABDA OF THE GLORIOUS HUTT CARTEL.>
SLKK
<LOURNA DEE ATTEMPTED TO ASSASSINATE ME IN MY OWN COMPOUND, MAY HER LEKKU BE BLIGHTED!>
<SHE IS AN **ENEMY** OF THE CARTEL AND MUST BE STOPPED AT **ALL** COSTS.>
<YOUR EXCELLENCY, THIS IS JEDI KNIGHT TEREC OF THE GALACTIC REPUBLIC.>
<CALL OFF YOUR FOOT SOLDIERS AND WE CAN ASSIST IN APPREHENDING THE TRAITOR.>

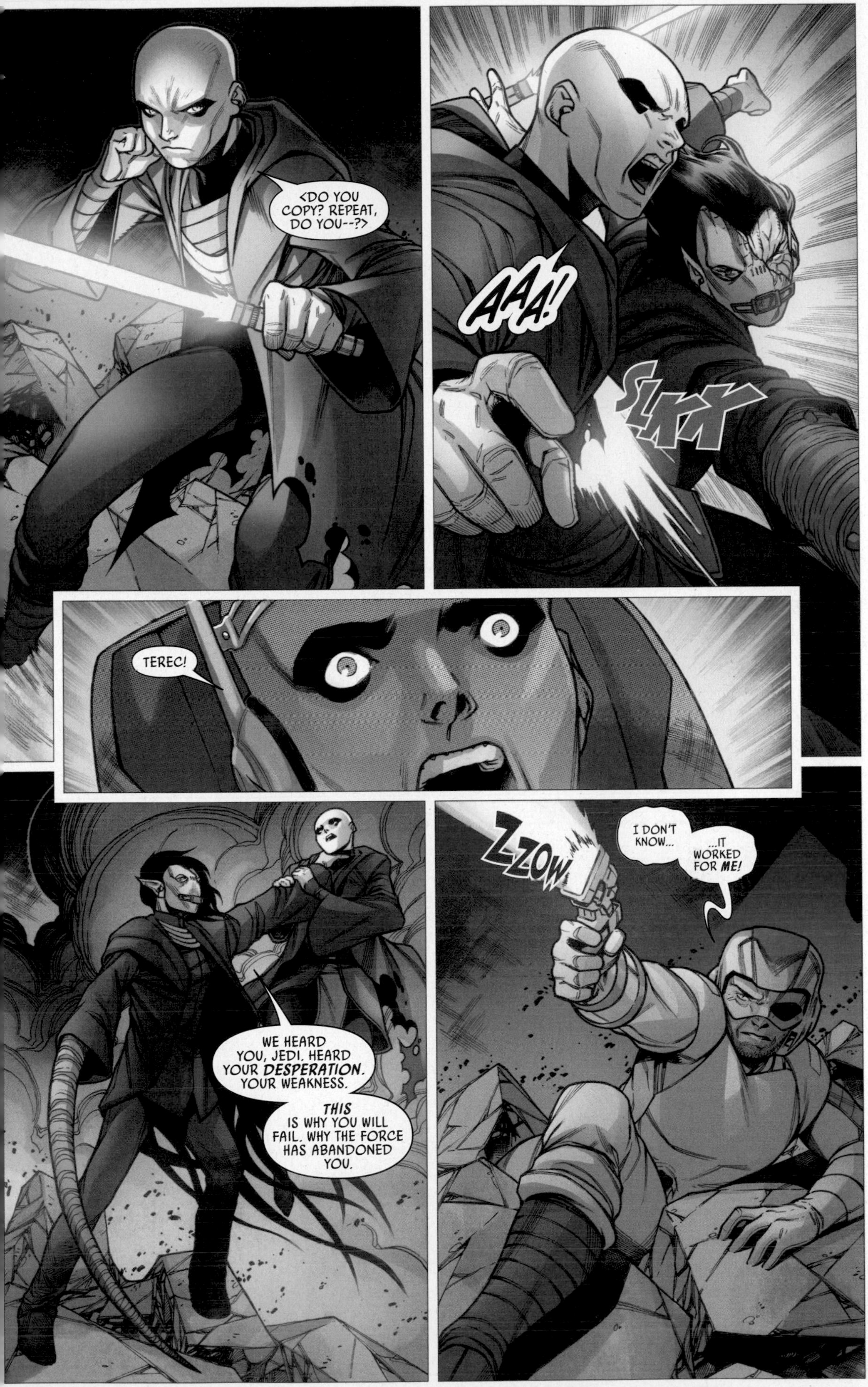

<DO YOU COPY? REPEAT, DO YOU--?>
AAA!
SLKK
TEREC!
WE HEARD YOU, JEDI. HEARD YOUR DESPERATION. YOUR WEAKNESS.
THIS IS WHY YOU WILL FAIL. WHY THE FORCE HAS ABANDONED YOU.
ZZOW
I DON'T KNOW...
...IT WORKED FOR ME!

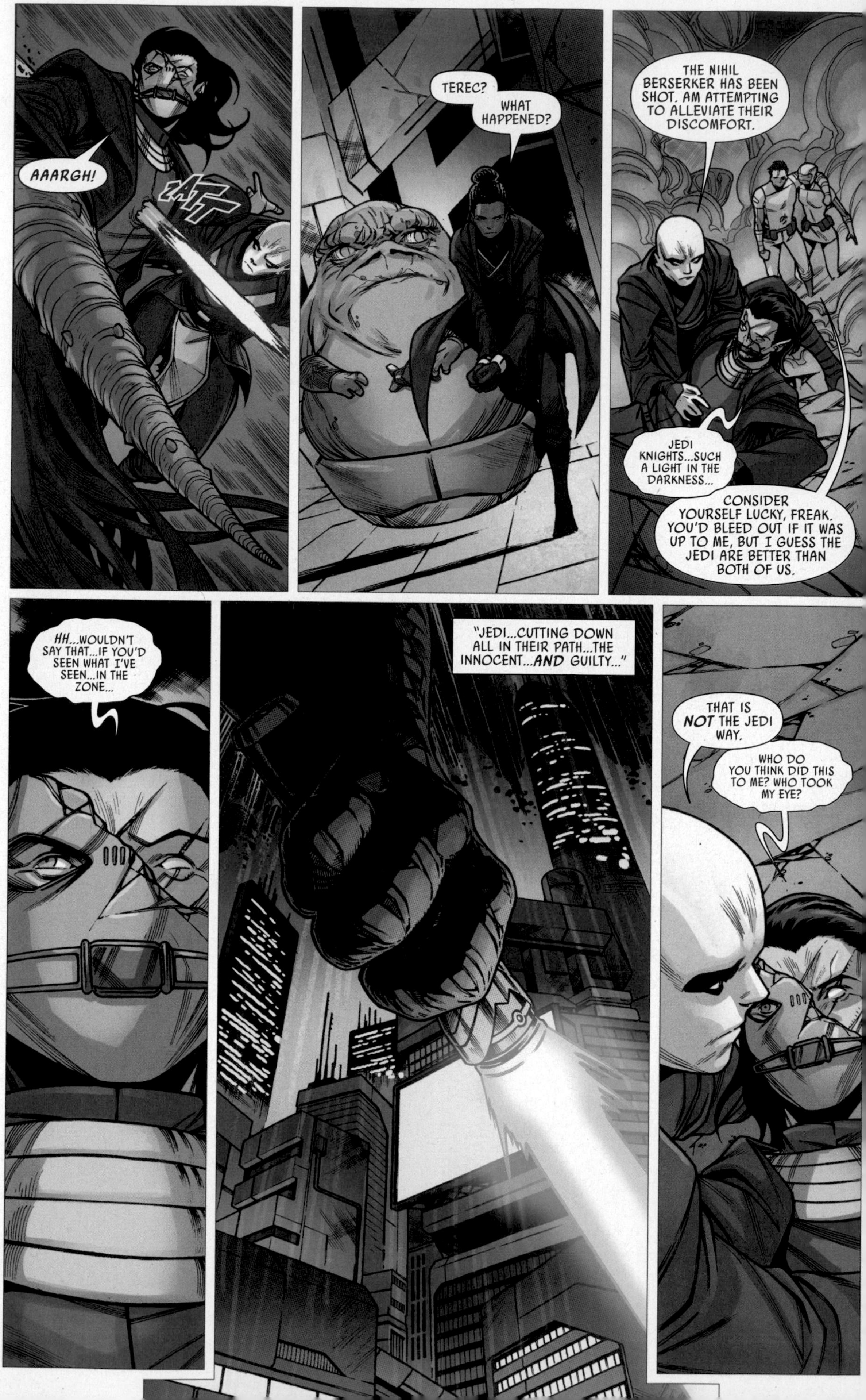
AAARGH!
ZAT
TEREC?
WHAT HAPPENED?
THE NIHIL BERSERKER HAS BEEN SHOT. AM ATTEMPTING TO ALLEVIATE THEIR DISCOMFORT.
JEDI KNIGHTS...SUCH A LIGHT IN THE DARKNESS...
CONSIDER YOURSELF LUCKY, FREAK. YOU'D BLEED OUT IF IT WAS UP TO ME, BUT I GUESS THE JEDI ARE BETTER THAN BOTH OF US.
HH...WOULDN'T SAY THAT...IF YOU'D SEEN WHAT I'VE SEEN...IN THE ZONE...
"JEDI...CUTTING DOWN ALL IN THEIR PATH...THE INNOCENT...AND GUILTY..."
THAT IS NOT THE JEDI WAY.
WHO DO YOU THINK DID THIS TO ME? WHO TOOK MY EYE?

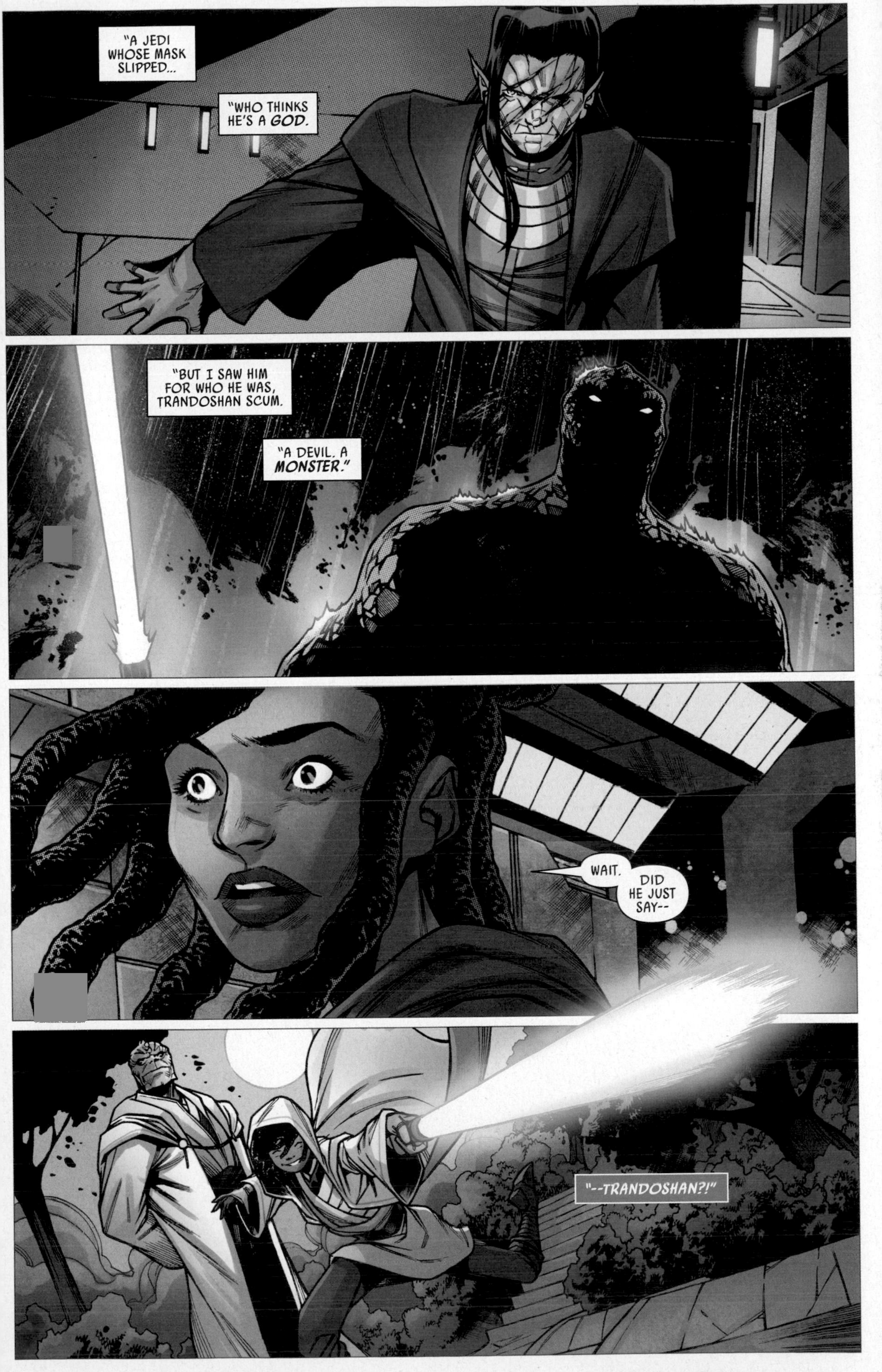
"A JEDI WHOSE MASK SLIPPED...
"WHO THINKS HE'S A GOD.
"BUT I SAW HIM FOR WHO HE WAS, TRANDOSHAN SCUM.
"A DEVIL, A MONSTER."
WAIT.
DID HE JUST SAY--
"--TRANDOSHAN?!"

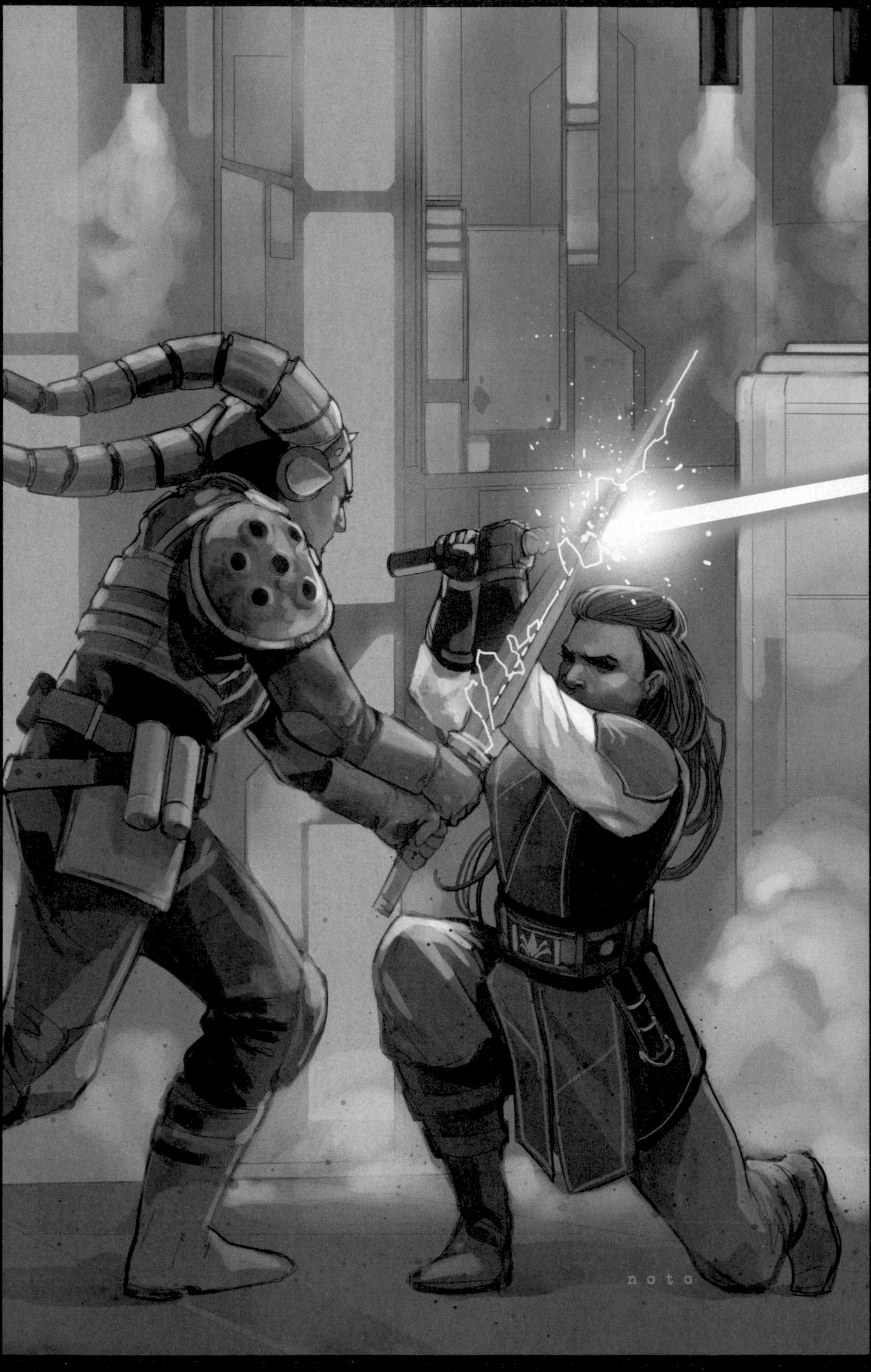
noto

3 | THE TAKING OF THE *ATARAXIA*

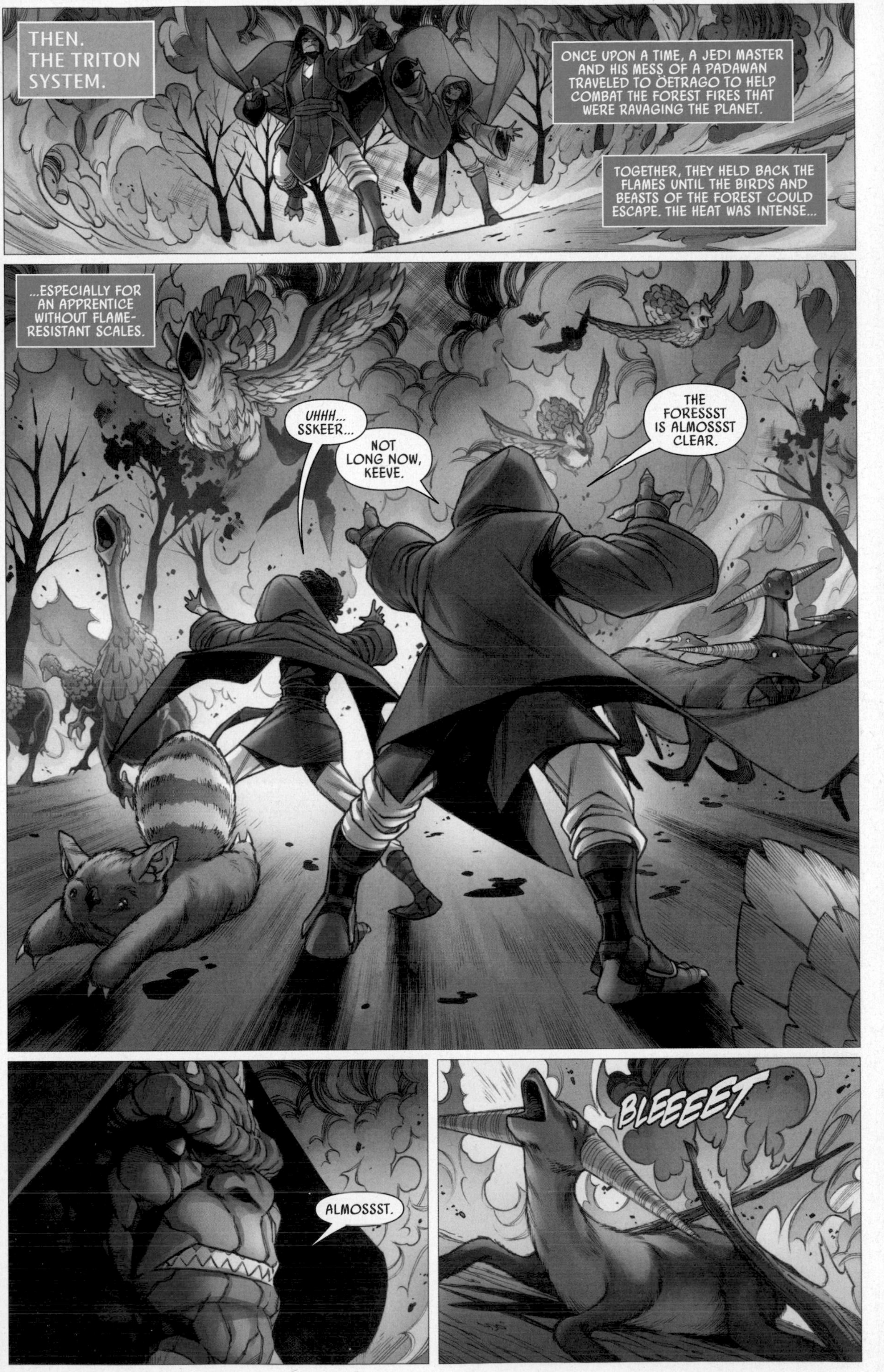
THEN. THE TRITON SYSTEM.
ONCE UPON A TIME, A JEDI MASTER AND HIS MESS OF A PADAWAN TRAVELED TO ÖETRAGO TO HELP COMBAT THE FOREST FIRES THAT WERE RAVAGING THE PLANET.
TOGETHER, THEY HELD BACK THE FLAMES UNTIL THE BIRDS AND BEASTS OF THE FOREST COULD ESCAPE. THE HEAT WAS INTENSE...
...ESPECIALLY FOR AN APPRENTICE WITHOUT FLAME-RESISTANT SCALES.
UHHH... SSKEER...
NOT LONG NOW, KEEVE.
THE FORESSST IS ALMOSSST CLEAR.
ALMOSSST.
BLEEEET

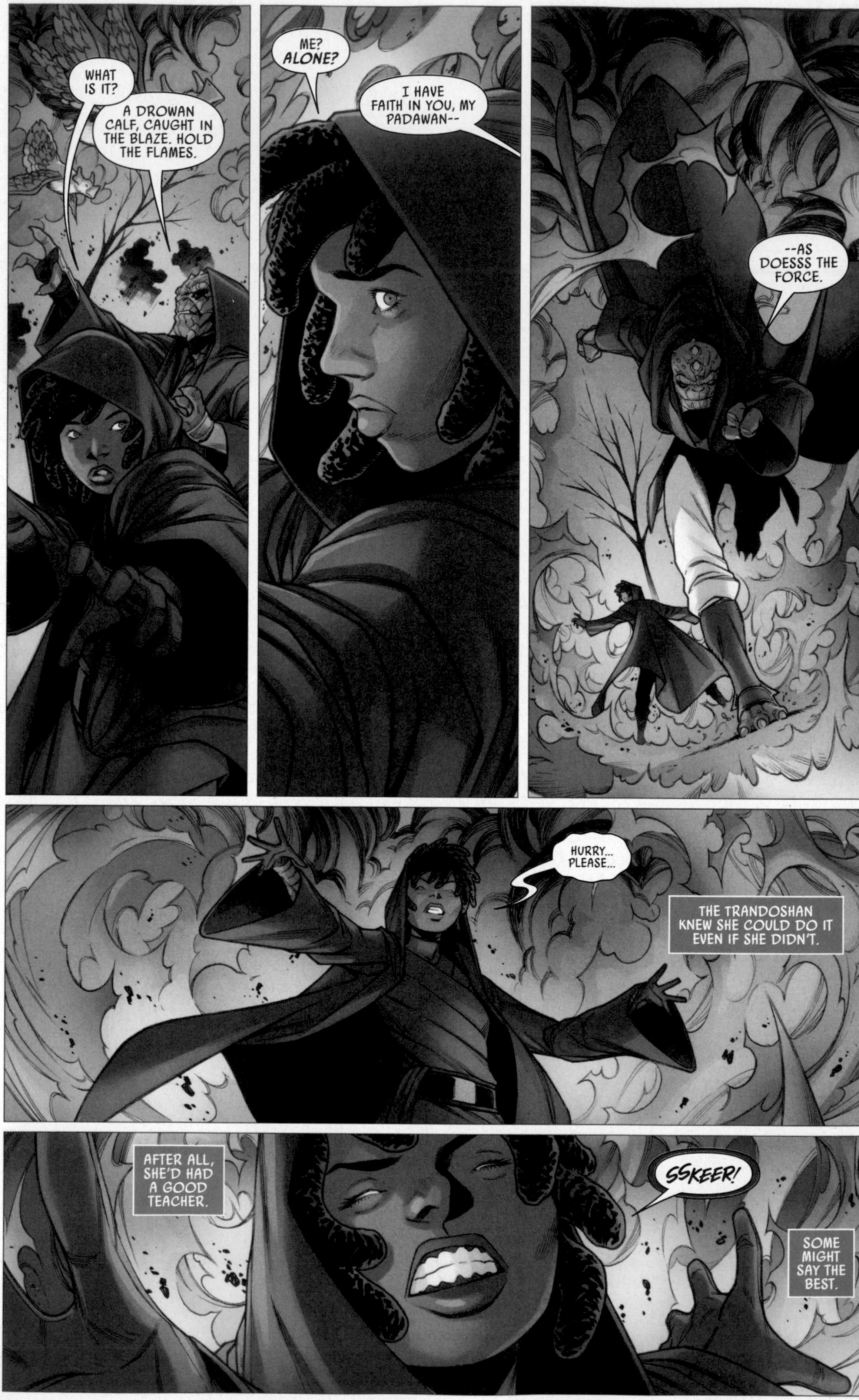
WHAT IS IT?
A DROWAN CALF, CAUGHT IN THE BLAZE. HOLD THE FLAMES.
ME? ALONE?
I HAVE FAITH IN YOU, MY PADAWAN--
--AS DOESSS THE FORCE.
HURRY... PLEASE...
THE TRANDOSHAN KNEW SHE COULD DO IT EVEN IF SHE DIDN'T.
AFTER ALL, SHE'D HAD A GOOD TEACHER.
SSKEER!
SOME MIGHT SAY THE BEST.

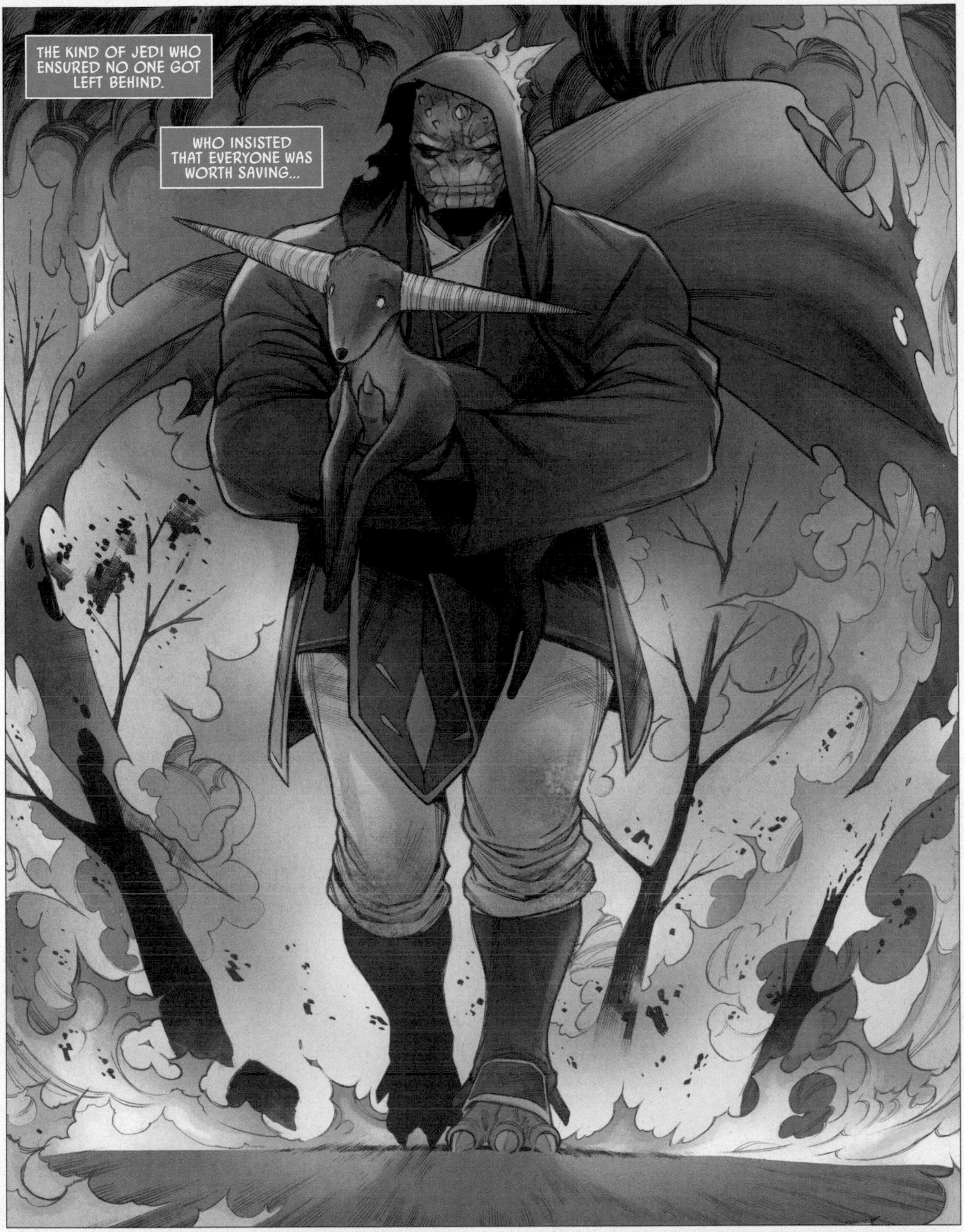
THE KIND OF JEDI WHO ENSURED NO ONE GOT LEFT BEHIND.
WHO INSISTED THAT EVERYONE WAS WORTH SAVING...

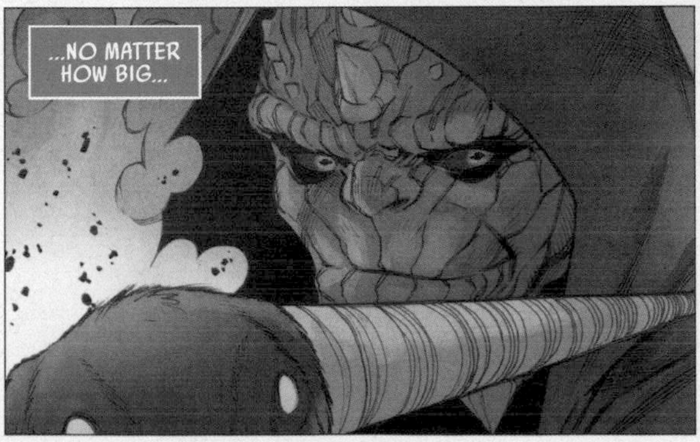
...NO MATTER HOW BIG...

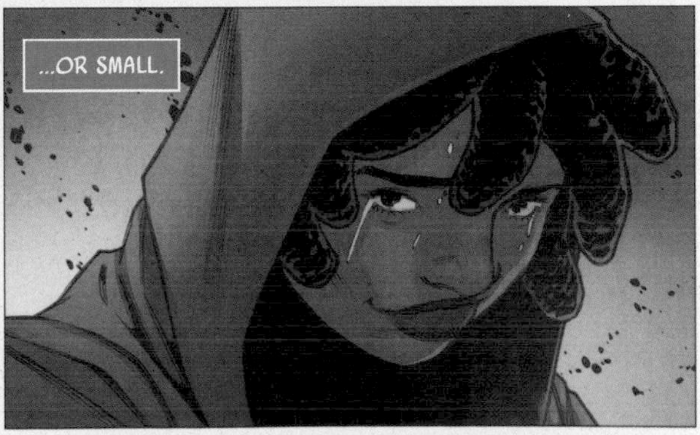
...OR SMALL.

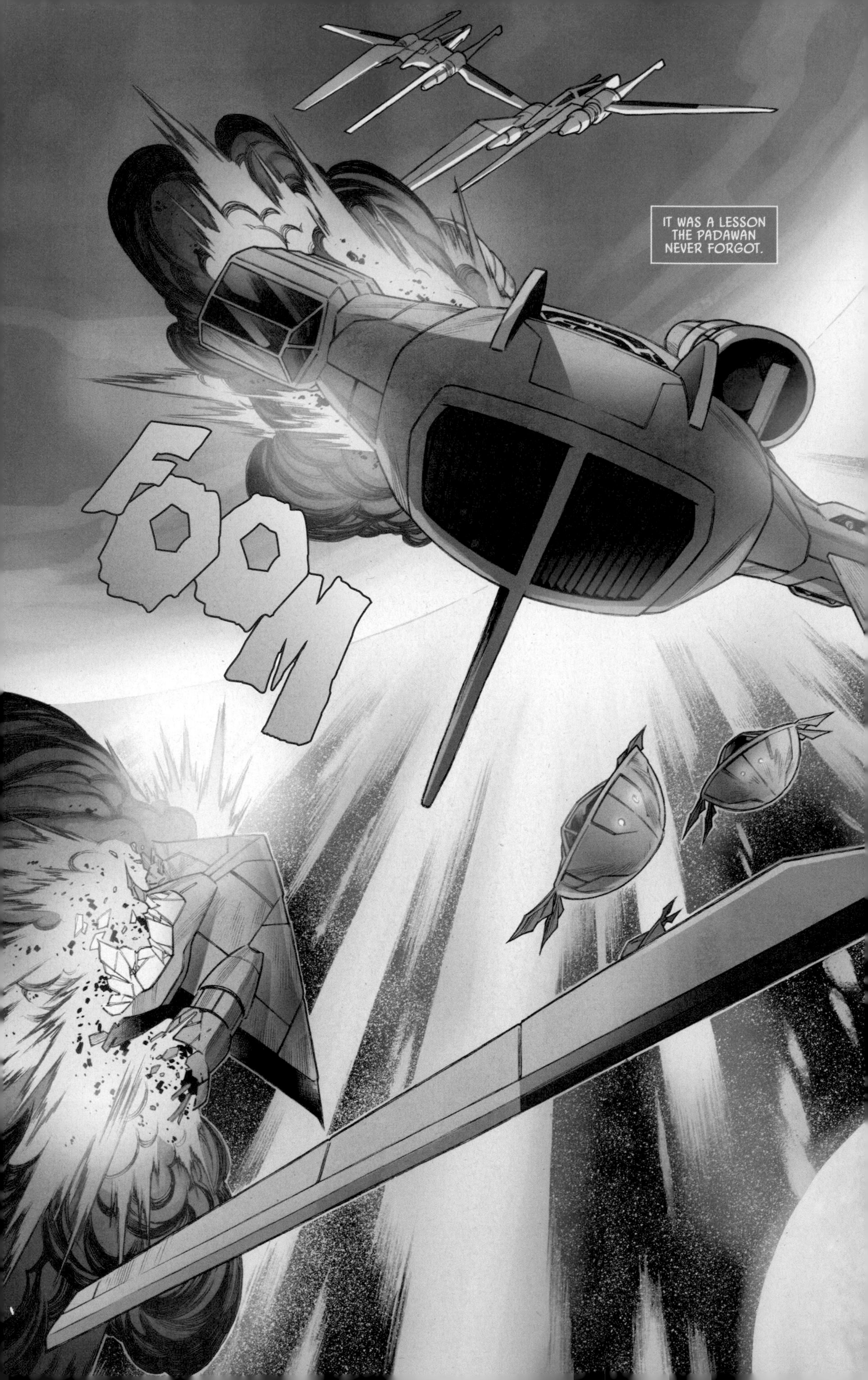
IT WAS A LESSON
THE PADAWAN
NEVER FORGOT.
FOOM

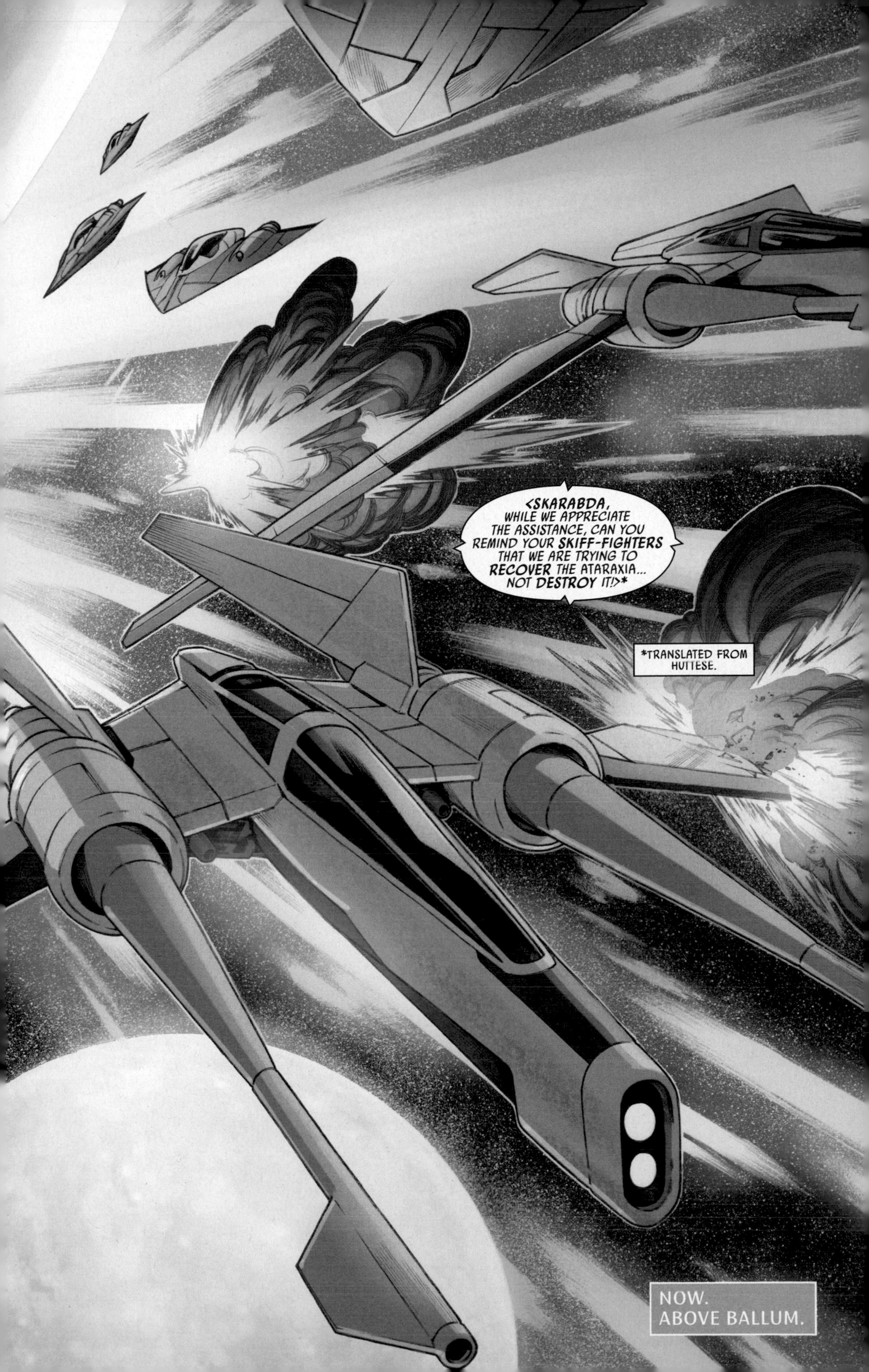
<SKARABDA, WHILE WE APPRECIATE THE ASSISTANCE, CAN YOU REMIND YOUR SKIFF-FIGHTERS THAT WE ARE TRYING TO RECOVER THE ATARAXIA... NOT DESTROY IT!>*
*TRANSLATED FROM HUTTESE.
NOW. ABOVE BALLUM.

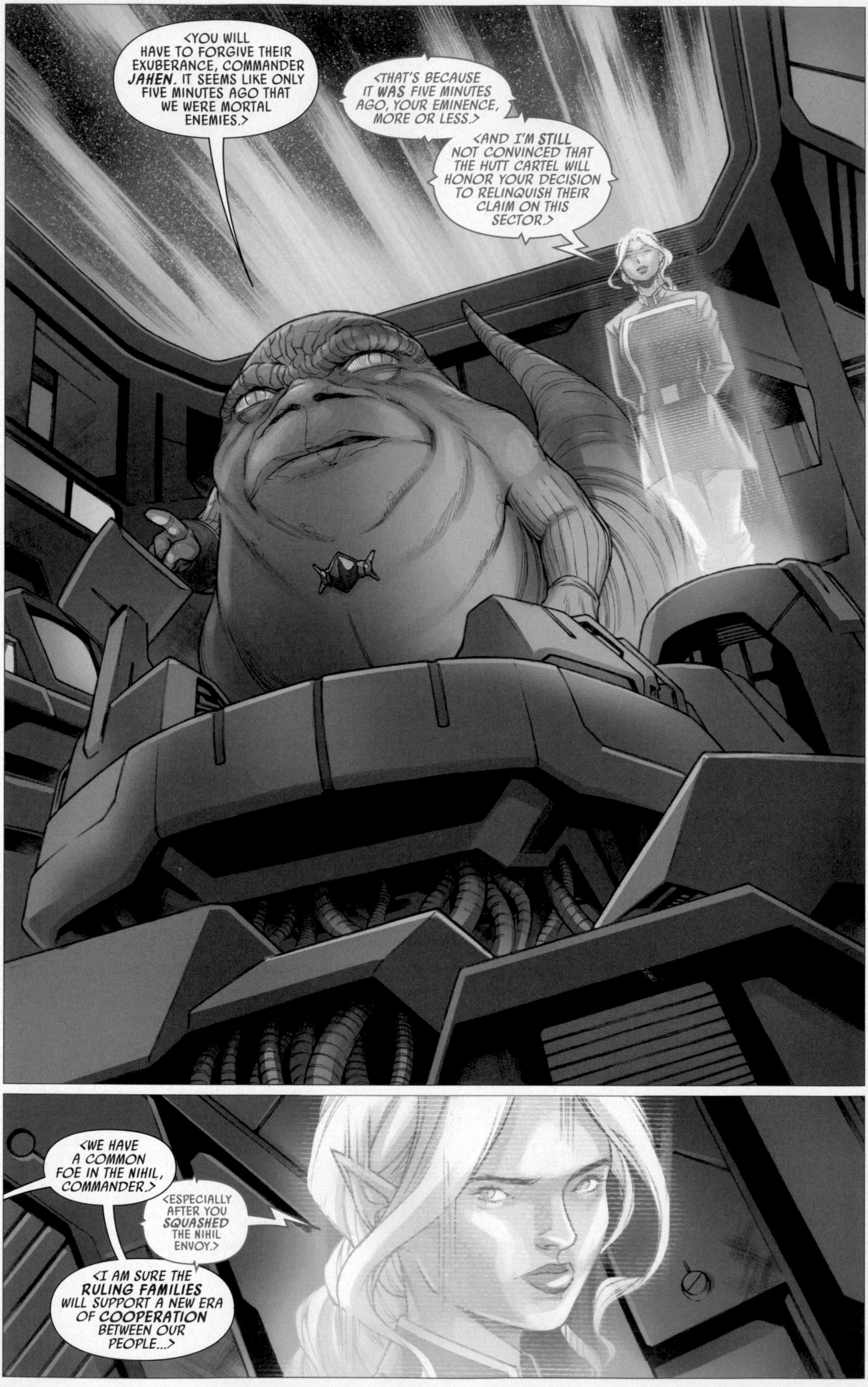

<YOU WILL HAVE TO FORGIVE THEIR EXUBERANCE, COMMANDER JAHEN. IT SEEMS LIKE ONLY FIVE MINUTES AGO THAT WE WERE MORTAL ENEMIES.>
<THAT'S BECAUSE IT WAS FIVE MINUTES AGO, YOUR EMINENCE, MORE OR LESS.>
<AND I'M STILL NOT CONVINCED THAT THE HUTT CARTEL WILL HONOR YOUR DECISION TO RELINQUISH THEIR CLAIM ON THIS SECTOR.>
<WE HAVE A COMMON FOE IN THE NIHIL, COMMANDER.>
<ESPECIALLY AFTER YOU SQUASHED THE NIHIL ENVOY.>
<I AM SURE THE RULING FAMILIES WILL SUPPORT A NEW ERA OF COOPERATION BETWEEN OUR PEOPLE...>

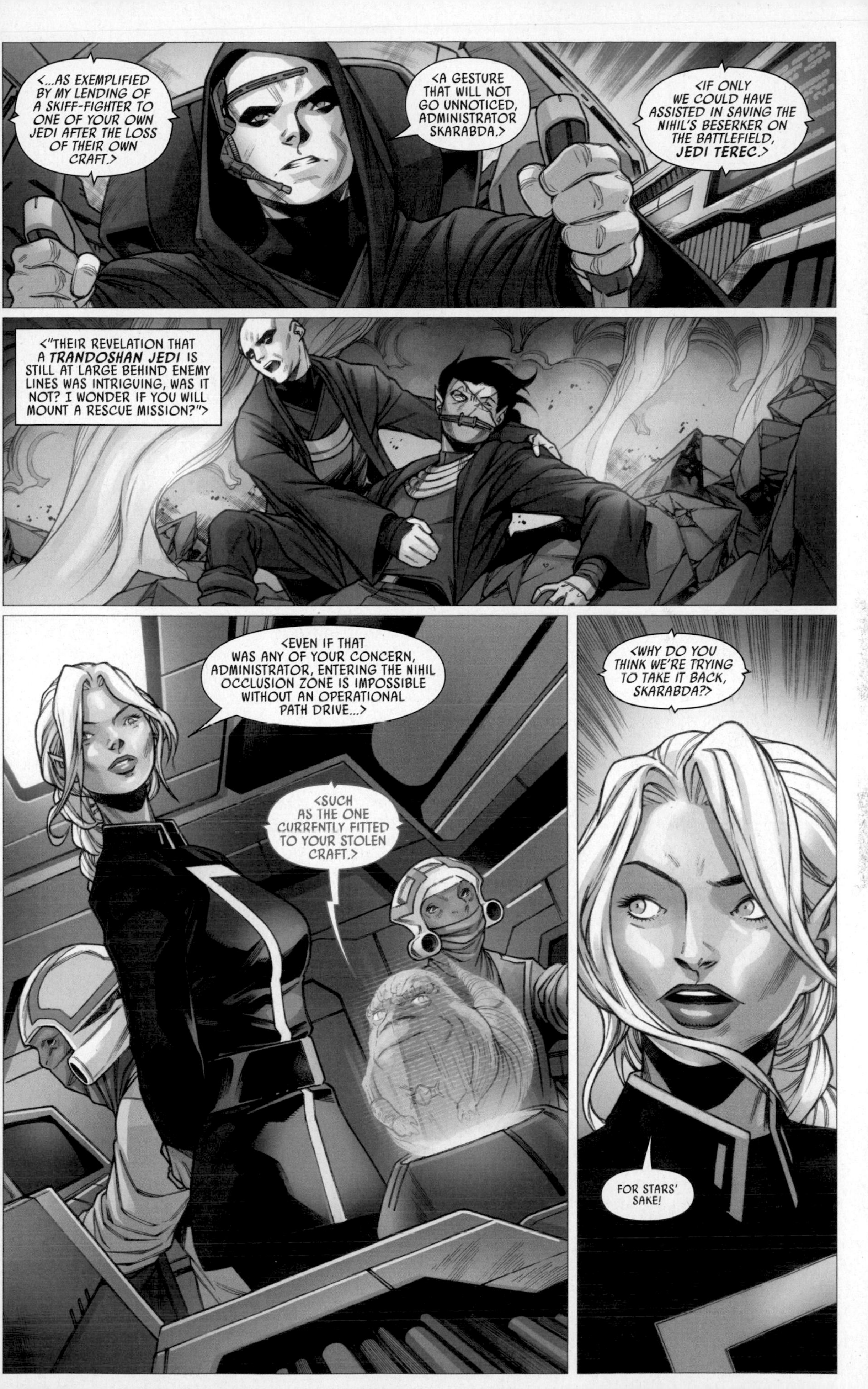

<...AS EXEMPLIFIED BY MY LENDING OF A SKIFF-FIGHTER TO ONE OF YOUR OWN JEDI AFTER THE LOSS OF THEIR OWN CRAFT.>
<A GESTURE THAT WILL NOT GO UNNOTICED, ADMINISTRATOR SKARABDA.>
<IF ONLY WE COULD HAVE ASSISTED IN SAVING THE NIHIL'S BESERKER ON THE BATTLEFIELD, JEDI TEREC.>
<"THEIR REVELATION THAT A TRANDOSHAN JEDI IS STILL AT LARGE BEHIND ENEMY LINES WAS INTRIGUING, WAS IT NOT? I WONDER IF YOU WILL MOUNT A RESCUE MISSION?">
<EVEN IF THAT WAS ANY OF YOUR CONCERN, ADMINISTRATOR, ENTERING THE NIHIL OCCLUSION ZONE IS IMPOSSIBLE WITHOUT AN OPERATIONAL PATH DRIVE...>
<SUCH AS THE ONE CURRENTLY FITTED TO YOUR STOLEN CRAFT.>
<WHY DO YOU THINK WE'RE TRYING TO TAKE IT BACK, SKARABDA?>
FOR STARS' SAKE!

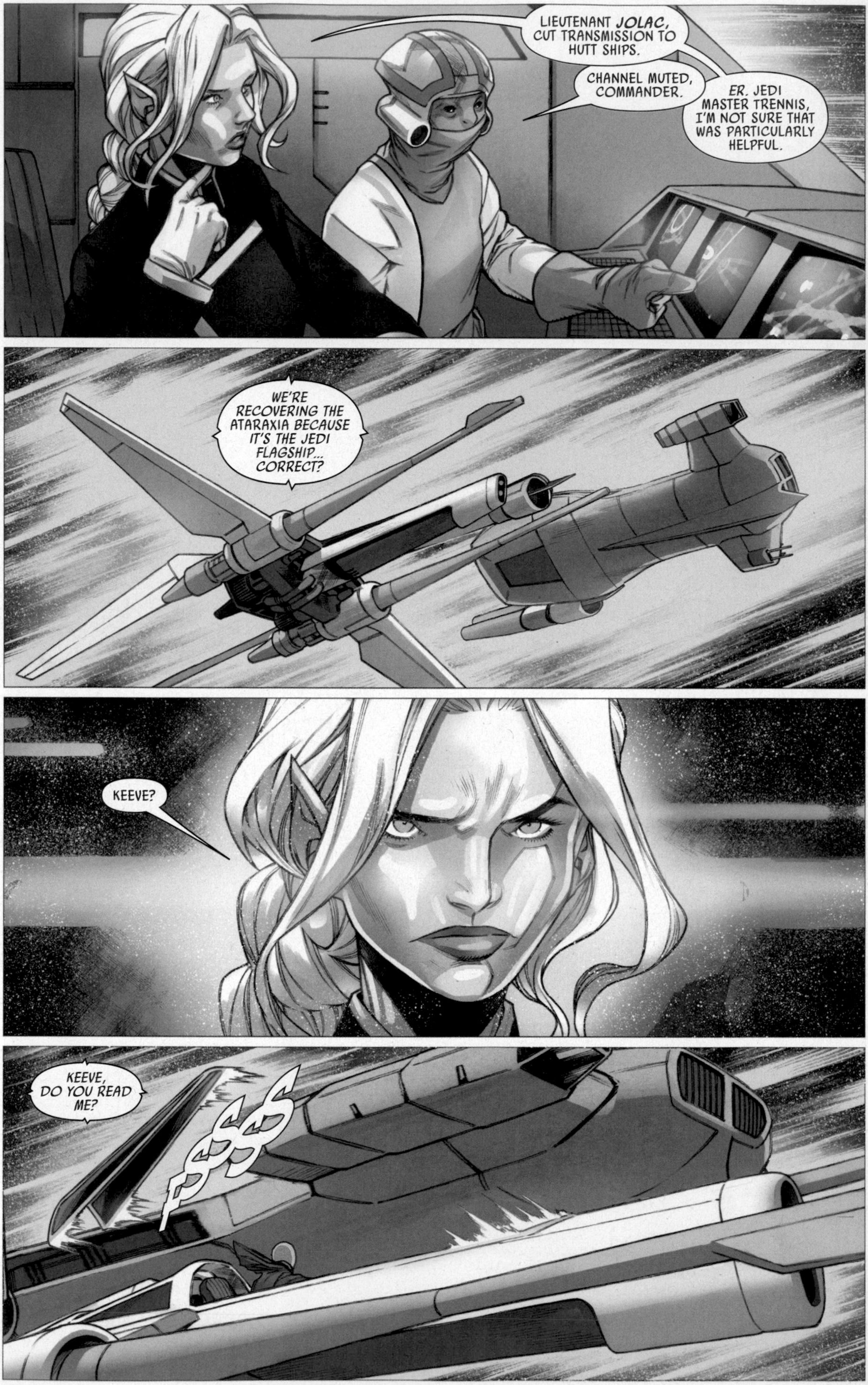
LIEUTENANT JOLAC, CUT TRANSMISSION TO HUTT SHIPS.
CHANNEL MUTED, COMMANDER.
ER. JEDI MASTER TRENNIS, I'M NOT SURE THAT WAS PARTICULARLY HELPFUL.
WE'RE RECOVERING THE ATARAXIA BECAUSE IT'S THE JEDI FLAGSHIP... CORRECT?
KEEVE?
KEEVE, DO YOU READ ME?
FSSSS

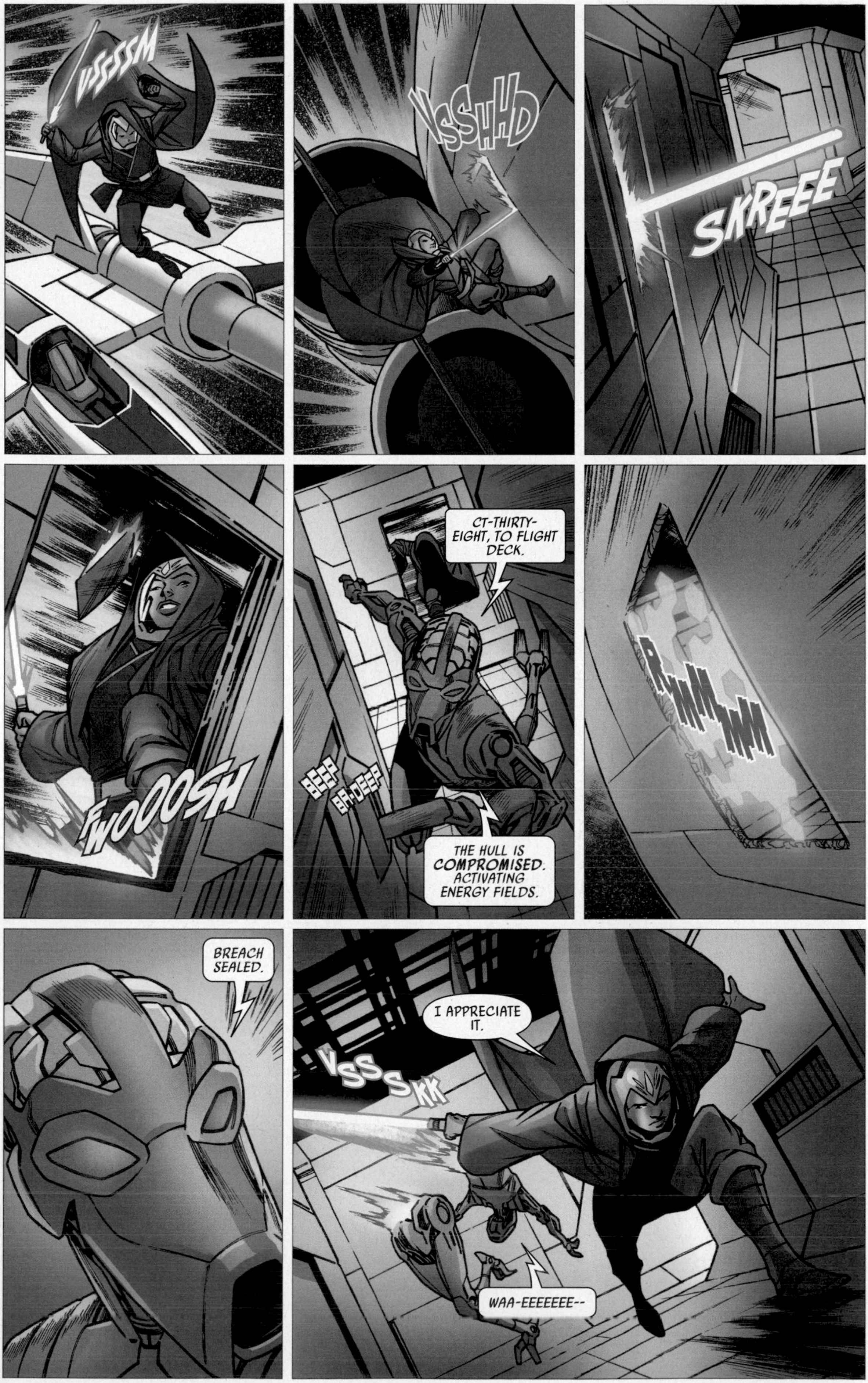
VSSSSM
VSSHHD
SKREEE
FWOOOSH
CT-THIRTY-EIGHT, TO FLIGHT DECK.
BEEP BA-DEEP
THE HULL IS COMPROMISED. ACTIVATING ENERGY FIELDS.
BREACH SEALED.
VSSSKK
I APPRECIATE IT.
WAA-EEEEEEE--

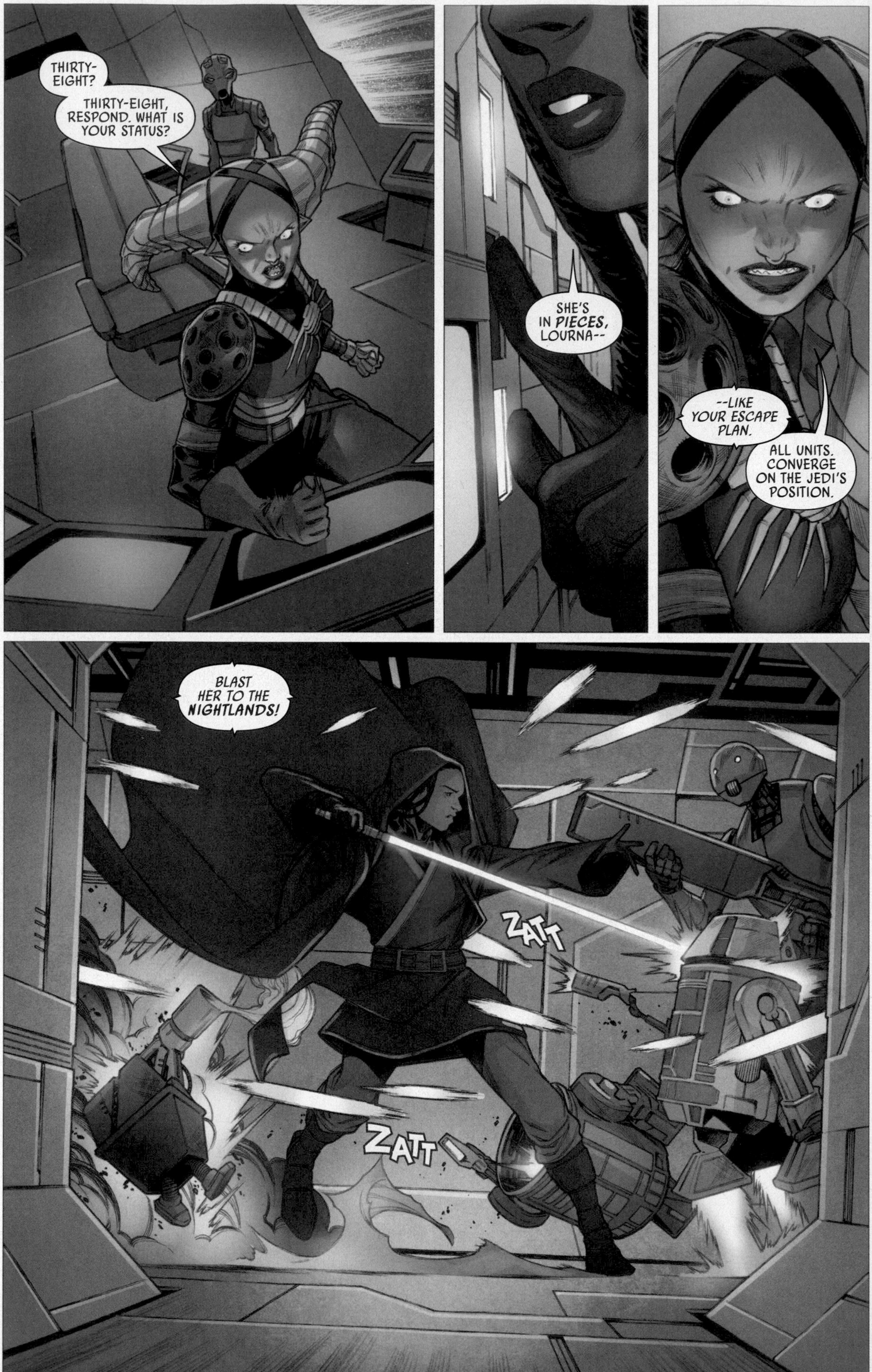
THIRTY-EIGHT?
THIRTY-EIGHT, RESPOND. WHAT IS YOUR STATUS?
SHE'S IN *PIECES*, LOURNA--
--LIKE YOUR ESCAPE PLAN.
ALL UNITS. CONVERGE ON THE JEDI'S POSITION.
BLAST HER TO THE **NIGHTLANDS!**
ZATT
ZATT

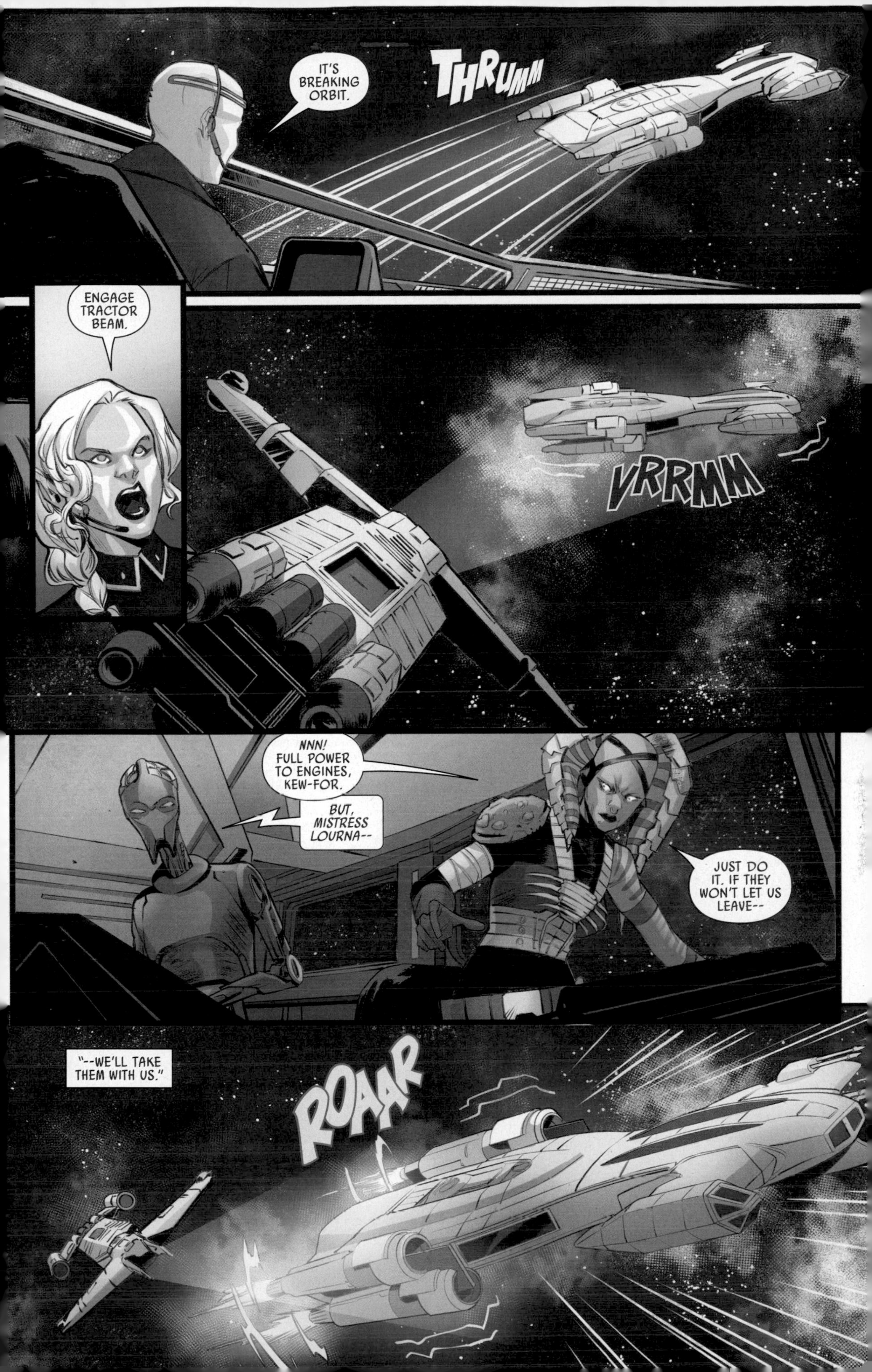
IT'S BREAKING ORBIT.
THRUMM
ENGAGE TRACTOR BEAM.
VRRMM
NNN! FULL POWER TO ENGINES, KEW-FOR.
BUT, MISTRESS LOURNA--
JUST DO IT. IF THEY WON'T LET US LEAVE--
"--WE'LL TAKE THEM WITH US."
ROAAR

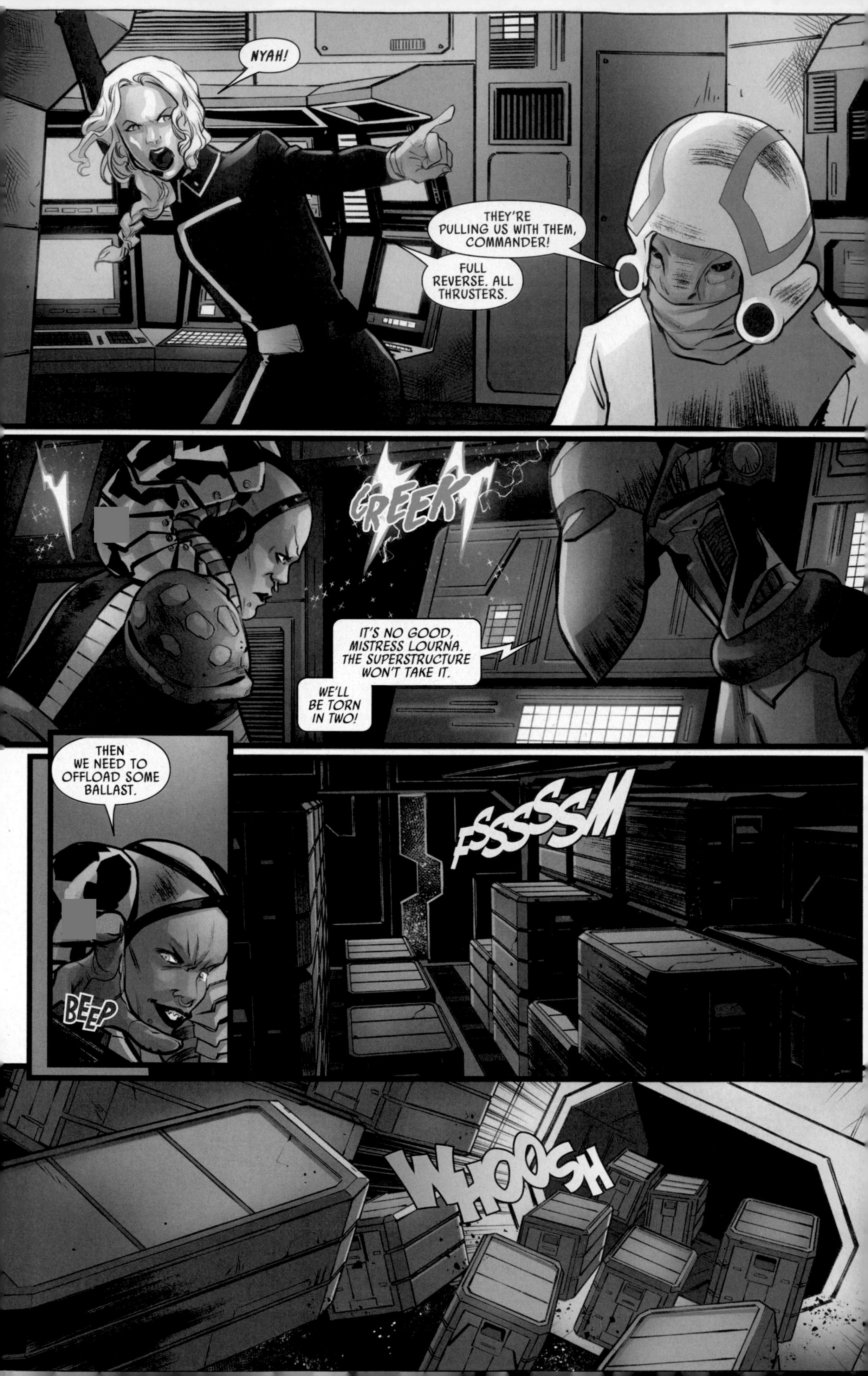
NYAH!
THEY'RE PULLING US WITH THEM, COMMANDER!
FULL REVERSE. ALL THRUSTERS.
CREEK
IT'S NO GOOD, MISTRESS LOURNA. THE SUPERSTRUCTURE WON'T TAKE IT.
WE'LL BE TORN IN TWO!
THEN WE NEED TO OFFLOAD SOME BALLAST.
BEEP
FSSSSM
WHOOSH

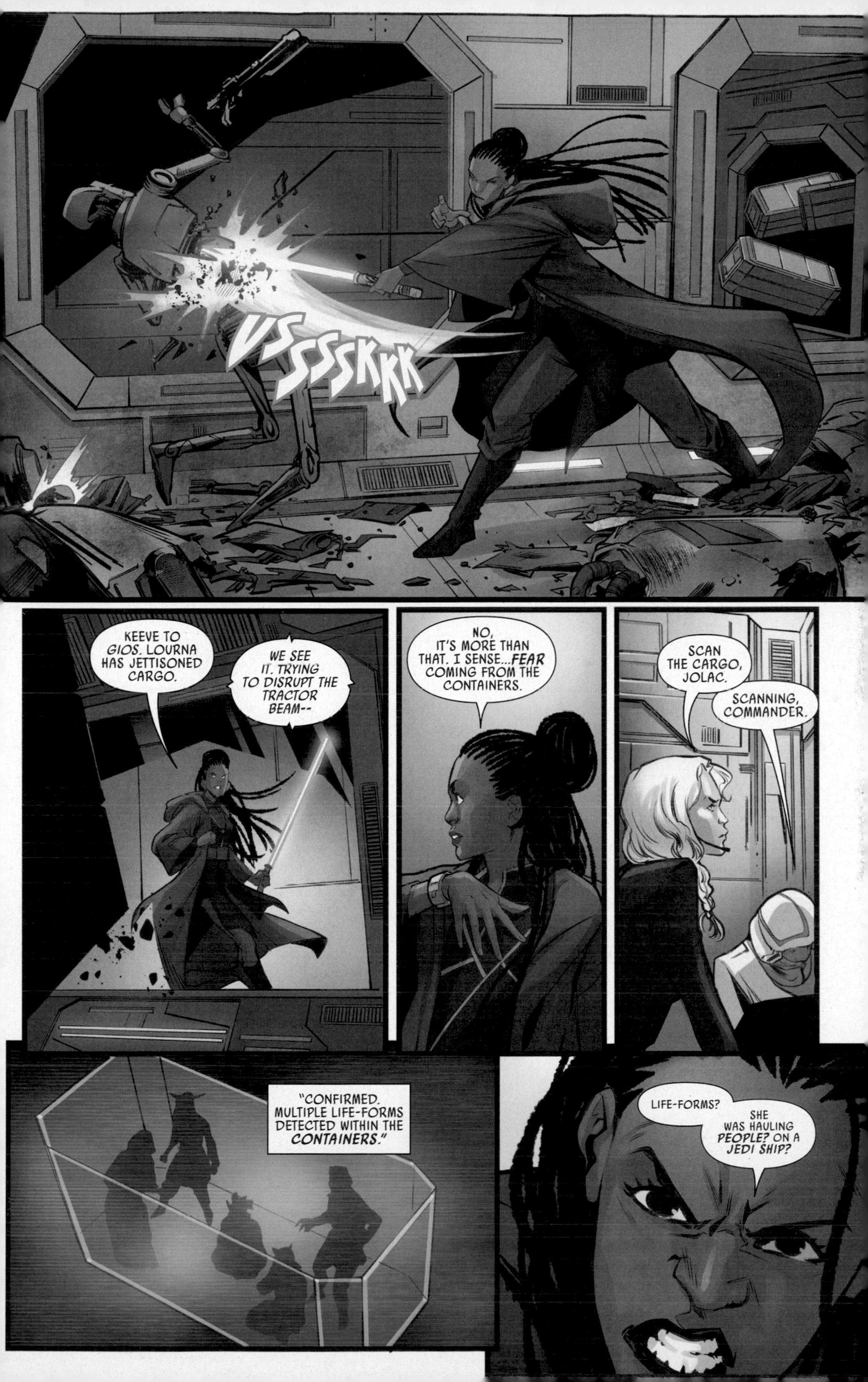
VSSSSKKK
KEEVE TO GIOS. LOURNA HAS JETTISONED CARGO.
WE SEE IT. TRYING TO DISRUPT THE TRACTOR BEAM--
NO, IT'S MORE THAN THAT. I SENSE...FEAR COMING FROM THE CONTAINERS.
SCAN THE CARGO, JOLAC.
SCANNING, COMMANDER.
"CONFIRMED. MULTIPLE LIFE-FORMS DETECTED WITHIN THE CONTAINERS."
LIFE-FORMS?
SHE WAS HAULING PEOPLE? ON A JEDI SHIP?

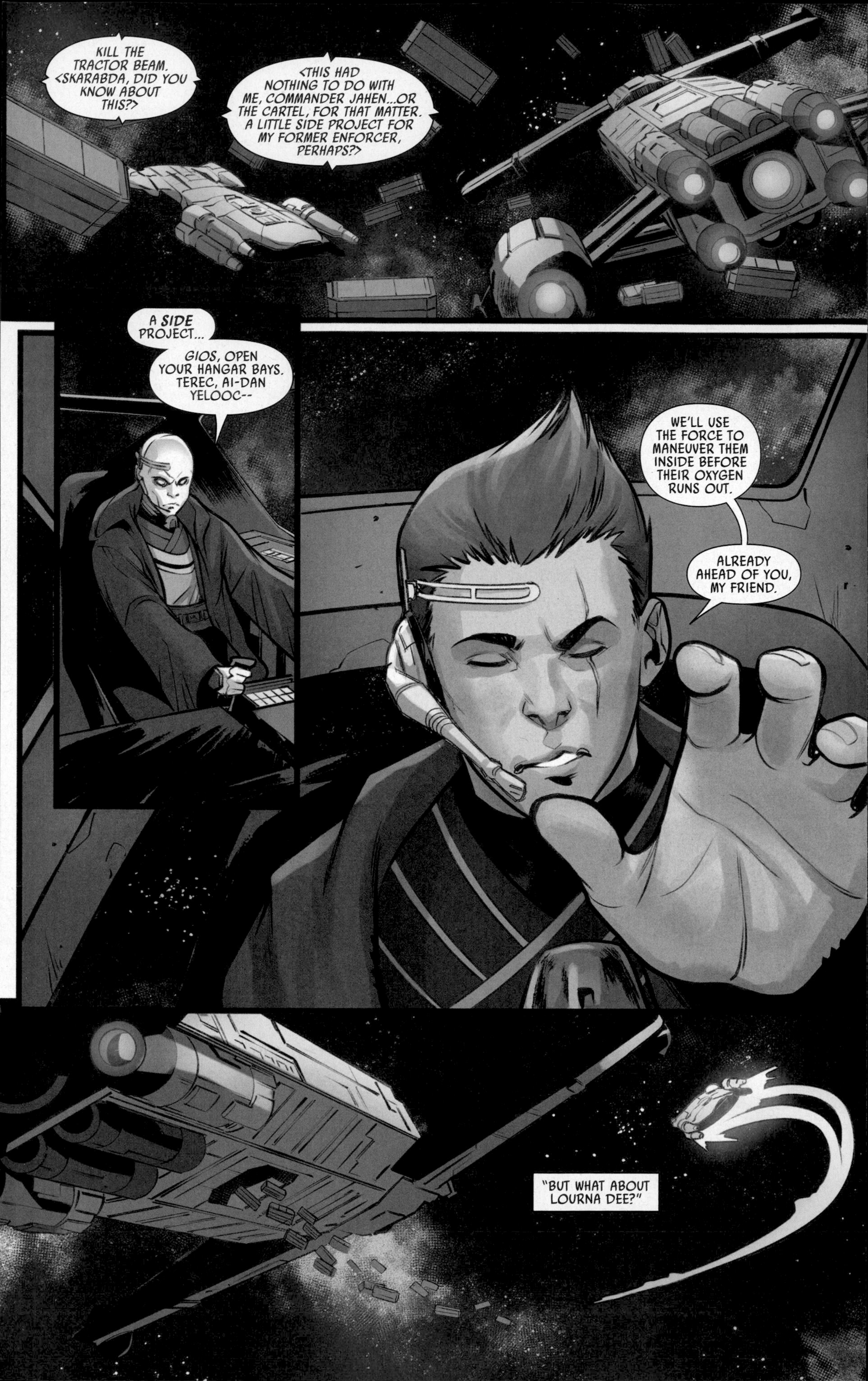
KILL THE TRACTOR BEAM. <SKARABDA, DID YOU KNOW ABOUT THIS?>
<THIS HAD NOTHING TO DO WITH ME, COMMANDER JAHEN...OR THE CARTEL, FOR THAT MATTER. A LITTLE SIDE PROJECT FOR MY FORMER ENFORCER, PERHAPS?>
A SIDE PROJECT...
GIOS, OPEN YOUR HANGAR BAYS. TEREC, AI-DAN YELOOC--
WE'LL USE THE FORCE TO MANEUVER THEM INSIDE BEFORE THEIR OXYGEN RUNS OUT.
ALREADY AHEAD OF YOU, MY FRIEND.
"BUT WHAT ABOUT LOURNA DEE?"

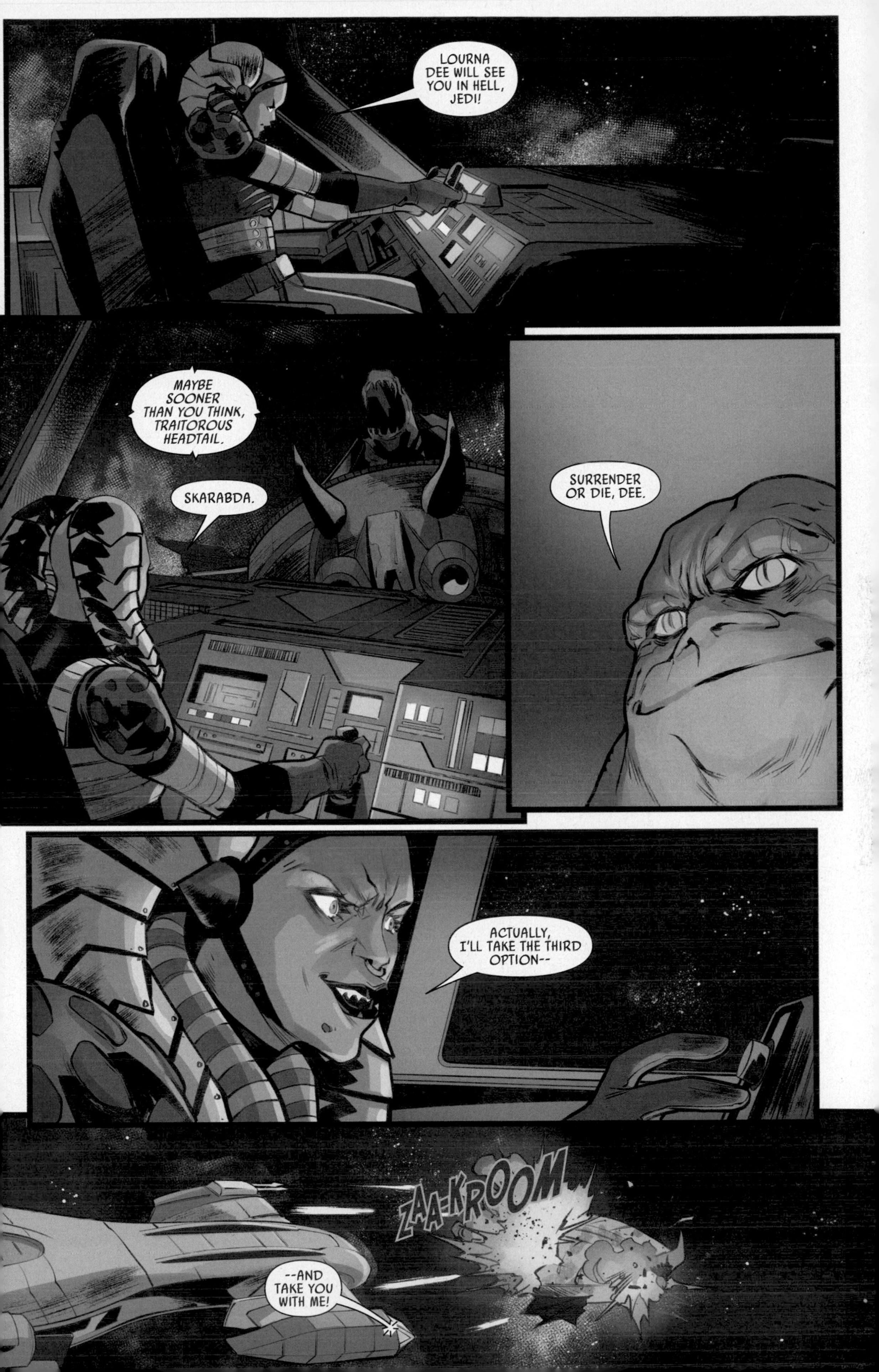
LOURNA DEE WILL SEE YOU IN HELL, JEDI!
MAYBE SOONER THAN YOU THINK, TRAITOROUS HEADTAIL.
SKARABDA.
SURRENDER OR DIE, DEE.
ACTUALLY, I'LL TAKE THE THIRD OPTION--
ZAA-KROOM
--AND TAKE YOU WITH ME!

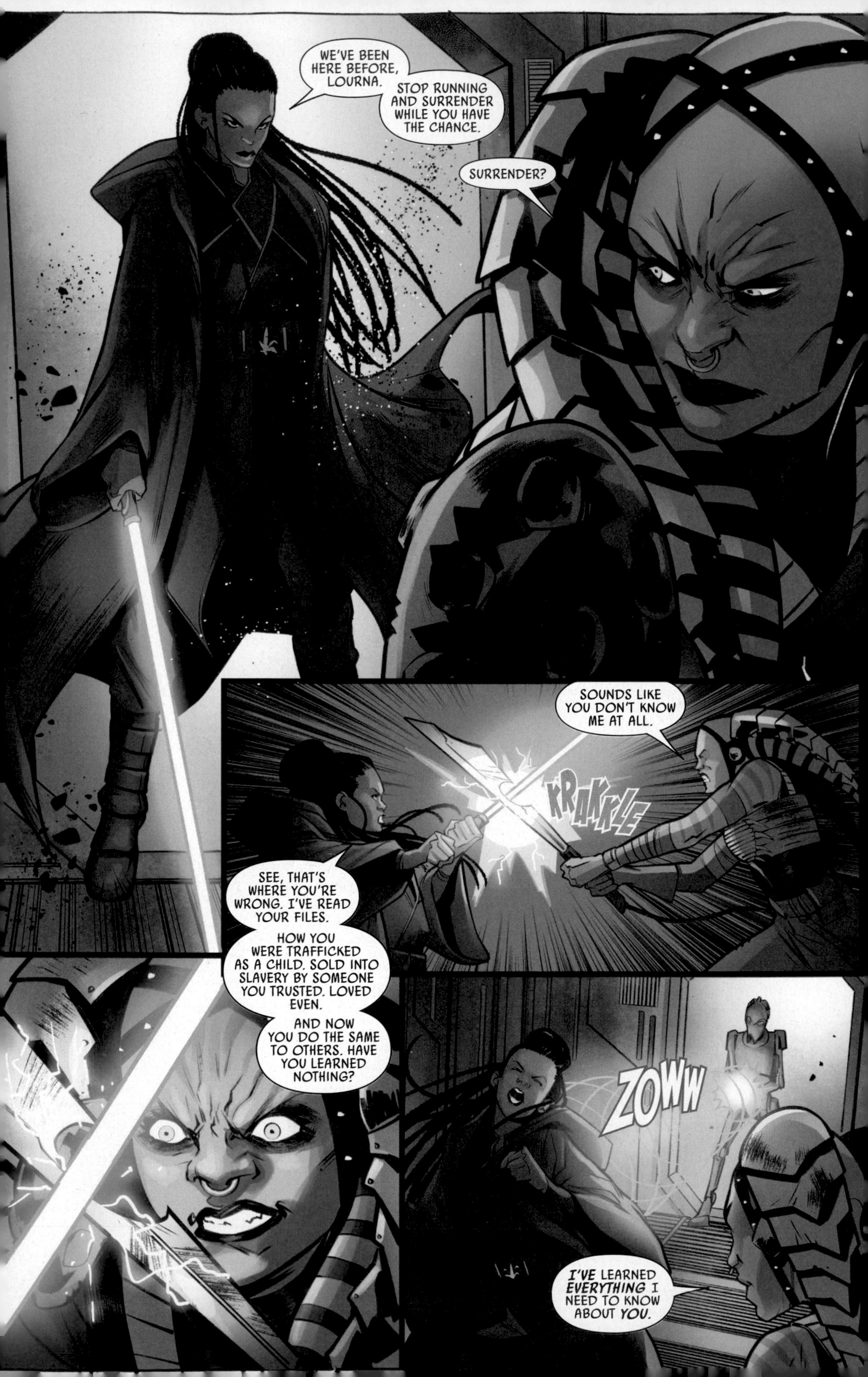
WE'VE BEEN HERE BEFORE, LOURNA.
STOP RUNNING AND SURRENDER WHILE YOU HAVE THE CHANCE.
SURRENDER?
SOUNDS LIKE YOU DON'T KNOW ME AT ALL.
KRAKKLE
SEE, THAT'S WHERE YOU'RE WRONG. I'VE READ YOUR FILES.
HOW YOU WERE TRAFFICKED AS A CHILD. SOLD INTO SLAVERY BY SOMEONE YOU TRUSTED. LOVED EVEN.
AND NOW YOU DO THE SAME TO OTHERS. HAVE YOU LEARNED NOTHING?
ZOWW
I'VE LEARNED **EVERYTHING** I NEED TO KNOW ABOUT *YOU*.

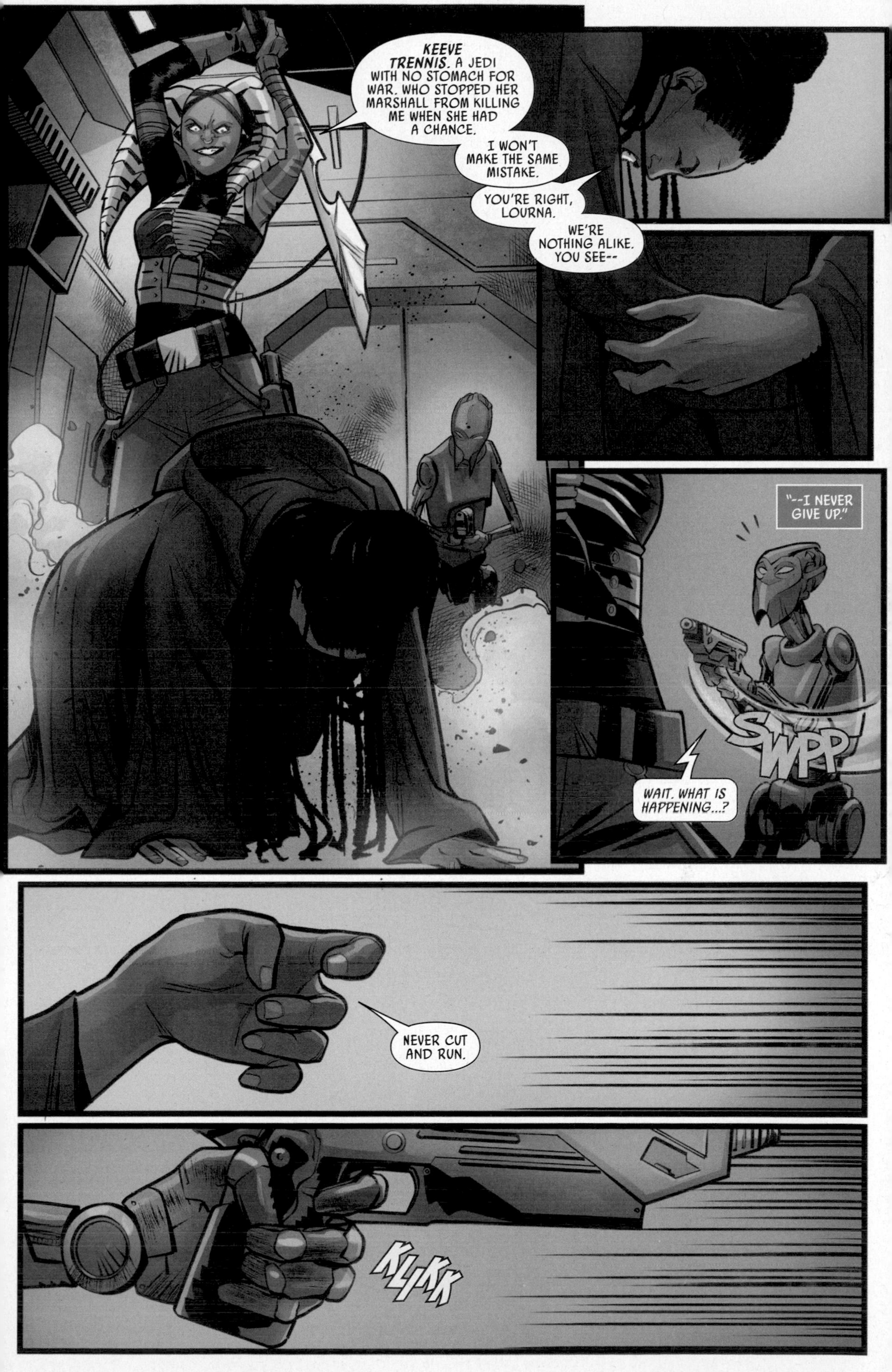
KEEVE TRENNIS. A JEDI WITH NO STOMACH FOR WAR. WHO STOPPED HER MARSHALL FROM KILLING ME WHEN SHE HAD A CHANCE.
I WON'T MAKE THE SAME MISTAKE.
YOU'RE RIGHT, LOURNA.
WE'RE NOTHING ALIKE. YOU SEE--
"--I NEVER GIVE UP."
SWPP
WAIT. WHAT IS HAPPENING...?
NEVER CUT AND RUN.
KLIKK

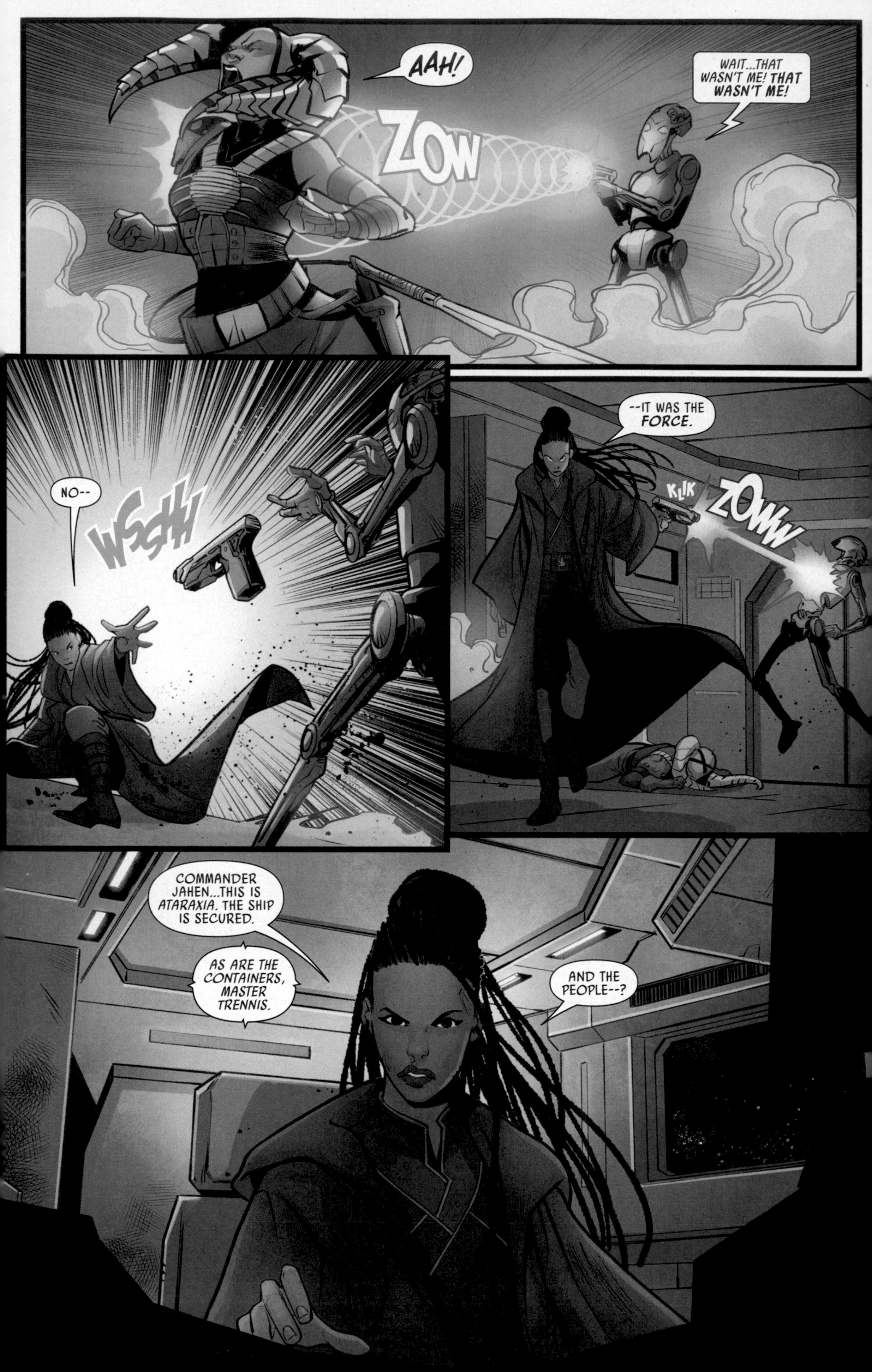
AAH!
WAIT...THAT WASN'T ME! THAT WASN'T ME!
ZOW
NO--
WSSHH
--IT WAS THE FORCE.
KLIK
ZOWW
COMMANDER JAHEN...THIS IS ATARAXIA. THE SHIP IS SECURED.
AS ARE THE CONTAINERS, MASTER TRENNIS.
AND THE PEOPLE--?

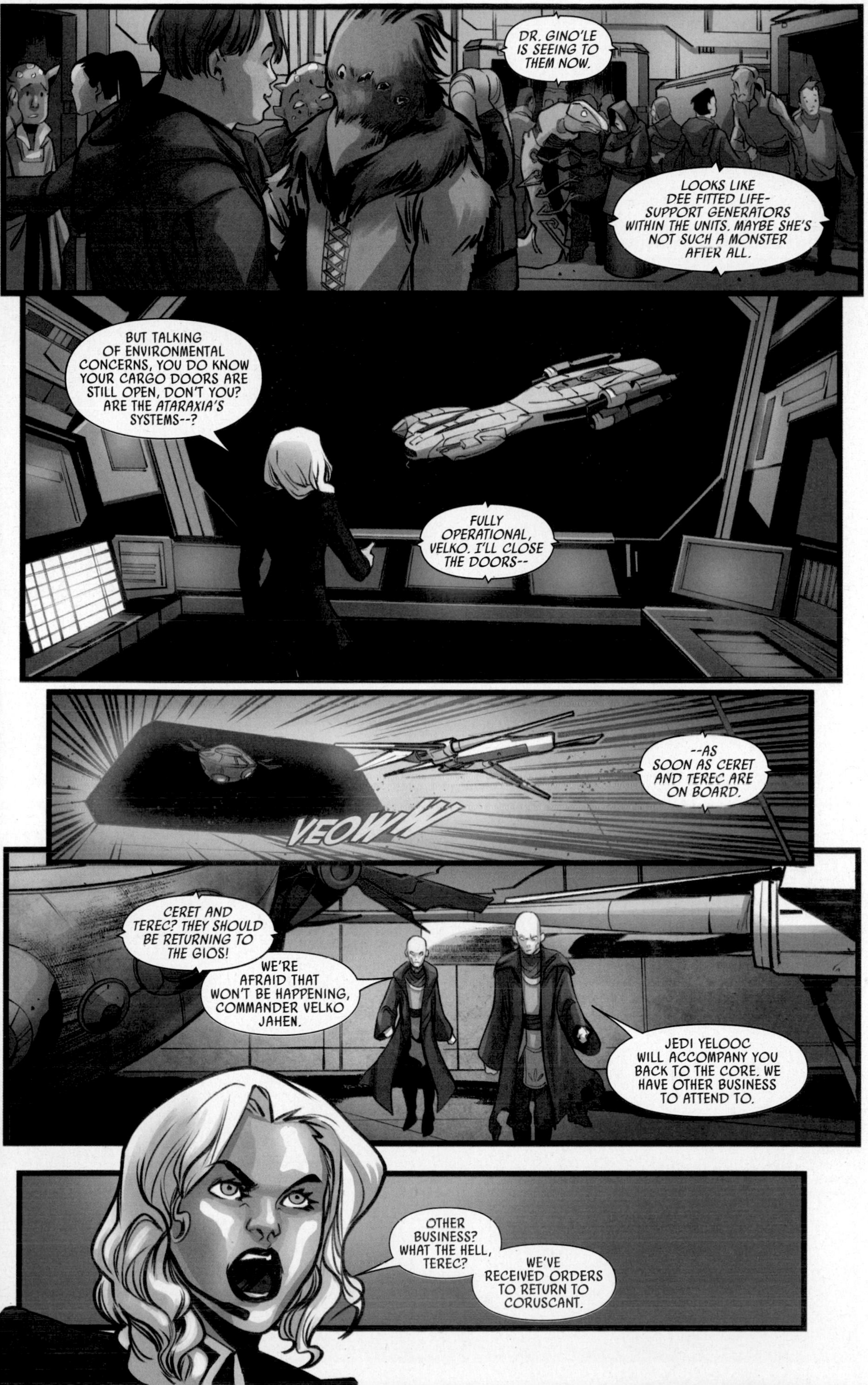
DR. GINO'LE IS SEEING TO THEM NOW.
LOOKS LIKE DEE FITTED LIFE-SUPPORT GENERATORS WITHIN THE UNITS. MAYBE SHE'S NOT SUCH A MONSTER AFTER ALL.
BUT TALKING OF ENVIRONMENTAL CONCERNS, YOU DO KNOW YOUR CARGO DOORS ARE STILL OPEN, DON'T YOU? ARE THE *ATARAXIA'S* SYSTEMS--?
FULLY OPERATIONAL, VELKO. I'LL CLOSE THE DOORS--
--AS SOON AS CERET AND TEREC ARE ON BOARD.
VEOWW
CERET AND TEREC? THEY SHOULD BE RETURNING TO THE GIOS!
WE'RE AFRAID THAT WON'T BE HAPPENING, COMMANDER VELKO JAHEN.
JEDI YELOOC WILL ACCOMPANY YOU BACK TO THE CORE. WE HAVE OTHER BUSINESS TO ATTEND TO.
OTHER BUSINESS? WHAT THE HELL, TEREC?
WE'VE RECEIVED ORDERS TO RETURN TO CORUSCANT.

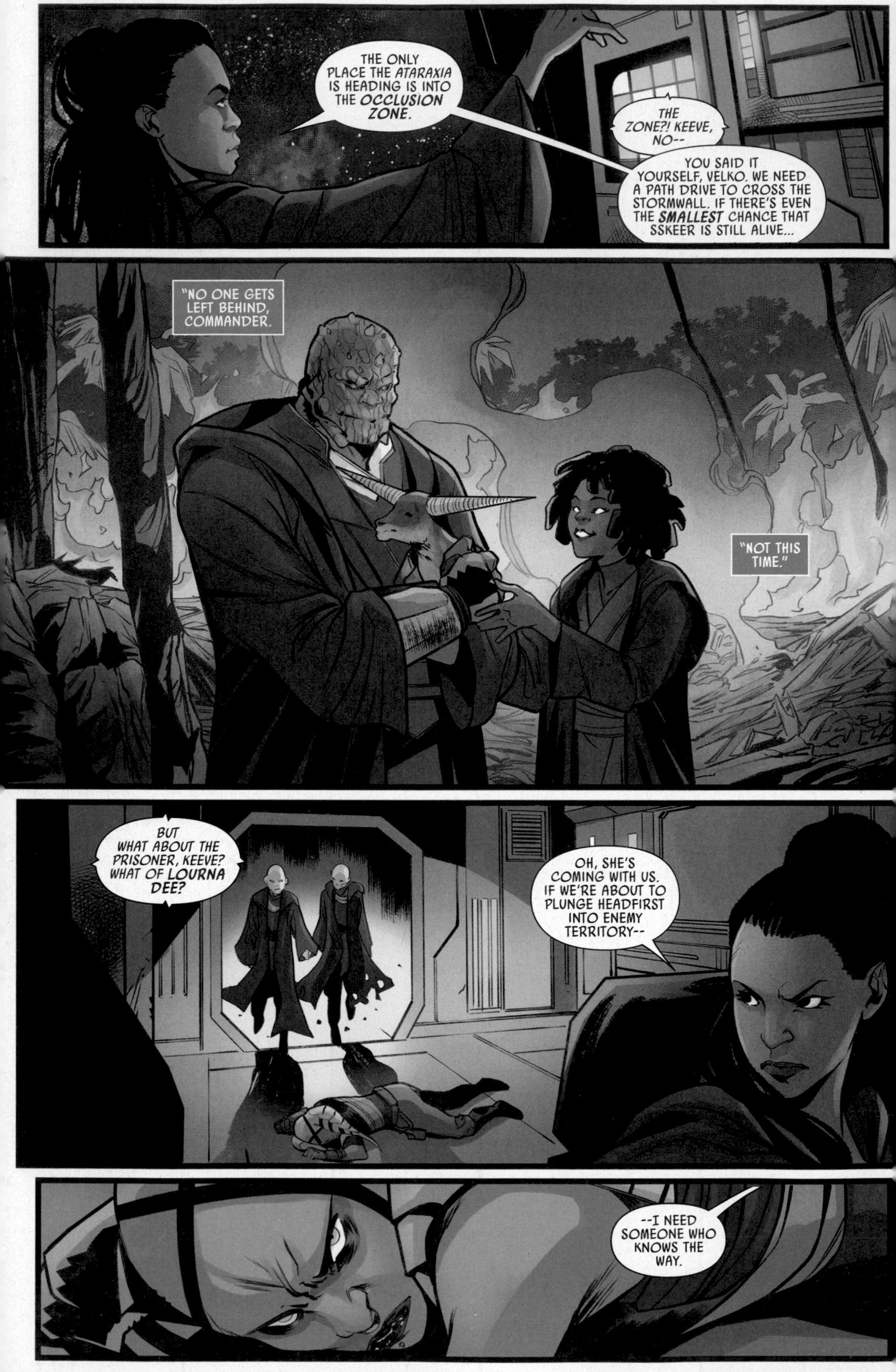
THE ONLY PLACE THE ATARAXIA IS HEADING IS INTO THE OCCLUSION ZONE.
THE ZONE?! KEEVE, NO--
YOU SAID IT YOURSELF, VELKO. WE NEED A PATH DRIVE TO CROSS THE STORMWALL. IF THERE'S EVEN THE SMALLEST CHANCE THAT SSKEER IS STILL ALIVE...
"NO ONE GETS LEFT BEHIND, COMMANDER.
"NOT THIS TIME."
BUT WHAT ABOUT THE PRISONER, KEEVE? WHAT OF LOURNA DEE?
OH, SHE'S COMING WITH US. IF WE'RE ABOUT TO PLUNGE HEADFIRST INTO ENEMY TERRITORY--
--I NEED SOMEONE WHO KNOWS THE WAY.

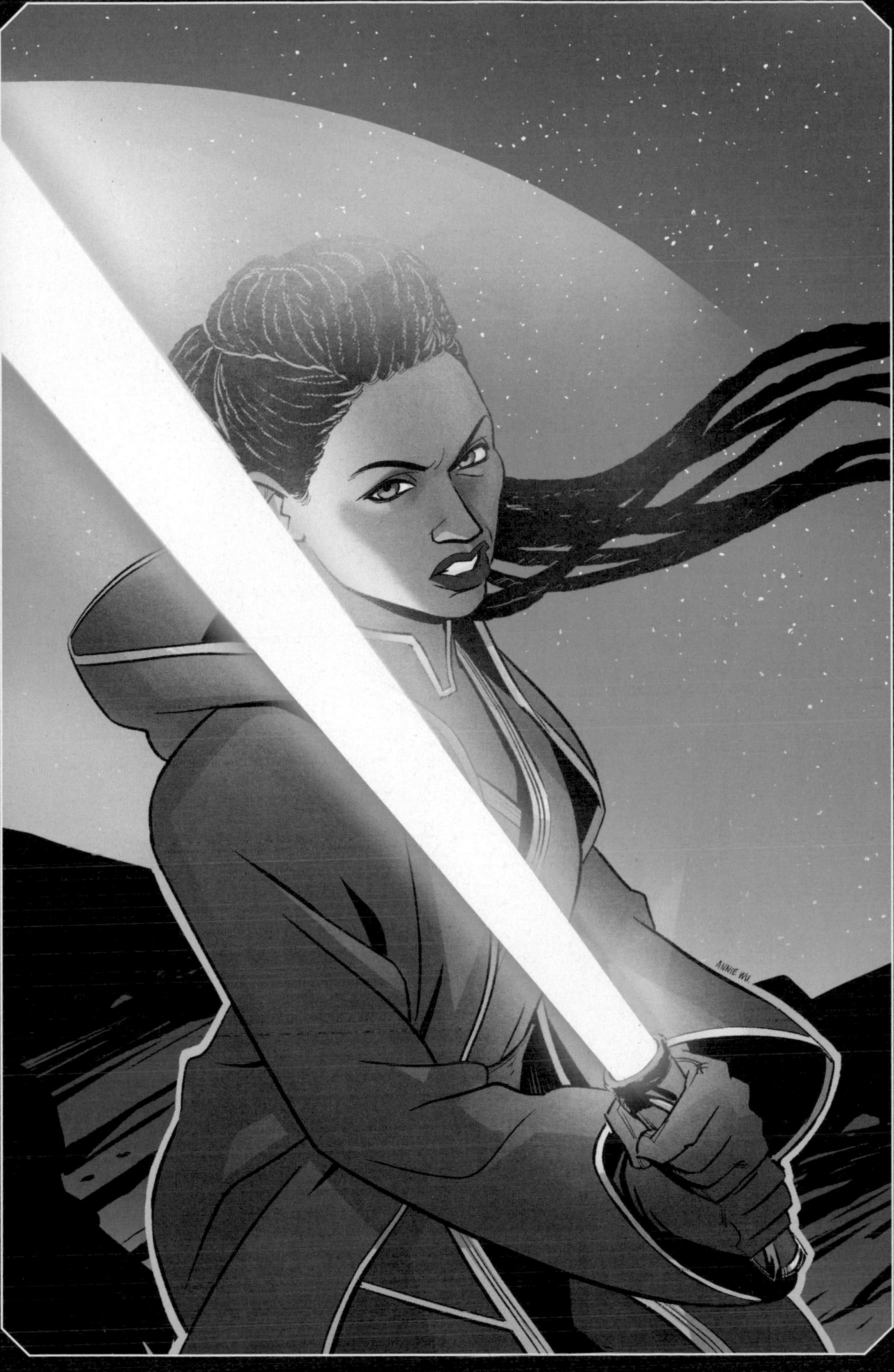
ANNIE WU.

#1 Variant by
ANNIE WU

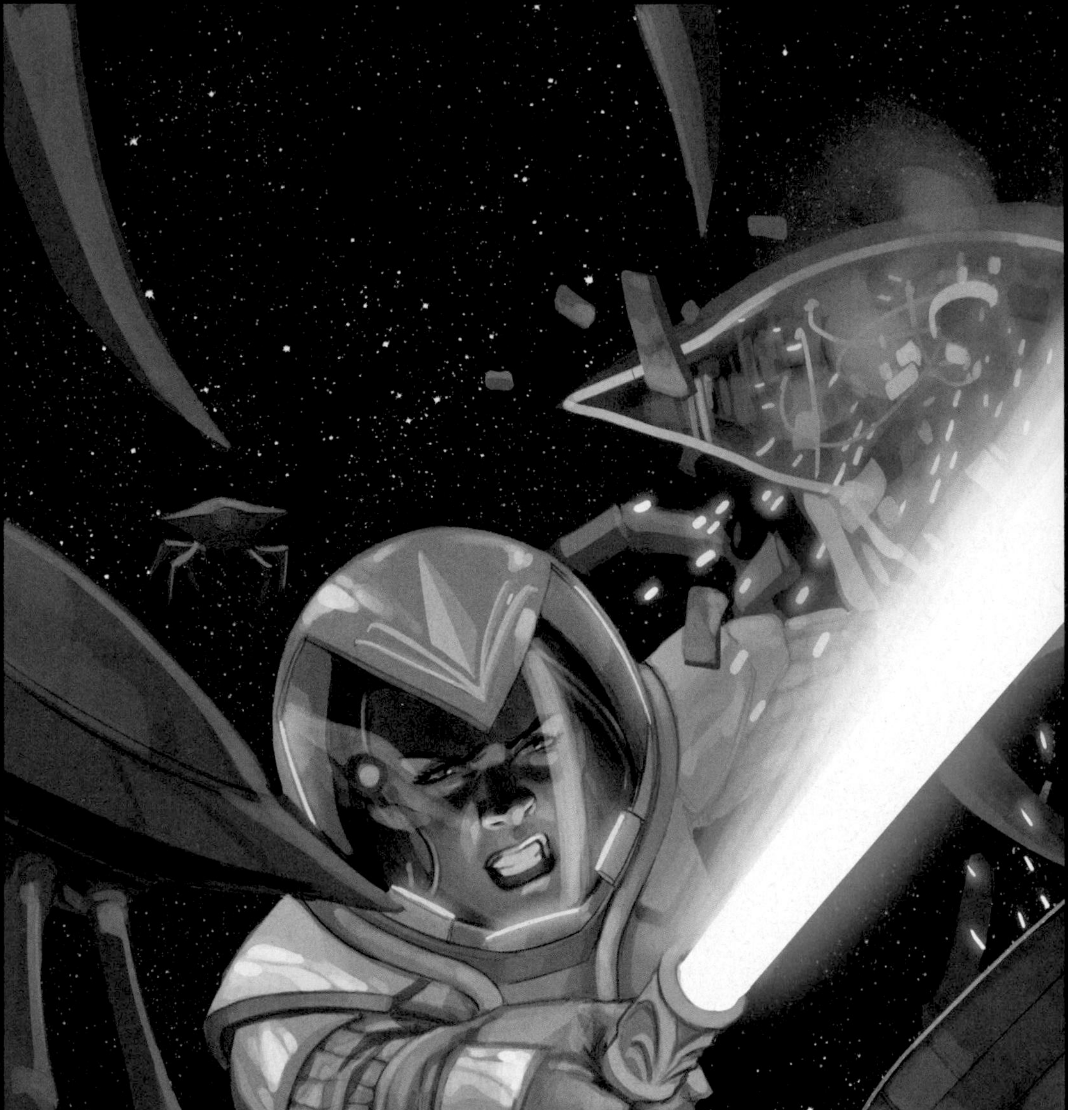
noto

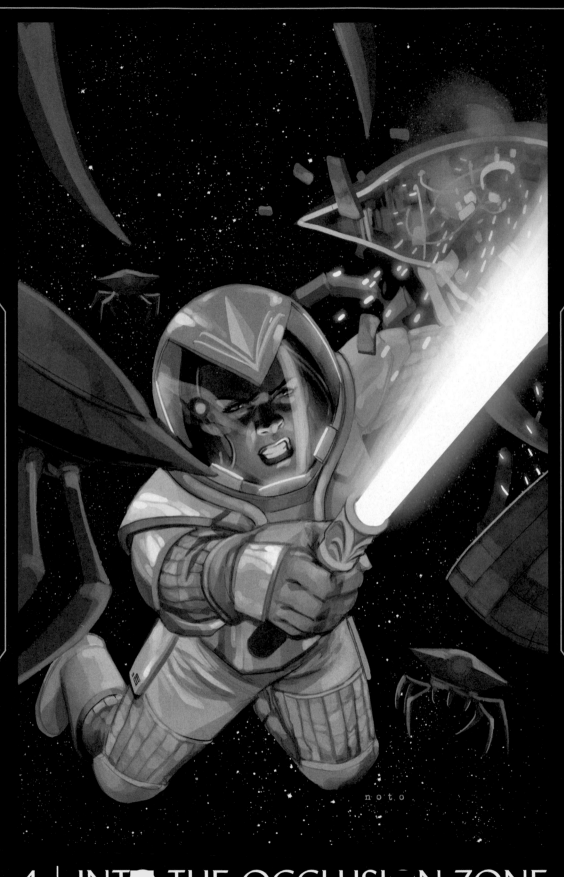

4 | INTO THE OCCLUSION ZONE

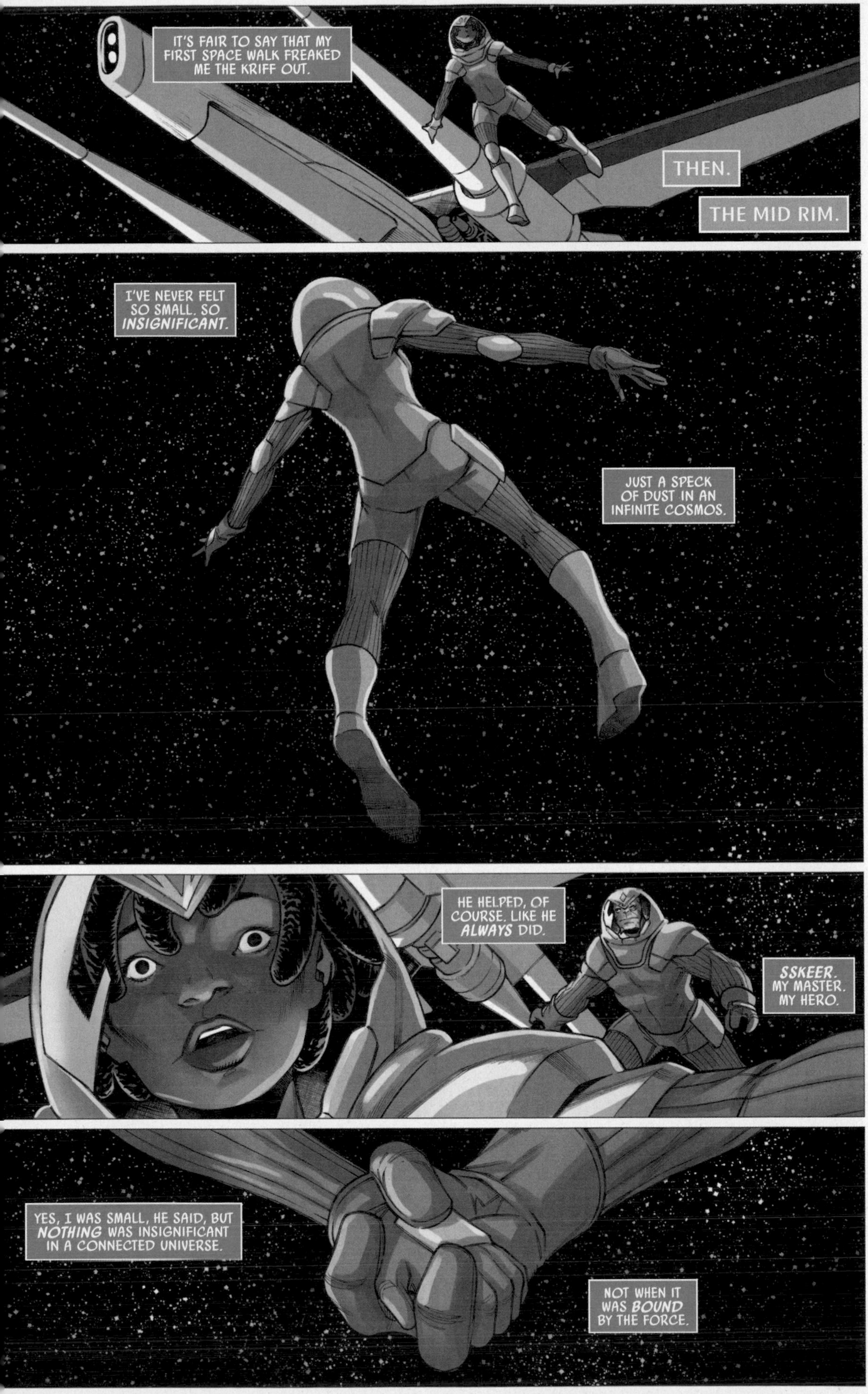
IT'S FAIR TO SAY THAT MY FIRST SPACE WALK FREAKED ME THE KRIFF OUT.
THEN.
THE MID RIM.
I'VE NEVER FELT SO SMALL. SO *INSIGNIFICANT*.
JUST A SPECK OF DUST IN AN INFINITE COSMOS.
HE HELPED, OF COURSE. LIKE HE *ALWAYS* DID.
SSKEER. MY MASTER. MY HERO.
YES, I WAS SMALL, HE SAID, BUT *NOTHING* WAS INSIGNIFICANT IN A CONNECTED UNIVERSE.
NOT WHEN IT WAS *BOUND* BY THE FORCE.

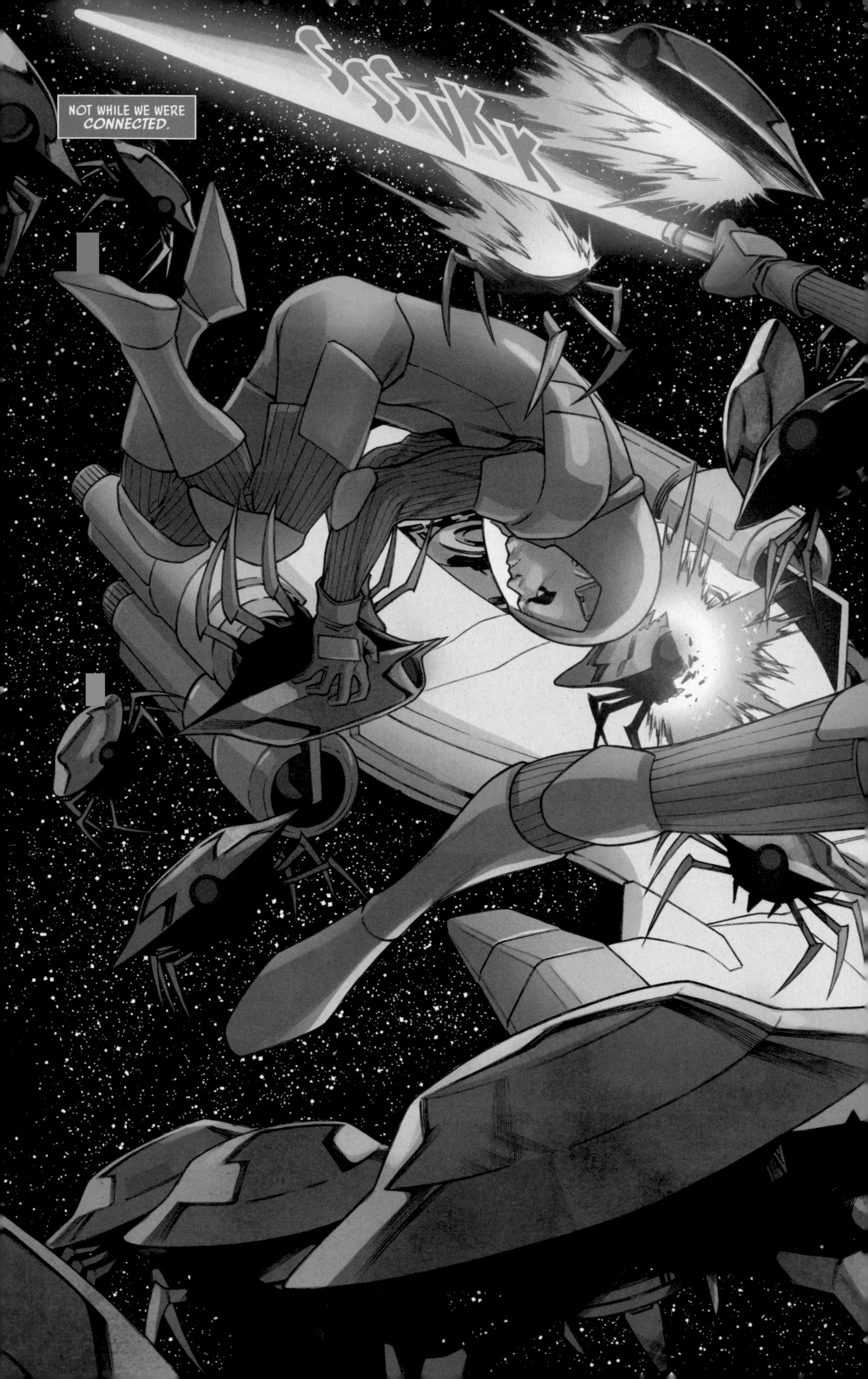
NOT WHILE WE WERE CONNECTED.
SSSSUKKK

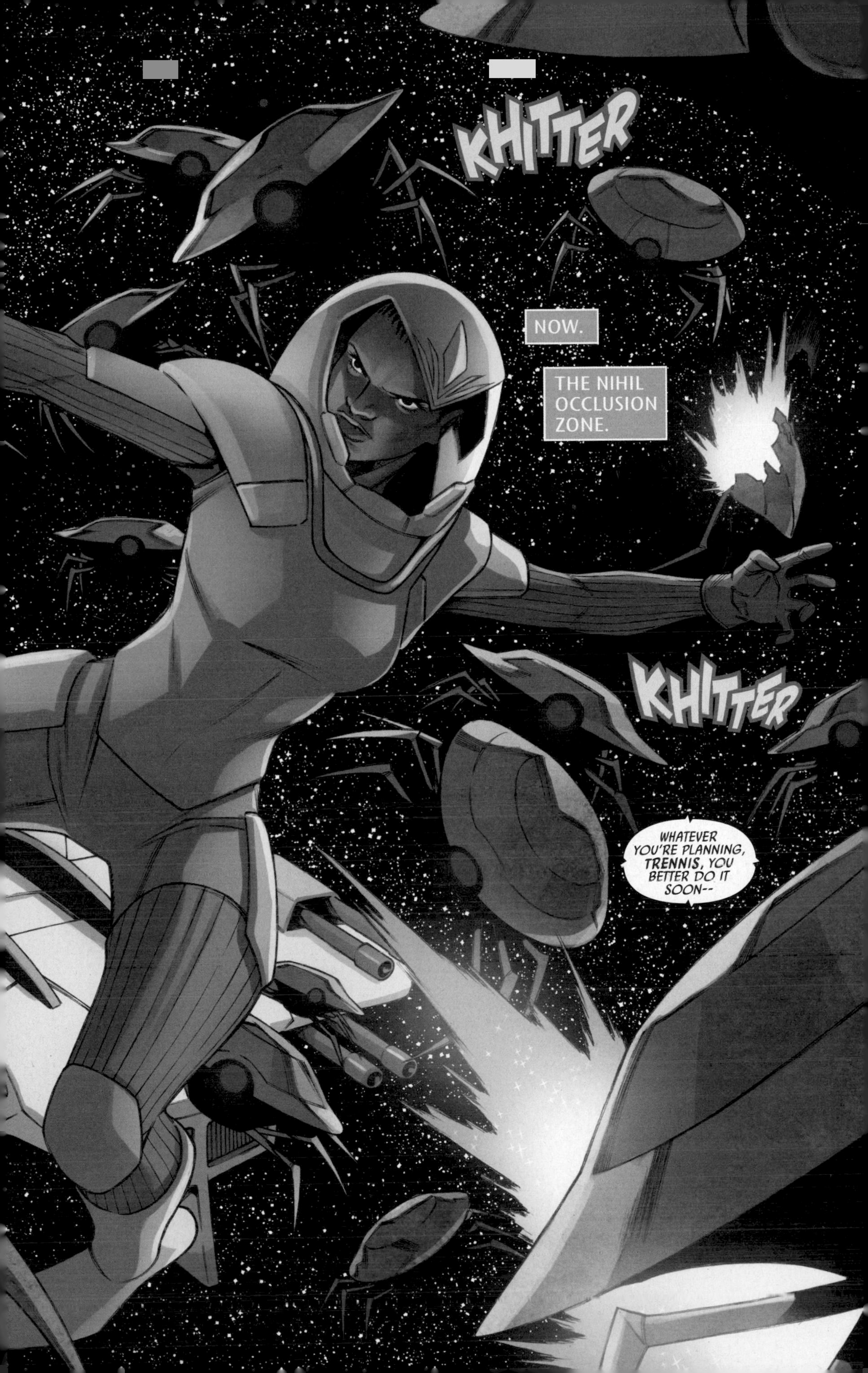
KHITTER
NOW.
THE NIHIL OCCLUSION ZONE.
KHITTER
WHATEVER YOU'RE PLANNING, TRENNIS, YOU BETTER DO IT SOON--

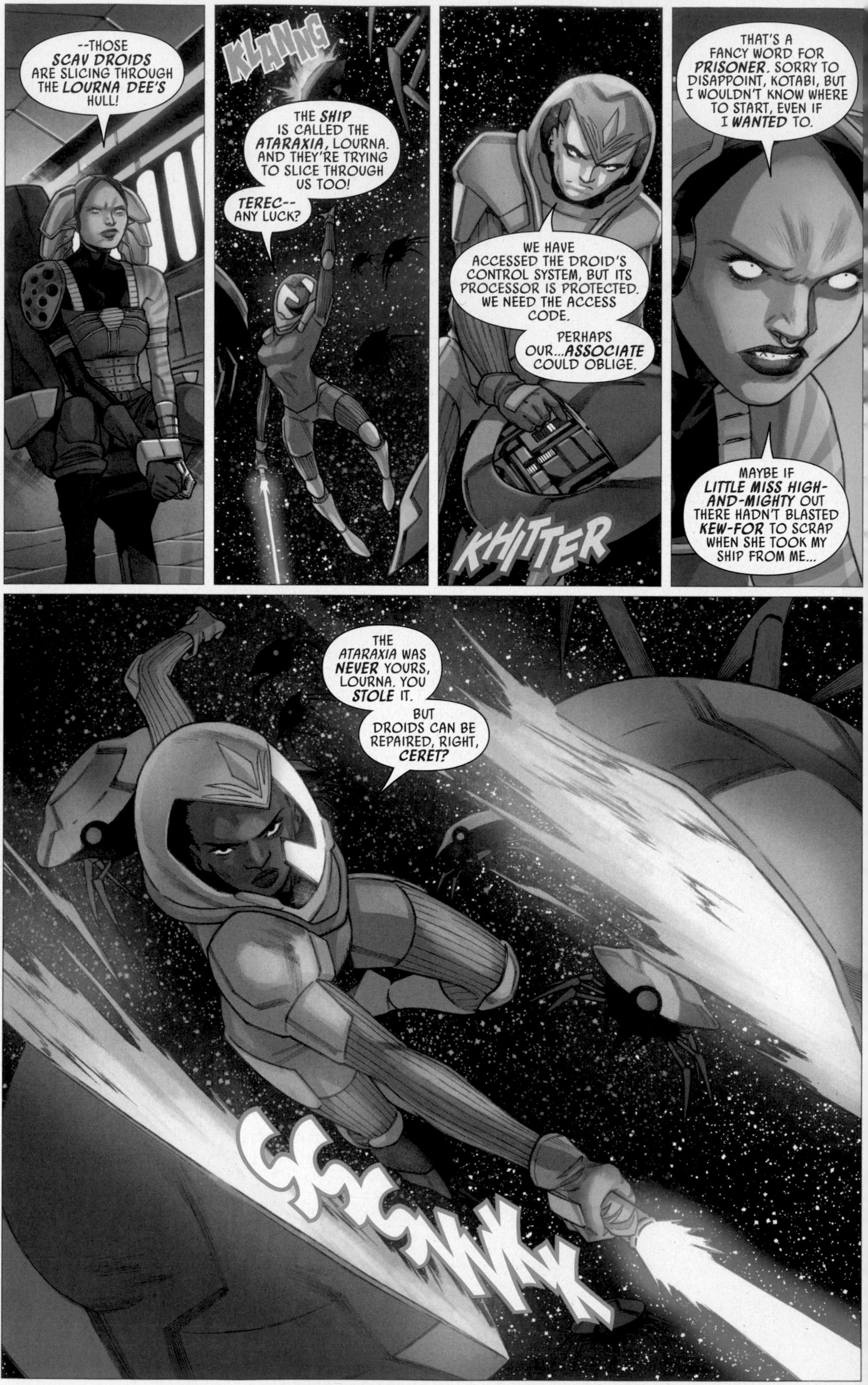
KLANNG
--THOSE SCAV DROIDS ARE SLICING THROUGH THE LOURNA DEE'S HULL!
THE SHIP IS CALLED THE ATARAXIA, LOURNA. AND THEY'RE TRYING TO SLICE THROUGH US TOO!
TEREC-- ANY LUCK?
WE HAVE ACCESSED THE DROID'S CONTROL SYSTEM, BUT ITS PROCESSOR IS PROTECTED. WE NEED THE ACCESS CODE.
PERHAPS OUR...ASSOCIATE COULD OBLIGE.
KHITTER
THAT'S A FANCY WORD FOR PRISONER. SORRY TO DISAPPOINT, KOTABI, BUT I WOULDN'T KNOW WHERE TO START, EVEN IF I WANTED TO.
MAYBE IF LITTLE MISS HIGH-AND-MIGHTY OUT THERE HADN'T BLASTED KEW-FOR TO SCRAP WHEN SHE TOOK MY SHIP FROM ME...
THE ATARAXIA WAS NEVER YOURS, LOURNA. YOU STOLE IT.
BUT DROIDS CAN BE REPAIRED, RIGHT, CERET?

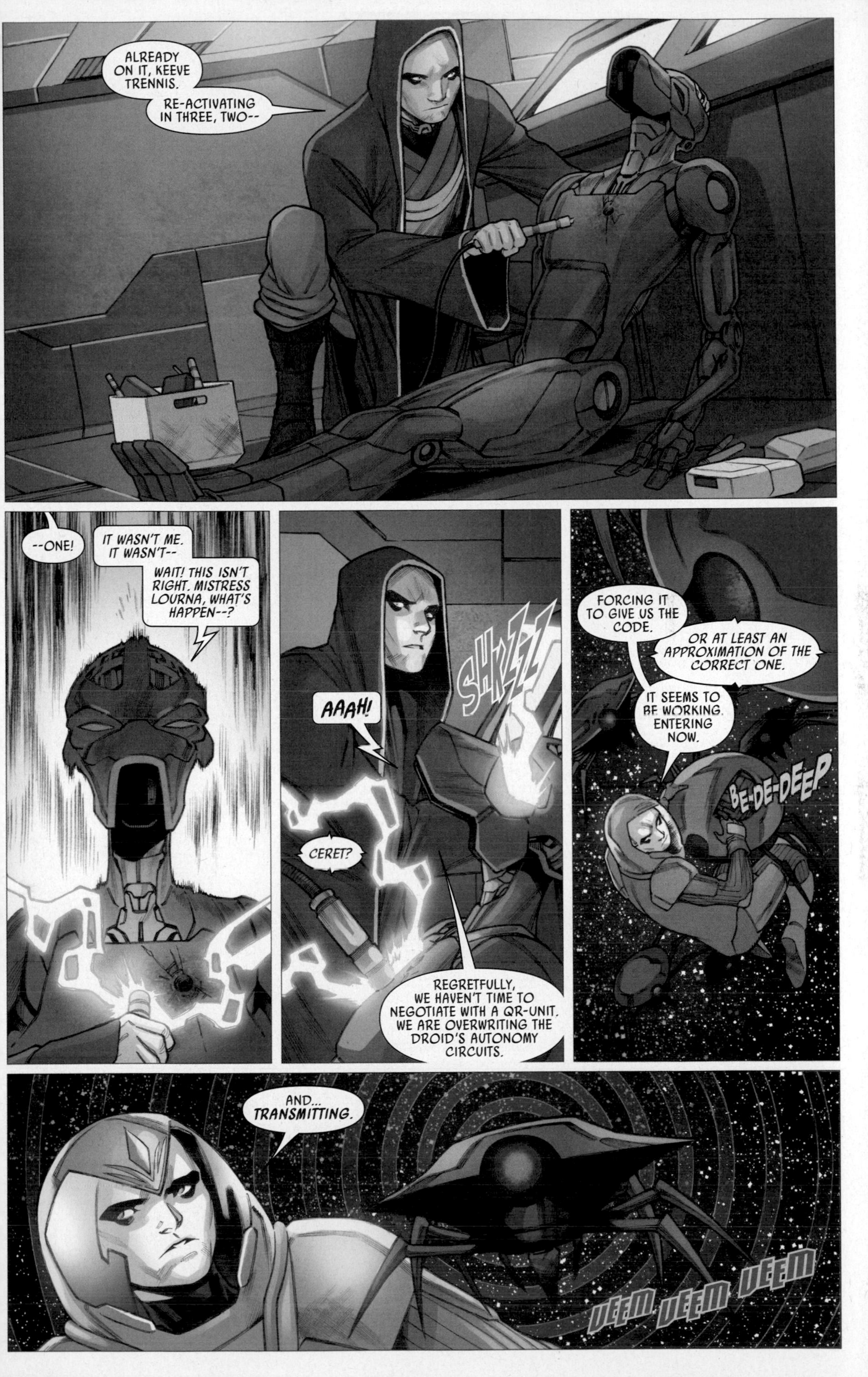
ALREADY ON IT, KEEVE TRENNIS.
RE-ACTIVATING IN THREE, TWO--
--ONE!
IT WASN'T ME. IT WASN'T--
WAIT! THIS ISN'T RIGHT. MISTRESS LOURNA, WHAT'S HAPPEN--?
SHRZZZ
AAAH!
CERET?
REGRETFULLY, WE HAVEN'T TIME TO NEGOTIATE WITH A QR-UNIT. WE ARE OVERWRITING THE DROID'S AUTONOMY CIRCUITS.
FORCING IT TO GIVE US THE CODE.
OR AT LEAST AN APPROXIMATION OF THE CORRECT ONE.
IT SEEMS TO BE WORKING. ENTERING NOW.
BE-DE-DEEP
AND... TRANSMITTING.
VEEM VEEM VEEM

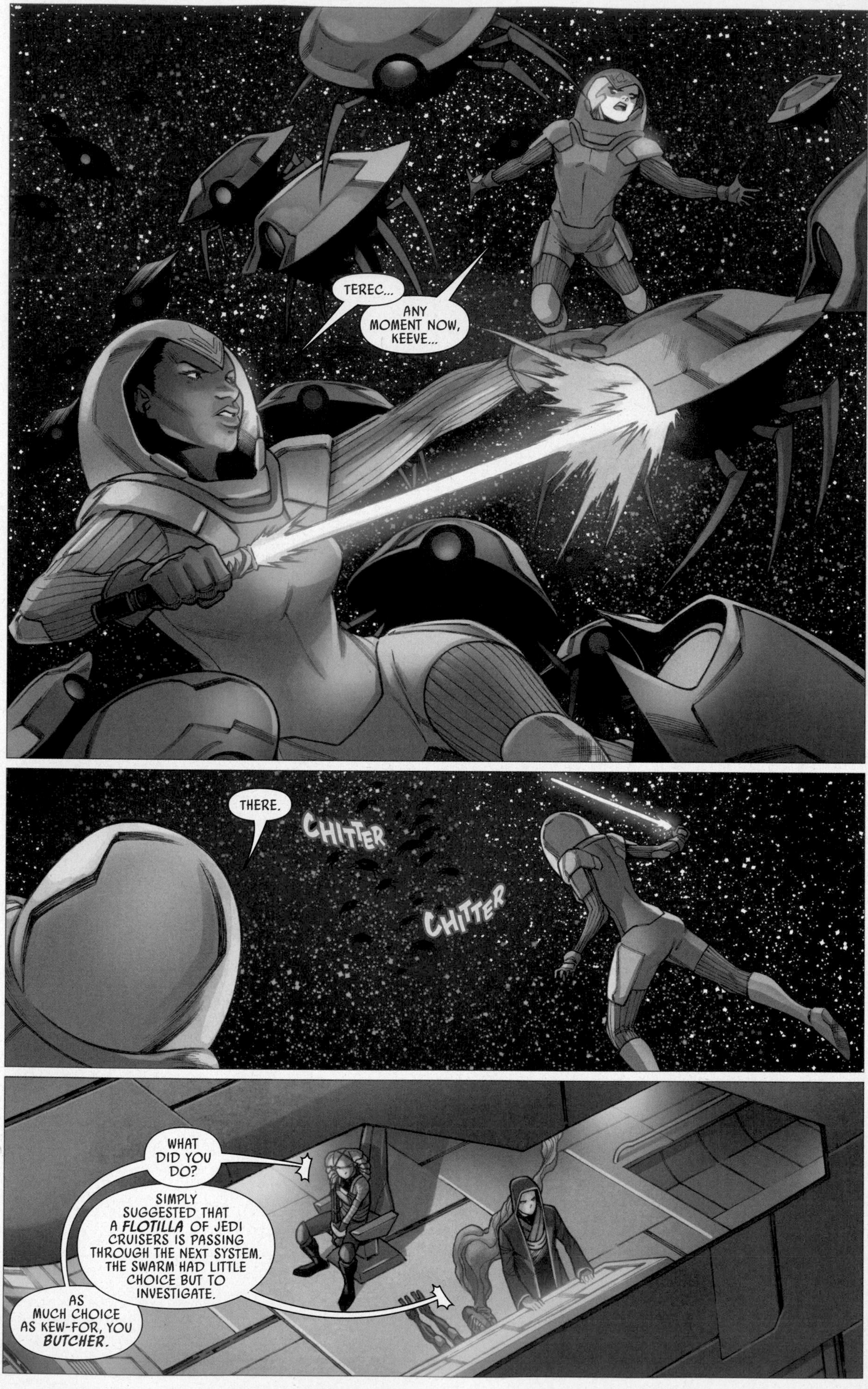
TEREC...
ANY MOMENT NOW, KEEVE...
THERE.
CHITTER
CHITTER
WHAT DID YOU DO?
SIMPLY SUGGESTED THAT A FLOTILLA OF JEDI CRUISERS IS PASSING THROUGH THE NEXT SYSTEM. THE SWARM HAD LITTLE CHOICE BUT TO INVESTIGATE.
AS MUCH CHOICE AS KEW-FOR, YOU BUTCHER.

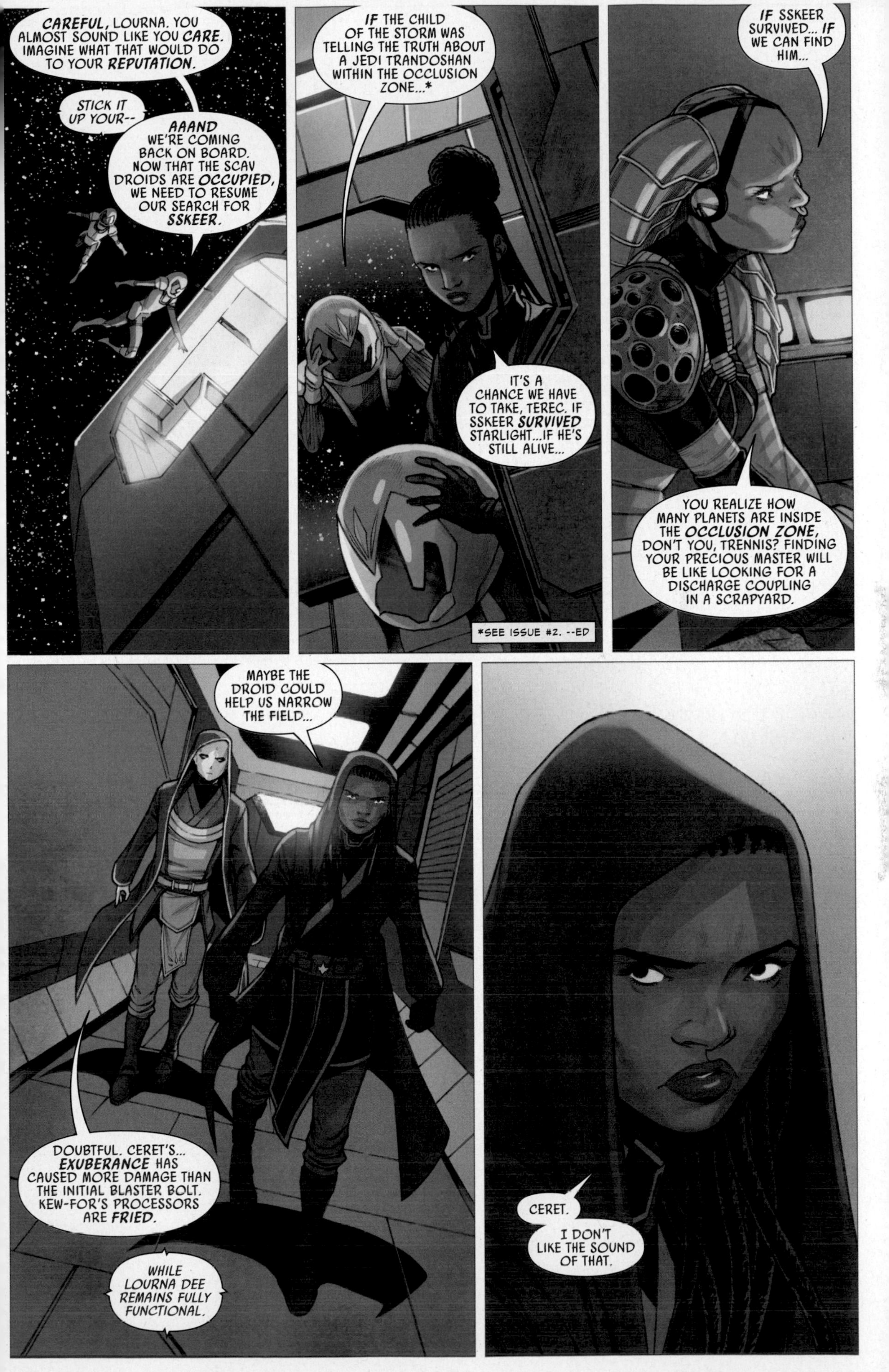
CAREFUL, LOURNA. YOU ALMOST SOUND LIKE YOU CARE. IMAGINE WHAT THAT WOULD DO TO YOUR REPUTATION.
STICK IT UP YOUR--
AAAND WE'RE COMING BACK ON BOARD. NOW THAT THE SCAV DROIDS ARE OCCUPIED, WE NEED TO RESUME OUR SEARCH FOR SSKEER.
IF THE CHILD OF THE STORM WAS TELLING THE TRUTH ABOUT A JEDI TRANDOSHAN WITHIN THE OCCLUSION ZONE...*
IT'S A CHANCE WE HAVE TO TAKE, TEREC. IF SSKEER SURVIVED STARLIGHT...IF HE'S STILL ALIVE...
*SEE ISSUE #2. --ED
IF SSKEER SURVIVED... IF WE CAN FIND HIM...
YOU REALIZE HOW MANY PLANETS ARE INSIDE THE OCCLUSION ZONE, DON'T YOU, TRENNIS? FINDING YOUR PRECIOUS MASTER WILL BE LIKE LOOKING FOR A DISCHARGE COUPLING IN A SCRAPYARD.
MAYBE THE DROID COULD HELP US NARROW THE FIELD...
DOUBTFUL. CERET'S... EXUBERANCE HAS CAUSED MORE DAMAGE THAN THE INITIAL BLASTER BOLT. KEW-FOR'S PROCESSORS ARE FRIED.
WHILE LOURNA DEE REMAINS FULLY FUNCTIONAL.
CERET.
I DON'T LIKE THE SOUND OF THAT.

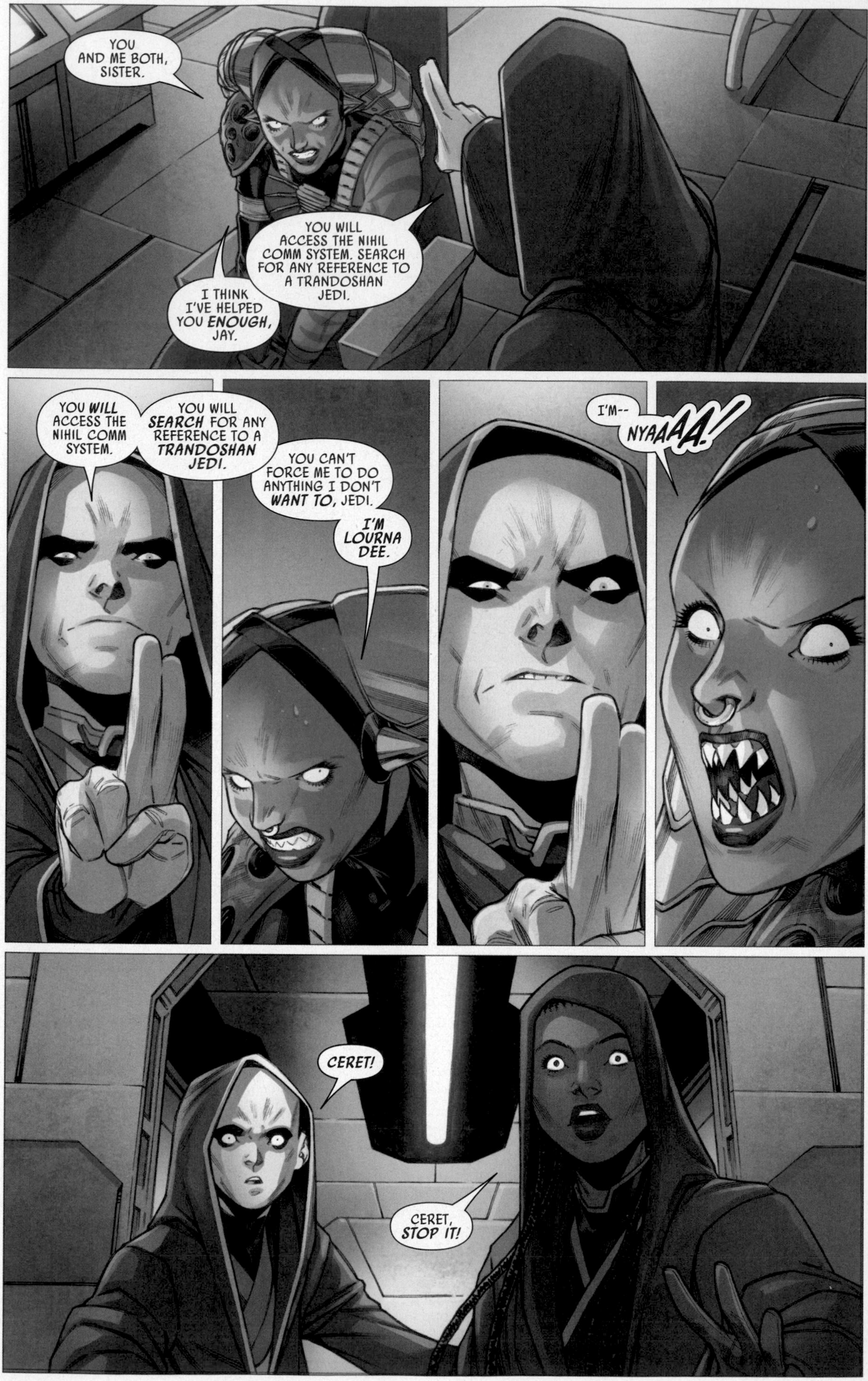
YOU AND ME BOTH, SISTER.
YOU WILL ACCESS THE NIHIL COMM SYSTEM. SEARCH FOR ANY REFERENCE TO A TRANDOSHAN JEDI.
I THINK I'VE HELPED YOU ENOUGH, JAY.
YOU WILL ACCESS THE NIHIL COMM SYSTEM.
YOU WILL SEARCH FOR ANY REFERENCE TO A TRANDOSHAN JEDI.
YOU CAN'T FORCE ME TO DO ANYTHING I DON'T WANT TO, JEDI.
I'M LOURNA DEE.
I'M--
NYAAAA!
CERET!
CERET, STOP IT!

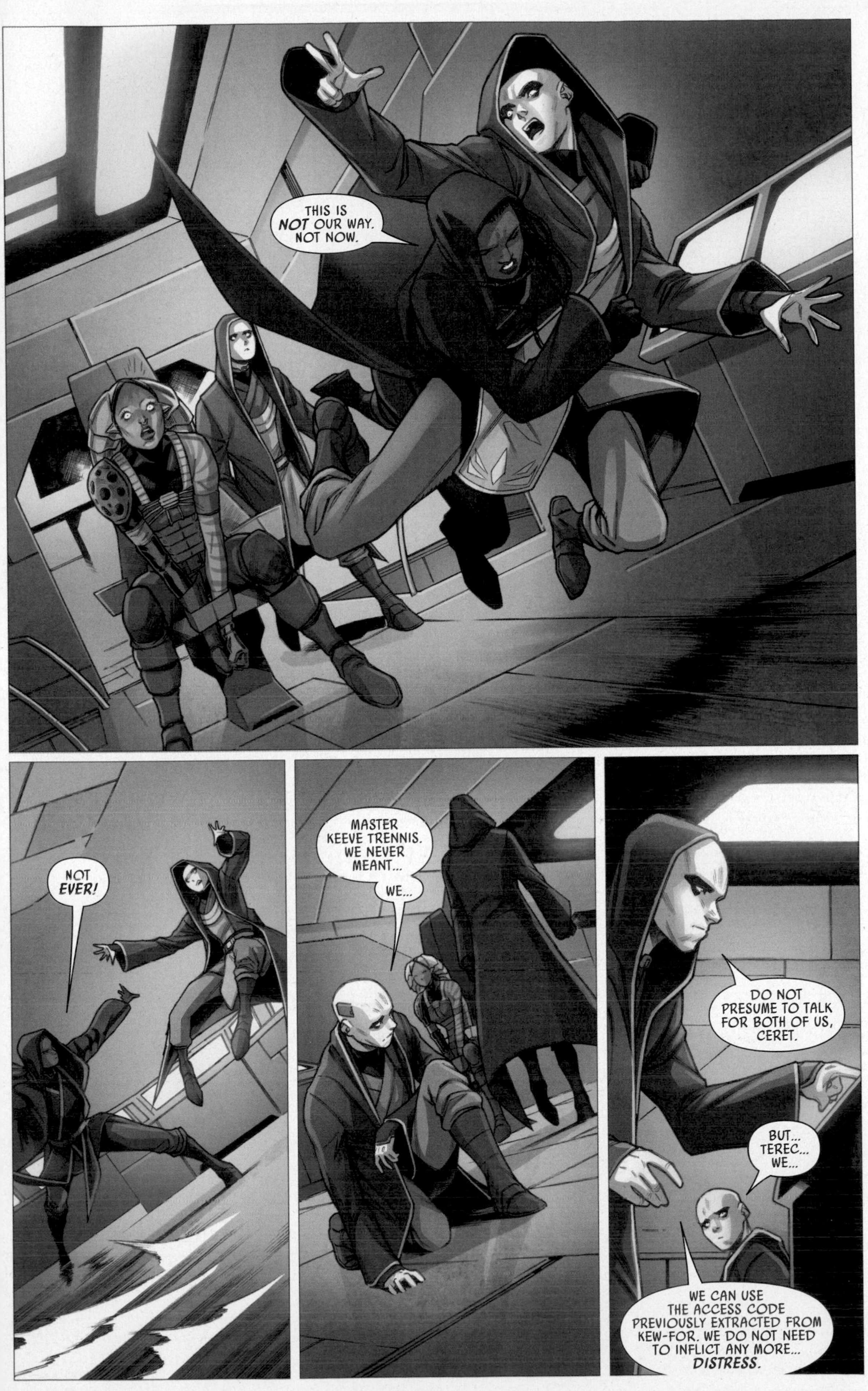
THIS IS NOT OUR WAY. NOT NOW.
NOT EVER!
MASTER KEEVE TRENNIS. WE NEVER MEANT...
WE...
DO NOT PRESUME TO TALK FOR BOTH OF US, CERET.
BUT... TEREC... WE...
WE CAN USE THE ACCESS CODE PREVIOUSLY EXTRACTED FROM KEW-FOR. WE DO NOT NEED TO INFLICT ANY MORE... DISTRESS.

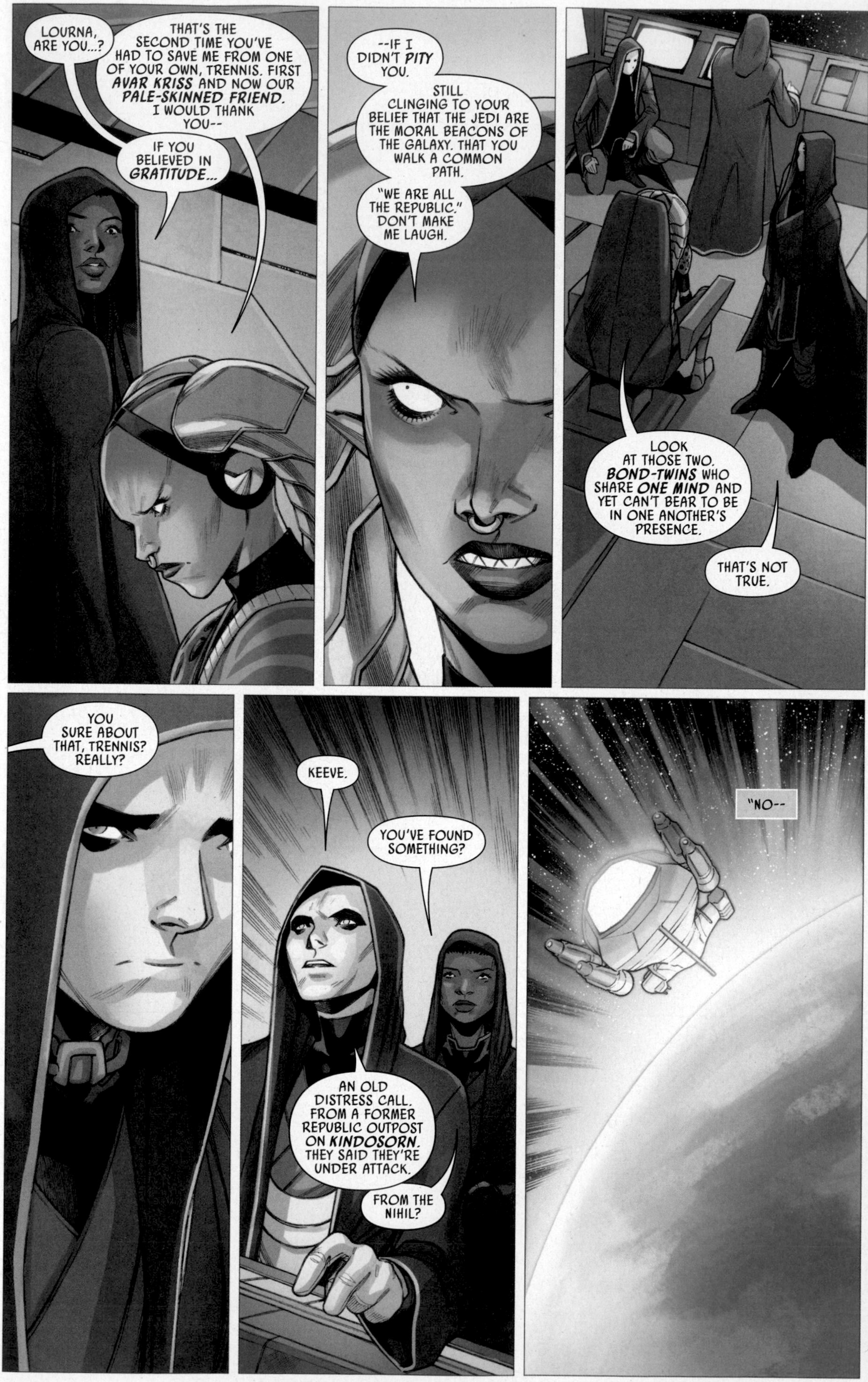
LOURNA, ARE YOU...?
THAT'S THE SECOND TIME YOU'VE HAD TO SAVE ME FROM ONE OF YOUR OWN, TRENNIS. FIRST AVAR KRISS AND NOW OUR PALE-SKINNED FRIEND. I WOULD THANK YOU--
IF YOU BELIEVED IN GRATITUDE...
--IF I DIDN'T PITY YOU.
STILL CLINGING TO YOUR BELIEF THAT THE JEDI ARE THE MORAL BEACONS OF THE GALAXY. THAT YOU WALK A COMMON PATH.
"WE ARE ALL THE REPUBLIC." DON'T MAKE ME LAUGH.
LOOK AT THOSE TWO. BOND-TWINS WHO SHARE ONE MIND AND YET CAN'T BEAR TO BE IN ONE ANOTHER'S PRESENCE.
THAT'S NOT TRUE.
YOU SURE ABOUT THAT, TRENNIS? REALLY?
KEEVE.
YOU'VE FOUND SOMETHING?
AN OLD DISTRESS CALL. FROM A FORMER REPUBLIC OUTPOST ON KINDOSORN. THEY SAID THEY'RE UNDER ATTACK.
FROM THE NIHIL?
"NO--

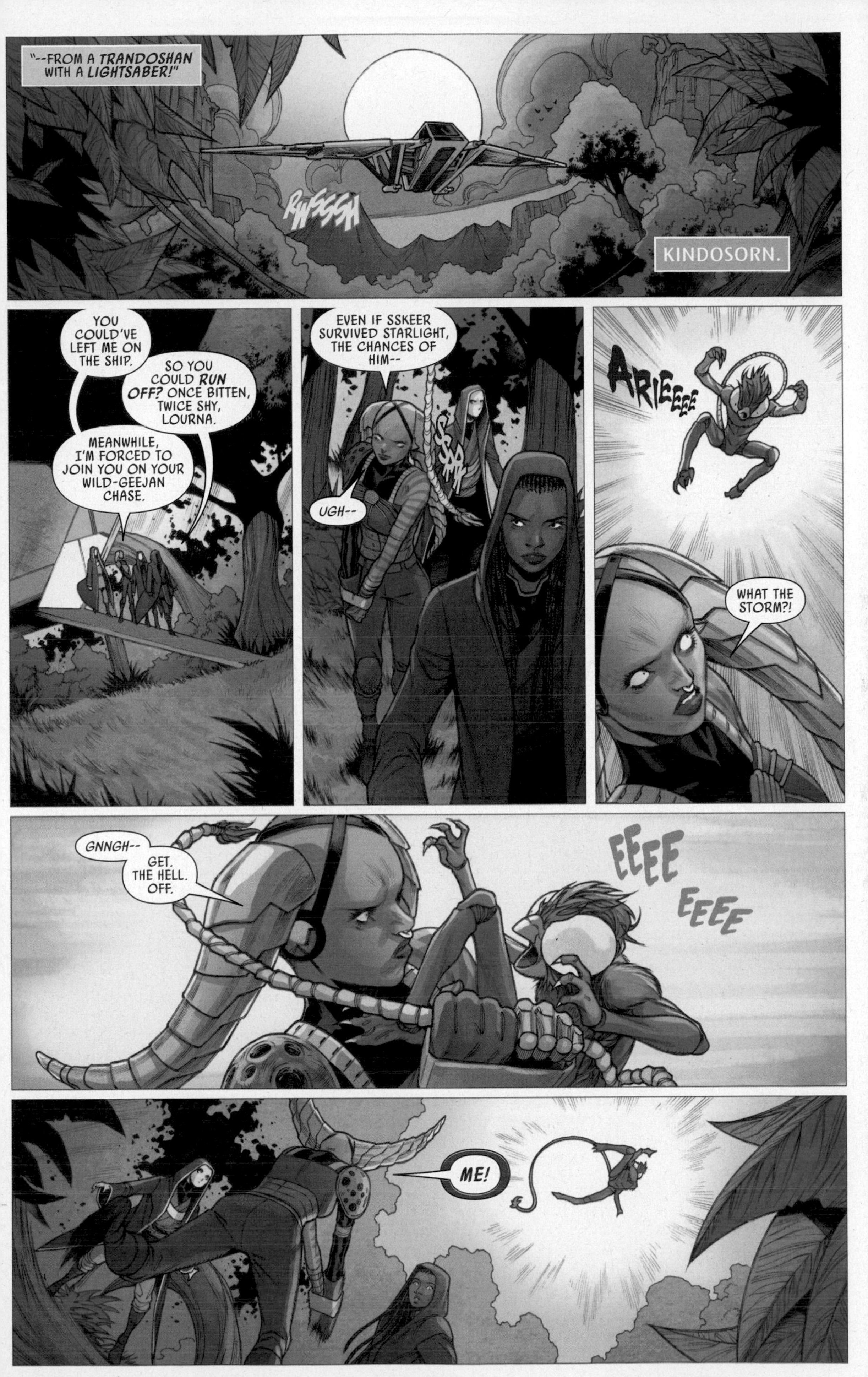
"--FROM A TRANDOSHAN WITH A LIGHTSABER!"
RWSSSH
KINDOSORN.
YOU COULD'VE LEFT ME ON THE SHIP.
SO YOU COULD RUN OFF? ONCE BITTEN, TWICE SHY, LOURNA.
MEANWHILE, I'M FORCED TO JOIN YOU ON YOUR WILD-GEEJAN CHASE.
EVEN IF SSKEER SURVIVED STARLIGHT, THE CHANCES OF HIM--
SSPAK
UGH--
ARIEEEE
WHAT THE STORM?!
GNNGH--
GET. THE HELL. OFF.
EEEE
EEEE
ME!

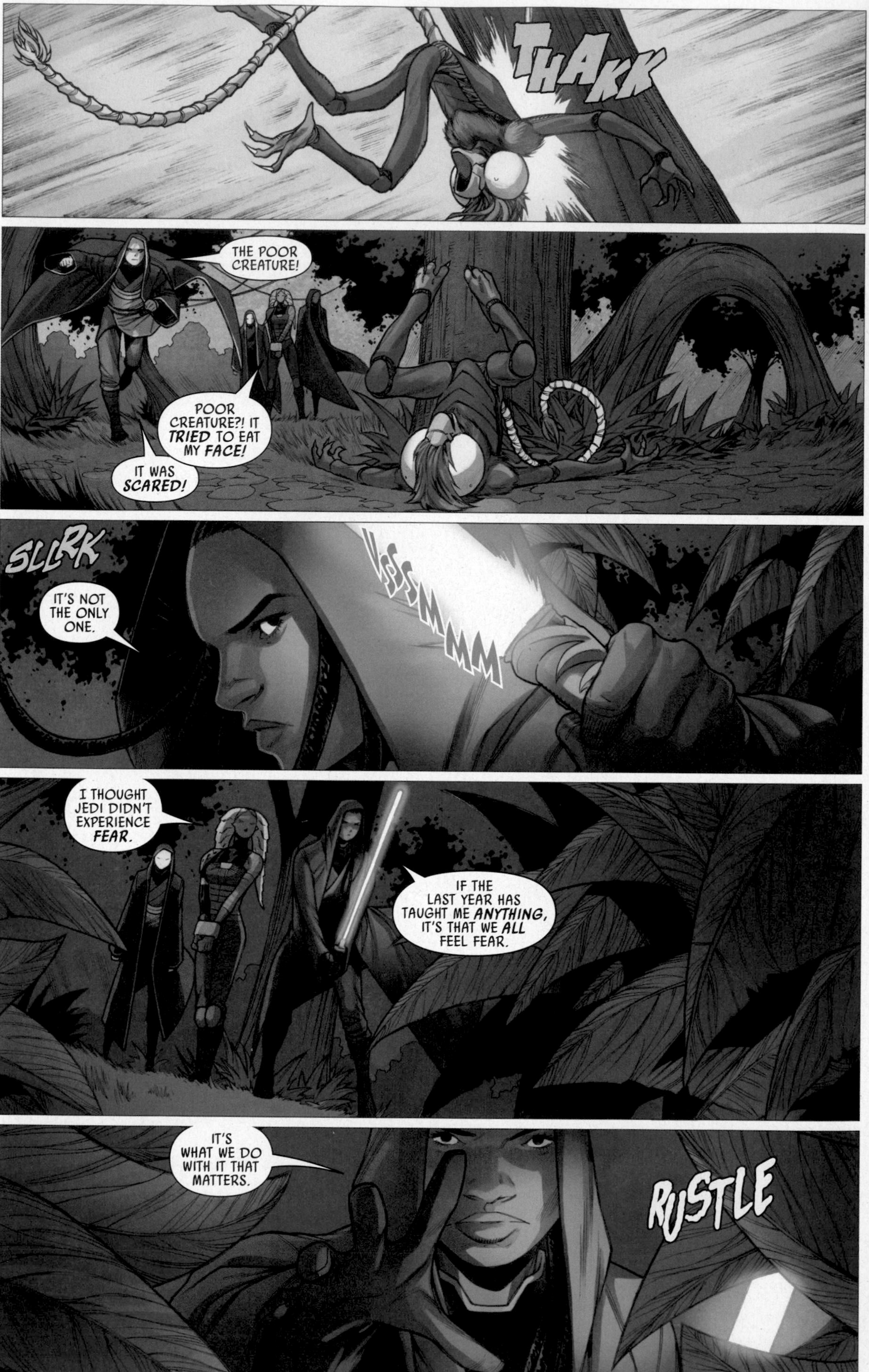
THAKK
THE POOR CREATURE!
POOR CREATURE?! IT TRIED TO EAT MY FACE!
IT WAS SCARED!
SLLRK
IT'S NOT THE ONLY ONE.
VSSSMMMM
I THOUGHT JEDI DIDN'T EXPERIENCE FEAR.
IF THE LAST YEAR HAS TAUGHT ME ANYTHING, IT'S THAT WE ALL FEEL FEAR.
IT'S WHAT WE DO WITH IT THAT MATTERS.
RUSTLE

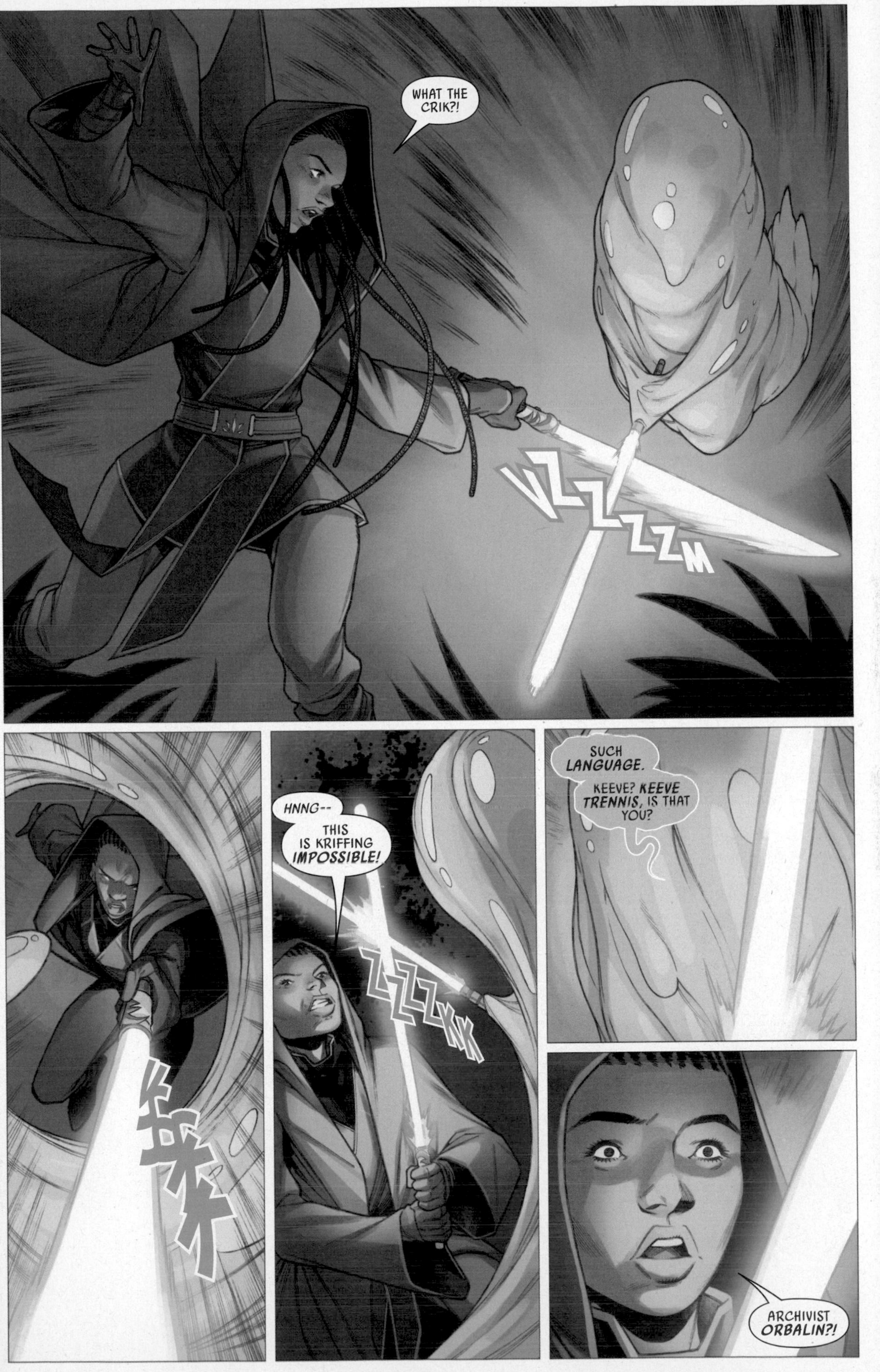
WHAT THE CRIK?!
VZZZZZM
HNNG--
THIS IS KRIFFING IMPOSSIBLE!
ZZZZKK
SUCH LANGUAGE.
KEEVE? KEEVE TRENNIS, IS THAT YOU?
ARCHIVIST ORBALIN?!

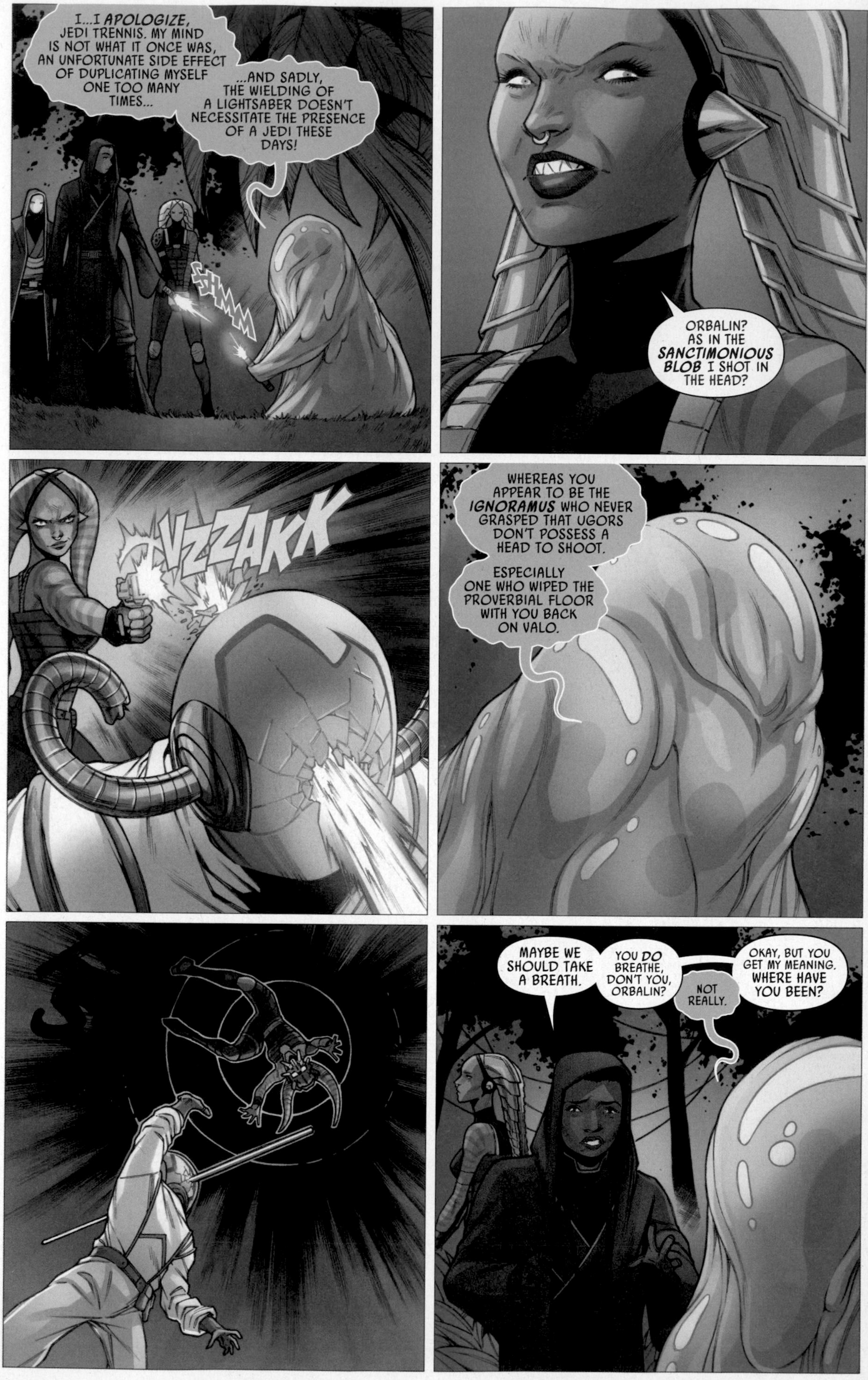
I...I APOLOGIZE, JEDI TRENNIS. MY MIND IS NOT WHAT IT ONCE WAS, AN UNFORTUNATE SIDE EFFECT OF DUPLICATING MYSELF ONE TOO MANY TIMES...
...AND SADLY, THE WIELDING OF A LIGHTSABER DOESN'T NECESSITATE THE PRESENCE OF A JEDI THESE DAYS!
SHMMM
ORBALIN? AS IN THE SANCTIMONIOUS BLOB I SHOT IN THE HEAD?
VZZAKK
WHEREAS YOU APPEAR TO BE THE IGNORAMUS WHO NEVER GRASPED THAT UGORS DON'T POSSESS A HEAD TO SHOOT.
ESPECIALLY ONE WHO WIPED THE PROVERBIAL FLOOR WITH YOU BACK ON VALO.
MAYBE WE SHOULD TAKE A BREATH.
YOU DO BREATHE, DON'T YOU, ORBALIN?
NOT REALLY.
OKAY, BUT YOU GET MY MEANING. WHERE HAVE YOU BEEN?

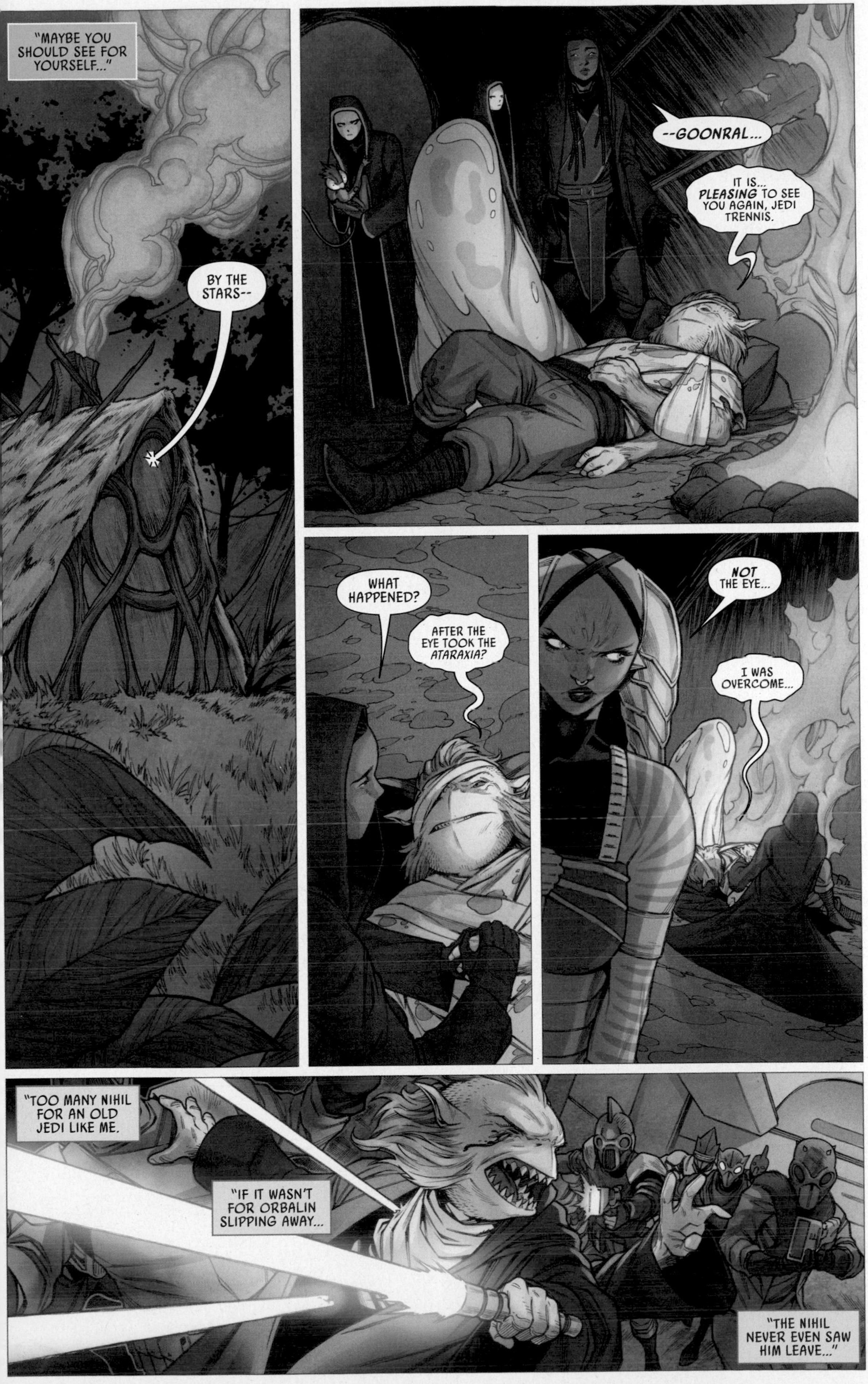
"MAYBE YOU SHOULD SEE FOR YOURSELF..."
BY THE STARS--
--GOONRAL...
IT IS... PLEASING TO SEE YOU AGAIN, JEDI TRENNIS.
WHAT HAPPENED?
AFTER THE EYE TOOK THE ATARAXIA?
NOT THE EYE...
I WAS OVERCOME...
"TOO MANY NIHIL FOR AN OLD JEDI LIKE ME.
"IF IT WASN'T FOR ORBALIN SLIPPING AWAY...
"THE NIHIL NEVER EVEN SAW HIM LEAVE..."

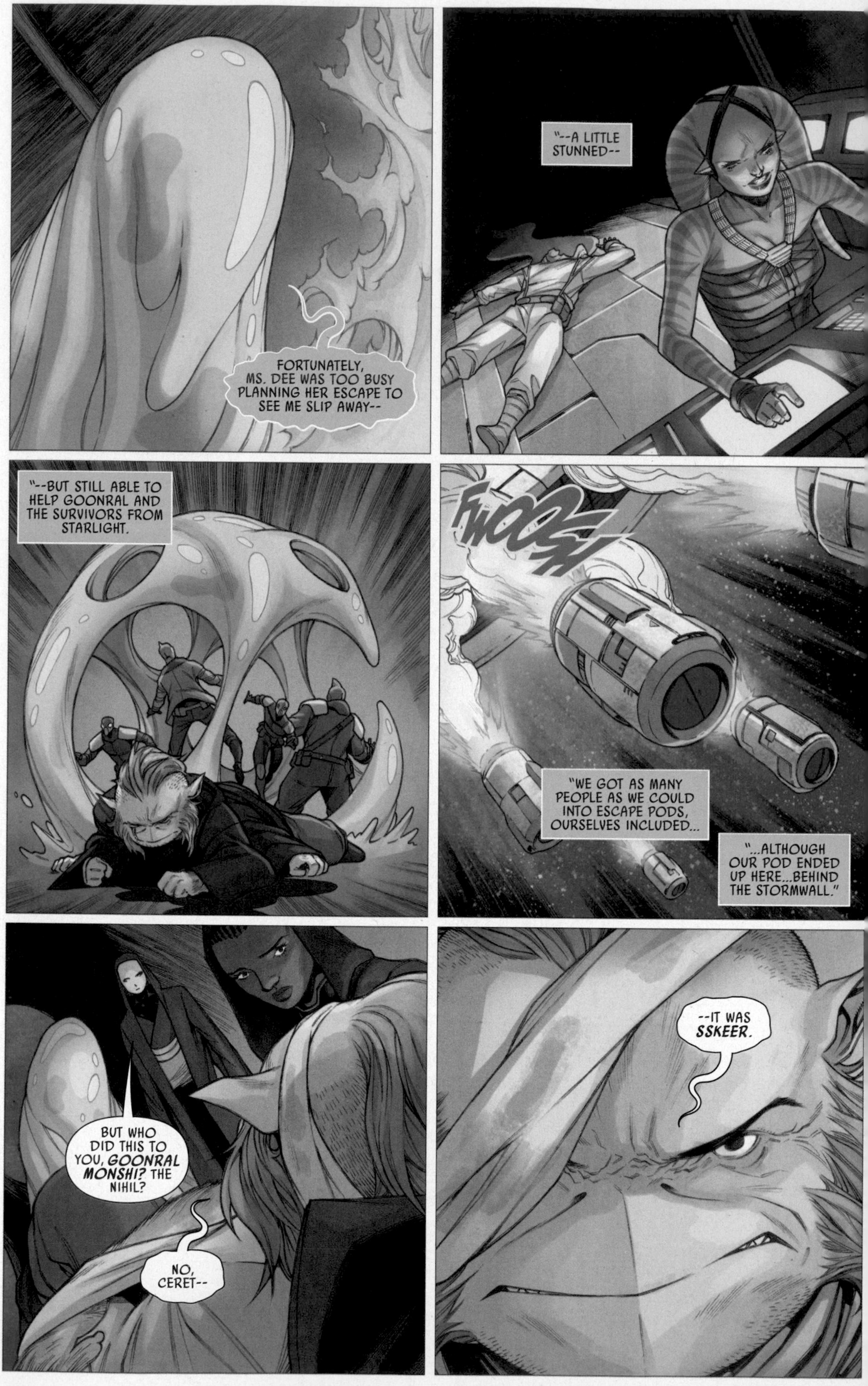
FORTUNATELY, MS. DEE WAS TOO BUSY PLANNING HER ESCAPE TO SEE ME SLIP AWAY--
"--A LITTLE STUNNED--
"--BUT STILL ABLE TO HELP GOONRAL AND THE SURVIVORS FROM STARLIGHT.
FWOOSH
"WE GOT AS MANY PEOPLE AS WE COULD INTO ESCAPE PODS, OURSELVES INCLUDED...
"...ALTHOUGH OUR POD ENDED UP HERE...BEHIND THE STORMWALL."
BUT WHO DID THIS TO YOU, GOONRAL MONSHI? THE NIHIL?
NO, CERET--
--IT WAS SSKEER.

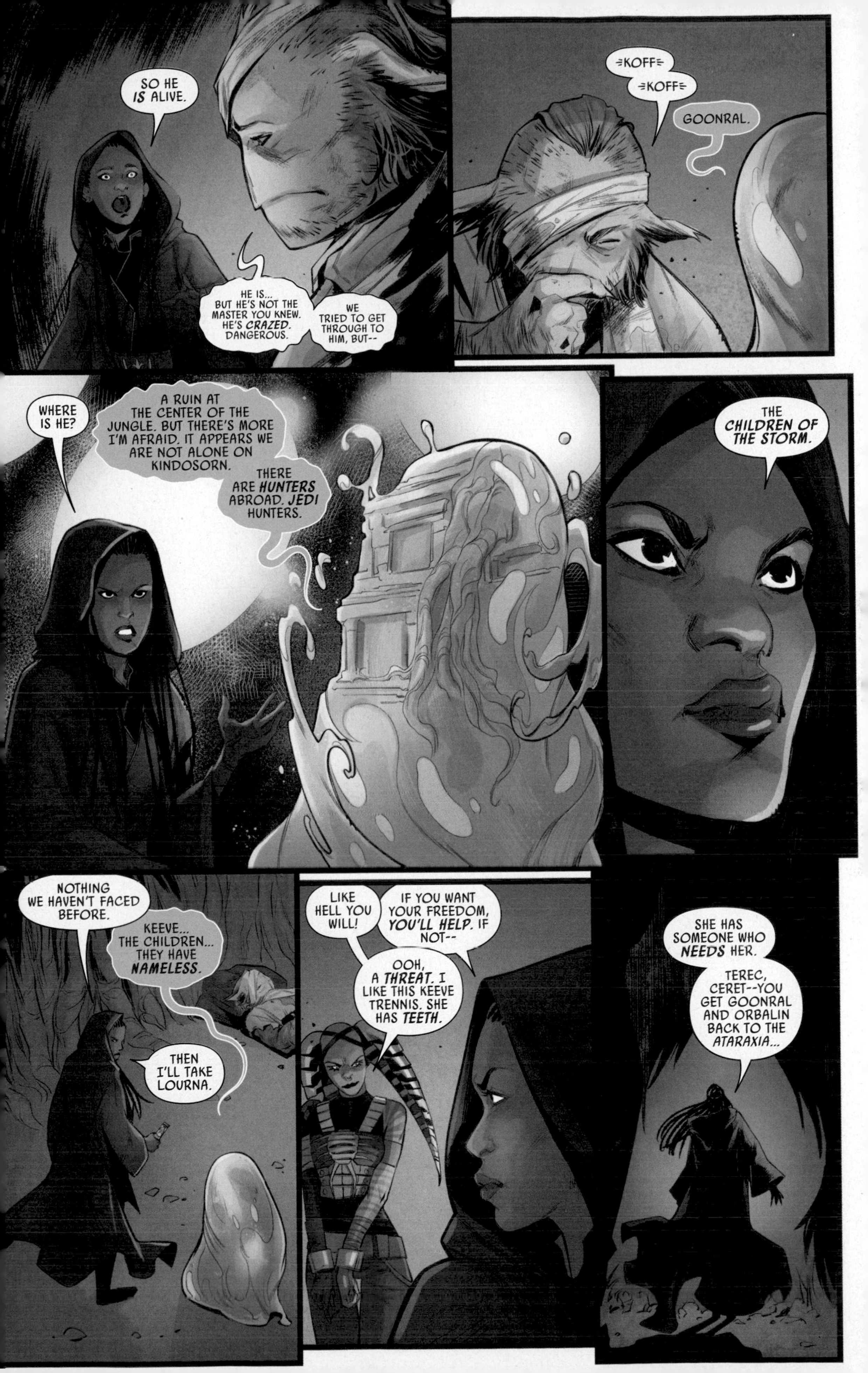
SO HE IS ALIVE.
HE IS... BUT HE'S NOT THE MASTER YOU KNEW. HE'S CRAZED. DANGEROUS.
WE TRIED TO GET THROUGH TO HIM, BUT--
=KOFF=
=KOFF=
GOONRAL.
WHERE IS HE?
A RUIN AT THE CENTER OF THE JUNGLE. BUT THERE'S MORE I'M AFRAID. IT APPEARS WE ARE NOT ALONE ON KINDOSORN.
THERE ARE HUNTERS ABROAD. JEDI HUNTERS.
THE CHILDREN OF THE STORM.
NOTHING WE HAVEN'T FACED BEFORE.
KEEVE... THE CHILDREN... THEY HAVE NAMELESS.
THEN I'LL TAKE LOURNA.
LIKE HELL YOU WILL!
IF YOU WANT YOUR FREEDOM, YOU'LL HELP. IF NOT--
OOH, A THREAT. I LIKE THIS KEEVE TRENNIS. SHE HAS TEETH.
SHE HAS SOMEONE WHO NEEDS HER.
TEREC, CERET--YOU GET GOONRAL AND ORBALIN BACK TO THE ATARAXIA...

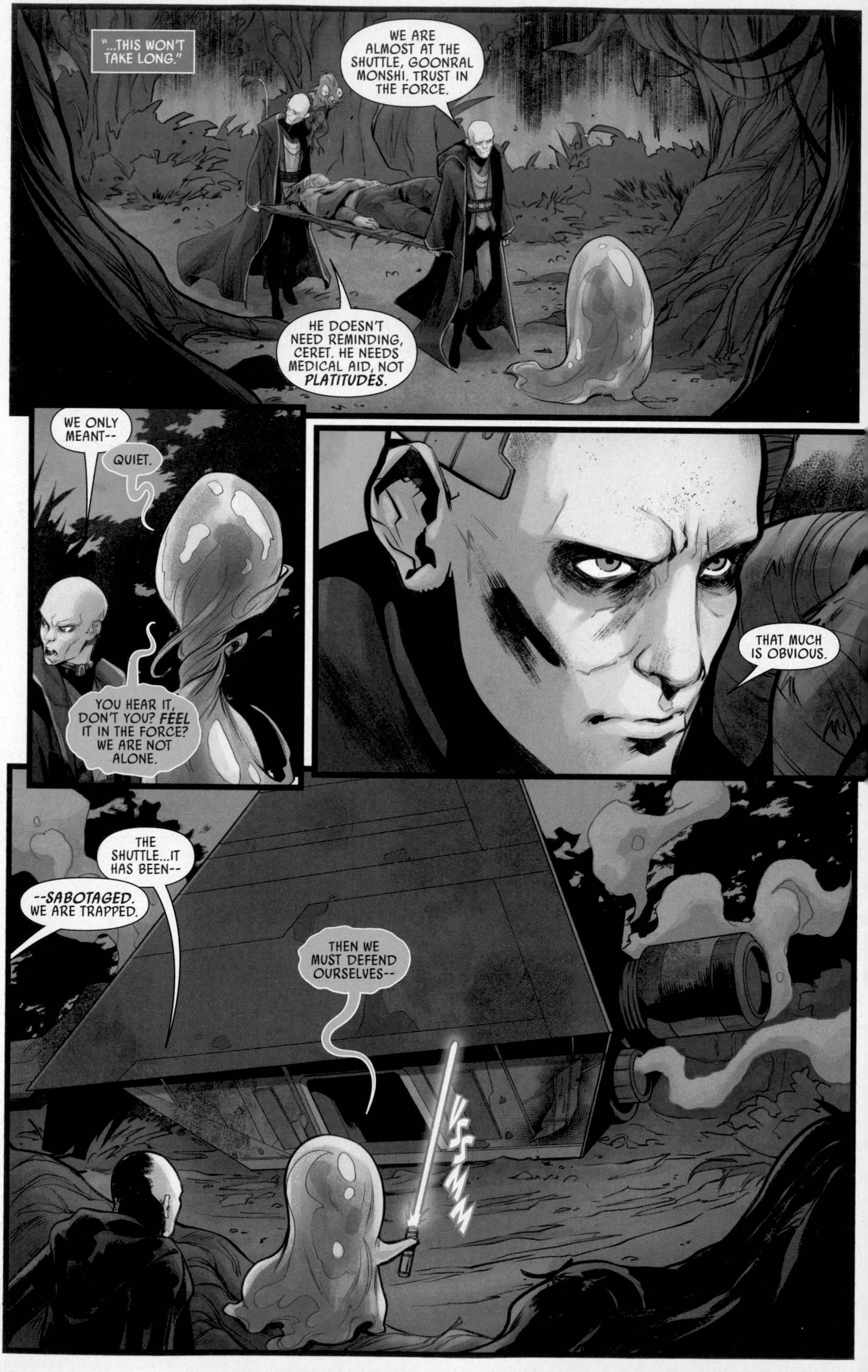
"...THIS WON'T TAKE LONG."
WE ARE ALMOST AT THE SHUTTLE, GOONRAL MONSHI. TRUST IN THE FORCE.
HE DOESN'T NEED REMINDING, CERET. HE NEEDS MEDICAL AID, NOT *PLATITUDES.*
WE ONLY MEANT--
QUIET.
YOU HEAR IT, DON'T YOU? *FEEL* IT IN THE FORCE? WE ARE NOT ALONE.
THAT MUCH IS OBVIOUS.
THE SHUTTLE...IT HAS BEEN--
--*SABOTAGED.* WE ARE TRAPPED.
THEN WE MUST DEFEND OURSELVES--
VSSMM

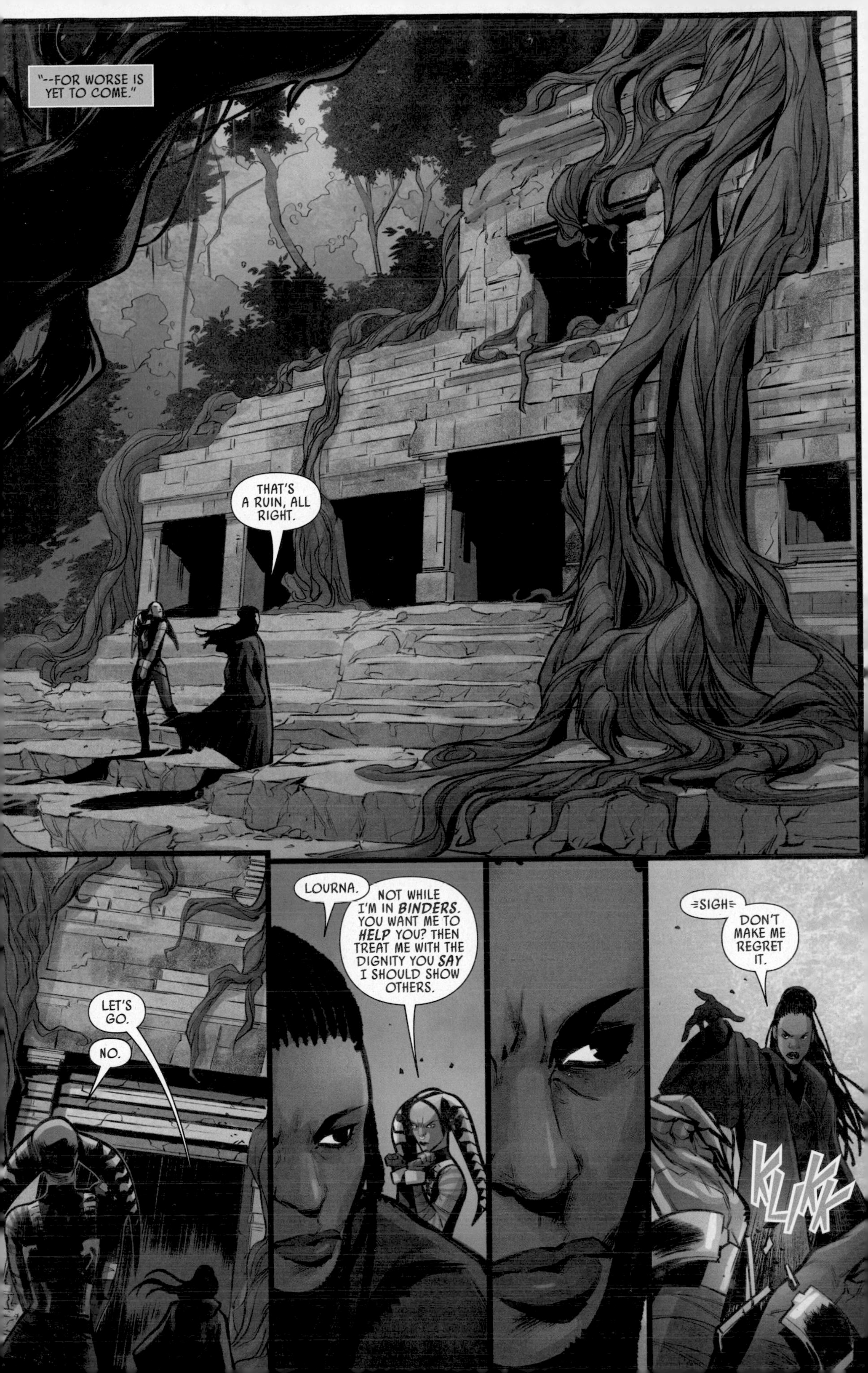
"--FOR WORSE IS YET TO COME."
THAT'S A RUIN, ALL RIGHT.
LET'S GO.
NO.
LOURNA.
NOT WHILE I'M IN BINDERS. YOU WANT ME TO HELP YOU? THEN TREAT ME WITH THE DIGNITY YOU SAY I SHOULD SHOW OTHERS.
SIGH
DON'T MAKE ME REGRET IT.
KLIKK

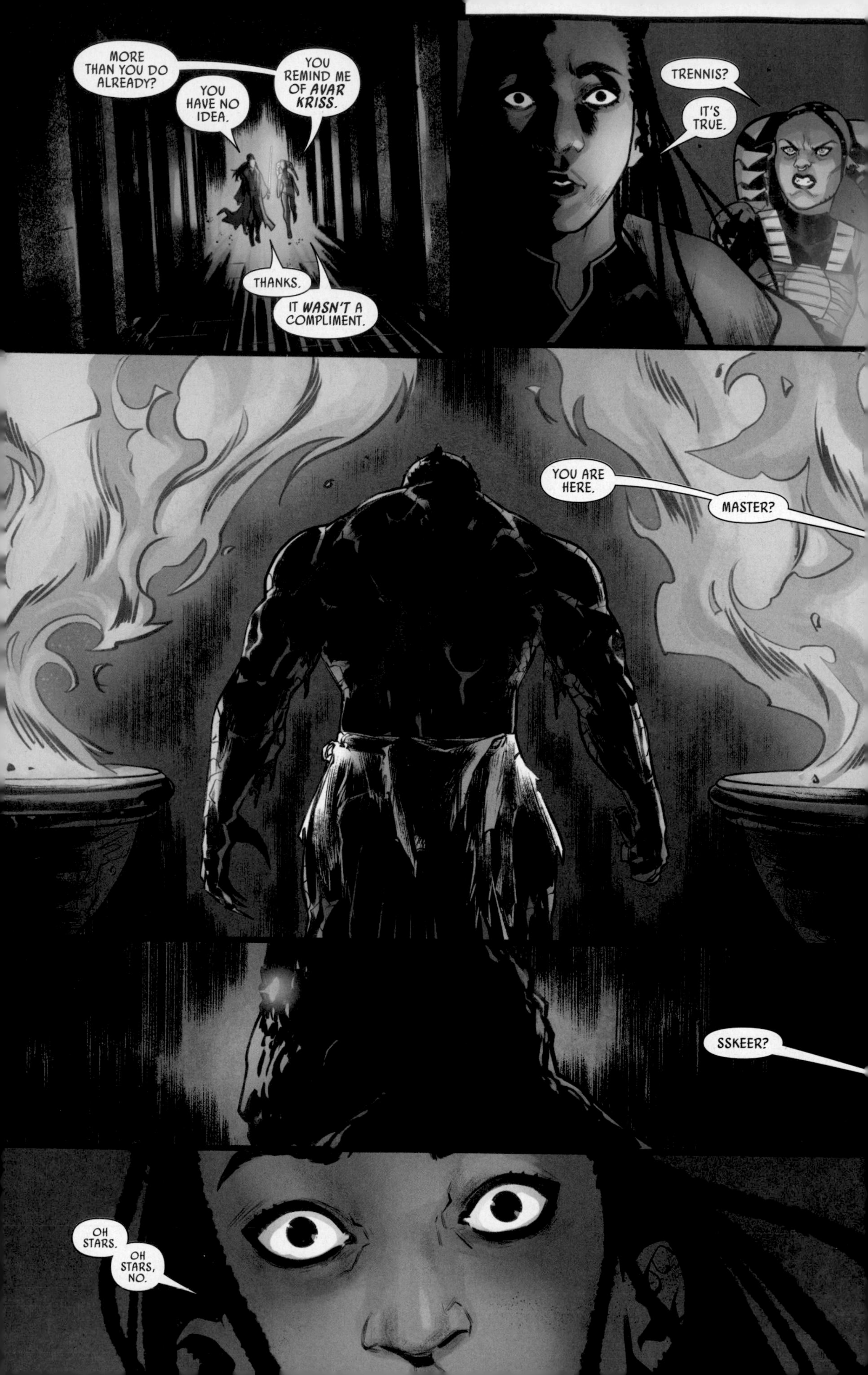
MORE THAN YOU DO ALREADY?
YOU REMIND ME OF AVAR KRISS.
YOU HAVE NO IDEA.
THANKS.
IT WASN'T A COMPLIMENT.
TRENNIS?
IT'S TRUE.
YOU ARE HERE.
MASTER?
SSKEER?
OH STARS.
OH STARS, NO.

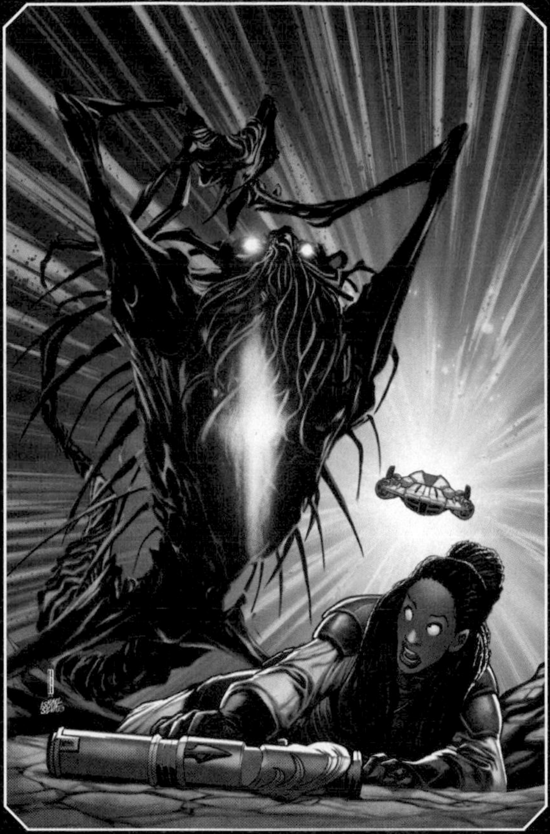

#1 Variant by
DAVID BALDEÓN & ISRAEL SILVA

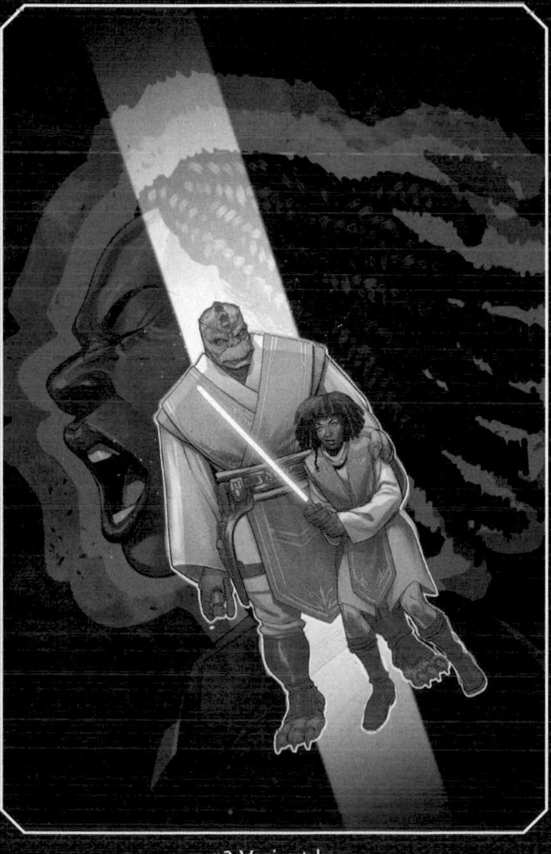

#2 Variant by
RACHAEL STOTT

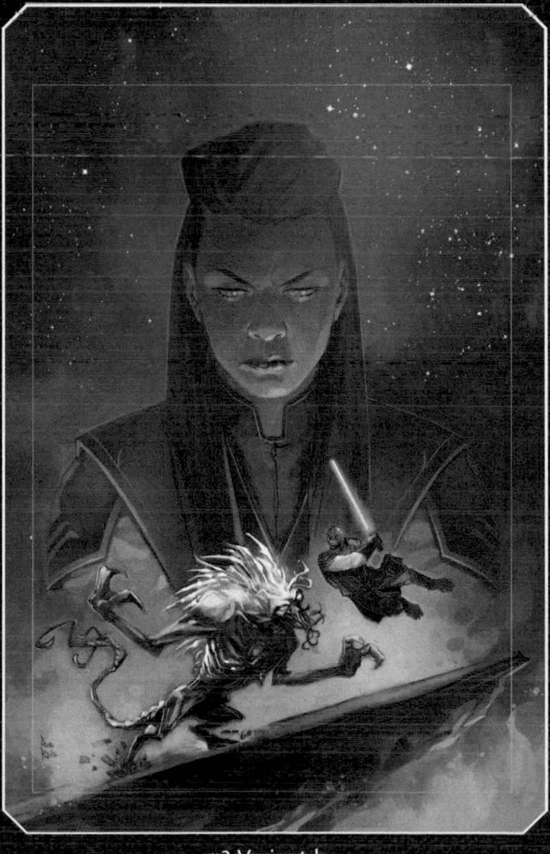

#2 Variant by
ROD REIS

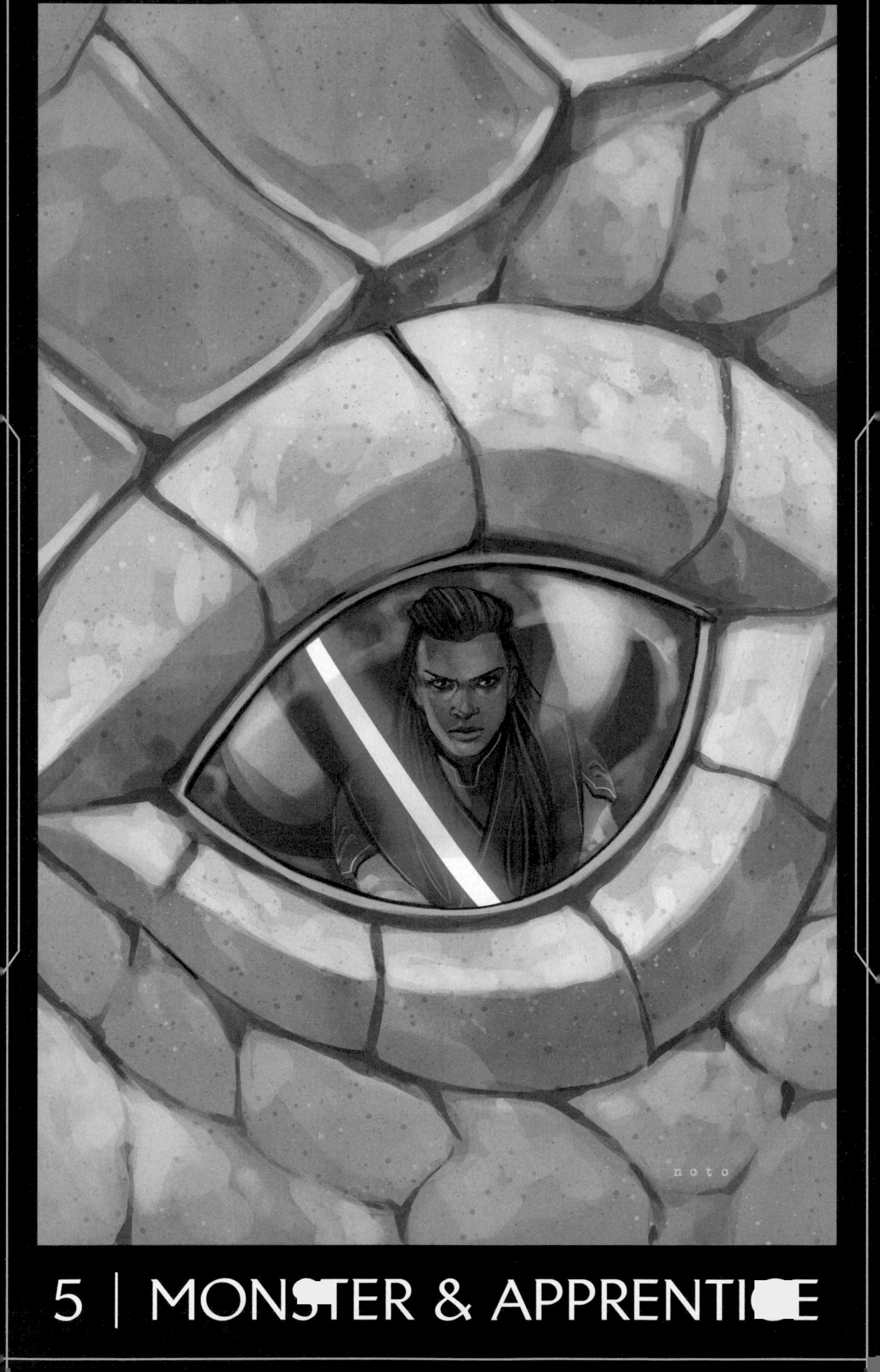
noto

5 | MONSTER & APPRENTICE

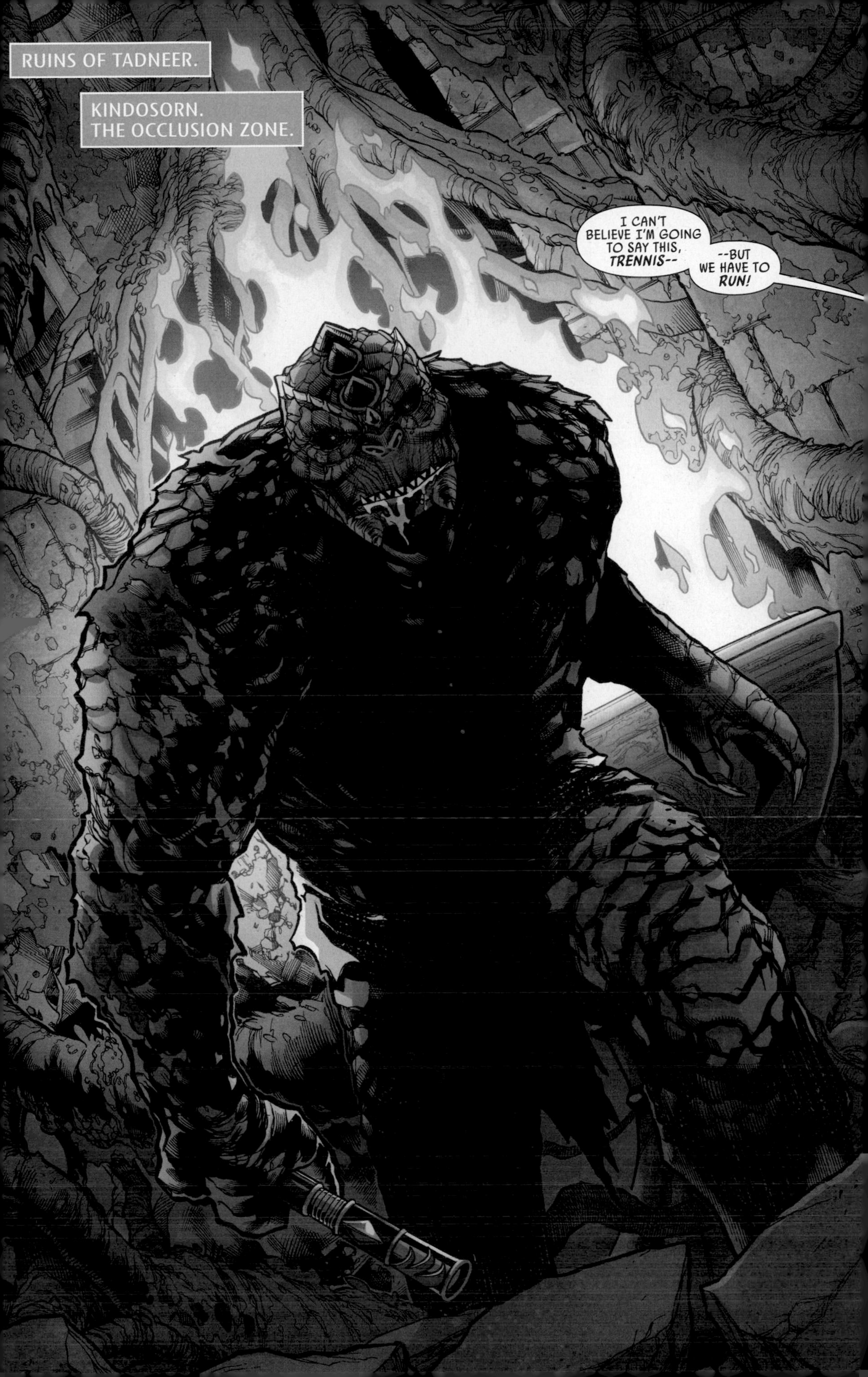
RUINS OF TADNEER.
KINDOSORN. THE OCCLUSION ZONE.
I CAN'T BELIEVE I'M GOING TO SAY THIS, TRENNIS--
--BUT WE HAVE TO RUN!

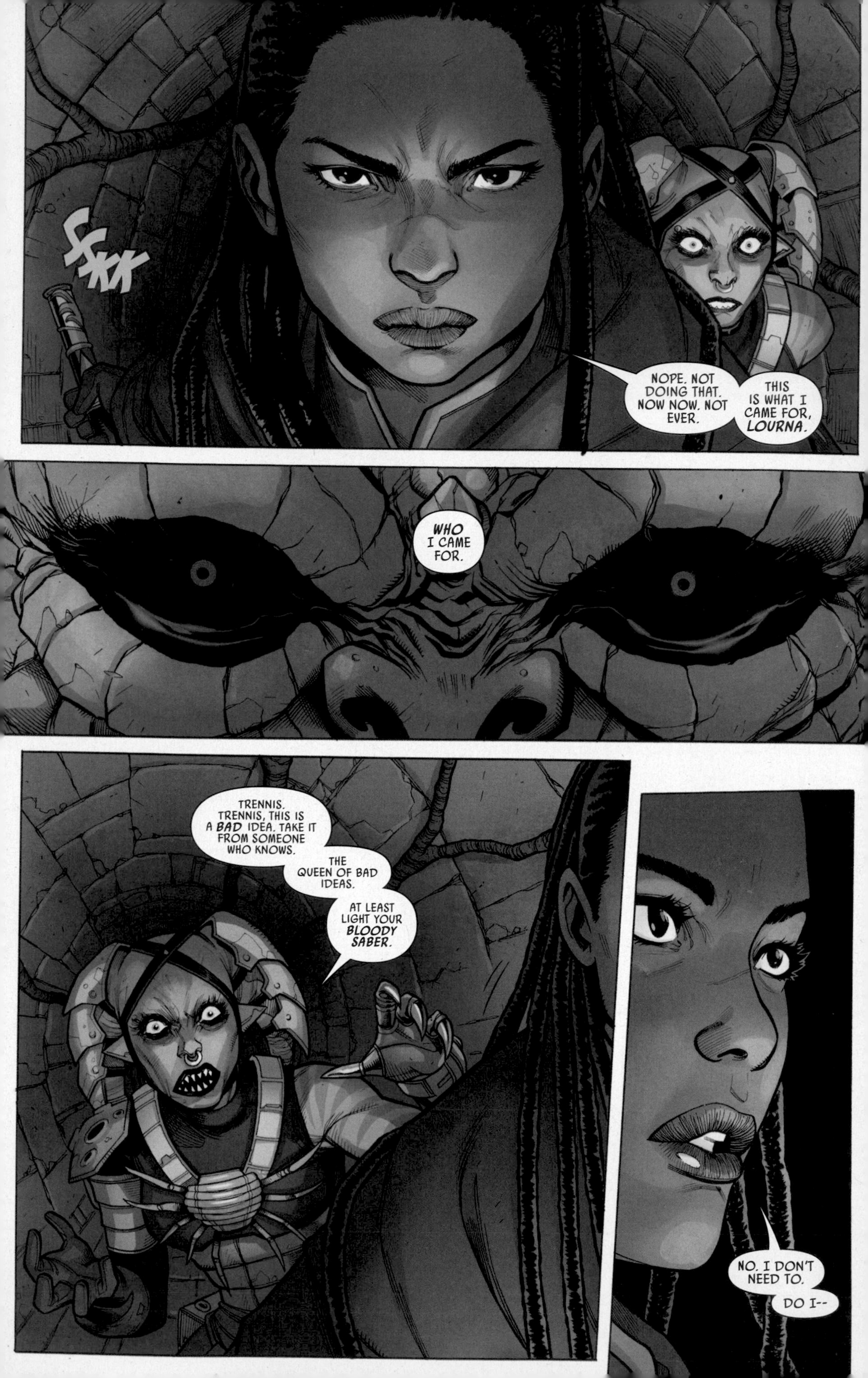

SKKK
NOPE. NOT DOING THAT. NOW NOW. NOT EVER.
THIS IS WHAT I CAME FOR, LOURNA.
WHO I CAME FOR.
TRENNIS. TRENNIS, THIS IS A BAD IDEA. TAKE IT FROM SOMEONE WHO KNOWS.
THE QUEEN OF BAD IDEAS.
AT LEAST LIGHT YOUR BLOODY SABER.
NO. I DON'T NEED TO.
DO I--

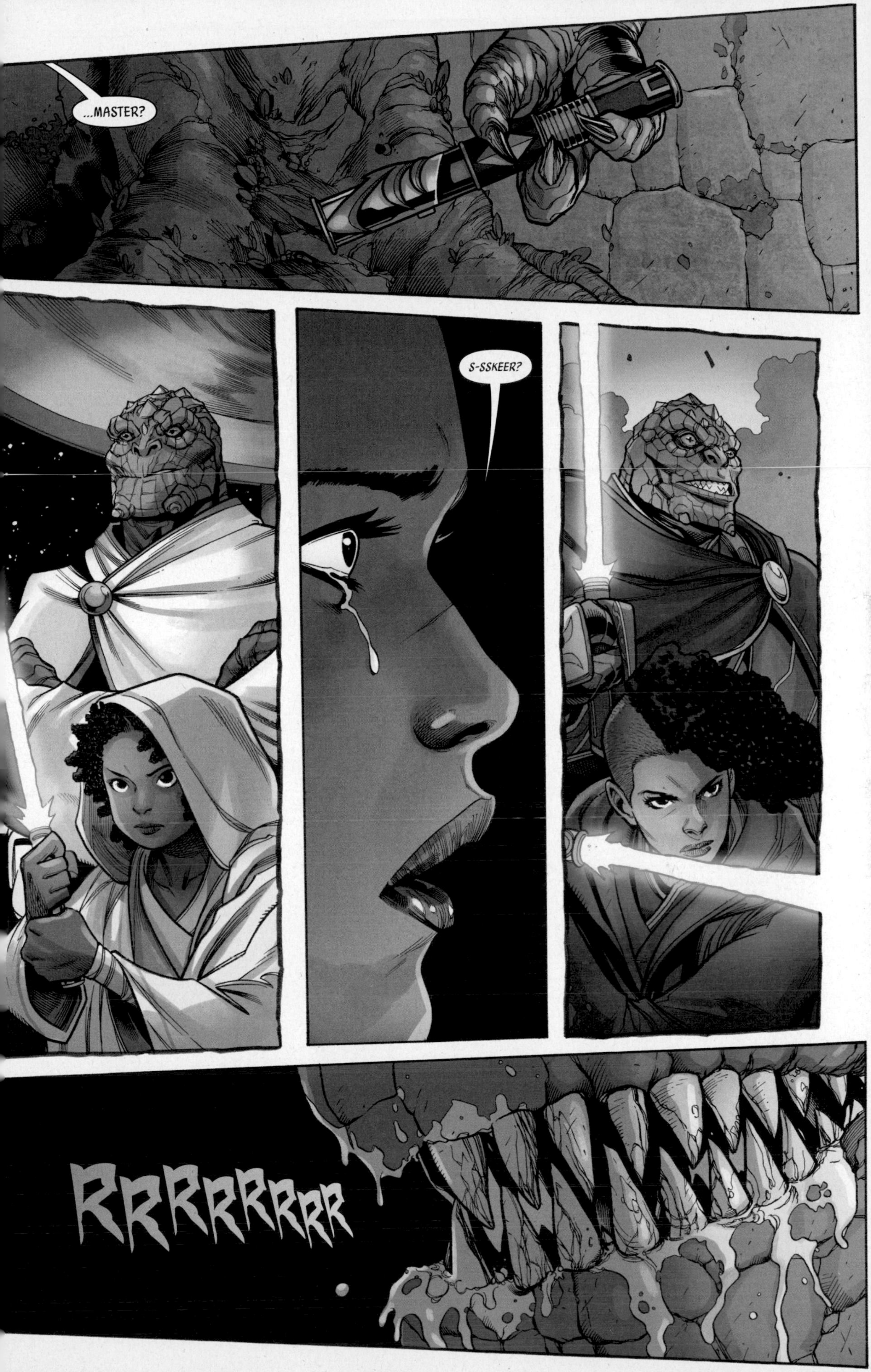

...MASTER?
S-SSKEER?
RRRRRRRR

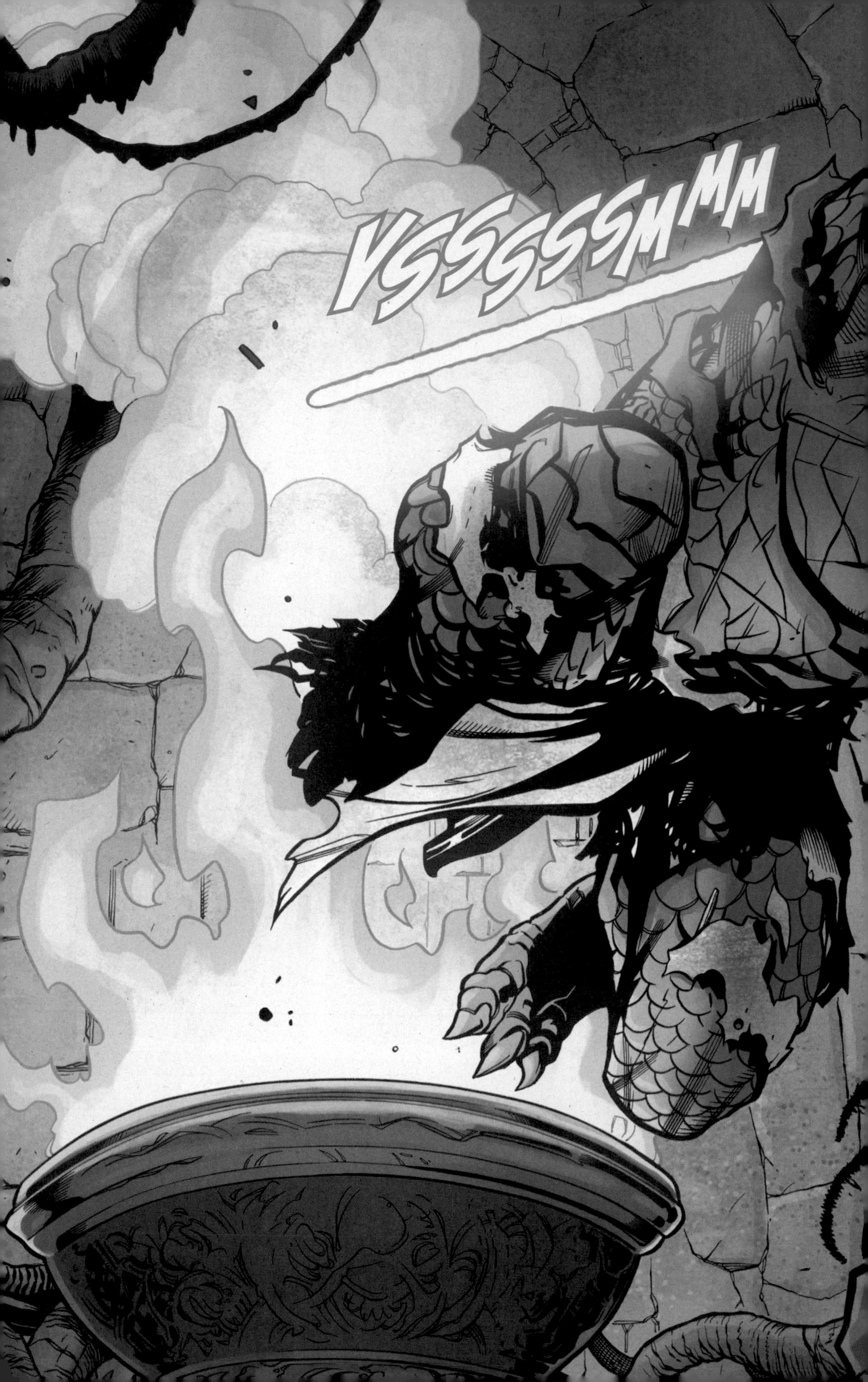
VSSSSSMMM

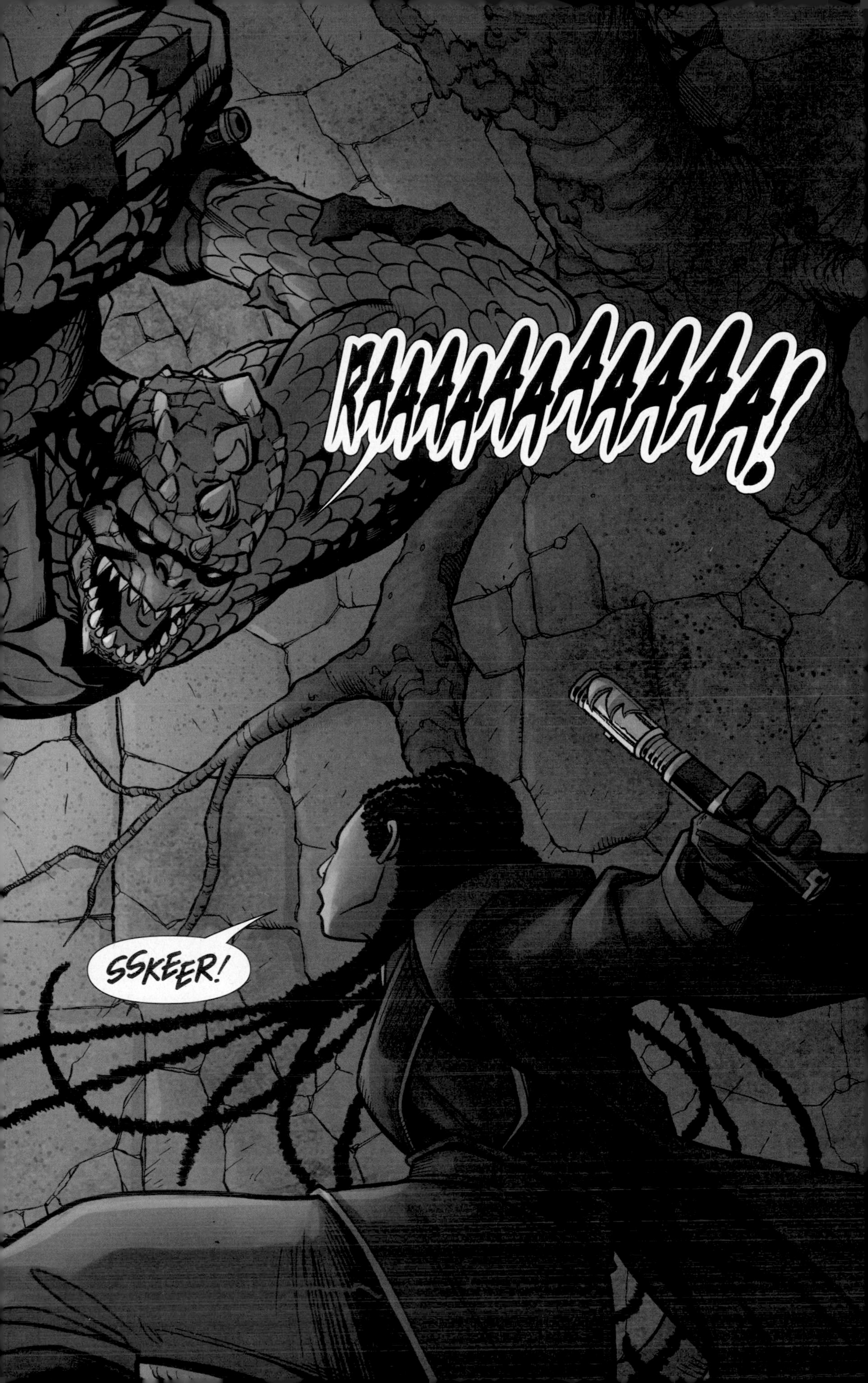
RAAAAAAAAAAAA!
SSKEER!

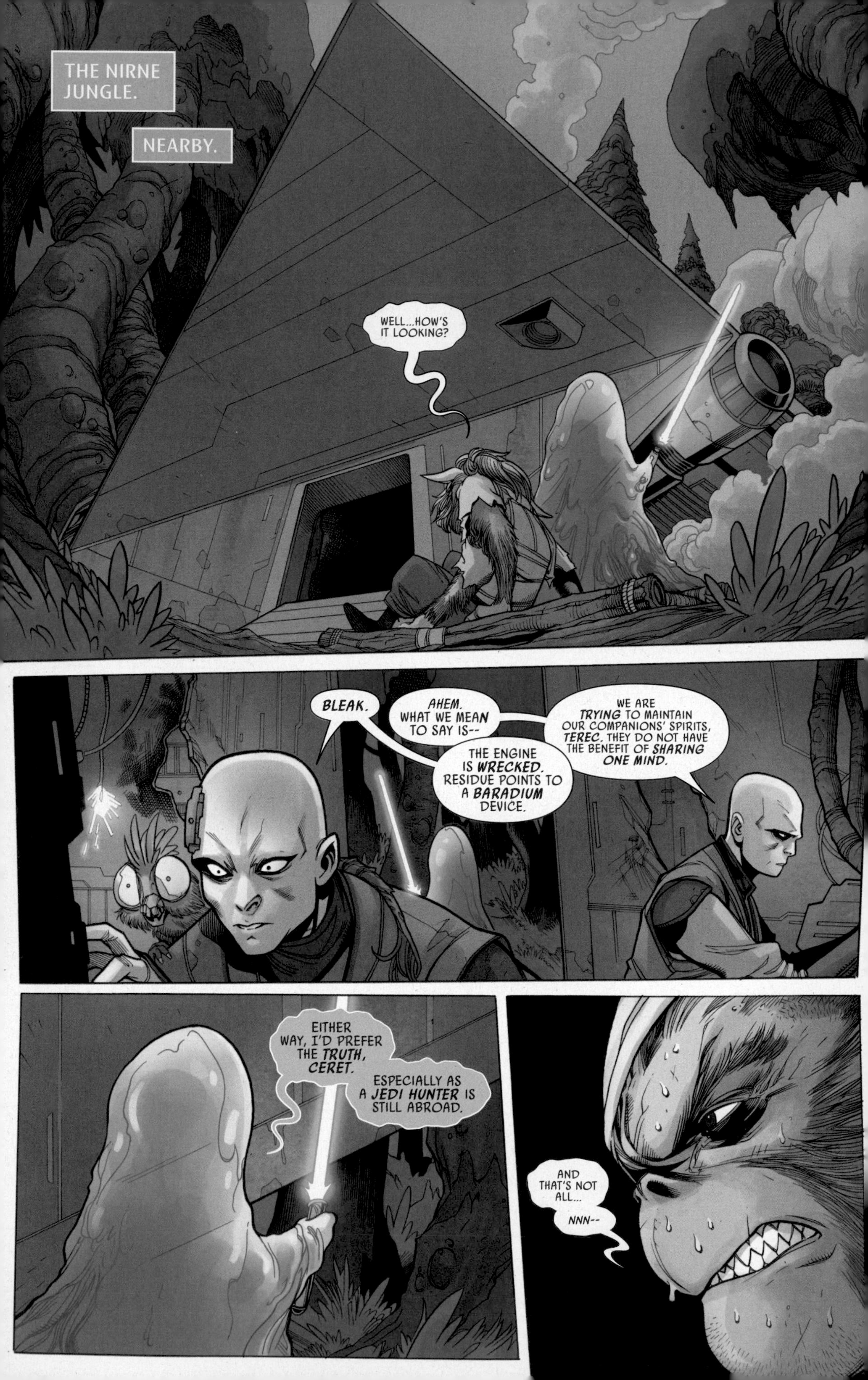

THE NIRNE JUNGLE.
NEARBY.
WELL...HOW'S IT LOOKING?
BLEAK.
AHEM. WHAT WE MEAN TO SAY IS--
THE ENGINE IS WRECKED. RESIDUE POINTS TO A BARADIUM DEVICE.
WE ARE TRYING TO MAINTAIN OUR COMPANIONS' SPIRITS, TEREC. THEY DO NOT HAVE THE BENEFIT OF SHARING ONE MIND.
EITHER WAY, I'D PREFER THE TRUTH, CERET.
ESPECIALLY AS A JEDI HUNTER IS STILL ABROAD.
AND THAT'S NOT ALL...
NNN--

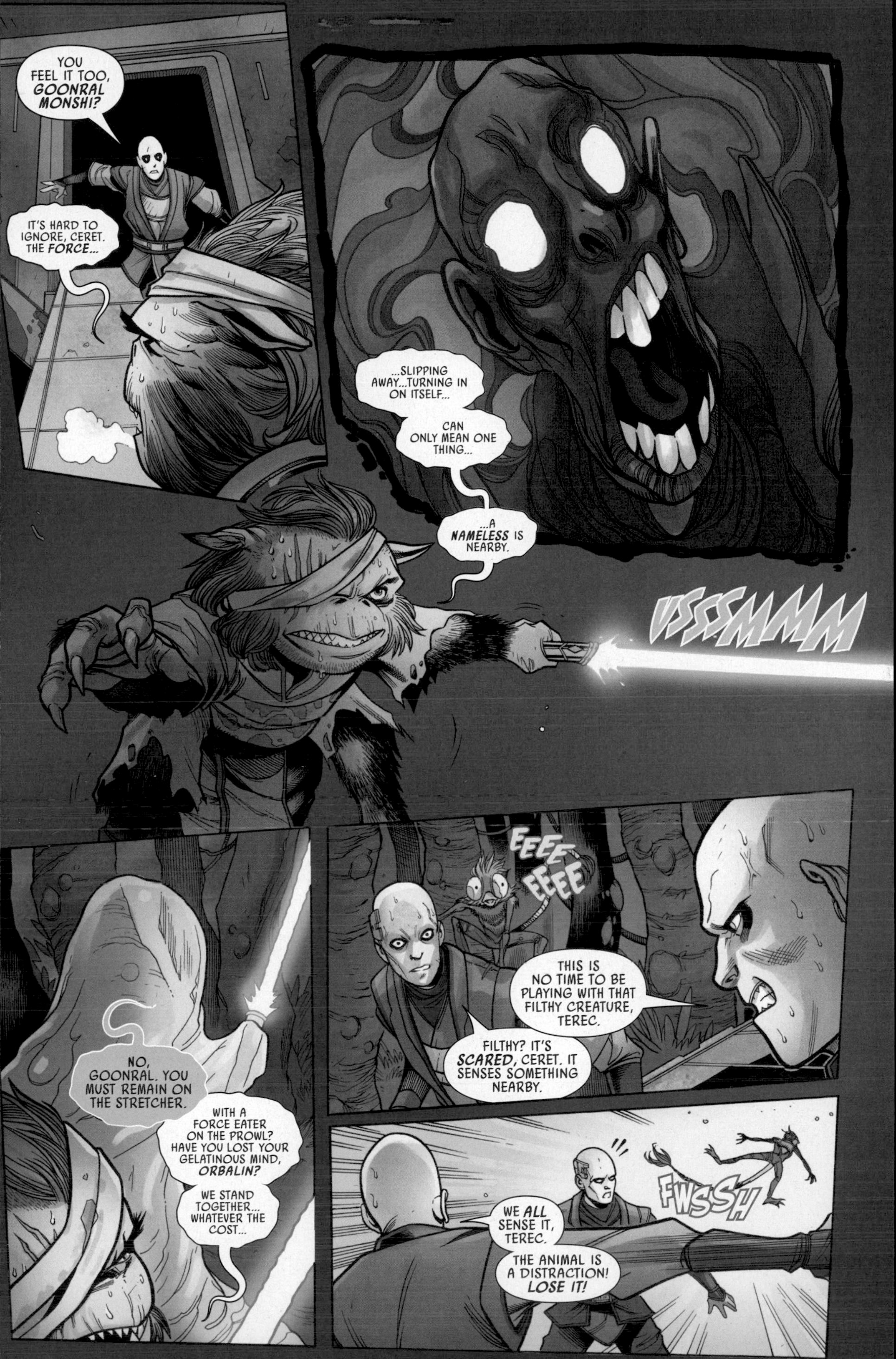

YOU FEEL IT TOO, GOONRAL MONSHI?
IT'S HARD TO IGNORE, CERET. THE FORCE...
...SLIPPING AWAY...TURNING IN ON ITSELF...
CAN ONLY MEAN ONE THING...
...A NAMELESS IS NEARBY.
VSSSMMM
NO, GOONRAL. YOU MUST REMAIN ON THE STRETCHER.
WITH A FORCE EATER ON THE PROWL? HAVE YOU LOST YOUR GELATINOUS MIND, ORBALIN?
WE STAND TOGETHER... WHATEVER THE COST...
EEEE EEEE
THIS IS NO TIME TO BE PLAYING WITH THAT FILTHY CREATURE, TEREC.
FILTHY? IT'S SCARED, CERET. IT SENSES SOMETHING NEARBY.
FWSSH
WE ALL SENSE IT, TEREC.
THE ANIMAL IS A DISTRACTION! LOSE IT!

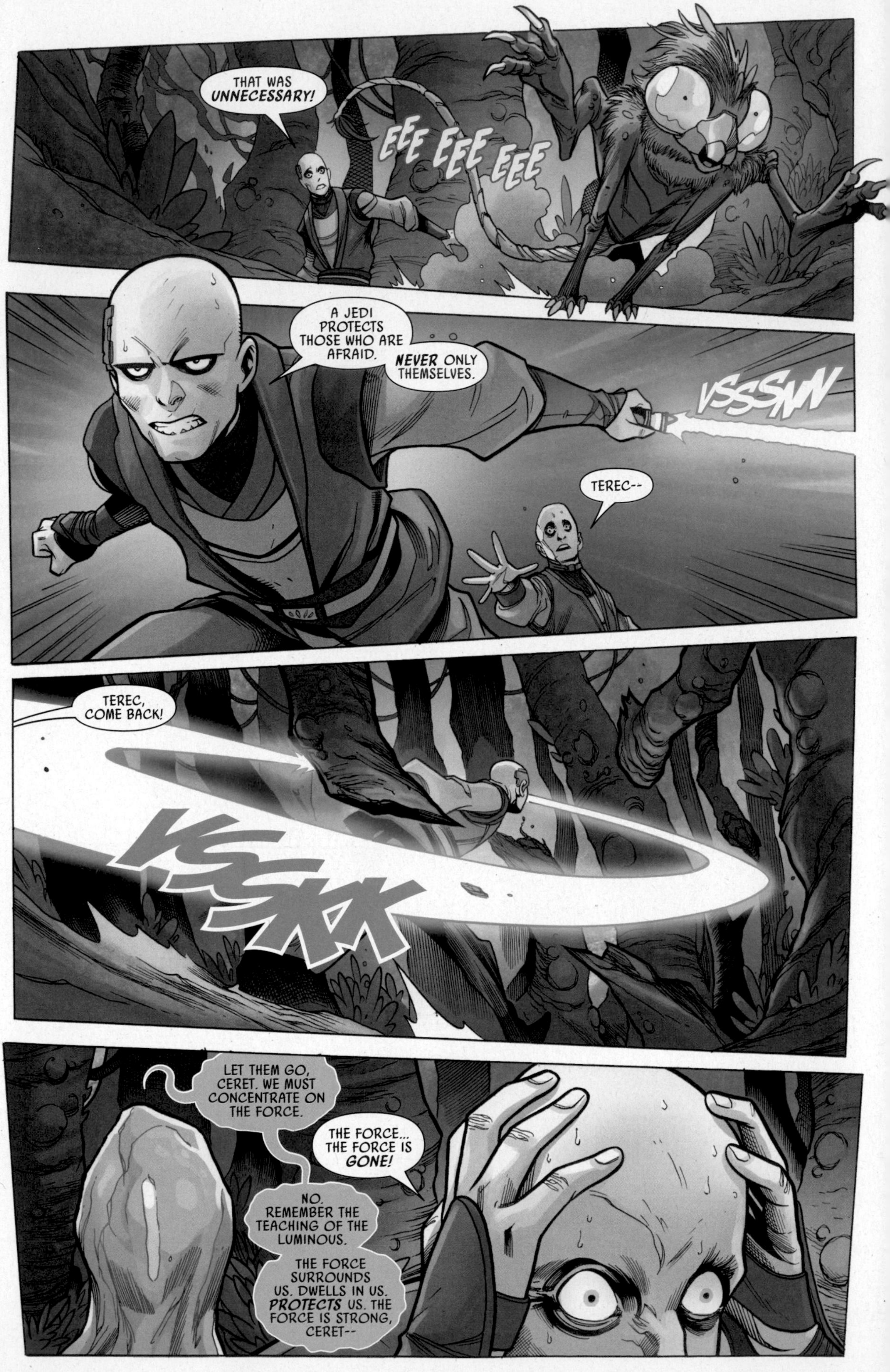

THAT WAS UNNECESSARY!
EEE EEE EEE
A JEDI PROTECTS THOSE WHO ARE AFRAID.
NEVER ONLY THEMSELVES.
VSSSNN
TEREC--
TEREC, COME BACK!
VSSKK
LET THEM GO, CERET. WE MUST CONCENTRATE ON THE FORCE.
THE FORCE... THE FORCE IS GONE!
NO. REMEMBER THE TEACHING OF THE LUMINOUS.
THE FORCE SURROUNDS US. DWELLS IN US. PROTECTS US. THE FORCE IS STRONG, CERET--

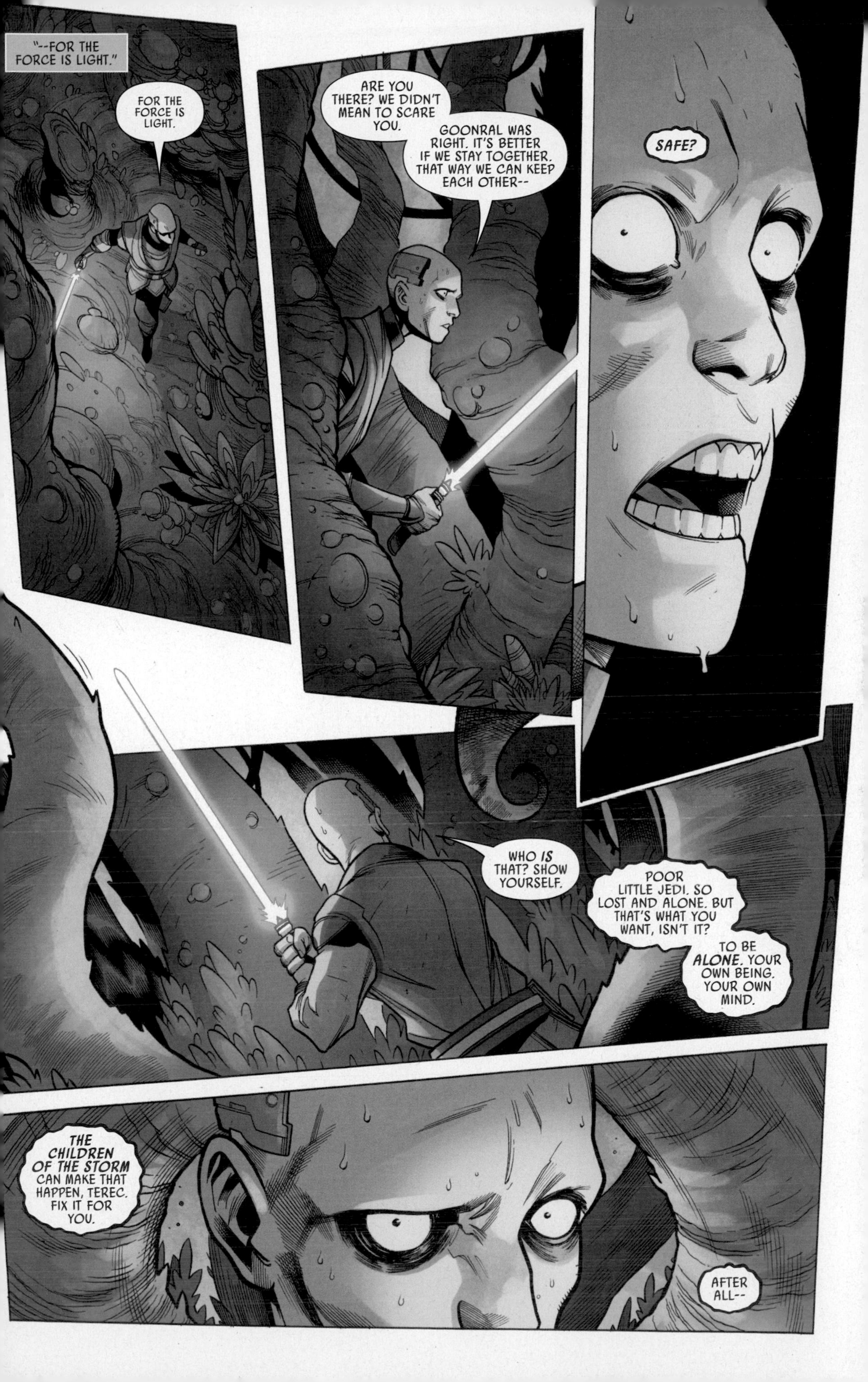
"--FOR THE FORCE IS LIGHT."
FOR THE FORCE IS LIGHT.
ARE YOU THERE? WE DIDN'T MEAN TO SCARE YOU.
GOONRAL WAS RIGHT. IT'S BETTER IF WE STAY TOGETHER. THAT WAY WE CAN KEEP EACH OTHER--
SAFE?
WHO IS THAT? SHOW YOURSELF.
POOR LITTLE JEDI. SO LOST AND ALONE. BUT THAT'S WHAT YOU WANT, ISN'T IT?
TO BE ALONE. YOUR OWN BEING. YOUR OWN MIND.
THE CHILDREN OF THE STORM CAN MAKE THAT HAPPEN, TEREC. FIX IT FOR YOU.
AFTER ALL--

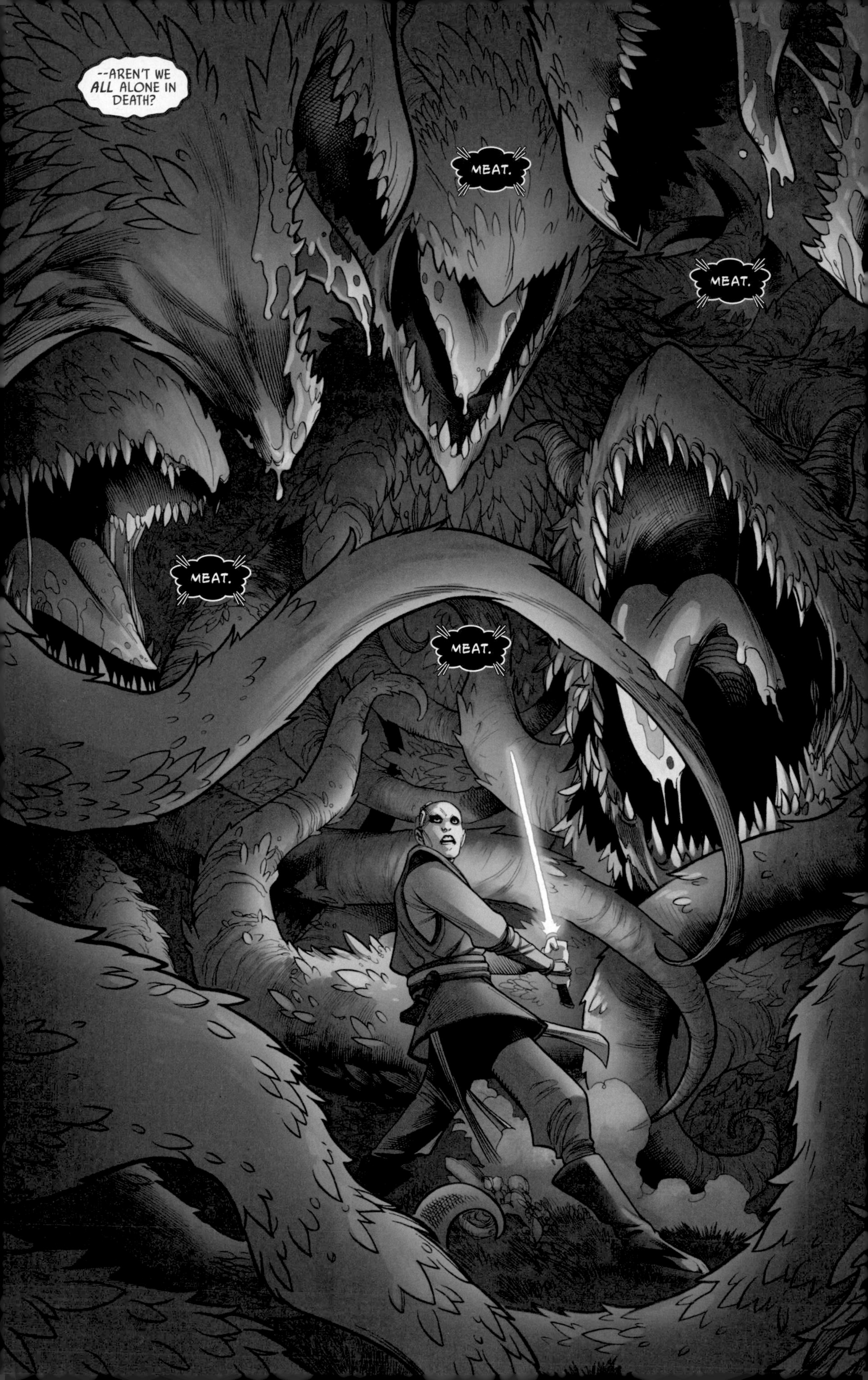
--AREN'T WE ALL ALONE IN DEATH?
MEAT.
MEAT.
MEAT.
MEAT.

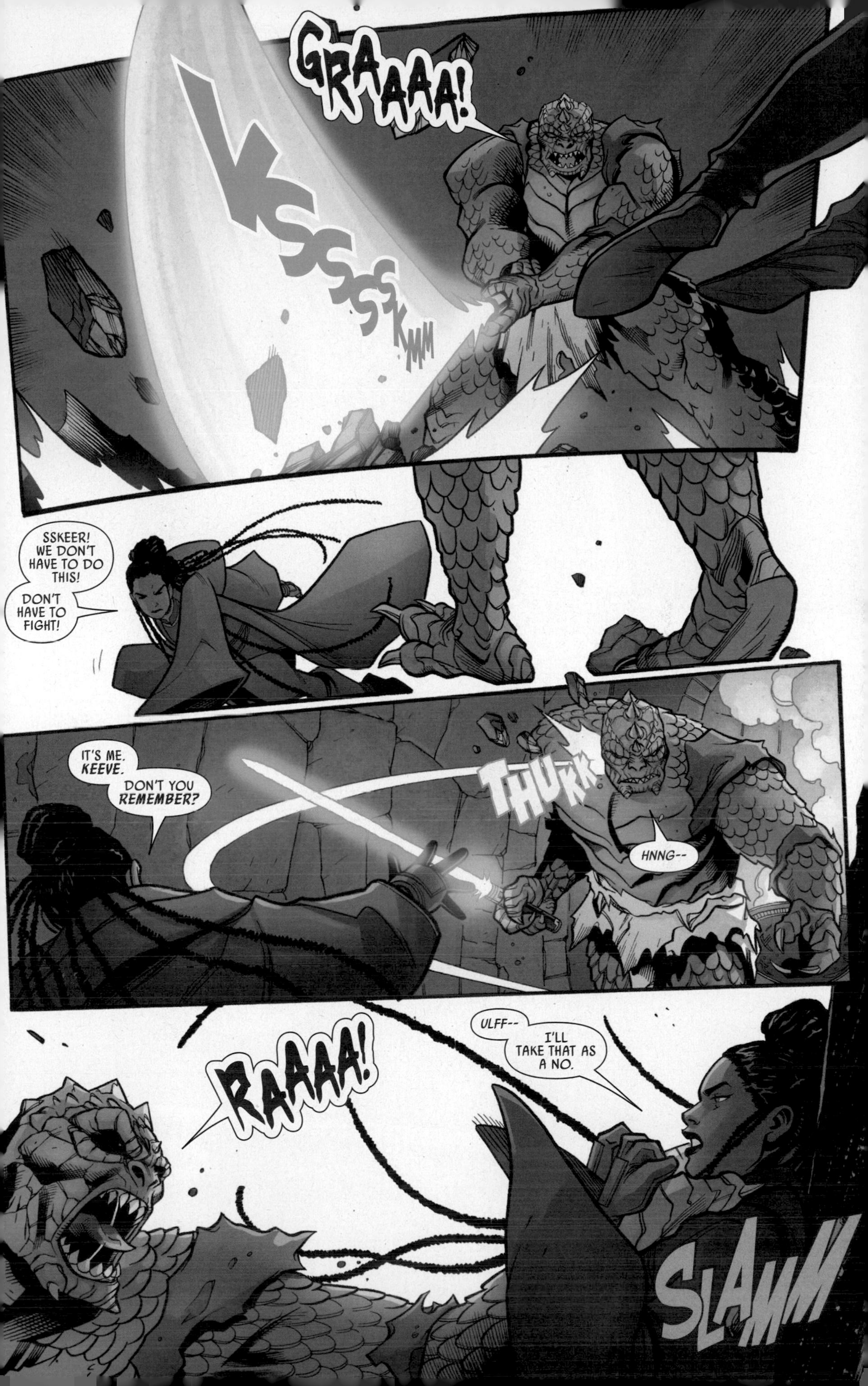
GRAAAA!
KSSSSSKMM
SSKEER! WE DON'T HAVE TO DO THIS!
DON'T HAVE TO FIGHT!
IT'S ME. KEEVE.
DON'T YOU REMEMBER?
THUKK
HNNG--
RAAAA!
ULFF--
I'LL TAKE THAT AS A NO.
SLAMM

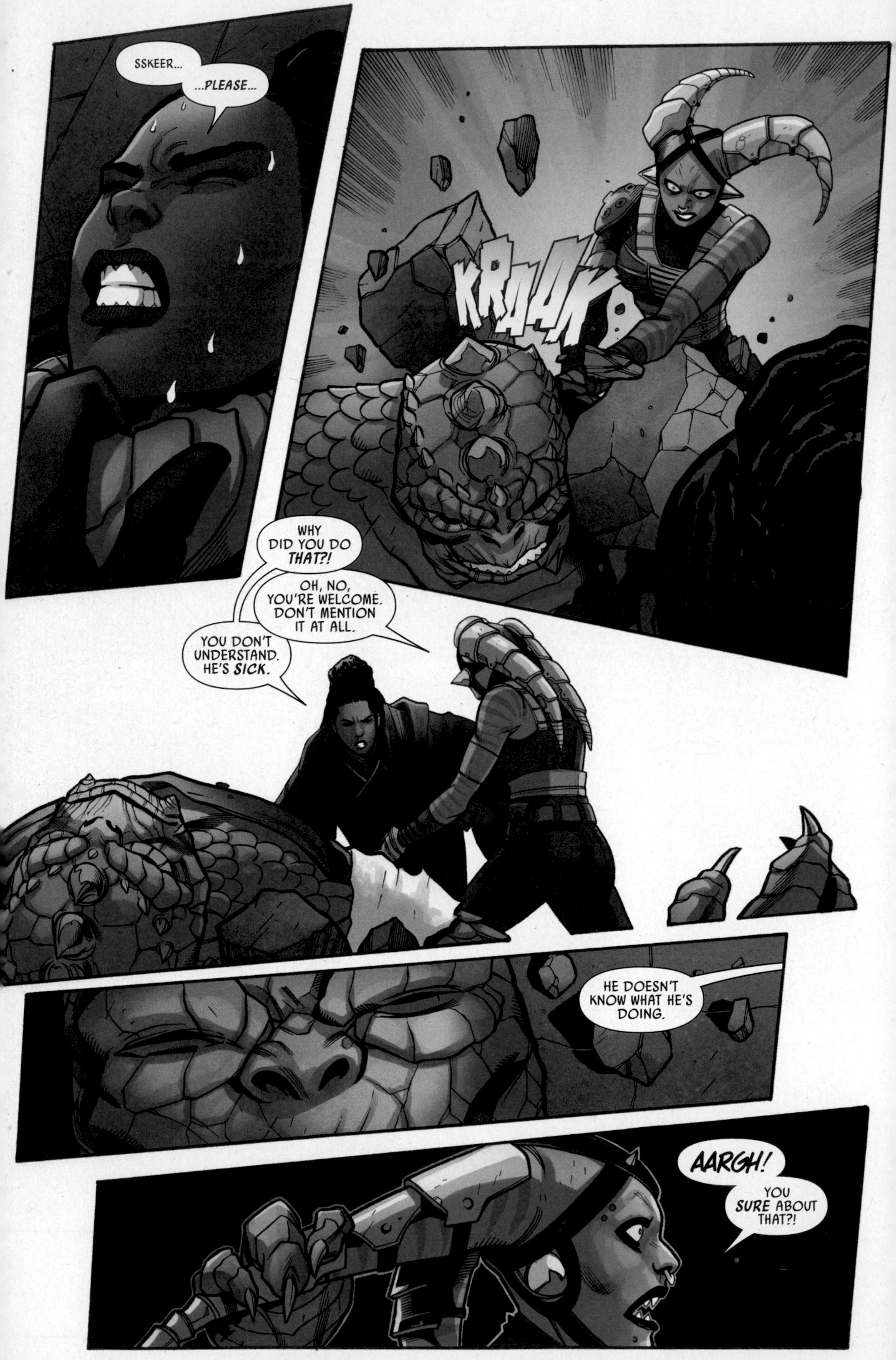
SSKEER...
...PLEASE...
KROOK
WHY DID YOU DO THAT?!
OH, NO, YOU'RE WELCOME. DON'T MENTION IT AT ALL.
YOU DON'T UNDERSTAND. HE'S SICK.
HE DOESN'T KNOW WHAT HE'S DOING.
AARGH!
YOU SURE ABOUT THAT?!

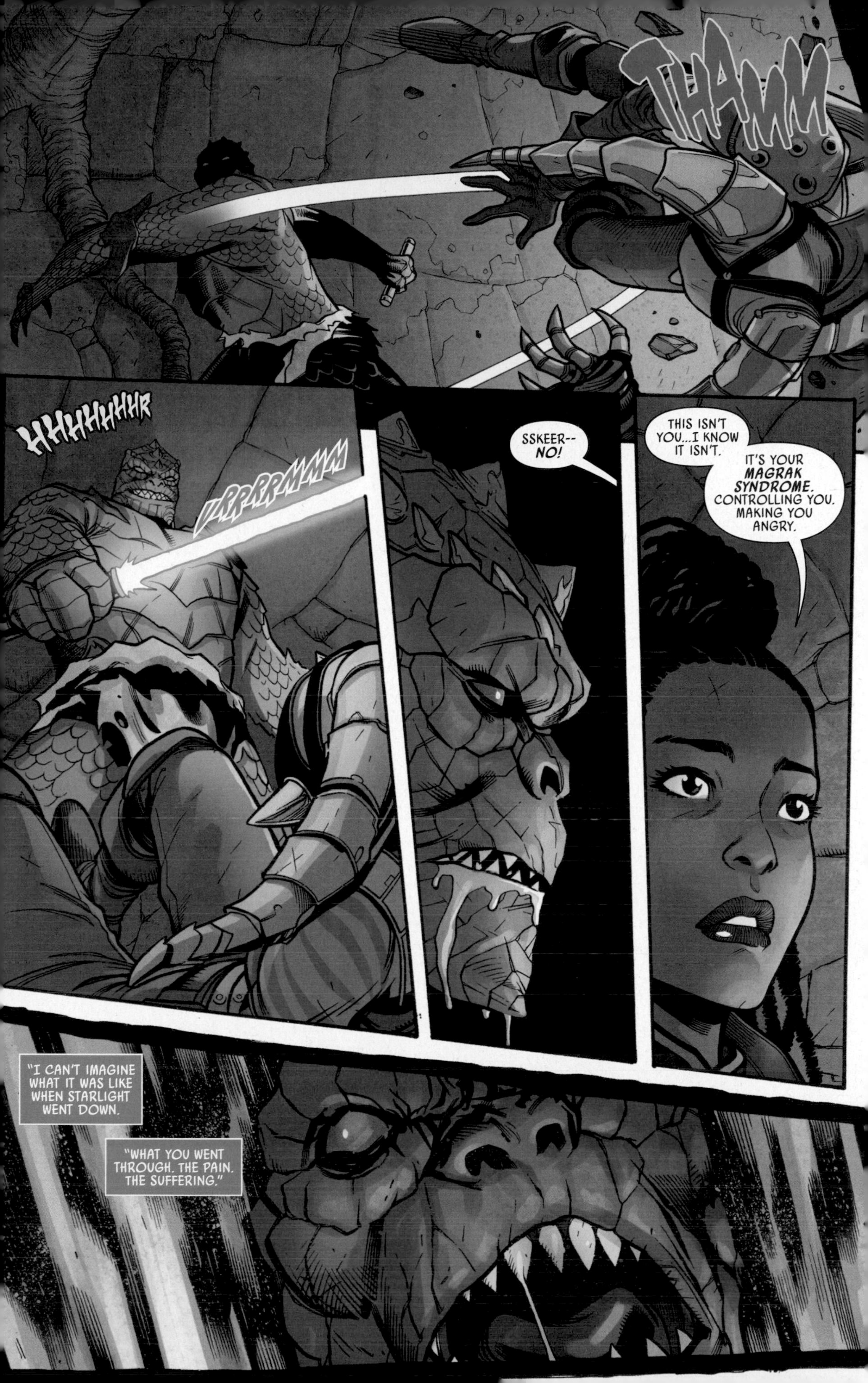
THAMM
HHHHHHHR
VRRRRMMM
SSKEER-- NO!
THIS ISN'T YOU...I KNOW IT ISN'T.
IT'S YOUR MAGRAK SYNDROME. CONTROLLING YOU. MAKING YOU ANGRY.
"I CAN'T IMAGINE WHAT IT WAS LIKE WHEN STARLIGHT WENT DOWN.
"WHAT YOU WENT THROUGH. THE PAIN. THE SUFFERING."

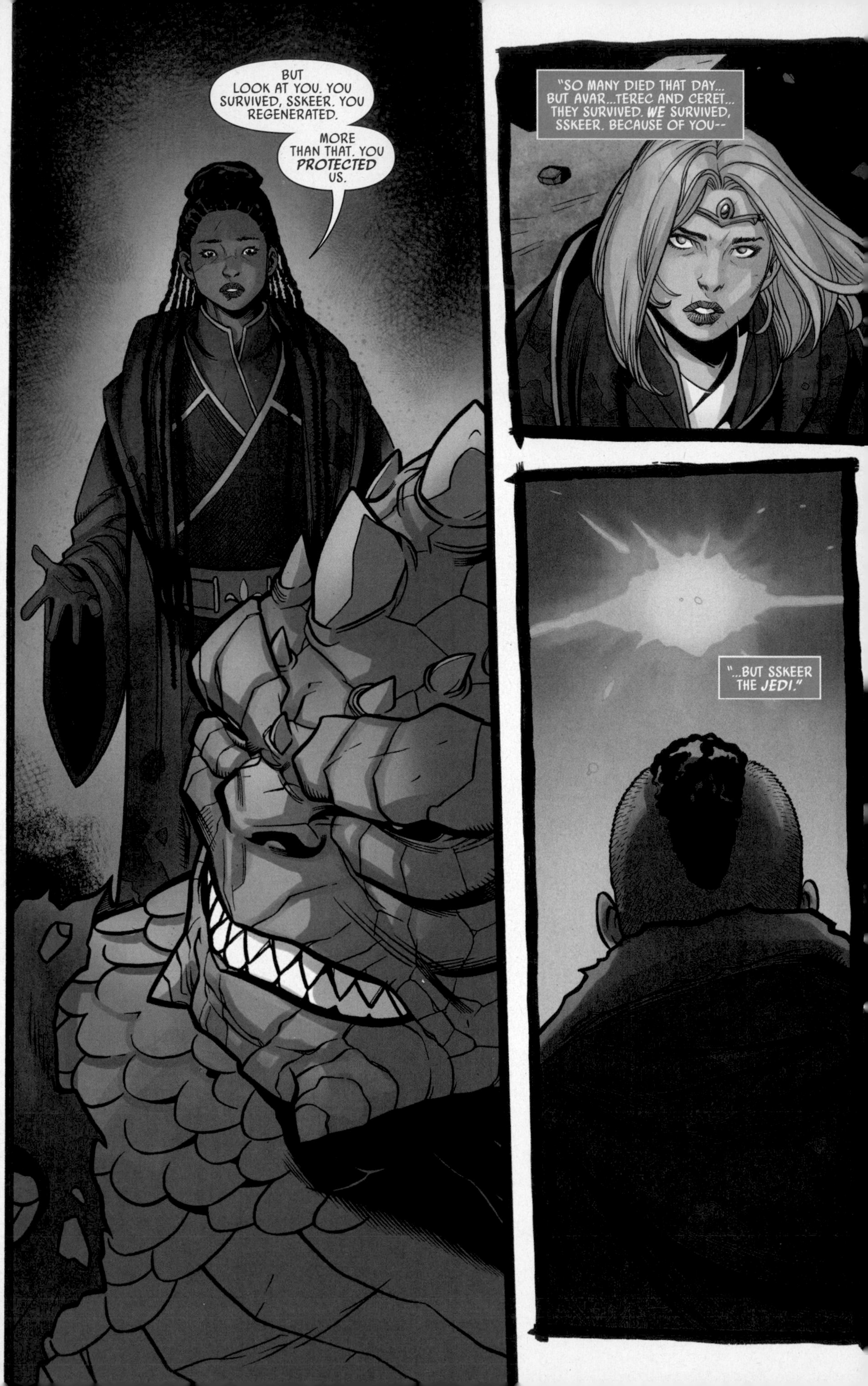
BUT LOOK AT YOU. YOU SURVIVED, SSKEER. YOU REGENERATED.
MORE THAN THAT. YOU PROTECTED US.
"SO MANY DIED THAT DAY... BUT AVAR...TEREC AND CERET... THEY SURVIVED. WE SURVIVED, SSKEER. BECAUSE OF YOU--
"...BUT SSKEER THE JEDI."

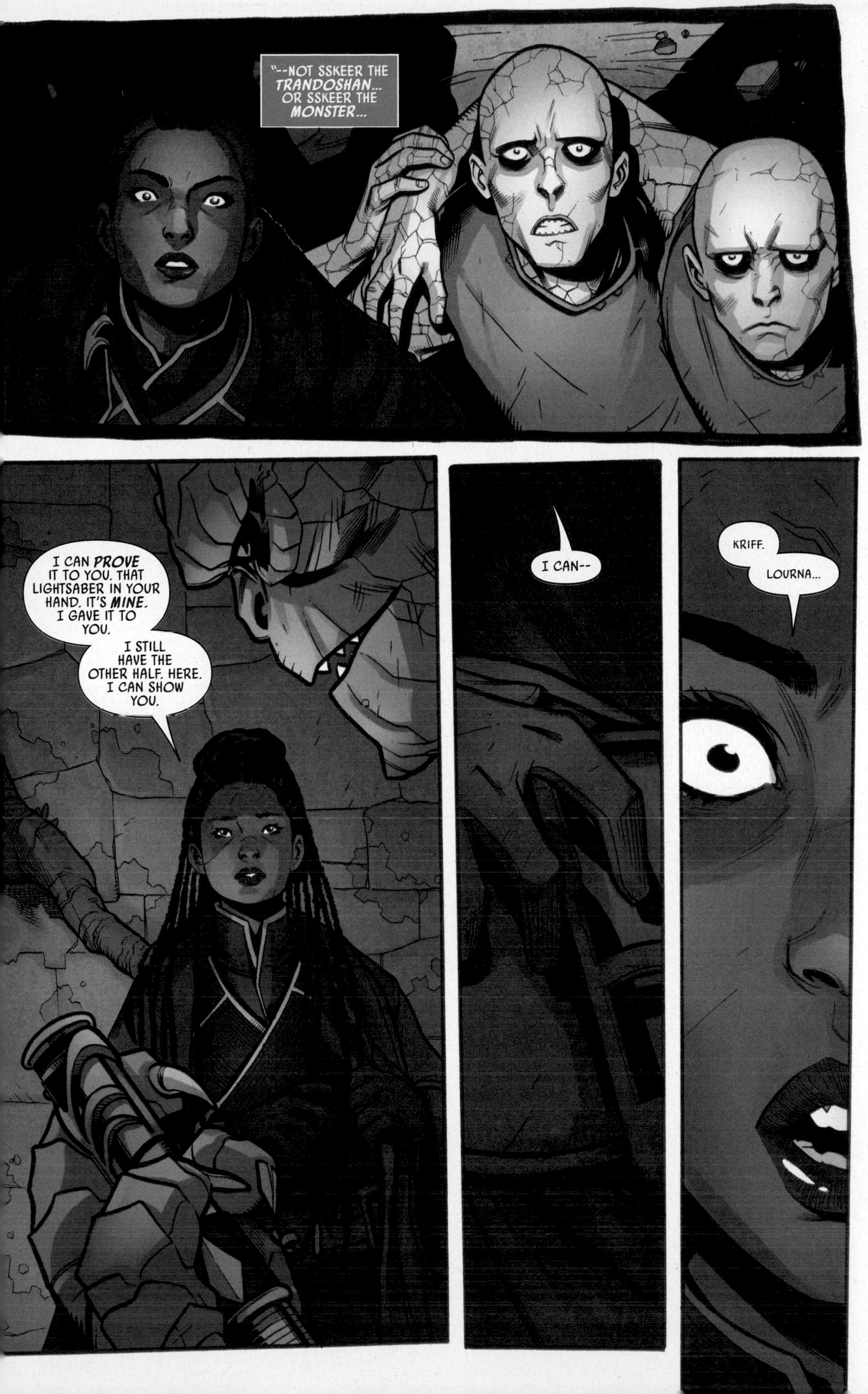
"--NOT SSKEER THE *TRANDOSHAN*... OR SSKEER THE *MONSTER*...
I CAN *PROVE* IT TO YOU. THAT LIGHTSABER IN YOUR HAND. IT'S *MINE.* I GAVE IT TO YOU.
I STILL HAVE THE OTHER HALF. HERE. I CAN SHOW YOU.
I CAN--
KRIFF.
LOURNA...

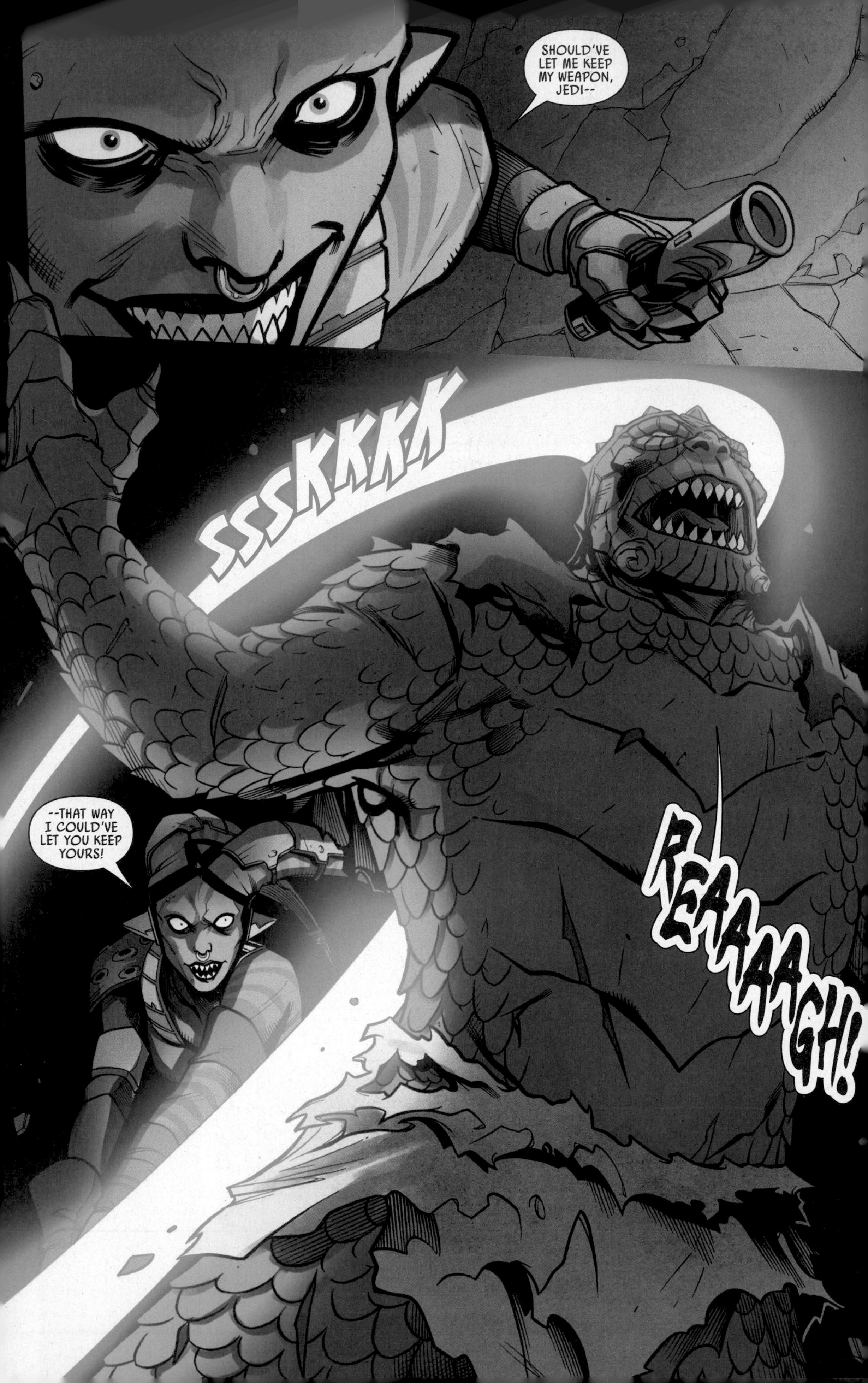
SHOULD'VE LET ME KEEP MY WEAPON, JEDI--
SSSKKKK
--THAT WAY I COULD'VE LET YOU KEEP YOURS!
REAAAAGH!

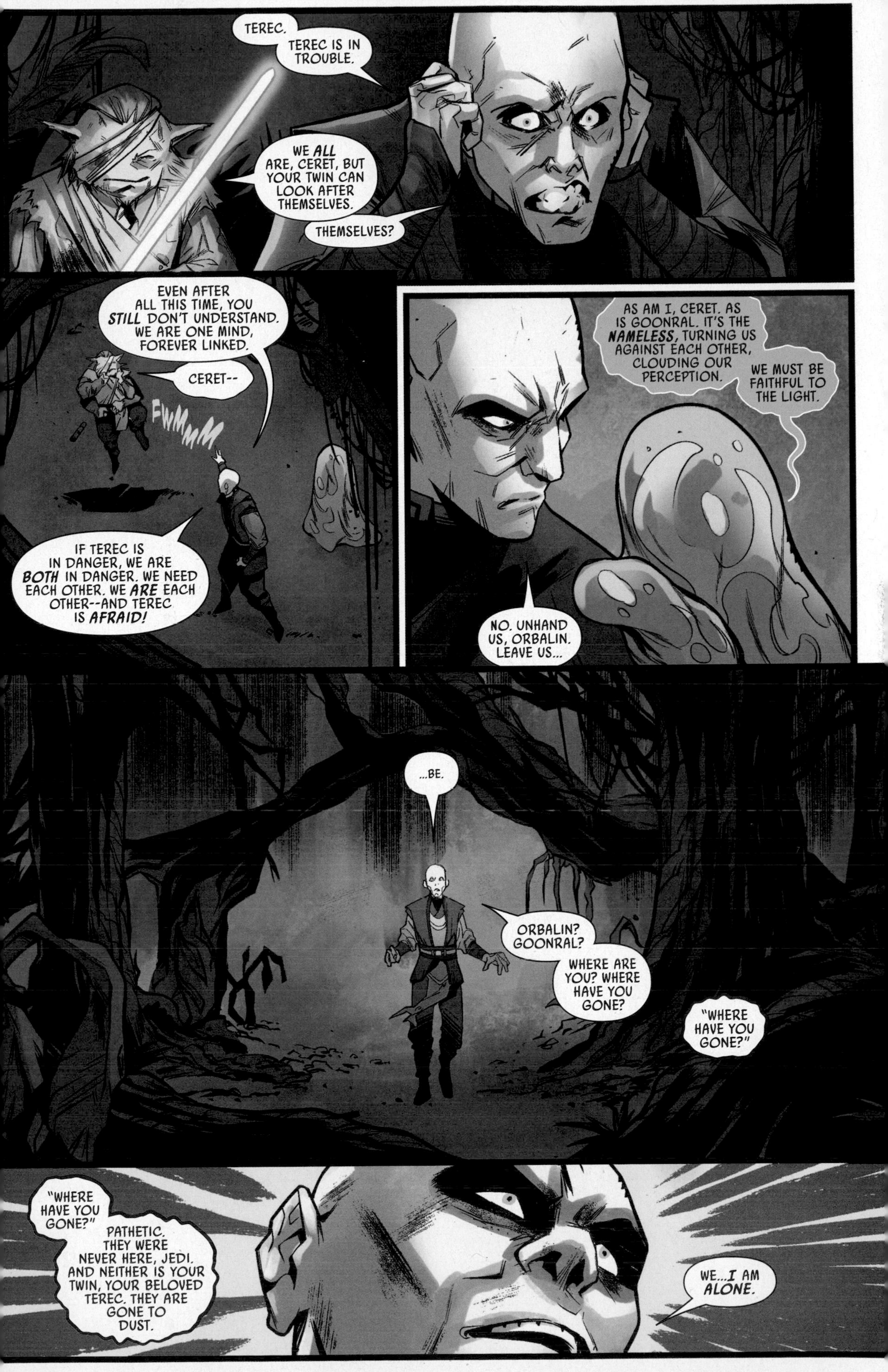
TEREC.
TEREC IS IN TROUBLE.
WE ALL ARE, CERET, BUT YOUR TWIN CAN LOOK AFTER THEMSELVES.
THEMSELVES?
EVEN AFTER ALL THIS TIME, YOU STILL DON'T UNDERSTAND. WE ARE ONE MIND, FOREVER LINKED.
CERET--
FWMMM
IF TEREC IS IN DANGER, WE ARE BOTH IN DANGER. WE NEED EACH OTHER. WE ARE EACH OTHER--AND TEREC IS AFRAID!
AS AM I, CERET. AS IS GOONRAL. IT'S THE NAMELESS, TURNING US AGAINST EACH OTHER, CLOUDING OUR PERCEPTION.
WE MUST BE FAITHFUL TO THE LIGHT.
NO. UNHAND US, ORBALIN. LEAVE US...
...BE.
ORBALIN? GOONRAL?
WHERE ARE YOU? WHERE HAVE YOU GONE?
"WHERE HAVE YOU GONE?"
"WHERE HAVE YOU GONE?"
PATHETIC. THEY WERE NEVER HERE, JEDI. AND NEITHER IS YOUR TWIN, YOUR BELOVED TEREC. THEY ARE GONE TO DUST.
WE...I AM ALONE.

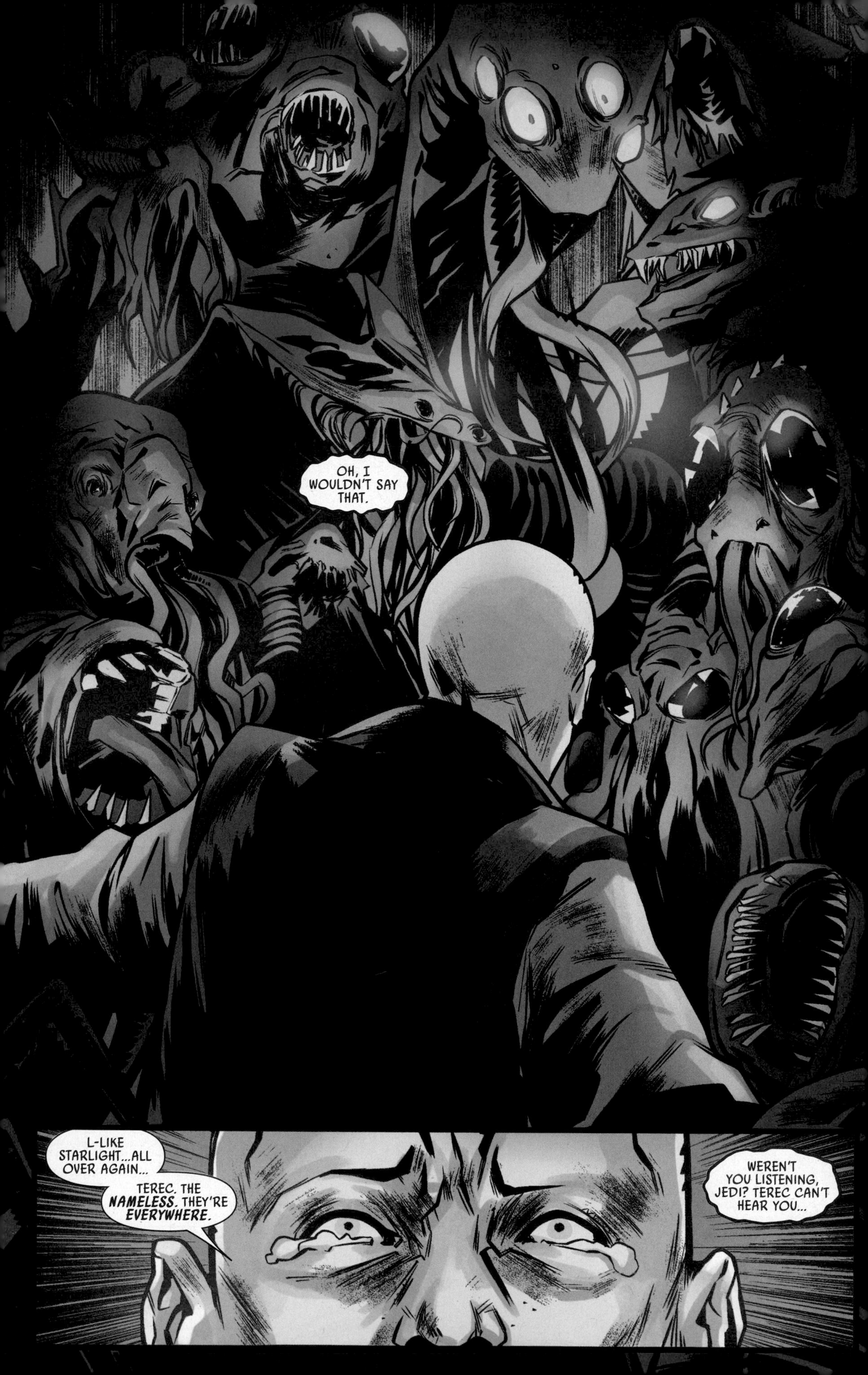
OH, I WOULDN'T SAY THAT.
L-LIKE STARLIGHT...ALL OVER AGAIN...
TEREC. THE *NAMELESS*. THEY'RE *EVERYWHERE*.
WEREN'T YOU LISTENING, JEDI? TEREC CAN'T HEAR YOU...

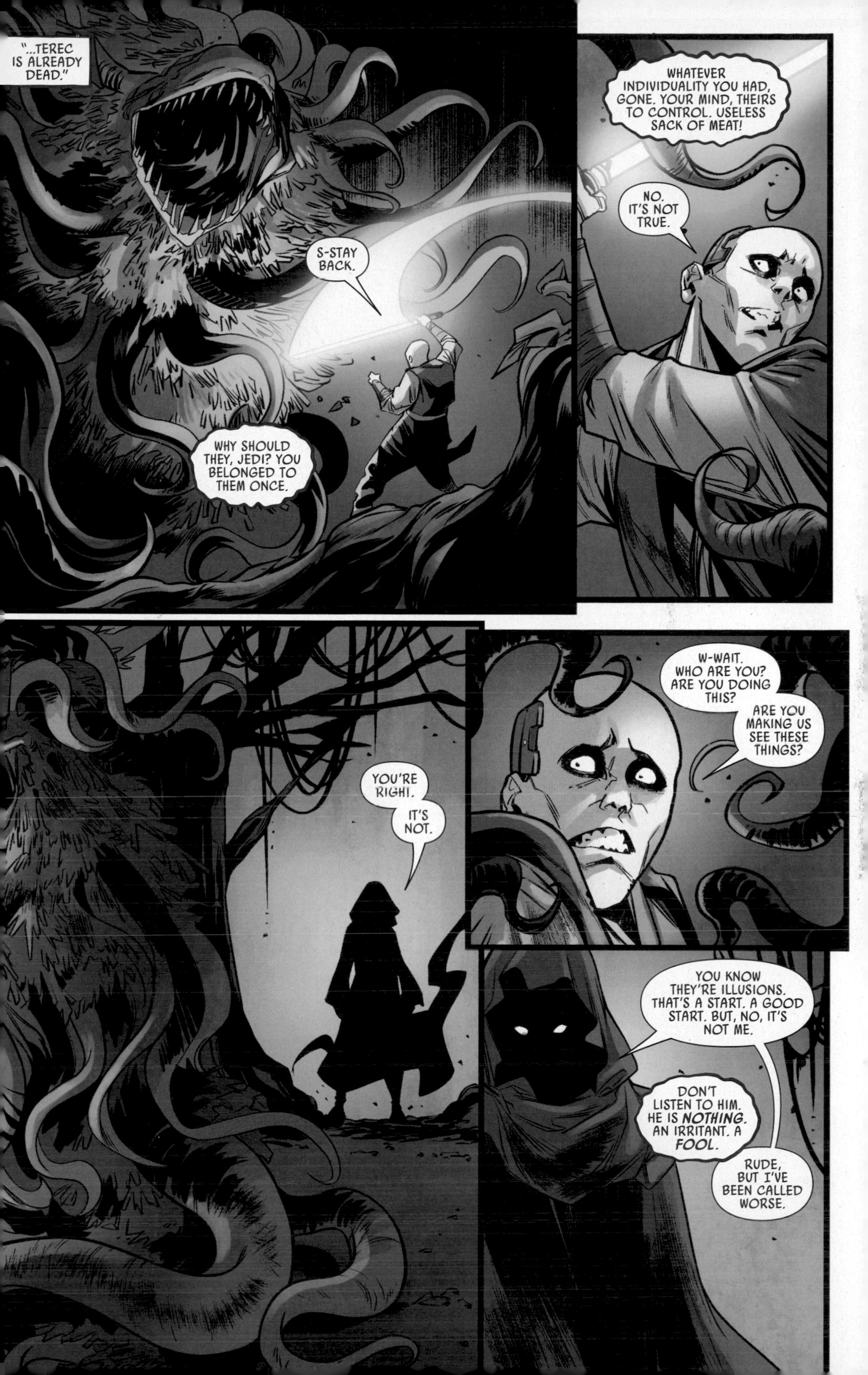
"...TEREC IS ALREADY DEAD."
S-STAY BACK.
WHY SHOULD THEY, JEDI? YOU BELONGED TO THEM ONCE.
WHATEVER INDIVIDUALITY YOU HAD, GONE. YOUR MIND, THEIRS TO CONTROL. USELESS SACK OF MEAT!
NO. IT'S NOT TRUE.
YOU'RE RIGHT.
IT'S NOT.
W-WAIT. WHO ARE YOU? ARE YOU DOING THIS?
ARE YOU MAKING US SEE THESE THINGS?
YOU KNOW THEY'RE ILLUSIONS. THAT'S A START. A GOOD START. BUT, NO, IT'S NOT ME.
DON'T LISTEN TO HIM. HE IS *NOTHING.* AN IRRITANT. A *FOOL.*
RUDE, BUT I'VE BEEN CALLED WORSE.

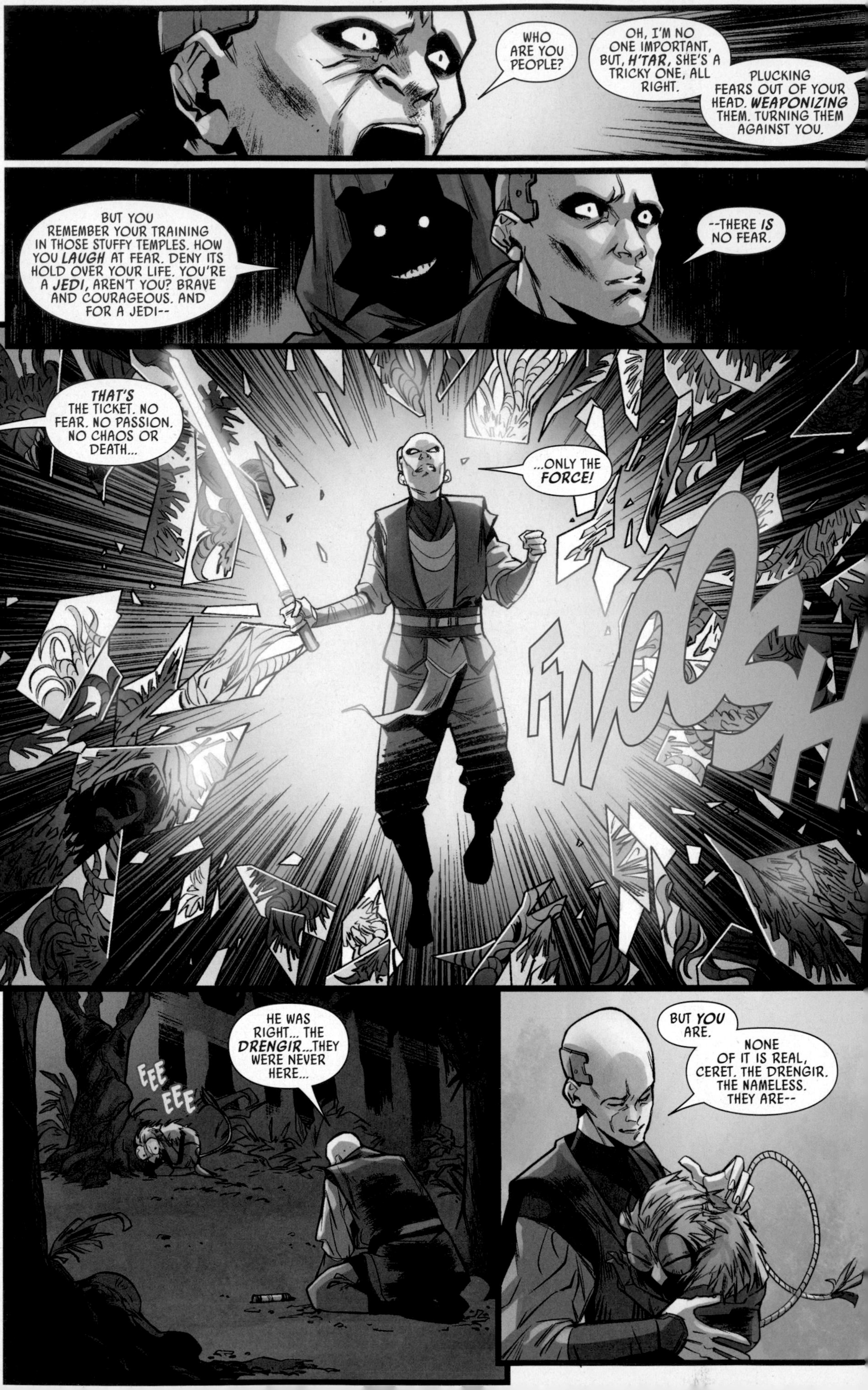
WHO ARE YOU PEOPLE?
OH, I'M NO ONE IMPORTANT, BUT, H'TAR, SHE'S A TRICKY ONE, ALL RIGHT.
PLUCKING FEARS OUT OF YOUR HEAD. WEAPONIZING THEM. TURNING THEM AGAINST YOU.
BUT YOU REMEMBER YOUR TRAINING IN THOSE STUFFY TEMPLES. HOW YOU LAUGH AT FEAR. DENY ITS HOLD OVER YOUR LIFE. YOU'RE A JEDI, AREN'T YOU? BRAVE AND COURAGEOUS. AND FOR A JEDI--
--THERE IS NO FEAR.
THAT'S THE TICKET. NO FEAR. NO PASSION. NO CHAOS OR DEATH...
...ONLY THE FORCE!
FWOOSH
HE WAS RIGHT... THE DRENGIR...THEY WERE NEVER HERE...
EEE
EEE
BUT YOU ARE.
NONE OF IT IS REAL, CERET. THE DRENGIR. THE NAMELESS. THEY ARE--

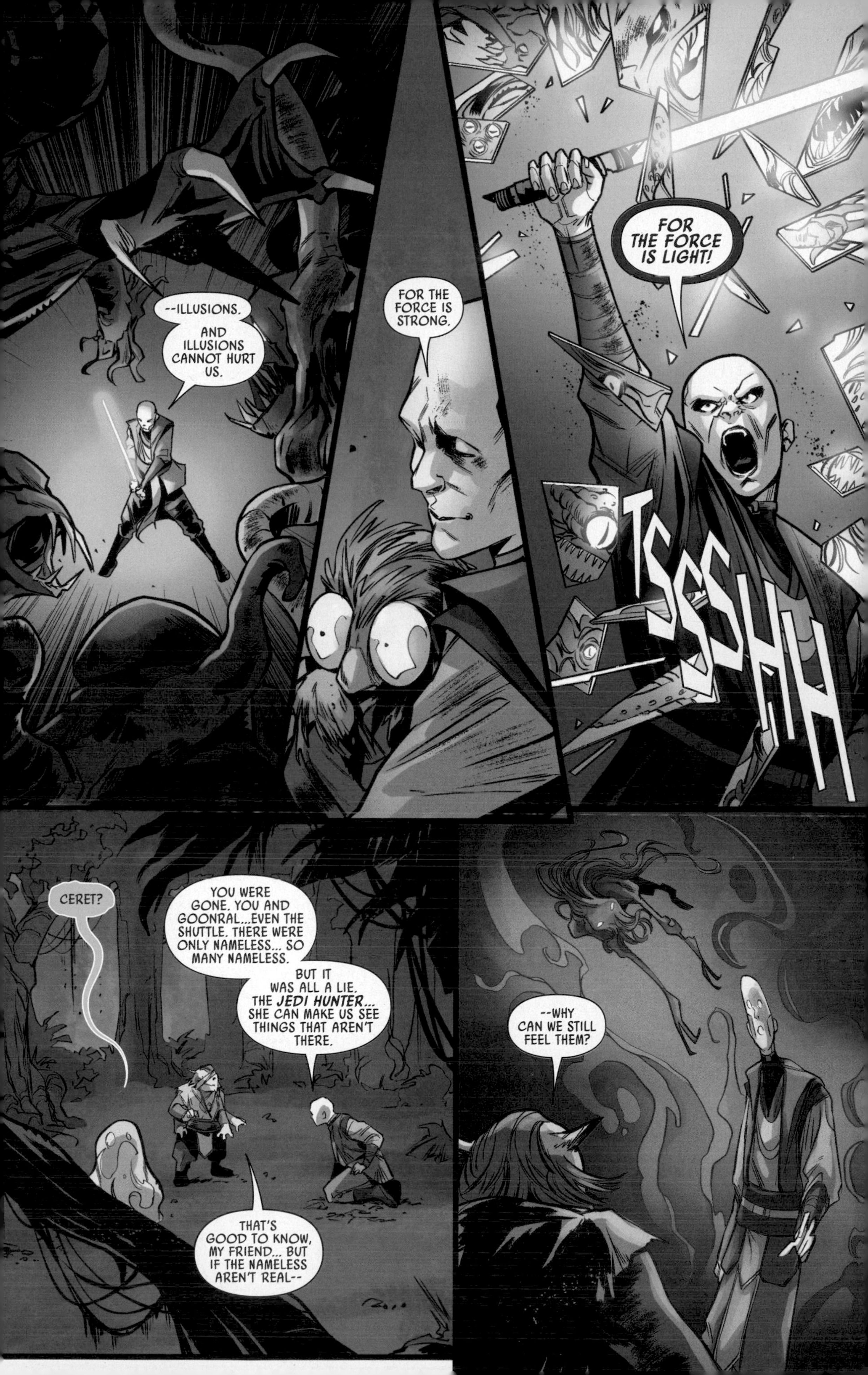
--ILLUSIONS.
AND ILLUSIONS CANNOT HURT US.
FOR THE FORCE IS STRONG.
FOR THE FORCE IS LIGHT!
TSSSHHH
CERET?
YOU WERE GONE. YOU AND GOONRAL...EVEN THE SHUTTLE. THERE WERE ONLY NAMELESS... SO MANY NAMELESS.
BUT IT WAS ALL A LIE. THE *JEDI HUNTER*... SHE CAN MAKE US SEE THINGS THAT AREN'T THERE.
THAT'S GOOD TO KNOW, MY FRIEND... BUT IF THE NAMELESS AREN'T REAL--
--WHY CAN WE STILL FEEL THEM?

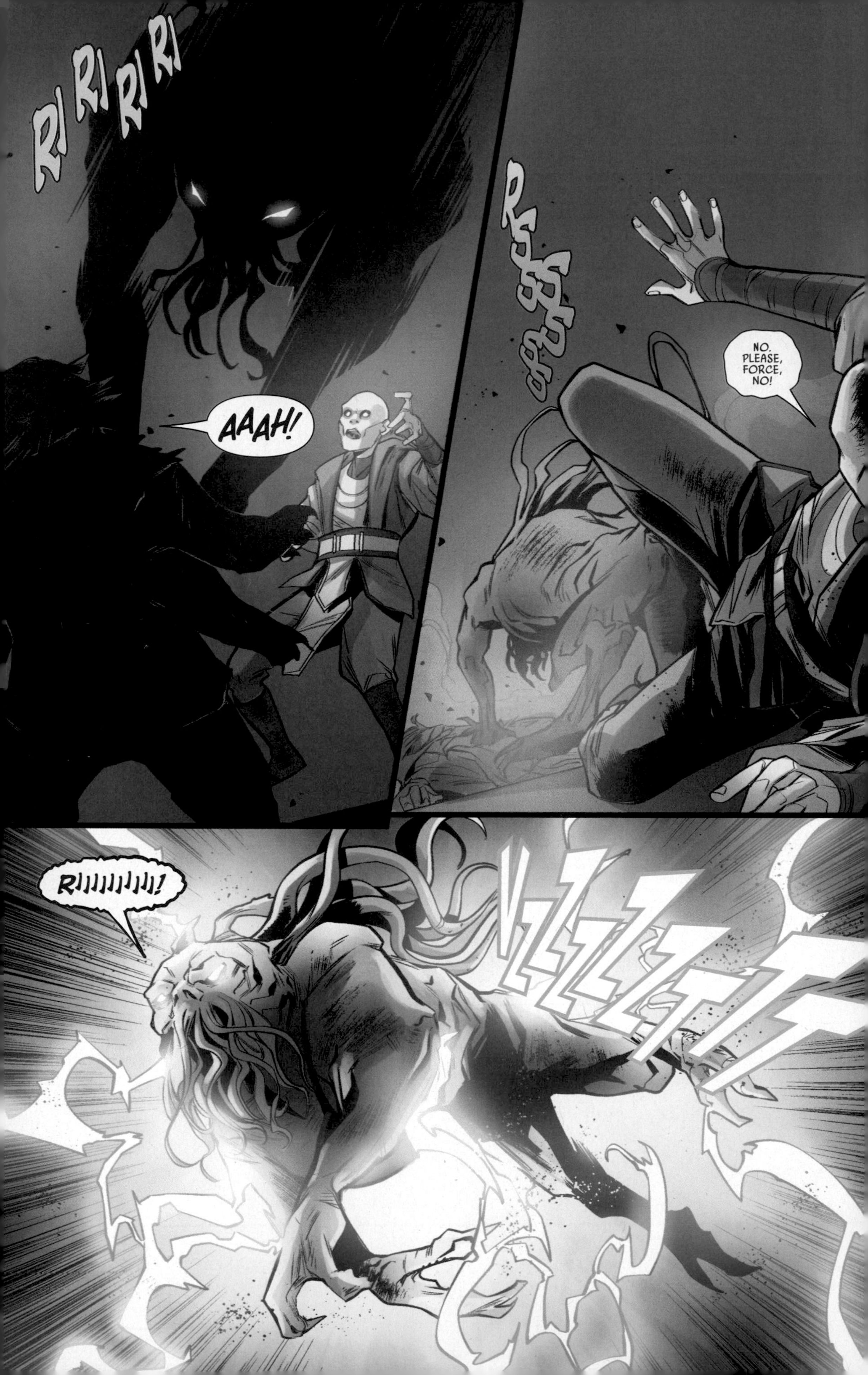

RI RI RI RI
AAAH!
RSSSSSS
NO. PLEASE, FORCE, NO!
RIIIIIIII!
VZZZZTT

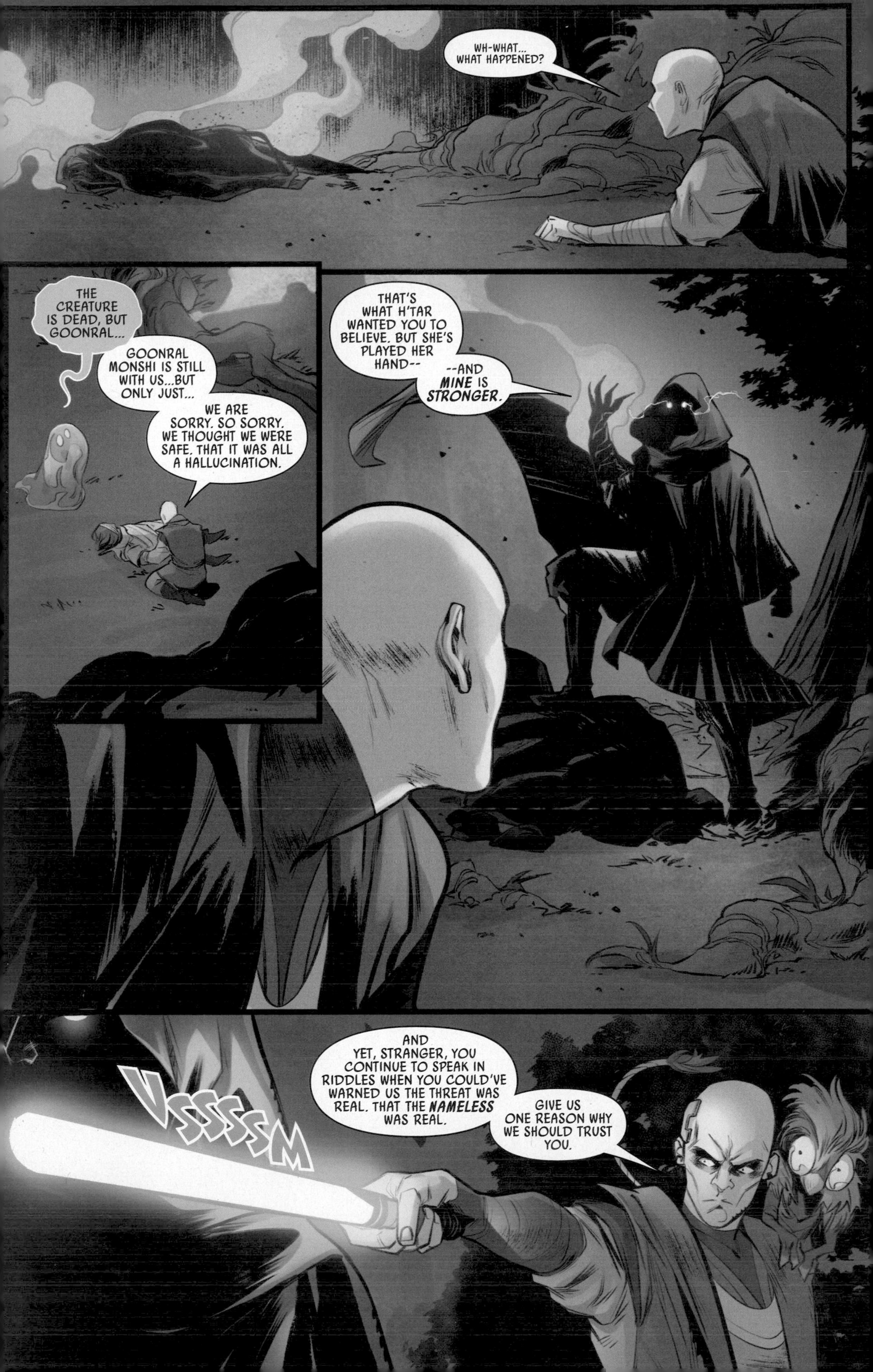
WH-WHAT... WHAT HAPPENED?
THE CREATURE IS DEAD, BUT GOONRAL...
GOONRAL MONSHI IS STILL WITH US...BUT ONLY JUST...
WE ARE SORRY. SO SORRY. WE THOUGHT WE WERE SAFE. THAT IT WAS ALL A HALLUCINATION.
THAT'S WHAT H'TAR WANTED YOU TO BELIEVE. BUT SHE'S PLAYED HER HAND--
--AND MINE IS STRONGER.
VSSSSM
AND YET, STRANGER, YOU CONTINUE TO SPEAK IN RIDDLES WHEN YOU COULD'VE WARNED US THE THREAT WAS REAL. THAT THE NAMELESS WAS REAL.
GIVE US ONE REASON WHY WE SHOULD TRUST YOU.

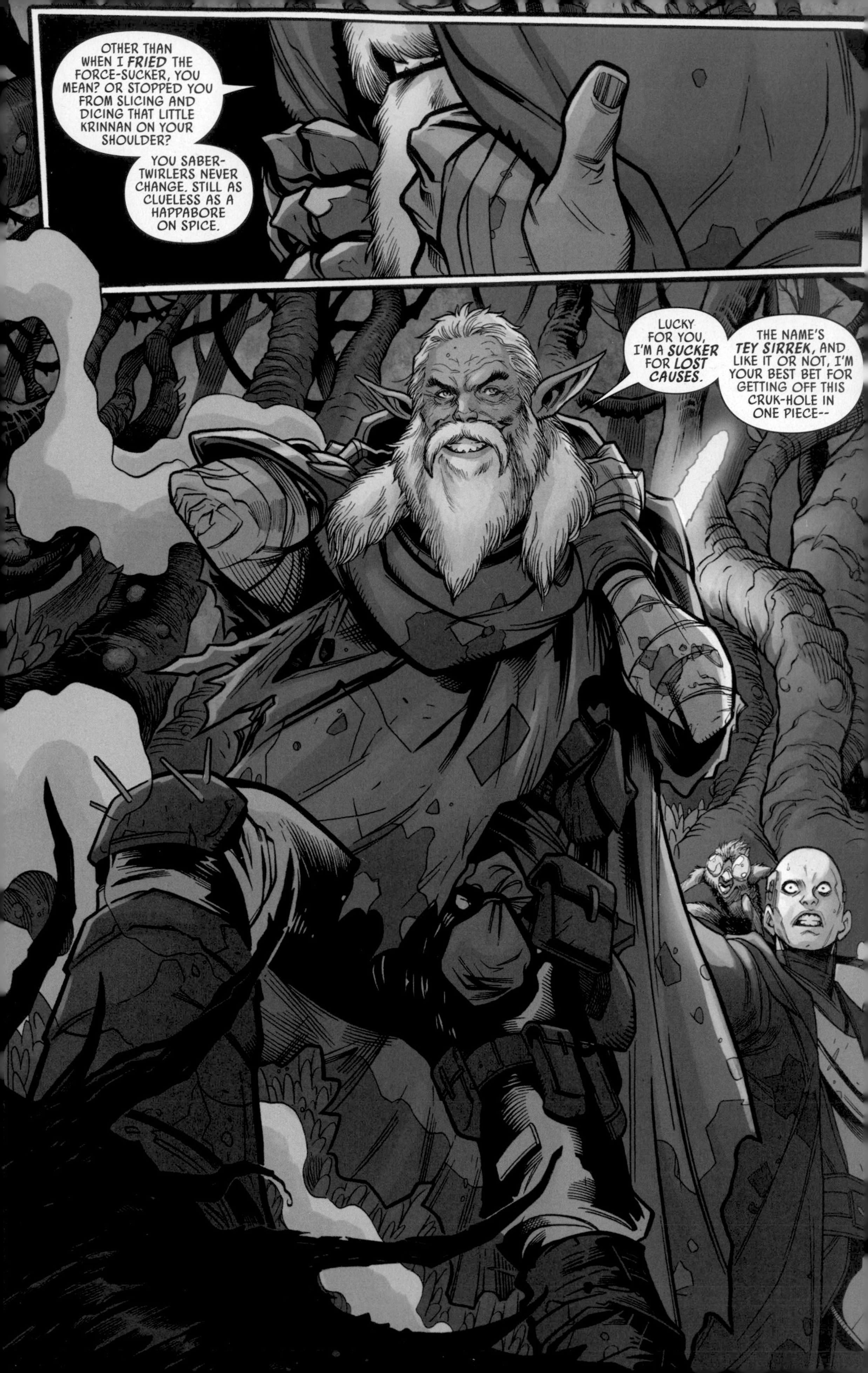
OTHER THAN WHEN I FRIED THE FORCE-SUCKER, YOU MEAN? OR STOPPED YOU FROM SLICING AND DICING THAT LITTLE KRINNAN ON YOUR SHOULDER?
YOU SABER-TWIRLERS NEVER CHANGE. STILL AS CLUELESS AS A HAPPABORE ON SPICE.
LUCKY FOR YOU, I'M A SUCKER FOR LOST CAUSES.
THE NAME'S TEY SIRREK, AND LIKE IT OR NOT, I'M YOUR BEST BET FOR GETTING OFF THIS CRUK-HOLE IN ONE PIECE--

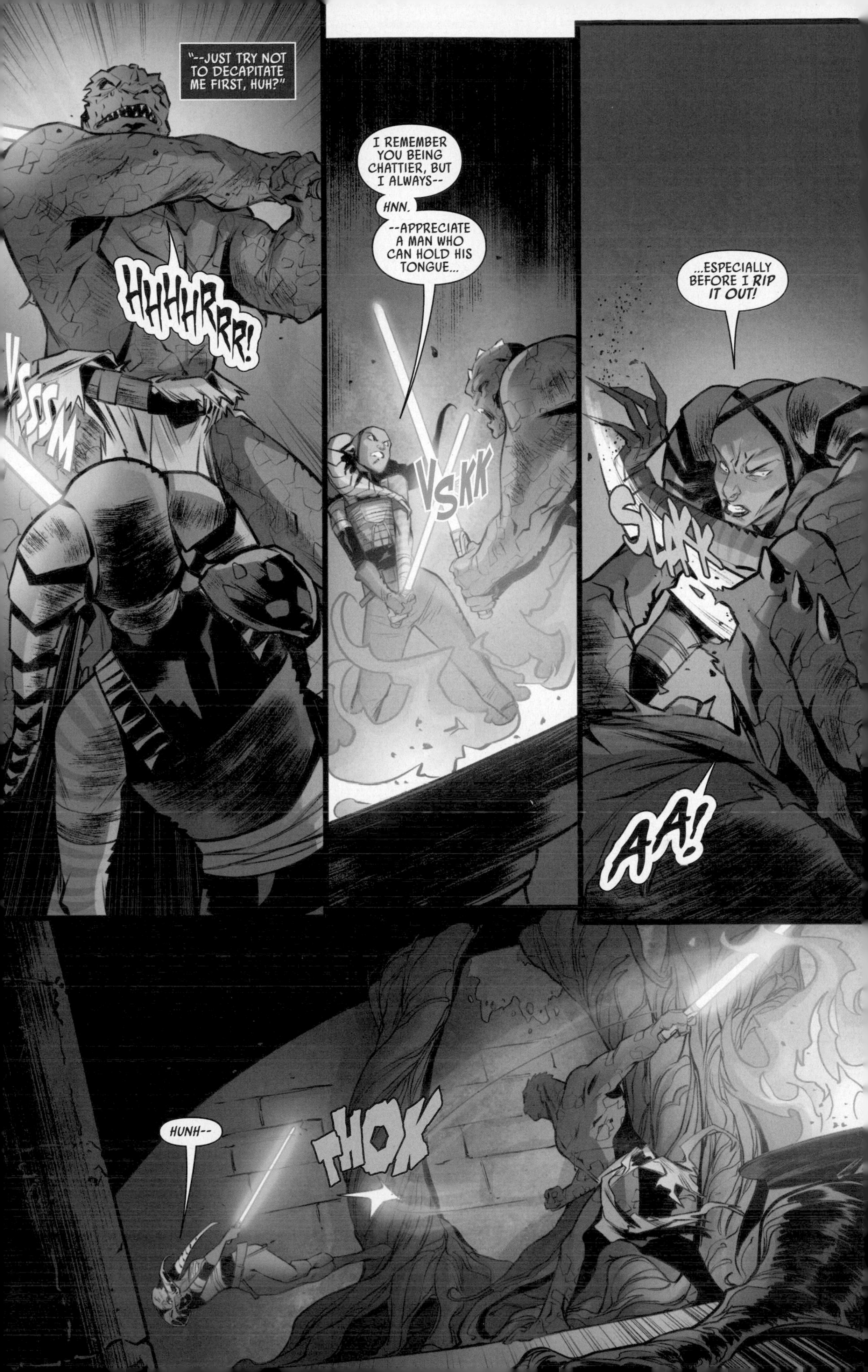
"--JUST TRY NOT TO DECAPITATE ME FIRST, HUH?"
HHHHRRRR!
VSSSM
I REMEMBER YOU BEING CHATTIER, BUT I ALWAYS--
HNN.
--APPRECIATE A MAN WHO CAN HOLD HIS TONGUE...
VSKK
...ESPECIALLY BEFORE I RIP IT OUT!
SLAKK
AA!
HUNH--
THOK

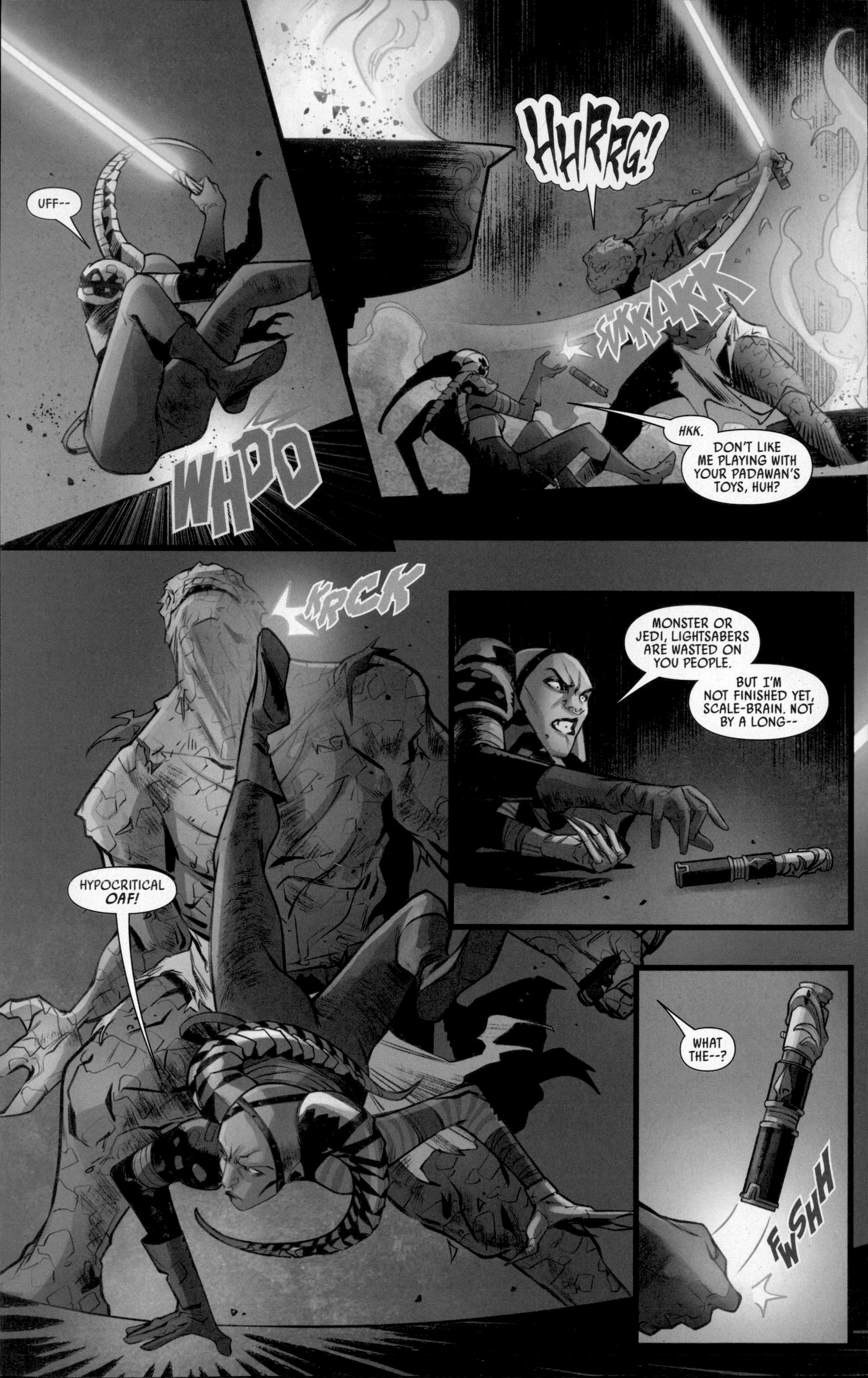
UFF--
WHDO
HURRG!
KKAKK
HKK.
DON'T LIKE ME PLAYING WITH YOUR PADAWAN'S TOYS, HUH?
KRCK
MONSTER OR JEDI, LIGHTSABERS ARE WASTED ON YOU PEOPLE.
BUT I'M NOT FINISHED YET, SCALE-BRAIN. NOT BY A LONG--
HYPOCRITICAL OAF!
WHAT THE--?
FWSHH

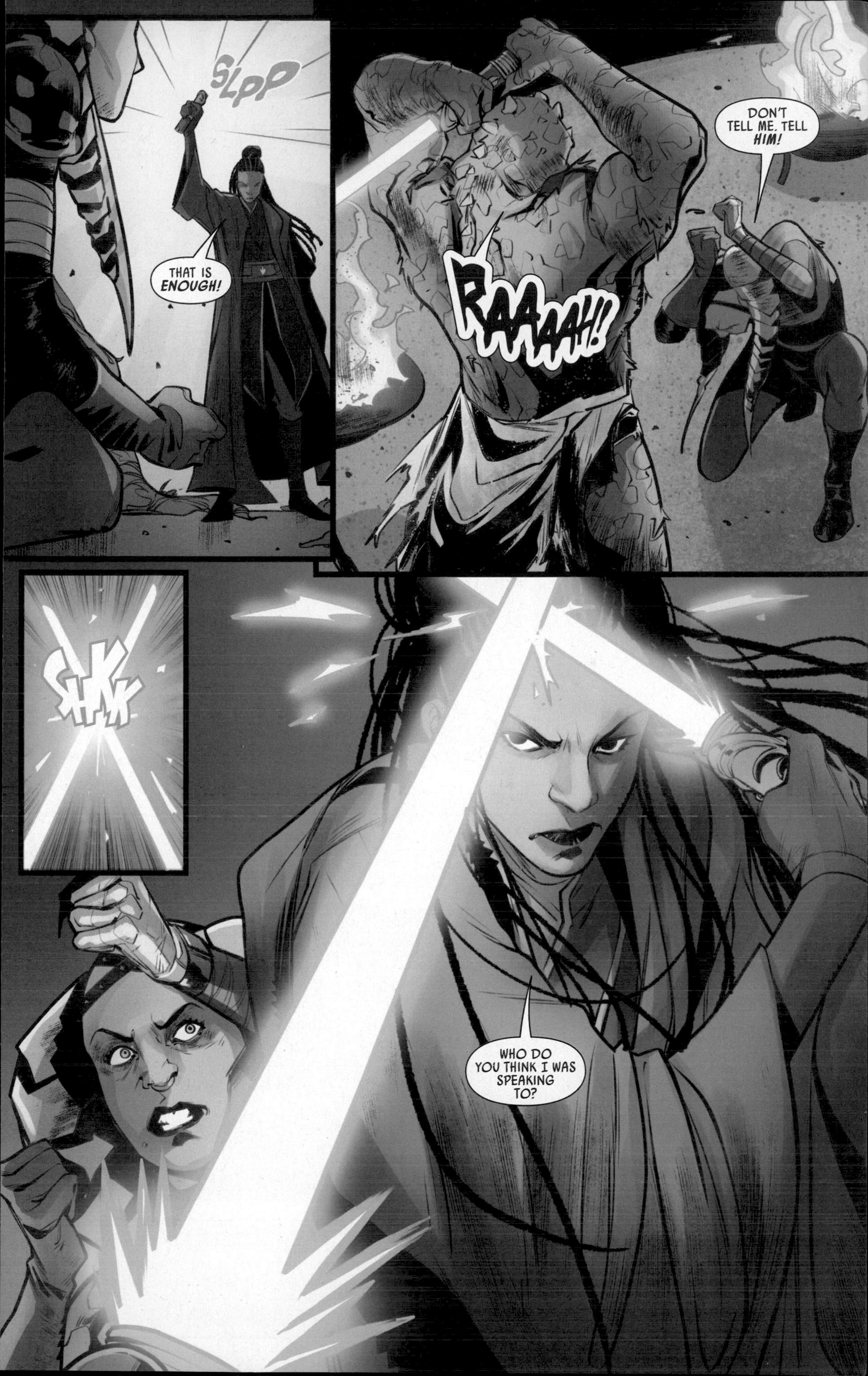
SLPP
THAT IS ENOUGH!
RAAAAH!!
DON'T TELL ME. TELL HIM!
SHKK
WHO DO YOU THINK I WAS SPEAKING TO?

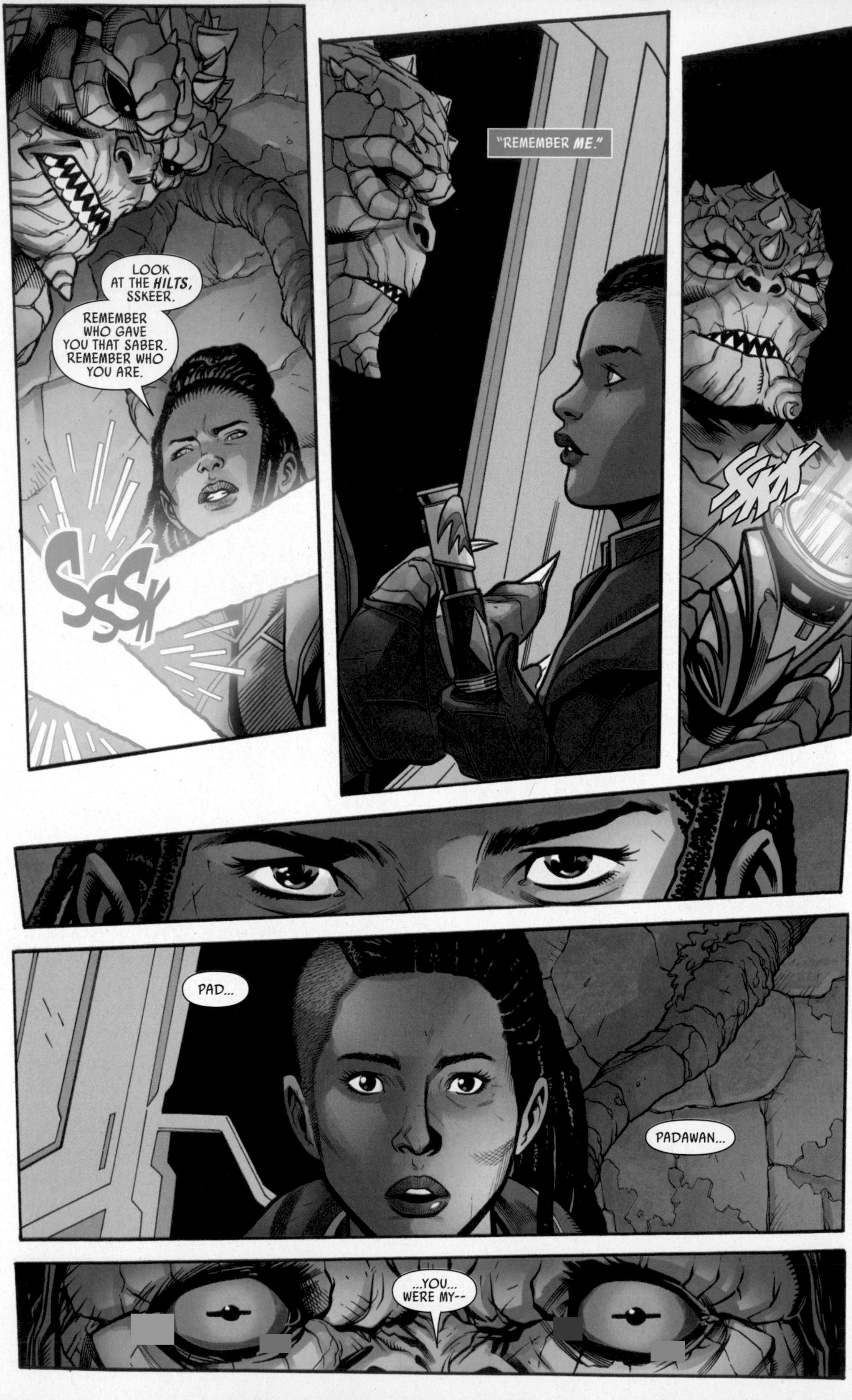
LOOK AT THE *HILTS*, SSKEER.
REMEMBER WHO GAVE YOU THAT SABER. REMEMBER WHO YOU ARE.
SSSK
"REMEMBER *ME*."
PAD...
PADAWAN...
...YOU... WERE MY--

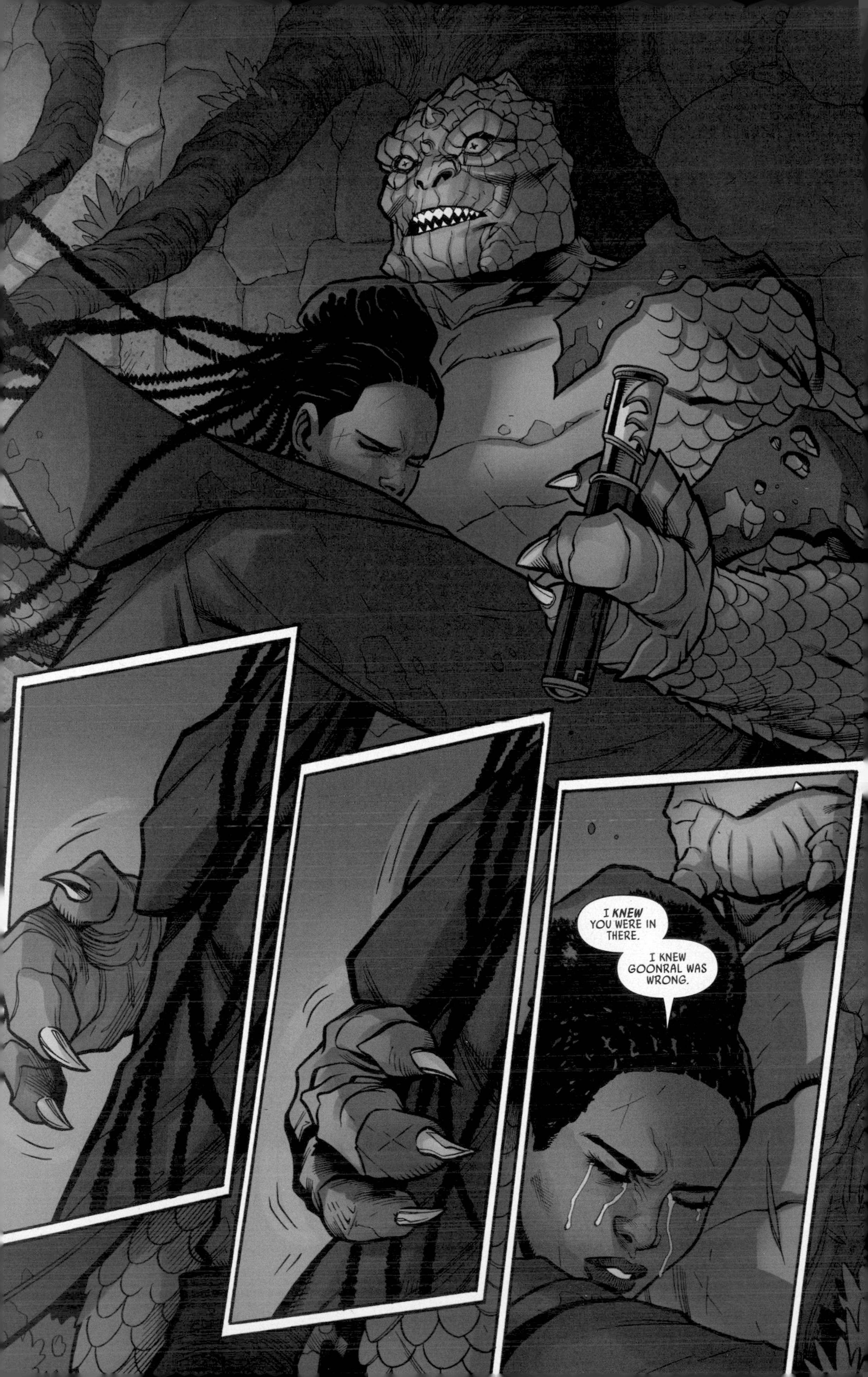
I KNEW YOU WERE IN THERE.
I KNEW GOONRAL WAS WRONG.

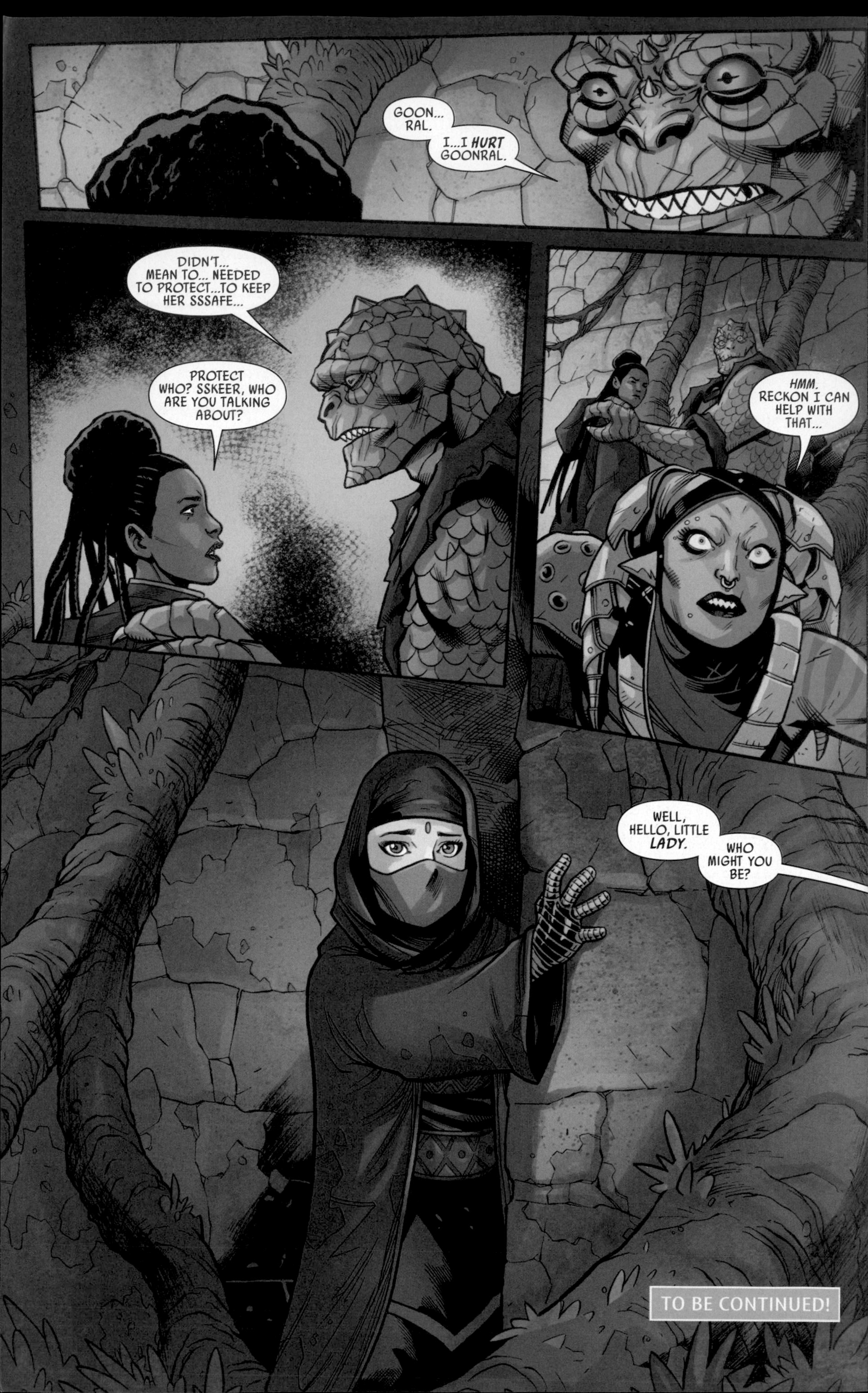
GOON... RAL.
I...I HURT GOONRAL.
DIDN'T... MEAN TO... NEEDED TO PROTECT...TO KEEP HER SSSAFE...
PROTECT WHO? SSKEER, WHO ARE YOU TALKING ABOUT?
HMM. RECKON I CAN HELP WITH THAT...
WELL, HELLO, LITTLE LADY.
WHO MIGHT YOU BE?
TO BE CONTINUED!

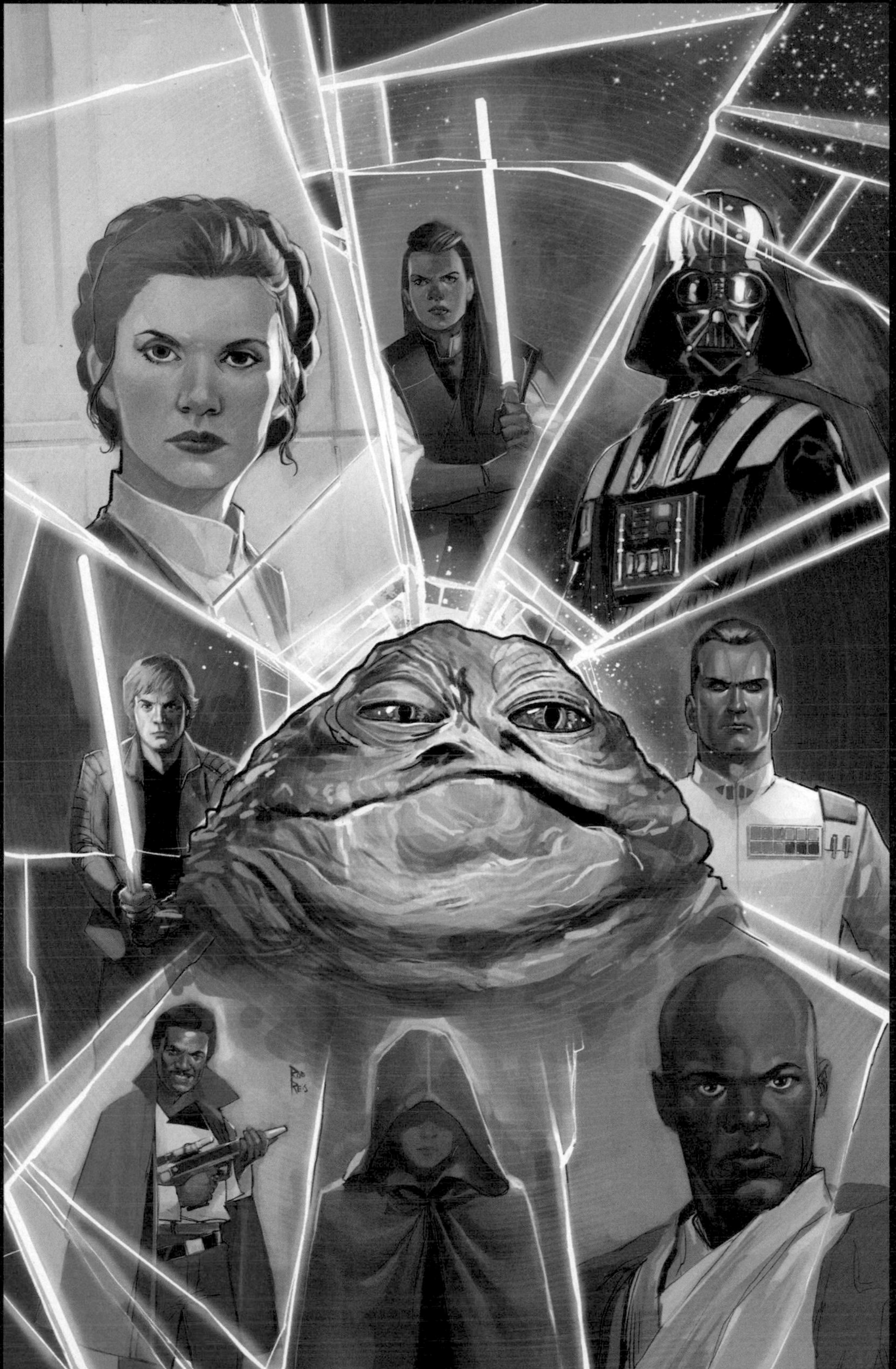

REVELATIONS | ALL THE REPUBLIC

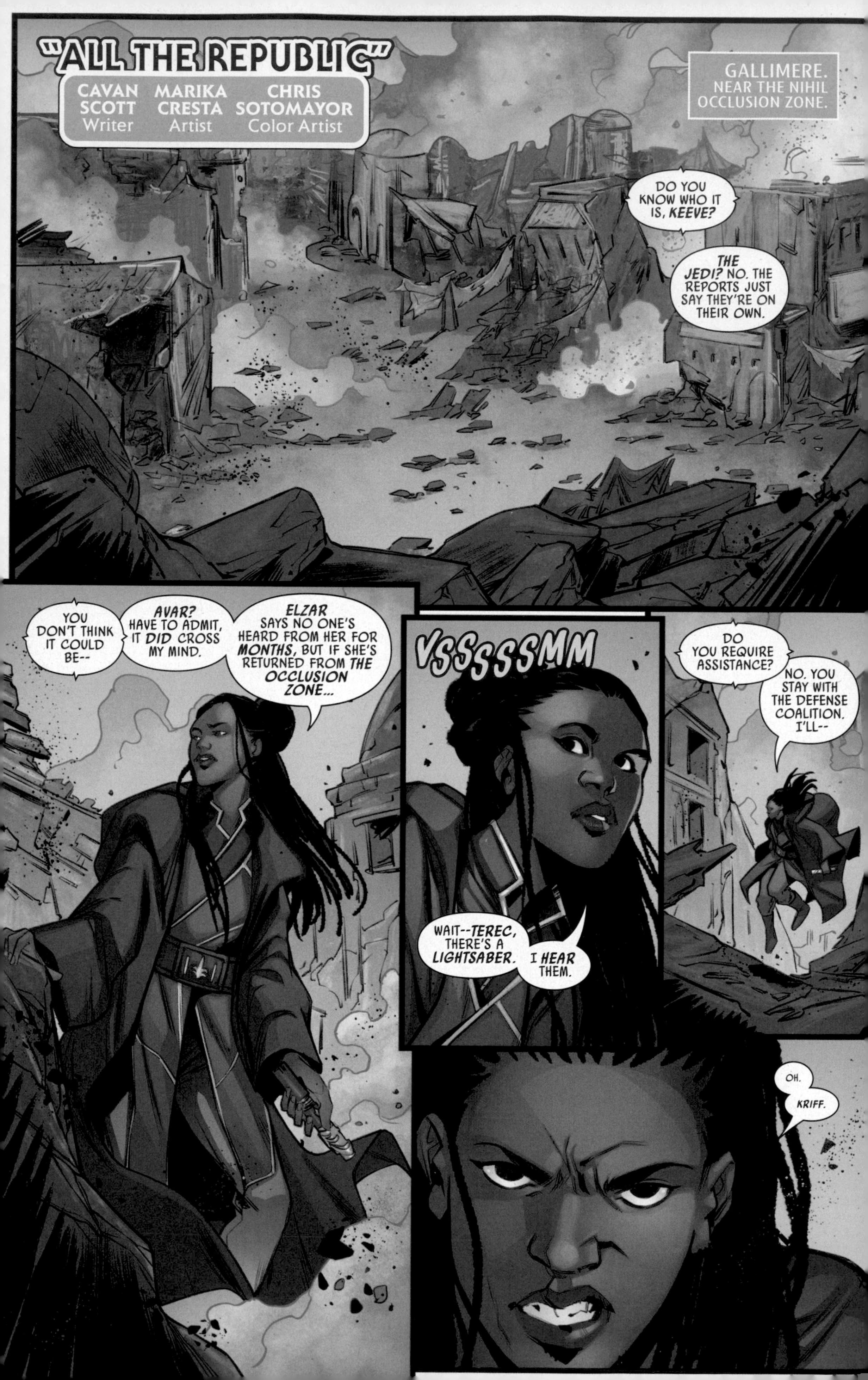
"ALL THE REPUBLIC"
CAVAN SCOTT Writer
MARIKA CRESTA Artist
CHRIS SOTOMAYOR Color Artist
GALLIMERE. NEAR THE NIHIL OCCLUSION ZONE.
DO YOU KNOW WHO IT IS, KEEVE?
THE JEDI? NO. THE REPORTS JUST SAY THEY'RE ON THEIR OWN.
YOU DON'T THINK IT COULD BE--
AVAR? HAVE TO ADMIT, IT DID CROSS MY MIND.
ELZAR SAYS NO ONE'S HEARD FROM HER FOR MONTHS, BUT IF SHE'S RETURNED FROM THE OCCLUSION ZONE...
VSSSSSMM
WAIT--TEREC, THERE'S A LIGHTSABER.
I HEAR THEM.
DO YOU REQUIRE ASSISTANCE?
NO. YOU STAY WITH THE DEFENSE COALITION. I'LL--
OH.
KRIFF.

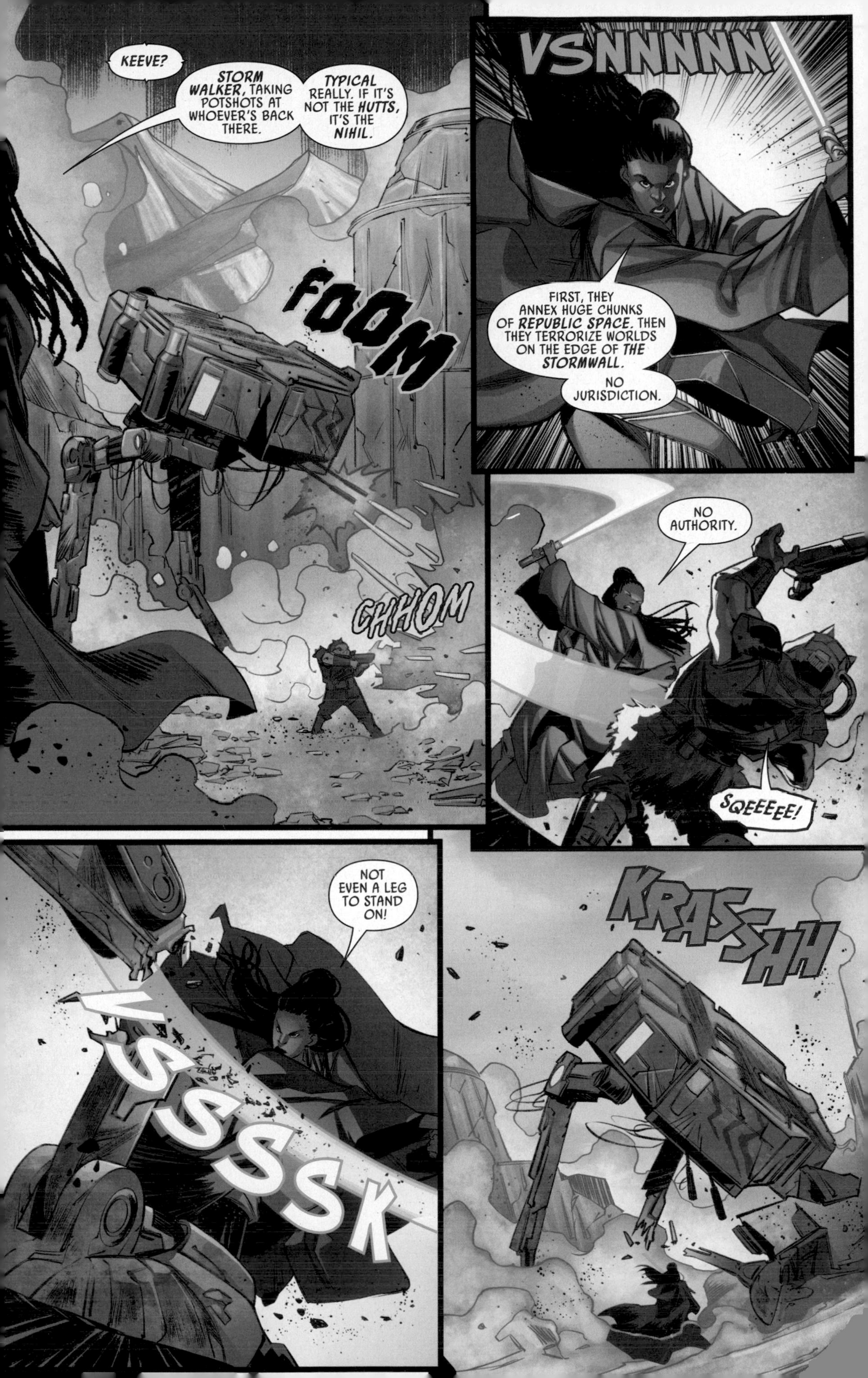
KEEVE?
STORM WALKER, TAKING POTSHOTS AT WHOEVER'S BACK THERE.
TYPICAL REALLY. IF IT'S NOT THE HUTTS, IT'S THE NIHIL.
FOOM
CHHOM
VSNNNNN
FIRST, THEY ANNEX HUGE CHUNKS OF REPUBLIC SPACE. THEN THEY TERRORIZE WORLDS ON THE EDGE OF THE STORMWALL.
NO JURISDICTION.
NO AUTHORITY.
SQEEEEE!
NOT EVEN A LEG TO STAND ON!
VSSSSK
KRASSHH

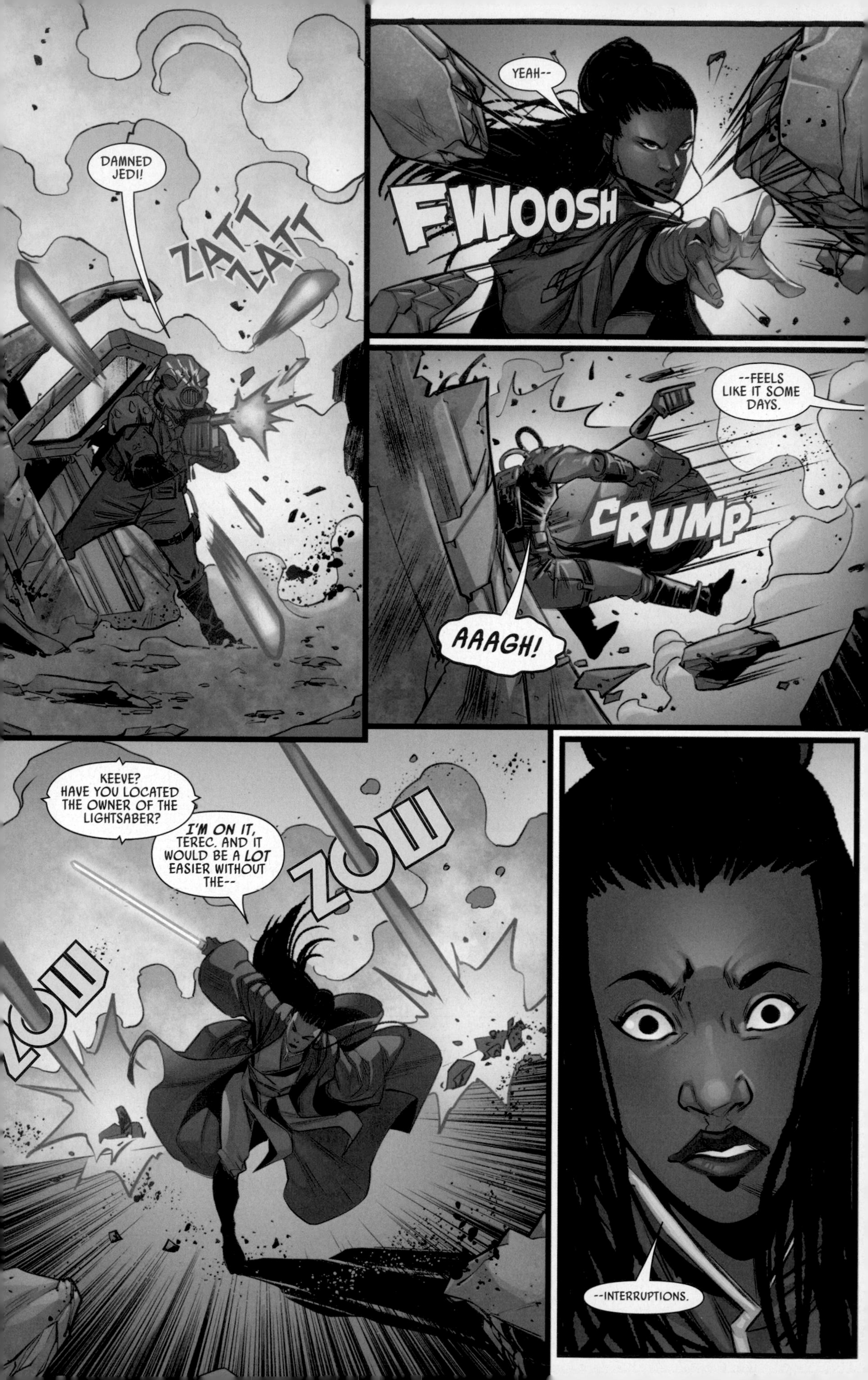
DAMNED JEDI!
ZATT ZATT
YEAH--
FWOOSH
--FEELS LIKE IT SOME DAYS.
CRUMP
AAAGH!
KEEVE? HAVE YOU LOCATED THE OWNER OF THE LIGHTSABER?
I'M ON IT, TEREC. AND IT WOULD BE A LOT EASIER WITHOUT THE--
ZOW
ZOW
--INTERRUPTIONS.

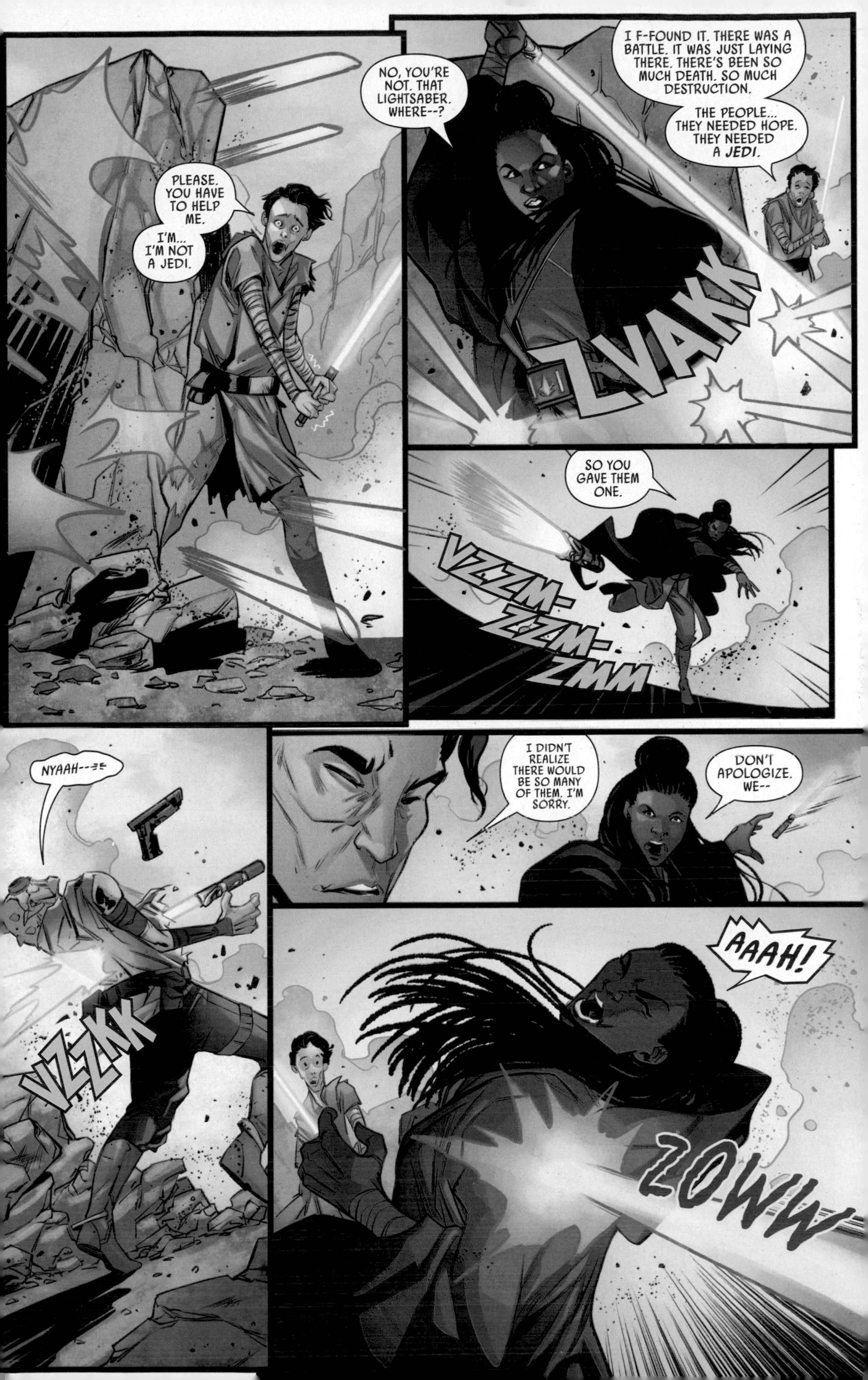
PLEASE. YOU HAVE TO HELP ME.
I'M... I'M NOT A JEDI.
NO, YOU'RE NOT. THAT LIGHTSABER. WHERE--?
I F-FOUND IT. THERE WAS A BATTLE. IT WAS JUST LAYING THERE. THERE'S BEEN SO MUCH DEATH. SO MUCH DESTRUCTION.
THE PEOPLE... THEY NEEDED HOPE. THEY NEEDED A JEDI.
ZVAKK
SO YOU GAVE THEM ONE.
VZZZM-ZZZM-ZMM
NYAAH--
VZZKK
I DIDN'T REALIZE THERE WOULD BE SO MANY OF THEM. I'M SORRY.
DON'T APOLOGIZE. WE--
AAAH!
ZOWW

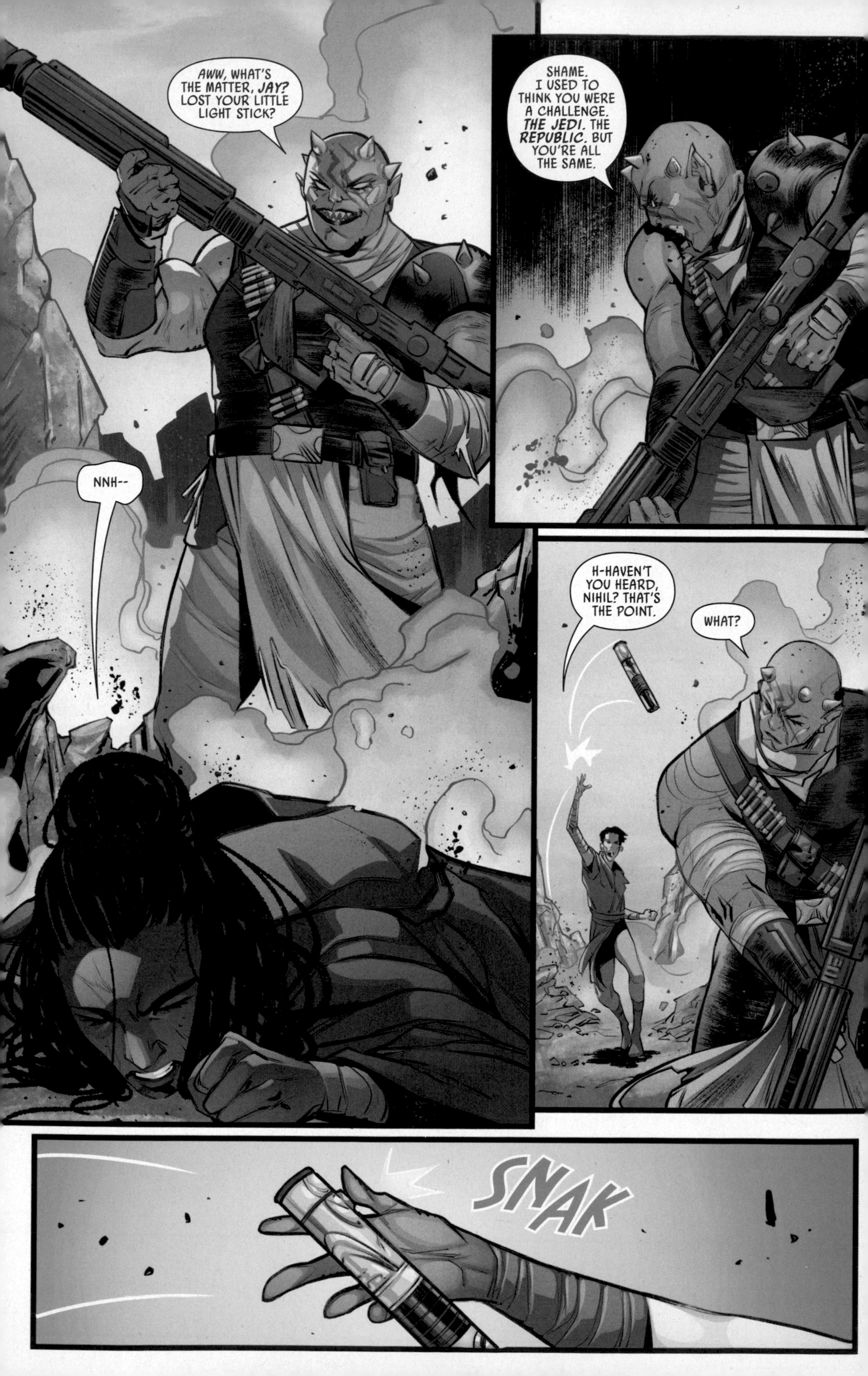
AWW, WHAT'S THE MATTER, JAY? LOST YOUR LITTLE LIGHT STICK?
SHAME. I USED TO THINK YOU WERE A CHALLENGE. THE JEDI. THE REPUBLIC. BUT YOU'RE ALL THE SAME.
NNH--
H-HAVEN'T YOU HEARD, NIHIL? THAT'S THE POINT.
WHAT?
SNAK

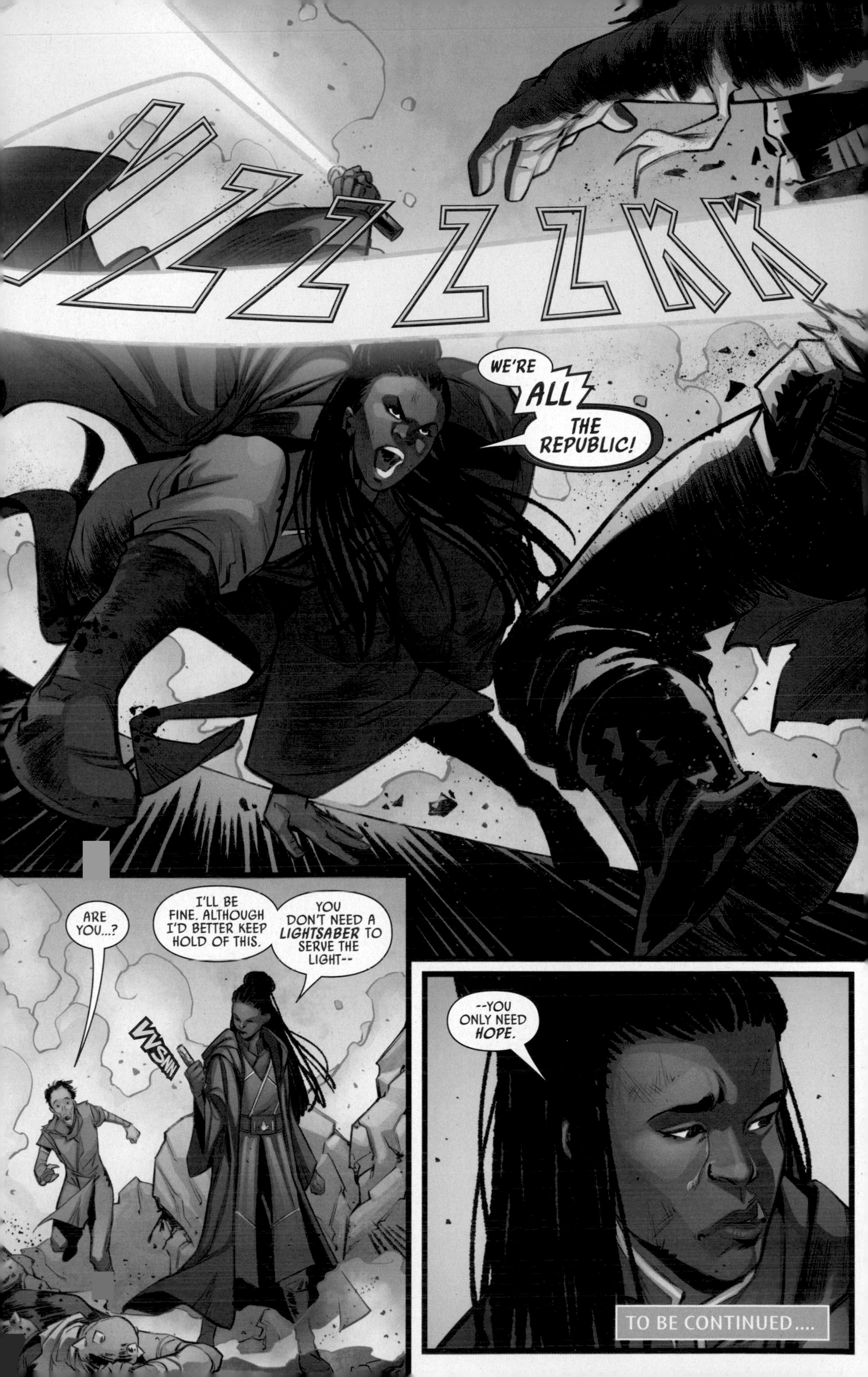
VZZZZKK
WE'RE ALL THE REPUBLIC!
ARE YOU...?
I'LL BE FINE. ALTHOUGH I'D BETTER KEEP HOLD OF THIS.
YOU DON'T NEED A LIGHTSABER TO SERVE THE LIGHT--
VVSNN
--YOU ONLY NEED HOPE.
TO BE CONTINUED....

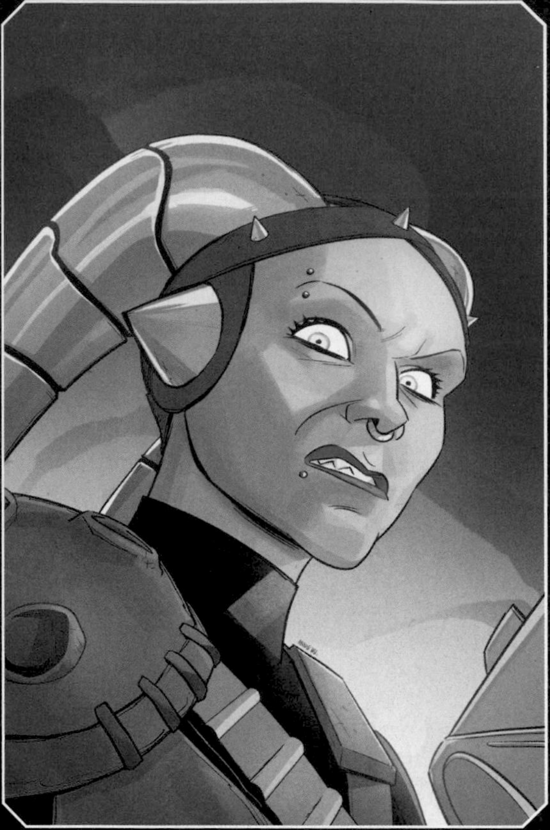

#3 Variant by
ANNIE WU

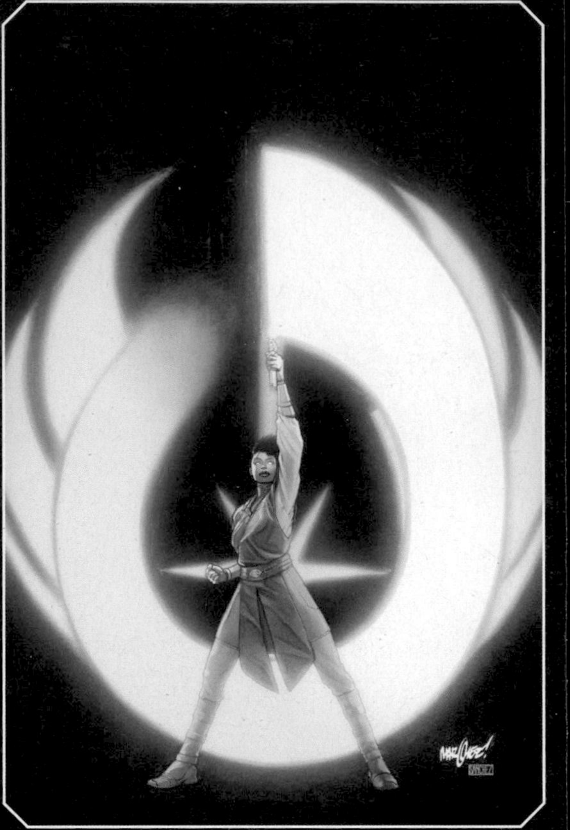

#3 Variant by
DAVID MARQUEZ

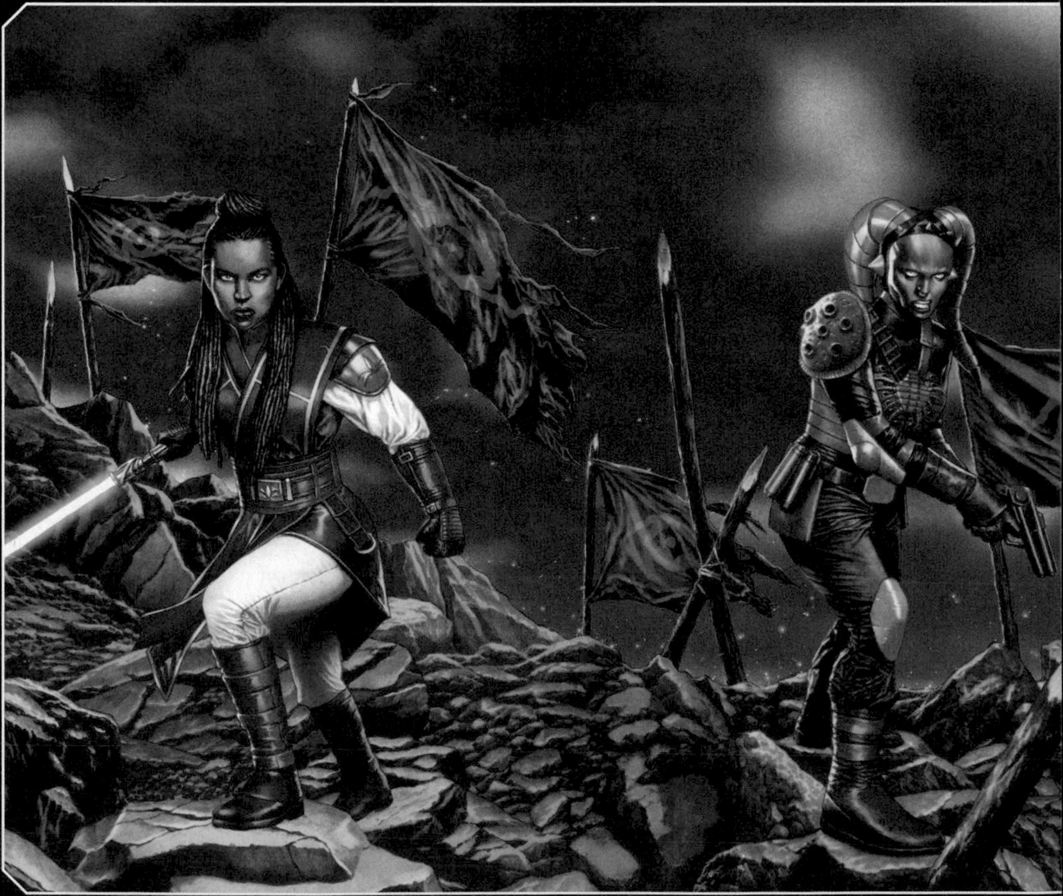

#1-4 Connecting Variants by
MICO SUAYAN & BRIAN REBER

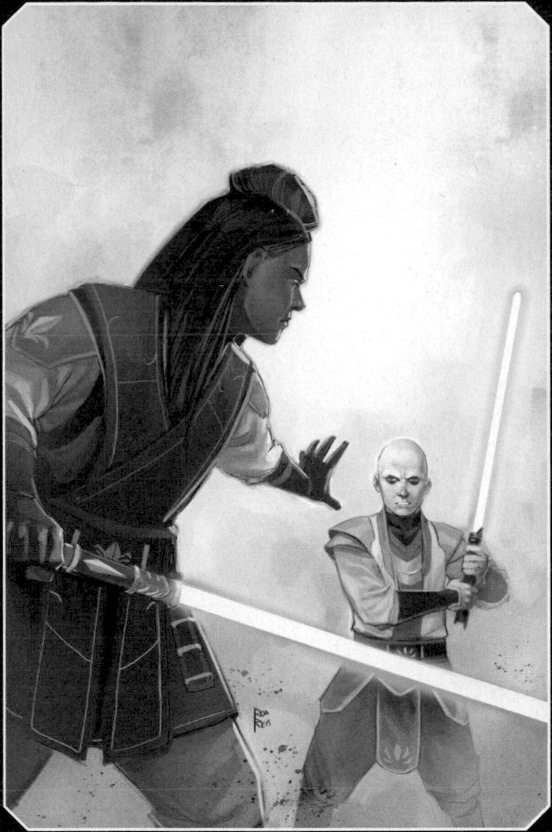

#4 Variant by
ROD REIS

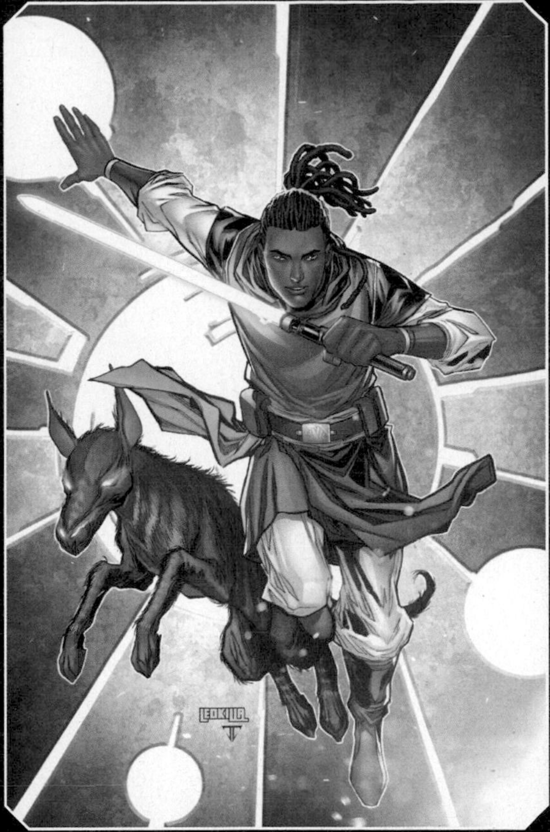

#4 Black History Month Variant by
KEN LASHLEY & JUAN FERNANDEZ

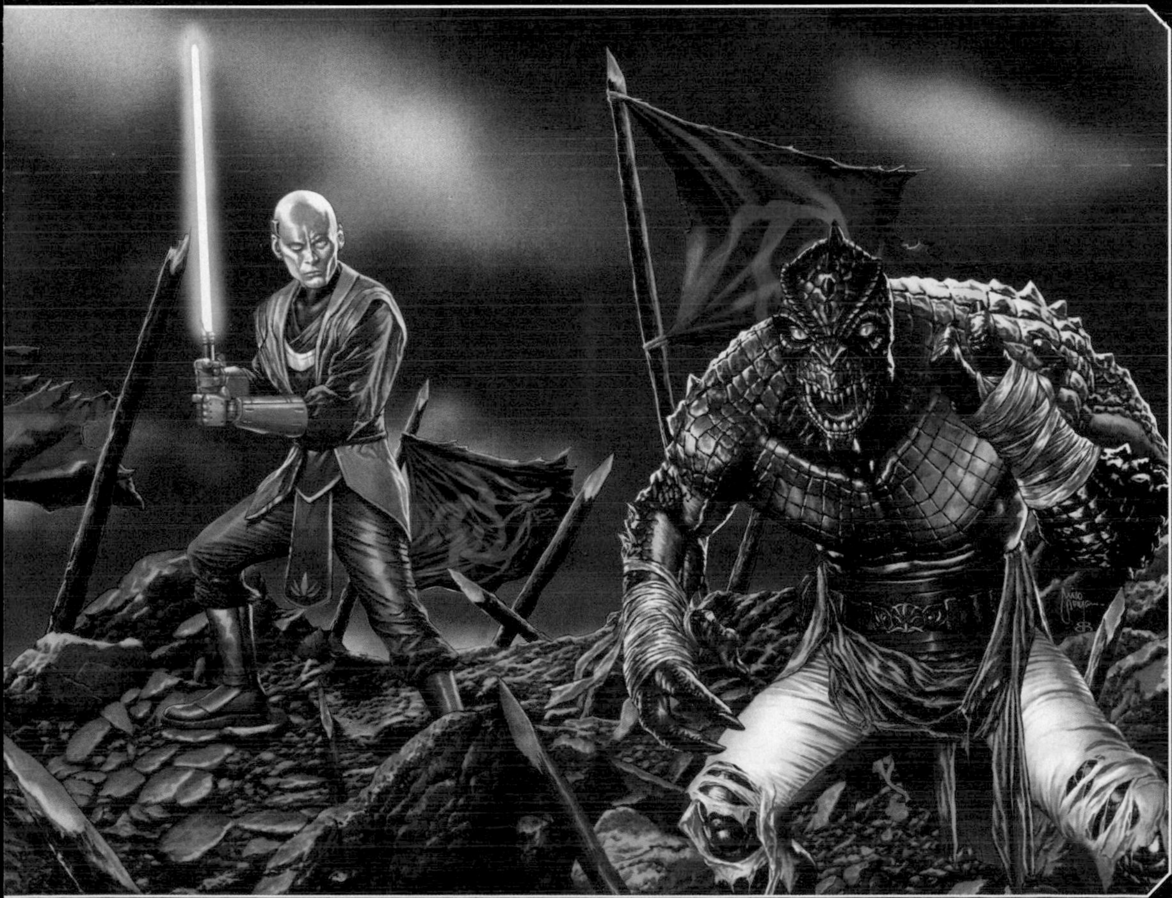

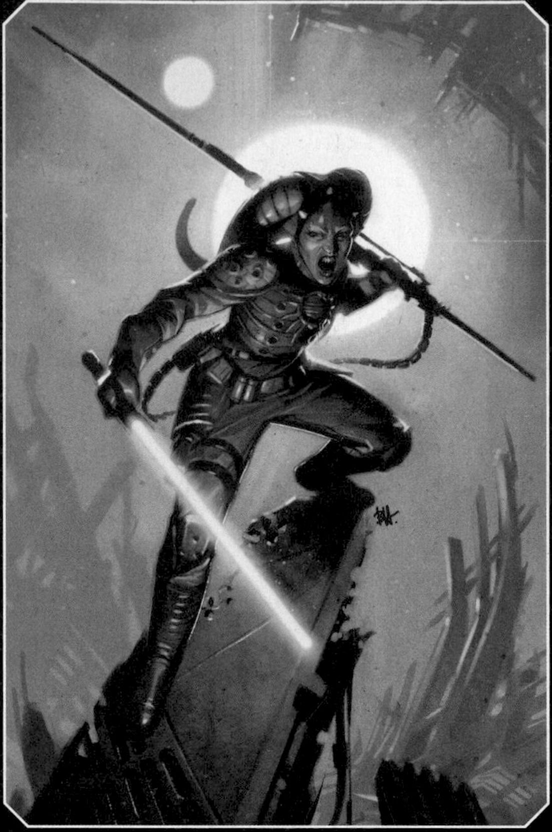

#4 Variant by
BEN HARVEY

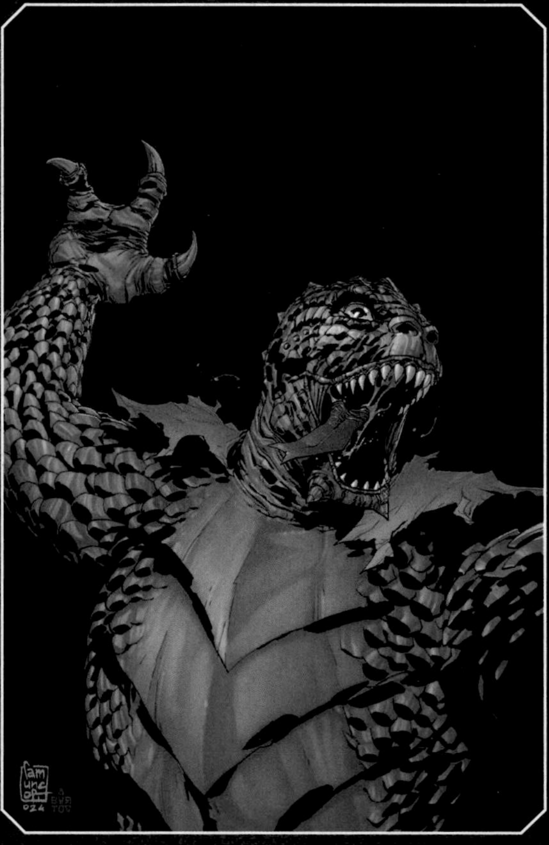

#5 Variant by
GIUSEPPE CAMUNCOLI & JESUS ABURTOV

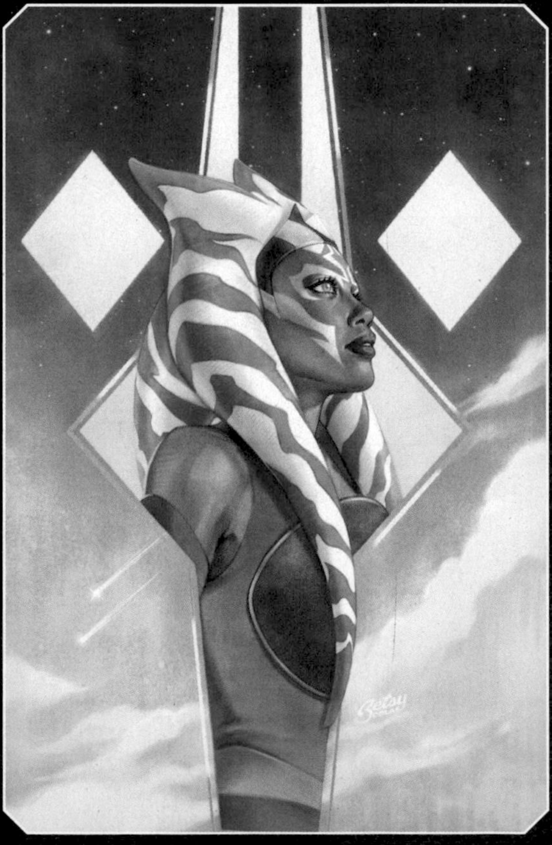

#5 Women's History Month Variant by
BETSY COLA